# A MURDER OF SAINTS

"5 Stars...A fast paced suspense-thriller that will keep you on the edge of your seat. Chris Miller made an unforgettable tale with his spine chilling suspense combined with hatred, revenge, and faith. Then the ending just blindsided me. You will never see that coming. I look forward to more spine-chilling tales from Chris Miller."

–Rebecca Larsen, All Things Book-Review

"...[Miller has] crafted a story of near Shakespearean power and depth. I just finished [his] novel, "A Murder of Saints", and my hands are still shaking as I write this. I celebrate [Miller's] amazing talent and this novel, which I believe, will stand out among the greats in this genre. [The] characters faithfully personify the bitterness, hatred, hypocrisy, dedication, heartbreak, and faith that I believe [he] intended to portray in them. The story is gripping, hard to put down. I read it through beginning yesterday. It is a real "page turner"."

–Michael, Amazon Customer

"I very rarely find a book that I want to stay up all night reading—literally. It has been a very long since there has been one. THIS IS IT. I was on the edge of my seat with every page. AND THE ENDING! Totally blind-sided by that one. Incredible first book from this author and [I] can't wait for the next one."

–Nancy, Amazon Customer

"A great read. [Miller] grabs you with one aspect of life, then gets you with another. You hear the saying "couldn't put the book down". Well,

*I literally couldn't. Fully intend on getting his next work. MASTER-PIECE!"*

—Amazon Customer

*"[A Murder of Saints] is full of suspense and thrill-riding emotions. It shows the destruction [created by] secrets as well as what can happen in the minds and hearts of victims and the souls left behind to deal with [a] tragedy. I loved it. And I…could not put it down."*

—Bobbie Brown-Wilson

*"If you're looking for a book that you can't put down, this is your book! I personally was hooked at the prologue. From the beginning [Miller] has you on the edge of your seat wanting more. Then the twist hits about half way through the book (don't want to spoil). If you're needing a good book to read…this is your book."*

—Trevin, Amazon Customer

*"'A Murder of Saints', [the] new novel by Chris Miller, is a chilling story of suspense, revenge, and the evil born of intense hatred. A young boy witnesses the annihilation of his family at the hands of someone he trusts. The pain he feels fuels a life of revenge and carnage. The reader is drawn into a tale that explores the abuse of power and the limits of cruelty in a titanic struggle of one man with his own soul. Meanwhile, the two mystified lawmen who grapple with this case also battle each other in a test of…ideology and the limits of the law. To call this novel a struggle of good and evil is to put it lightly, and the softer, quieter moments battle the plot for dominance. Steel yourself for a violent page-turner…and keep the antacid tablets nearby."*

—Fran Rathburn, Ret.,<br>Adjunct Professor of English, East Tennessee State University

For Rori

Enjoy!

# A MURDER OF SAINTS

## A NOVEL

CHRIS MILLER

**A Murder of Saints**
**A Novel**

Crimson Saint Press books may be ordered through booksellers or by contacting:

Crimson Saint Press
7355 E SH 154
Winnsboro, TX 75494
www.chrismillerauthor.com

ISBN: 978-0-692-04526-8 (sc)

Library of Congress Control Number: 2017914723

Second Edition

*To Aliana, my wife, my love, my heart, and to my children, Joanna, Jack, and Sloane. You are my motivation and my strength. Thank you, Ali, for believing in me. I would never have finished this without your support.*

# PROLOGUE

"*Come on over here, little girly. Have a seat right here!*"

The echoing, nightmarish words swirled inside the girl's young mind, swelling up and drifting back out to a black sea like a menacing tide.

"*Daddy D wants to show ya something!*"

Sophie Fields blinked the memories away furiously as she stood uneasily upon the peak of her parent's roof. Her toes clenched and curled inside her small shoes, and she heard the soles of her sneakers scrape on the grit of the shingles. In her hand was a small note, something she'd scribbled with crayons just moments before making her way to the roof. Tears streaked her pale face, and dark, brown hair matted her cheeks in tangles.

She felt ashamed and tormented, her very soul wrenched into a tangled knot. The same relentless nightmares terrified her every single night.

She was at his house, sleeping on the floor. He was an elder at the church her family had gone for years. Her whole life, as a matter of fact, at least until Daddy D had done what he did.

Her dreams haunted her, all the way down to the smallest details: the hardwood floors, the adjoining tile, the game room with the billiard table and dart boards, the swimming pool, the tennis courts.

And the dark bedrooms.

It was there—in her dreams—where she would open her eyes, and there he would be. Standing over her, a sick grin polluting his deceivingly charming face. Perfectly manicured fingers attached to soft, weathered hands would reach for her out of the dark. His shadow-smeared face would begin to emerge from the inky abyss, scarcely masking his repugnant perversion.

*"Come to Daddy D, darling! I wanna show you some-thing!"*

Mercifully, she would awaken at that point, but that mercy could never cover the screams or stop the cold sweat that would burst forth from her goose-pimpled flesh. She was always relieved at waking, but she always dreaded the inevitability of slumber. Creeping ever closer to her, relentless and unstoppable; she would, after all, have to sleep sometime. And when that time came, when exhaustion overcame her and she could hold her eyes open no longer, he would be there.

Even more frightening was the thought that perhaps her dream might not start from the beginning, though so far it always had. But what if?

*What if?*

That great and terrible question lingered over her, an ever-present torment in times of despair. She dreaded the thought that her dream might pick back up right where it had left off.

She shuddered at the thought.

Sometimes, she thought that was the worst part of her waking, unending nightmare. What happened next. After his sick grin. After his perverse glare. After the hands stretching out from the gloom.

*"I wanna show you something!"*

The part after all that was too frightening for her to relive.

Of course, when she was honest with herself she knew that even that wasn't the worst part of the nightmare. No, the truth was that the most horrible part of the whole thing was they weren't really nightmares at all. At least not in the traditional sense. Most nightmares were mere fables, unreasonable fears that transformed into fictions in the night. Little more than that. Those at least could be rea-soned away, comforted by the loving arms of an under-standing parent.

But the dreams that were tormenting her did not come from childish phobias of the dark and spook stories of boogeymen creeping under beds. These memories were real, manifesting the real horrors of her real life.

His name was Damien Smith. The much-loved and respected church elder with a secret lust for the unmen-tionable. Yet he had walked away from the whole thing, his integrity intact. It was more than her twelve-year-old mind could stand.

Damien had had help, too. She'd heard the rumors, the whisperings, the hushed remarks. Damien Smith, un-touchable behind the hedge of elders standing in absolute unity and assurance. The pastor, too, absolutely convincing in both his sermons and his impassioned defense of Smith.

And, of course, there was money, that great arbiter of freedom. Daddy D had plenty.

They had covered up the whole thing. Paid off everyone that could be bought and made the two families that wouldn't take the money—who had the integrity to refuse to be bought—look like bitter, mean-spirited malcontents. Made to look like utter fools; self-seeking, divisive, trouble-makers with a briar up their craw, grasping at anything they could to make the church look bad. Almost as if they were doing Satan's work. It was as sick as it was ironic.

Yet her family's story was true. Every ugly detail. But, as is so often the case with such things, none of that mattered. To the world, and, more importantly, to the residents of Longview Texas, the leadership of Glorious Rising Church were saints.

And now, it was over. Her family was one of only two who'd had the backbone to stand up to the church leadership and refuse the money. They'd put their trust in the law. In the system. Truth and justice.

She thought about one of the scriptures she'd been taught in that den of lies.

*The truth shall set you free.*

Only it hadn't. Truth had never made it into the light of day. In fact, the only thing that did see the light of day was the twisted fabrication the pastor and elders had spun to the congregation, the media, and to the judges. They'd smugly sold their fabrication, and heaped contempt on any who dared to challenge it.

Yes, it was all over. It was time to move on. The other family had. They'd picked up and moved, far from all the lies, hurts, manipulation, and backstabbing.

Sophie's family, however, couldn't afford to do the same. They simply didn't have the means. But Longview wasn't a tiny town by any definition. Easy enough to avoid people on a day to day basis. Plenty of places to shop and eat. No real reason to worry about bumping into any of those people, and even if you did, it was easy enough to turn around and go the other way. It was perfectly reasonable, and entirely necessary.

But the pain—the horror—wasn't going away. She couldn't deal with it any longer.

She shuffled closer to the edge of the roof, and saw her big brother in the yard. Little Charlie, as people liked to call him, was kicking a soccer ball around the yard, going this way and that, oblivious to his sister's whereabouts. His dark hair, almost black, hung past his ears and danced about his head as he moved. His bucked teeth—their parents had been discussing getting them fixed before the business with Daddy D came to light, but afterward seemed to have totally forgotten about—were exposed behind lips that were pulled back in concentration as his brown eyes focused on the ball. He was already tall, despite his nickname, and ropey muscles bulged under tight skin on his arms and legs.

A soft, whimper of a smile braved her face for just a moment before being swallowed whole by her angst.

Charlie had been the only one she could totally trust. The only one who really grasped the depth of her pain. Their parents cared, of course, a great deal, but they were so hurt, so emotionally destroyed themselves, that they were unable to be there for her. At least not in a meaningful way. The way she needed. The way little Charlie had.

Only little Charlie wasn't enough.

Their quaint little neighborhood, a small subdivision filled with cookie-cutter houses with only slight variations in brick and siding and landscaping, was a typical lower-middle-class setting. The small street that ran between the rows of homes curved back around to her right to more of the same homes on the next street. Cars were parked here and there in driveways and a few on the street itself. A few of the driveways had basketball goals in them, some free-standing, some atop garages, while others had none of this. Yards were littered with bicycles and skateboards, left behind when children had abandoned them to run into their houses for snacks, sweet tea, lemonade, or watching the afternoon ball game on TV.

It was the picture of the American dream.

Sophie snapped—as if out of a trance—as her fears and despair rushed back on her. Fresh tears surged from her eyes. Tears for the death of their once God-centered family, which had shattered into a thousand pieces.

*But Charlie...*

She loved her big brother deeply. She thought about how he'd held her in his arms, for hours sometimes, as she wept openly, unable to face the pain and humiliation of what that horrible man had done to her. Charlie had stroked her hair and rocked her, telling her it was all going to be okay. She had almost believed him, too. She wanted to believe him. More than anything.

But it wasn't okay. It just wasn't true. Nothing was ever going to be okay so long as Daddy D could enter her nightmares every night. Not even Charlie could fix that.

No. She couldn't deal with it anymore. Everything she had been taught about God had to be a lie. She had tried to believe, but her belief—her faith—had failed her.

*How could this happen to me? To my family? To God's people?*

How cruel would a God have to be to let such horrors befall her? He was supposed to be her strength and her shield. Yet, she'd been shielded from absolutely nothing.

She inched closer, nearing the edge of the roof. The rain-gutter caught her eye, desperately in need of attention and cleaning. She supposed her family would never touch it again.

Reaching the edge, her foot slipped slightly on the shingles. It made a gravely, scraping sound.

Charlie heard it and looked up. His face transformed from a look of care-free indifference to one of abject terror instantly.

"What are you *doing*, Sophie?" he screamed at her as he stumbled back a few steps to get a better view. "You're going to get hurt!"

Sophie smiled at her brother, brushing her wet, matted hair off cheeks that had begun to glow pink. She sniffed and choked back her tears. She shook her head.

"I'm going to be free, Charlie," she said with an unfamiliar finality.

Charlie was becoming visibly frantic. His face paled to the color of skim milk.

"What do you mean?" he screamed.

She shook her head slowly.

"You can't understand, Charlie. He didn't do it to you!"

Finally, Charlie stopped backing up and stepped toward the house.

"I know, baby girl! I *know*! But this won't stop him! This won't fix anything!" His eyes darted around the yard at nothing for a moment, and then went back to her. "What about me? What about Mom and Dad?"

She shook her head again, tears streaming from her eyes.

"Mom and dad, they…they don't understand. They're so angry. I need them, Charlie! So much! But they're just…gone."

Charlie gasped. His eyes frantically searched hers, desperation permeating from them.

"But I haven't," he said, his body shaking. "I haven't forgotten! I know Mom and Dad are angry, but not at you! They care, Sophie! They love you! I just know it!"

She nodded. "I know they do, Charlie. I really do. But I…I can't take this anymore. No more."

Fear seemed to quake from Charlie in waves. He took another step forward. He stumbled, as though he had to fight to keep his footing.

"God hasn't forgotten you," he piped at her, his voice cracking.

Sophie stopped nodding at that, and began to shake her head angrily. Instant rage covered her face.

"No!" she screamed. "God is *DEAD!*"

Charlie shrank back at her words. His face drained of what little hope may have been there, and tears filled his eyes. He was having no effect on her, and she thought he was starting to see that.

And there was nothing that he, or anyone else, could do to stop her.

"But…" she continued, pausing to gulp back her tears and lock eyes with her brother, "Daddy D isn't."

She jumped.

---

When their eyes locked, Charlie was seized by horror. This horror exploded into full-on terror as she threw herself head-long from the roof. As if it were slow-motion, her little frame flipped upside-down in the air in a quick arc. It was so fast, yet seemed so slow. Her hair blew back and streamed behind her, as if a gentle summer breeze were brushing her face. Her eyes were closed. Her arms were outspread, palms turned up.

She looked so…*peaceful.*

Then her face—so sad, but smiling now—rushed into the driveway.

Her head cracked loudly on the concrete. Sick, sharp snapping sounds pierced Charlie's soul as he watched her little body twist in ways it was never meant to go. It was an image that would be seared into his mind forever.

Charlie screamed, collapsing to his knees, tears bursting from his eyes like rain.

He forced himself to his feet and staggered towards her a few steps, seeing a pool of scarlet collect around her head. He could smell the metallic tang of blood—his little Sophie's blood. He got sick.

Her head was twisted around backwards, and her mouth hung open. Lifeless eyes, still wet with tears, stared into Charlie, beyond him, at nothing. The note, the crayon note, lay in her limp hand.

She wasn't crying anymore.

He fell to his knees, shaking with horror. His heart felt like it had been ripped into a thousand pieces. His fists clenched white, his fingernails digging into the flesh of his palms, drawing blood. His eyes stung, and he felt as though he were choking. He realized he wasn't breathing. With a monumental effort, he wrenched his lungs free from their prison and drew in a horrible, rasping breath.

Little Charlie looked to the sky and screamed.

# CHAPTER
# 1

Harry Fletcher wiped the sweat from his forehead and took a deep breath.

He stood outside a rather large but rundown house in a rough part of town wearing his usual attire: slacks, a button up shirt and tie, with the omission of his sport jacket and the addition of a dark blue Kevlar vest. At forty-one years old, he was still in decent shape, though his midsection was beginning to get the middle-age bulge. Still, at least the bulge had not yet begun to *roll.* He even retained most of his lightly salted, brown hair, though it wasn't as thick as it once had been, and he maintained a thick and neatly trimmed mustache.

Fletcher was a Detective, First Grade for the Longview Police Department. He was surrounded by a group of other officers, some dressed in similar attire, others in more traditional uniforms. They had just been tipped off that Jimmy Mitchell, a lowlife of the *lowest* order, was hiding out at 5235 First St.

They were gearing up to execute a raid.

Fletcher took stock of his gear, making sure he was ready. He had to be ready when dealing with Jimmy Mitchell. This scumbag had been arrested for suspicion of sexual assault of a minor. After his arraignment, the judge ordered his bail at five hundred thousand dollars. Jimmy wasn't going to be able to come up with the money for bail, so he had jumped the officers as they were taking him back to his cell. He managed to relieve one officer of his gun, knocking him senseless, and shot the other. Quickly retrieving the handcuff keys from the stunned officer, he freed himself and proceeded to beat the poor man to death with his own expandable baton. A chase had ensued, but Jimmy managed to slip away.

LPD began an area wide search, with Channel Seven News highlighting it on Crime Stoppers. Two days later, Fletcher and his partner, Marvin Gaston, were leading a small group of officers in the raid at the home of Natalie Jenkins, Jimmy's on-again, off-again girlfriend.

Fletcher winked at his partner and gave a signal to the other officers to let them know they were about to go in. One officer around the side of the house signaled to an officer at the back door. Fletcher racked his pump shotgun and Gaston cocked the hammer of his revolver.

They were ready.

Fletcher gave the go signal and kicked in the front door. He heard the rear door splinter as it too was kicked in. His partner rushed in the open door, his gun raised. Fletcher was a second behind him, his shotgun up, the stock pressed firmly against his shoulder. There was no one in the front hallway.

His partner yelled, "Clear!"

Somewhere near the back of the house, Fletcher heard a voice yell the same thing as he and Gaston made their way down the hall towards the living room that was connected through a doorway on the left. Old pictures hung crooked and covered in dust on the walls of the hallway. Fletcher could hear a TV blaring up ahead in the living room.

*Shit.*

The TV volume was loud, making it difficult—no, *impossible*—to sort out what was going on. Noise like that could be fatal, Fletcher knew, robbing an officer of one of his crucial senses. Whatever was going down, it was impossible to tell by listening.

Gaston got to the doorway and dived into the room without hesitation. This behavior always bothered Fletcher. It was reckless. The kind of thing that got people killed. Fletcher might expect this from an over-zealous rookie, but Gaston should know better. Hell, he *did* know better. Being a bachelor, as Gaston was, seemed to make him careless.

Fletcher hated that.

His worry though, as usual, was uncalled-for. The room was clear. This time. Gaston turned off the TV, silence filling the auditory vacuum.

"Clear!" he announced.

Fletcher had begun to think they may have gotten here too late when he heard movement coming from an upstairs room. Fletcher's eyes met Gaston's, who then bolted past Fletcher and up the stairs. Fletcher bounded close behind. Ahead of him on the stairs, Gaston paused for a quick peek around the corner, then rolled into the hallway with his gun raised. Fletcher moved past him into the upstairs hallway, surveying the layout with his twelve-gauge leveled.

There was a brief moment of strained silence as their muscles tensed and their eyes strained to open wider than they were meant to. They were listening hard, waiting. Waiting for whomever had made the sound to show themselves.

Then, suddenly, someone burst across the hallway from one room to another in a blur.

"Freeze! Police!" Fletcher shouted, but was met with only silence.

They crept down the hallway, cautiously, nervous energy flowing off them in waves. The floor creaked ever so quietly with each step. Fletcher's face beaded with sweat. He could hear his heart pounding in his ears. He looked over at his partner and saw that he was likewise transfixed in the moment. Unlike Fletcher, though, adrenaline made Gaston even more aggressive. Fletcher could see it in his partner's eye. That gleam. That singularity of focus. He had seen it all too often in their years together on the force.

"Don't!" Fletcher hissed at his partner. "I mean it! Just wait for the others!"

He pulled his radio off his belt and started briefing the other officers in the house of the situation. No sooner had he started the transmission, Gaston rushed down the hall toward the door where the blur of a person disappeared.

*"For fuck's sake!"* Fletcher blurted across the radio before he could think to release the mic.

Fletcher snapped the radio back on his belt as he ran after his partner. As he hustled after him, he saw Gaston round the doorway of the room and vanish inside.

*"Freeze!"* Gaston's voice boomed.

Fletcher rushed faster, quickly glancing into the room across the hall from Gaston before spinning around to face him. He could see his partner commanding Natalie Jenkins to put her hands up and get on her knees. She was complying, ever so slowly, but laughing maniacally as she did so.

"You're so dead, cop!" she laughed. "Jimmy's gonna light you up!"

She continued laughing as she laced her fingers together behind her head and dropped to her knees. Gaston moved across the room, holstering his weapon, and began cuffing the lunatic woman.

Fletcher moved to the doorway but didn't enter. His eyes were focused down the hallway, searching for any sign of movement.

It was then that he heard a very distinct clicking sound, the sound any cop or person familiar with guns knew.

It was coming from the room Gaston was in. The one Fletcher was still just outside of.

As he looked back in at Gaston, everything seemed to slow. His gaze met Gaston's, who was just coming up from securing the cuffs on Natalie, and Fletcher could see that he had heard it too.

Then Gaston looked just to the side of the doorway where Fletcher was. As Fletcher followed his gaze, he saw a closet door opening. The door, opening toward him, swung in a steady arc. He couldn't see who was behind that door, but he knew.

It was Jimmy Mitchell.

Fletcher's eyes swept back to Gaston. He started to open his mouth to tell him—to *scream* at him—to get down.

But he was too late. Gaston sighed, saying only one word. That one word didn't sound frightened or even surprised. Only disappointed.

"No."

A shot rang out like thunder in the night. A flash of flame licked into the room, searing the moment into Fletcher's mind forever. A small red dot appeared on Gaston's forehead. A splash of blood and brain matter sprayed across the wall behind him, sticking to it like some demented piece of modern art.

Gaston collapsed, unceremoniously.

Fletcher screamed at the top of his lungs as he swung his shotgun at the door. He fired. The twelve-gauge blast exploded through the door. A hole the size of a basketball appeared in it, accompanied by a splash of blood.

Jimmy Mitchell stumbled out from behind the door, his left arm shredded with pellets and streaming blood. He was raising the gun in his right hand as Fletcher racked another shell into the pipe of his shotgun. Jimmy shot, catching Fletcher squarely in his shoulder. Blood sprayed on the door frame and Fletcher fell to the ground with a loud grunt. Jimmy leveled the gun at Fletcher again and fired, but this time the bullet just missed him, slamming into the wall above his head and blasting splinters in every direction. Stunned, Fletcher tried to raise his own gun with one hand, fumbling with it, trying to ignore the symphony of pain screaming from his shoulder.

Jimmy stumbled forward, collapsing to the ground on his knees. Blood gushed freely out of his arm and upper thigh. Fletcher was still struggling to raise the shotgun at Jimmy.

"Stop!" Fletcher screamed.

Jimmy, slowly raising the pistol again, started laughing.

"STOP!"

Natalie had fallen on her chest behind Jimmy, her hands cuffed behind her back, her face speckled with Gaston's blood. She was laughing again now, louder than ever.

Fletcher could hear the officers below clambering up the stairs. They would be too late. It was going to be up to him to get control the situation—*fast*—or he would be dead.

He pulled the shotgun up again, sliding his right leg underneath it. Raising his knee up, he steadied the weapon at Jimmy's chest.

"Give it up Jimmy! It's over, just drop it!"

He could hear the other cops coming. They were only seconds away.

Jimmy grimaced, then smiled sadistically. He had no intention of being arrested or going back to prison.

His smile receded back to a grimace as he raised the pistol up, quicker now. Fletcher screamed.

And fired.

The twelve-gauge roared. Flames and searing pellets blasted squarely across Jimmy's chest, and it erupted in a shower of blood. In that same moment, Jimmy fired another round, this one ripping through Fletcher's left thigh. Fletcher winced as blood spat onto the floor and Jimmy's body sailed backwards across the room, smashing a bloody and grotesque hole in the drywall before falling face first to the floor.

In that moment, the rest of the officers burst into the room. Spreading out, they began securing the scene. Natalie Jenkins was no longer laughing, but screaming hysterically for Jimmy to get up.

*"Kill these pigs!"* she wailed.

Jimmy didn't move. Jimmy Mitchell would never move again.

Fletcher pushed away the officer checking him and began to crawl across the room toward Gaston. He dropped his shotgun, using his right arm and leg to push himself forward. His left arm was tucked up close to his side, his left leg dragging limply behind. Smears of blood followed him across the room as he pulled himself to Gaston.

Finally reaching his partner, he began to cry. To sob.

He clutched his partner's hand one last time, searching into his eyes. Searching for that gleam he had seen so many times.

The gleam was gone.

# CHAPTER
# 2

SIX MONTHS LATER...

Harry Fletcher pulled into the LPD's parking lot off Cotton Street. He stepped out of his truck, a mid-sized pickup, locked it, and shuffled towards the front door.

Fletcher was tired. He hadn't been sleeping much the past few months since the disastrous raid on Natalie Jenkins's house when his partner had been killed. Since then, he had not paired up with anyone else. He vowed to his Captain he would work alone for the remainder of his years on the force. The Captain had snorted at this, telling him for the time being that was fine, but as soon as he found someone reliable with half a brain in their skull, Fletcher would most certainly be paired up again.

This aggravated Fletcher, but so far it had been an empty promise. Six months along, he had yet to be partnered up with anyone.

*Don't make too many waves, they'll leave you alone.*

He reached the steps and bounded up them two at a time—a technique he used to help keep his leg strong after getting shot—to the front door of the Department. It was a warm day for October and Fletcher felt stuffy in his suit. In the short distance from his truck to the door, he could already feel impending sweat threatening to crop up on his back.

He opened the door and felt a blast of cold air conditioning. He soaked it in for a moment, relishing the retreat of perspiration under his clothes, then ambled towards his office. Sounds of clicking keyboards and ringing phones filled his ears. He could hear the squeaking caws of casters in desperate need of oil rolling this way and that, most often supporting the load of people heavier than they were ever meant to endure. Occasional squawks of radio transmissions from patrolmen floated through the air, and muffled conversations between colleagues rounded out the mild cacophony of a completely normal day at the office.

As he strode quietly on his way, his mind went to Gaston. He often thought about his deceased partner. He enjoyed remembering him, but the *way* he had been remembering him…that…was hell. The memories weren't of good times. Never the two of them at the bar sharing a pitcher of beer, or at a Department bar-b-que. Nothing like that. What consumed Fletcher's mind when he thought of his partner was drenched in blood and spattered brains. Dead eyes with no smart-ass gleam in them.

Screaming.

He had been having nightmares of those last moments before Marvin died. And it always ended the same way, sparing nothing. The flash of the gun. The smattering of gray-matter art. His partner's single, disappointed word.

*"No."*

He pushed the memory *(nightmare)* away from his mind as he rounded the corner to the Detectives' office. He went to his desk, dumping keys in a pile on top of paperwork, and sat down. Exhaling, he leaned down and turned on his computer. It whirred and beeped and booped. A fan kicked in loudly, rattling in its carriage. It was an old thing—not what it used to be—working hard to wake up.

While it was booting up, he leaned back in his chair, looking around the room. He exhaled again—he seemed to be doing this more and more lately—and laced his fingers behind his head. As he surveyed the familiar and as-yet-still-unpopulated area, his eyes went to the back of the room where the Captain's private office was.

He snapped up in his chair with a start. Someone was in the office with the Captain. The door was closed so he could hear nothing, but there were smiles back and forth and the shaking of hands.

The Captain was hiring a rookie.

The guy was young, maybe thirty, thirty-one at most, probably right out of the patrol car, and appeared to be in impeccable shape. He looked like an average height, perhaps five feet ten inches, and dark brown hair was perfectly styled atop his head in a spiked-up fashion that had become common amongst younger people. Yet, the kid still managed to look professional. Even his smile was perfect, Fletcher could see, the teeth inside it nearly sparkling when exposed.

Fletcher felt ill. This was it. His new, reliable partner had finally arrived, as the Captain had promised. What was worse was the kid was in textbook perfect shape. This made Fletcher feel self-conscious. Not that Fletcher was all that worried about his looks, but if he was going to have to start training a new partner on the ins and outs of detective work, he didn't want that partner to start outshining him in every aspect. That was all he needed, some punk coming in and putting an old man to shame.

*You're not old yet, Harry,* he thought, almost reassuring himself. *Kid's probably an arrogant hothead, like all the rookies. There's a reason old cops become old cops.*

Right.

As Fletcher was internally ironing out his ego, the Captain's eyes caught him through the window of his office. He motioned Fletcher to come, a fleshy, shit-eating grin donning his face. Fletcher obliged, grudgingly, and exhaled once again.

He crossed the room, searching for his smile but realizing he must have misplaced it. He'd known this day was coming, but he still wasn't prepared for it.

When he reached the door to the Captains office, he took a deep breath that was dangerously close in nature to his frequent exhales.

*Huffs, Harry. They're huffs. Call it what it is.*

He opened the door and stepped in.

"Harry, come on in," the Captain said, sweeping his hand towards the impeccable young cop. "I want ya to meet your new partner!"

Captain Dan Felt was a large man of fifty-six years. His hair was almost all gray, at least what was left of it. He was completely bald up top, with only a horseshoe of hair around the sides and back of his head. He had more than one chin that he kept cleanly shaved. He had a laugh like a freight train but he was also a good boss. He was stern but fair, and very intimidating when he needed to be.

Fletcher finally found his smile, dusted it off, and slapped it on. He shook hands with the young cop. The young cop beamed his smile again. Fletcher almost thought he heard a *'ding!'* coming from the kid's sparkling mouth.

"Harry Fletcher," Harry introduced himself with a bit more grunt than he'd intended.

The kid gripped Fletcher's hand firmly. "Elliot James Benson. My friends call me Jimmy!"

Fletcher tensed. The name bothered him, for obvious reasons.

"You'll excuse me if I just call you Elliot, or perhaps Benson." He released Benson's hand and turned to the door to leave.

"Hold on, Harry," Captain Felt said. "I want you to bring Detective Benson up to speed on everything you're working on and get him familiar with our procedures."

Harry glared, but bit his lip. "Yes sir."

He turned and walked out of the room. He went to his desk without saying a word. As he left, he overheard the Captain.

"He'll come around. Just give him time."

Fletcher heard Benson thanking the Captain for his courtesy, then heard the footsteps of the whippersnapper *(did you seriously just call him that?)* following him to his new desk, positioned directly across from Fletcher's own.

Benson sat down just as Fletcher did and immediately started trying to break the ice.

"So…" he started, searching for the words. "I just wanted to let you know it's an honor to work with you. I've heard a lot of great things about you. A lot of busts!"

He smiled broadly, with apparent admiration.

"Yeah," Fletcher responded with yet another exhale. "A lot of busts."

He tried to calm himself.

*Give the poor kid a chance, will ya?*

Maybe.

"So, what about you? Fresh out of the patrol car?"

"Yep," Benson chirped back with pride. "Seven years of driving up and down streets, working accidents, you know the drill. Been praying for this promotion. I'm ready to dive in."

Benson paused then, looking over his desk. He was looking at nothing, apparently, because there was nothing on it. Or maybe he was admiring its industrial sheen. Who knew? Fletcher had cleared the desk himself after Gaston's death and taken his things home.

Finally, Benson looked up. "So, what're you working on?" he asked, genuine intrigue in his voice.

Fletcher grunted, "Just, uh, some crack head killed another crack head. It's all but closed. I'm putting my report together to turn into the D.A."

"Cool."

Fletcher looked back at his computer screen. He pulled up a file he'd saved on his desktop. The screen redrew, and he checked his work over. Satisfied, he clicked print. A moment later, the printer at the center of the room spit several pages out, moaning and huffing as if in protest. Fletcher got up, retrieved his report, and put it into a manila envelope. With a black Magic Marker, he scribbled 'To: D.A Turner From: Detective Fletcher'. Under that he wrote, 'John Tyler Case'. He returned the marker and looked at his new partner.

Benson was sitting in his new chair *(that's Marvin's chair, goddamnit!)*, watching Fletcher intently with bright excitement in his eyes, his hands folded in his lap.

*What a chump,* Fletcher thought, managing to hide his contempt with an effort. He managed to stifle another exhale.

*Huff, Harry.*

Whatever.

"Come on," Fletcher said, holding up the envelope. "We'll go drop this off and grab some breakfast."

Benson smiled again and followed him eagerly out the door.

# CHAPTER
## 3

Charlton Fields watched from his car across the street as the Reverend walked out of the barbershop. This was going to be the beginning. The first one. Years, *decades*, of thought, hate, and preparation finally coming to fruition.

Game on.

The dogs, cats, fish, and birds had been therapeutic, but they weren't bringing him any justice.

When a dog or cat, or *any* animal for that matter, died, then sure, people were sad. Children cried and whined about their missing pets for a while, but they forgot about them once mommy and daddy bought a new one to replace it.

It had no staying power.

He needed to make a statement. A statement that would shock the world. Open their eyes. Make them see what was happening.

But most of all, he had to avenge Sophie.

Pain stung his soul when he thought of his sweet sister. As close as they had been, thinking of her these past twenty years hadn't brought joyful memories. The fact that he had to remember her at all was enough to suck the joy right out of him. Even when he thought of times when he and Sophie would tell little secrets back and forth during the sermons on Sunday mornings at church, when they would giggle, trying to be quiet, until their father would look over at them and give them one of his famous 'daggers-shooting-from-the-eyes' looks and they would hush up, silently eying each other for the rest of the service with laughter in their eyes, no joy would come. Only more pain. Pain of loss. Of injustice.

Because virtually all these memories, joyful in and of themselves, would lead to what consumed him all these years later. Like when the church services would end, the memory gave way to how they would all go eat at Hunan's Chinese Buffet. Their father would mildly scold them for their behavior in church, though all the while he was trying to hide his ever-widening smile. Little Charlie and Sophie would pile their plates and fill their bellies with Moo-Shoo pork, Lo Mien noodles, sesame chicken, and egg rolls. After they finished, they would go pile and fill again. More memories that should fetch fond feelings. But they did not. Because these would lead to more.

After their Chinese buffet lunch, they would inevitably go over to Damien Smith's house.

*Damien Smith.*

If ever there was a man who truly embodied Satan himself—not that Charlton *believed* in Satan—it was Damien Smith. Little Charlie's parents had loved him, of course, and thought he was a great man of God. Everybody had. He was filthy rich, tithed way more than the obligatory ten percent—if ever there were a Sunday service that didn't include a lengthy diatribe about giving so you could get, Charlton couldn't remember it—and seemed to have more knowledge of the Bible than anyone they knew, exceeding even their pastor and most others in the church. He was an official Elder *(capital 'E')* in the church and most people would look to him for wisdom and guidance in their walk with the Lord.

Smith had a large pool in the back yard of his large estate where all the churchgoer's children would swim, splash, and dunk each other. He held a gathering almost every Sunday afternoon at his house, and the whole church was invited.

*Such a great guy.*

The parents were all blind. None of them could see what was behind those soft, endearing blue eyes. Eyes that made most people feel comforted and welcome. That made children trust him. Even little Charlie hadn't seen it. Not until the damage was already done.

Charlton Fields snapped back. With sweat dripping off his face, he rubbed his locked jaw. The memories were horrible, alright. Void of joy. But he didn't dare suppress them. They were his fuel now. His drive.

*His passion.*

The Reverend got into his car after waving to a middle-aged couple he apparently knew.

*Probably covers up whatever they do, too. Hides it. Forgives them. Let them get away with whatever they want so long as the checkbook keeps clearing. Bastard proba-bly—*

But wait.

This wasn't a Catholic Priest or anything. This was your typical, run-o-the-mill Southern Baptist preacher. He didn't absolve any sins. At most, he would sit down with people in his church and offer counsel. Biblical advice. Nothing more.

But Charlton Fields didn't care about that. The church itself was a problem, big 'C' or little 'c', it made no difference. Anyone who claimed to do *God's* work was a manipulative con-artist. Nothing more. It didn't matter what denomination they hailed from. They were all the same to him. Baptist, Methodist, Catholic, Presbyterian, Church of Christ, *Non-Denominational*, it didn't matter, though the latter of those he hated more than any of them.

The *Non-Denominational* church was, essentially, its own denomination, despite the attempt to shed its labeling. They were the ones who claimed everyone else had it wrong and if one worshiped in his own way, namely a way different than they did, then you were another of the poor, pitiful lost souls.

Of course, all the other denominations believed this as well, but he hadn't attended any other denominations.

*Why bother with semantics?*

Charlton Fields hated church, religion, and anyone affiliated with it, and he was about to make his hatred known to mankind.

But first, he had to make a real kill.

This Reverend had nothing to do with what happened to Charlton and his family all those years ago, but that didn't matter. Going into his vendetta with only dogs, cats, fish, birds, and one very unfortunate gopher under his belt would just not do. No, he needed to kill a human being, one that believed in all the things he hated, before he could go forward. He needed to know what it felt like, for one thing, to take a human life, but also, he needed to know he could get away with it, at least long enough to finish what had to be done.

He needed to be prepared.

He shifted his car, a small sedan, into gear and began following the Reverend.

The Reverend lived in a nice neighborhood on Airline Road behind the High School baseball field. His house was a nice, single-story, gray brick home with a two-car garage. A lovely creek ran through the front yard until it turned around the East side of the house and vanished into the trees at the back of the property. There were trees encircling most of the house, except for the back where there was a rather large open yard with another tree-line beyond it where the creek disappeared. A screened porch that wrapped the front and Eastern sides of the house hid any view inside the home.

Charlton knew the Reverend was married to a very attractive woman—only about five years younger than the Reverend himself—and that made him furious. All his life, girls would hardly give Charlton the time of day much less go out with him. And as he passed from adolescence into manhood, the women he encountered continued to be no different from the girls of his youth. Only ones with far too much ugly on their face would date him, but he had grown tired of that. He couldn't be happy with an *ugly* girl. So soon, he began buying love. The pro's in town weren't of as high a class as Charlton would have liked, but they were still better than any girl he could get a date with that didn't demand the money up front.

And, if he was honest, he really didn't mind. They at least pretended to like him. Pretended to appreciate him.

To *want* him.

He glared as he watched the Reverend pull into his beautiful driveway, park his nice, sporty sedan in his nice, large garage, and go inside to his wonderful home and his enchanting life.

Charlton drove on past the house and out of the neighborhood. He pulled into a patch of woods two streets over he had scoped out earlier and parked his car, making sure no one saw him.

The sun was high in the October sky. Charlton guessed it was about 11 A.M. He had decided to do the deed in the daytime, before lunch, because there would most likely be almost no one home in this neighborhood. People who could afford to live here worked hard and worked a lot. They would all be gone by now, crunching numbers and making phone calls. A few would come home for a quick lunch, but that wouldn't be until nearly twelve-fifteen.

He checked his watch and found it was closer to eleven-thirty. He wanted to be done with his business and back to his car going home before noon.

He took a quick inventory of his gear. He had on a pair of running shorts and a light gray T-shirt. A fanny pack was fastened around his waist, and inside were a pair of latex gloves, a pair of hospital shoe covers, a .25 auto with a small silencer screwed onto the barrel, a box cutter knife, and a blond wig.

He zipped up his fanny pack. Charlton cautiously made his way to the road, looking to and fro for any sign of someone watching, and for oncoming traffic. When he reached the road, and was satisfied no one had seen him park or come out of the woods, he began to jog toward the Reverend's house.

He looked the part of the jogger. That afternoon, when police were investigating and asking questions of neighbors, Jerry McMahon would say he'd seen no one at all besides a *couple* of joggers and Mrs. Jeans in her car. He would say a *couple* because there had been a man with semi long black hair wearing a pair of running shorts with a gray T-shirt, and a blond man wearing running shorts with a white T-shirt, the latter moving at more of a run than a jog, unlike the first. They had been going in opposite directions at different times, though, and he didn't get a good look at their faces.

Charlton turned onto Airline Road at a brisk, even jog. He was beginning to sweat mildly, but he was in excellent shape, not even winding himself. To his right passed houses he guessed were in the three to five-hundred-thousand-dollar price-range and began to fume over how a full-time Reverend could afford to live here. Sure, he'd heard the stories about the Reverend's wife having money from an inheritance. There was even the fact that although the Reverend *was* full-time, he owned a successful body shop that was pulling in a great deal of money every month. But Charlton, again, knew better. The *good* Reverend was taking money right out of the tithe bowl and putting it into his own pocket.

No matter what anyone else said, that was the truth to Charlton Fields, little Charlie, Sophie's big brother. The big brother who had not been able to protect his little sister. The big brother who had watched her beautiful face crack into the driveway.

Charlton noticed he was biting down on his tongue, hard, and he could taste blood. He took a couple of deep, very controlled breaths to steady his emotions. He needed to be calm and collected when he went into the Reverend's house. Acting like a lunatic is what got people caught. Worse, it got people killed.

He saw the Reverend's house up ahead of him on the right. He ran his fingers through his long, black hair and shook out his goose bumps. He licked his lips across his immensely bucked teeth and scratched his crooked nose. He began to feel a light chill in his spine.

*This is it! This is really it! It's about to happen!*

Then a small tear came to his eye as the memory of his little sister filled his mind.

*This is for you, Sophie. It's all for you.*

He was right next to the wooded area at the front of the Reverend's house. He did a quick look about for any potential witnesses, saw none, and dashed into the woods. Then he sprinted quickly down next to the creek and squatted near the ground for a moment to take mental notes. No one was outside. He couldn't see in the windows because of the screened porch, but he was sure that no one inside could see him either because of his vantage point. He would stay in the cover of the trees until the last moment, then make a mad dash for the door to the screened porch.

He followed his mental plan, first putting on his latex gloves. After a few, cautious minutes, he was inside the screen door. It made a bit more noise than he would have liked, but no one seemed to hear. He immediately removed his shoes, retrieved the hospital foot covers and put them on. He put the shoes right next to the door and tried the knob.

Locked.

He then crept to the first window next to the door and peered inside. No one there. He dashed all the way to where the porch wrapped around the house to the left and pressed himself against the corner. As he peaked around the corner to look, he heard a car horn beep twice.

His heart leaped into his throat, and his lungs seized. The heat of the day pressed in on him, thicker now than before inside the screened porch, and goose-flesh rippled his arms.

He managed to unlock his lungs and take a steadying breath. Then he peered out the screened porch to the street.

The Reverend's house was right in the middle of a gradual curve and from this vantage point, Charlton could see up the road in each direction.

A small, white sedan was coming from Charlton's left and he could see a woman behind the wheel, waving energetically.

*She sees me! Oh, damn, she sees me!*

Then he saw a man's head pop up from behind a shrubbery in the adjacent yard. He was also waving, a pair of shears in one hand.

Charlton's pulse slowed momentarily as the car went on around the bend, finally drifting out of sight. The man in the next yard went back to his shrubbery.

He hoped the man hadn't seen him jogging, but he was sure he had. He *must* have. Charlton had jogged right past him and never seen him.

*Too careless. You should be more careful!*

He was still sure the man hadn't seen him come into the thin woods or up to the house, else the man would surely have come over or called to him.

He had not.

*Calm down, old boy. Pull it together.*

Charlton got his wits about him once again and began to creep around the corner of the porch. At the end of this section was another door, and this one had a large doggie door in it. Even if the door was locked, he felt relatively sure he could squeeze in through the dog's entrance. Charlton was in excellent shape and was very strong, but he was not overly big by any means. In fact, he was rather thin and wiry.

As he neared the next window, he detected movement in his periphery. He froze, pulled himself back out of sight, and peeked inside the window with one eye. The Reverend was walking out of the kitchen with a sandwich in hand, one large chunk already bitten out, his lips smacking on the food. He began loosening his tie with one hand as he moved down the hallway toward the bedroom, and took another chomp out of the sandwich.

When he was out of sight, Charlton made a mad dash for the door at the end of the porch. Once there, he tried the knob, and again found the door was locked.

*Bow-wow.*

Then a thought occurred to him. What about the dog? That little detail had slipped right past him and he cursed to himself for not thinking of it sooner. Dogs had a much greater sense of hearing, not to mention smell, and would likely detect him at any moment. He wouldn't have time to scramble through the doggie door and silence the little beast before the Reverend heard the ruckus.

Then he relaxed. If the dog were here, it would already be running marathons around the Reverend's feet and yapping like a crazed Yorkie always does. He had done his homework on the Reverend, planning the details and even following the Reverend and his wife around for more than a week to get a feel for their habits. He knew the Reverend always came home for lunch between eleven and twelve and usually stayed until late afternoon before going back out, if he did at all. The Reverend's wife went to lunch with a ladies group at their church every day and was never home before two in the afternoon.

And he also knew the dog went everywhere with the Reverend's wife.

He relaxed a bit, chuckling silently to himself.

*The pup is out with the woman. Chill.*

He crouched down and slowly stuck his head through the doggie door. It moved in a silent arc and rested atop his head.

He looked around and noticed that he was in the laundry room. Directly in front of him there was another door, open about a quarter of the way, and he could see a bedroom beyond that.

He began to squirm his way in silently. He writhed and twisted, careful to move slowly so as not to be heard, and managed to get his shoulders through. Then he placed his palms on the cold tile floor and began to pull himself the rest of the way. As his hips had just begun slipping through the small opening, he heard the Reverend's voice.

"Hello?"

Charlton froze. Cold, Antarctic fear solidified him in place. The Reverend had heard him, there was no doubt about that, and he was caught. Caught breaking and entering, and in a position that rendered him utterly defenseless, no less.

Beads of sweat began to form on his brow despite the frigid terror that held him captive. His mission, his vendetta, his *passion*, had ended before it had even begun. Surly the Reverend would have a gun or something in the house he would use against Charlton, little Charlie, forcing him to lie on the floor until the police arrived to take him away.

*Damn! Damn! DAMN!*

"Oh, John! How are you?" A pause. "I was calling to see if your brother was around?"

Charlton—wide-eyed and frantic—began to breath. The Reverend had made a phone call, that was all. Charlton had simply not heard the beeping of the buttons while he was squirming through the doggie door.

Released for the moment from his shackles of fear, he quickly got moving again, scrambling on through. He made some minor noises, but the Reverend didn't seem to hear, still too busy rambling away on his telephone call.

Charlton was inside.

He crept up to the door to the bedroom and peeked inside. The Reverend was sitting on the side of the bed, his tie gone now, the collar of his shirt unbuttoned and his shoes off. He was taking bites out of his sandwich whenever he shut up long enough for the person on the other end talk for a change.

Charlton grinned to himself as he pulled the .25 auto out of his fanny pack. He released the magazine, checked it, pressed it back into place. It clicked, and he pulled back the slide, chambering a round. He was ready.

He waited until the Reverend got off the phone before entering the room.

"Sounds good, John! We'll talk then. Bye now."

Charlton heard the phone returned to its cradle, no more than a soft, plastic scrape, and burst into the room.

The Reverend whirled around from the phone, his mouth hanging open and exposing half chewed sandwich mashed in his teeth. Charlton came towards him. The Reverend dropped his sandwich, quickly swallowing what he had in his mouth.

"What do you want?" the Reverend asked, terrified.

Charlton grinned. "Nothing in particular with you, *Reverend!*" The last part he hissed through hate-clenched teeth.

"J-just take whatever you want and go!" the Reverend pleaded. "Just go!"

Charlton shook his head. "You don't seem to understand. *You* are what I came here for. You're my guinea pig!"

Charlton laughed when he said the last part. The chortle spat out of him involuntarily, and he almost choked trying to reel it in. He didn't know why he had laughed. It just seemed funny.

He pulled his laugh back and replaced the grimace that had fallen away. The Reverend looked confused and bewildered.

Then Charlton, little Charlie, shot the Reverend.

There was no ceremony, no build up, no monologue. He didn't waste time trying to explain things to the Reverend, to make him understand why he had to die. None of that. This wasn't about the Reverend at all, really. It was about Charlton, and about preparing for a crusade.

The Reverend's confused bewilderment never changed as the bullet went through his neck, shattering a glass picture frame behind him, and speckling the wall with blood. His body gave a quick jolt when it happened, and nothing more.

The Reverend reached up to the spot on his neck where the bullet entered, which was now beginning to bleed profusely. He touched the blood and pulled his hand back, looking at it, that same bewilderment still present on his face.

"Oh, God," he uttered in a gurgling voice. "Oh, my Lord God!"

Those words. Those *wretched* words. They infuriated Charlton. Black fury stole over his vision in blots as he briskly crossed the room to where the Reverend was standing and put the barrel of the gun right between his eyes.

"God is *DEAD!*" he screamed, thoughts of his sister filling his mind.

He pulled the trigger.

The bullet whispered through the silencer and plunged its way through the Reverend's skull. His gray matter splattered the wall and bed. The man fell back onto his plush, white comforter, now decorated with the innards of his head, with a soft *flump*.

Charlton looked down at his dead prey. It had been easier to do than he thought it would be. He'd hardly felt anything other than rage when he'd done it. And now, only the surge of sweet adrenaline pulsating through his system remained.

In fact, it had been quite exhilarating.

He drew a broad smile across his face and began to chuckle. No sooner had he begun, he heard a door close at the other end of the house.

*The garage, maybe?*

The hair on the back of his neck rose and began dancing on the nape.

"Honey?" a woman's voice called.

It was the Reverend's wife. Had to be. Home much earlier than she should be. Not following her routine.

*Why?*

"Dear? What was that I heard? Were you screaming?" she said, and Charlton thought he heard a laugh in her voice as he heard keys dropping onto a table somewhere beyond the door.

Footsteps. At the end of the hall.

"Honey?"

Charlton heard her, closer to the bedroom now. He had to act quickly. No time to run. No use in hiding. She would see her husband's body. She would scream. She would cry. She would most certainly call the police. He didn't have time for all of that.

No time at all.

He was still standing next to the bed when she opened the door and took two steps into the bedroom. Then she paused, stumbling back a step, as the scene sunk in, a tiny Yorkshire Terrier in her arms with a pink bow on its head. The dog began to yip and yowl at once, even as the woman was only just absorbing what she was seeing. Charlton could see her eyes, darting around the room, trying to comprehend what she was seeing.

Her husband dead on the bed.

His brain matter and blood everywhere.

Some man in jogging attire standing over him, holding a small gun.

She opened her mouth to scream then, her chest heaving, brutally sucking in air. She barely got her mouth open.

Charlton raised the gun and shot a round right down her throat. The bullet ripped through the back of her neck, exiting just under the base of her skull. It tore through part of her brain stem and she was dead before she hit the ground.

In fact, she was dead before the blood hit the wall.

She slumped back against the wall and slid down to the floor like a wet napkin. As she settled on her buttocks, she slumped over on her side.

*That was even easier!*

And it was. Where there had been just a moment of hesitation with the Reverend, there had certainly been none with the man's wife. That was what he needed. No hesitation. Instant reaction.

The dog was shaking and shivering, but still managing a terrible yowling sound, something between a screaming woman and a dying cat.

Charlton snatched the shivering animal up in his hands and broke its neck. Mercifully, the shrieking howls ceased.

He felt like a new man now. He could taste something metallic in his mouth, something like copper. His head was euphoric. Spinning.

*You've done it! You've really done it!*

A few moments later, he finally got his bearings back. He put the gun back into his fanny pack with trembling hands, and retrieved the box cutter.

*Time to go to work.*

He walked first over to the Reverend's wife. She really was a beautiful woman. Long blond hair, sparkling blue eyes, and a perfect figure. The kind of woman who would never have given Charlton the time of day, never mind gone to bed with him. Not without money, anyway.

Charlton, little Charlie, smiled.

---

He cut off her head and placed it on the bed. Then he cut open the Reverend's belly. He had no forethought to any of this. It just happened. As if he were a spectator watching a macabre play acted out before him. He had no will in the matter, yet he relished it all the same.

He stared at his work for a moment, the severed head staring up at him with an open mouth, tongue lolling out, and the opened gullet of the Reverend. Then, as he again watched like a spectator, he stuffed her head inside the Reverend's stomach, careful not to get any blood on his clothes. It squished and slurped as he mashed it into the Reverend's guts, and he heard sounds like farts coming from the gore that made him laugh.

A little blood did, however, get on him. He searched the Reverend's chest-of-drawers and found a white T-shirt. He took off his gloves, placed them inside his fanny pack, then grabbed the shirt with his clean hands. He went to the bathroom and removed the blond wig from his fanny pack. He placed it and the shirt on the counter, then he pulled off his gray shirt with the Reverend's blood on it.

*Or is it his wife's?*

He couldn't tell. And didn't care.

He rolled it up and stuffed it into his fanny pack, which was starting to bulge now. Then he grabbed a hand towel next to the sink. He used it to keep finger prints off everything. After this, he went out the back door, found a garden hose, and washed off his wrists and forearms.

Then he returned to the bathroom and donned the white T-shirt and blond wig, picked up all the casings from his pistol, and made his way out the front door. He pulled his hospital booties off and put his shoes back on. Then he checked for people in the area. He didn't see any—not even the guy with the shears. He checked the time, and knew people would be coming in for lunch soon. He needed to get going.

He looked around one more time, then silently slipped out the screen door and darted into the thin woods. He was much quieter on the way out than on the way in. This made him smile.

*Got it under control now, baby. You're ready!*

He felt a hot tear sting the corner of his eye, and he realized he was thinking of Sophie.

*This is for you, baby girl. This is all for you.*

He made his way to the road—again seeing no one—and jogged into the street. The farther he got, the faster he ran. He had so much energy!

*Oh, man, this is good, huh?!*

He saw the man at his shrubbery now, popping up from his work. Charlton smiled at him. He even waved. The man waved back, oblivious to what had just transpired next door.

This made Charlton happy. He made his way over the two streets, trotting along as natural as could be. He checked once more for possible witnesses when he got to his destination, saw none, then sprinted up into the woods to his car. He got in, and pulled it out onto the street. Still, no one was around.

He drove home. He had covered every angle. There would be no impressions in the carpet of his shoes, no fingerprints, no nothing. He'd done it perfectly. Even with the curve ball of the Reverend's wife showing up, he had never faltered.

He smiled. It was time to begin the real game.

The only thing he didn't notice was the hand towel he'd dropped in the woods as he got into his car.

———

Later that day, Amelia Sanchez came to the house of Reverend William Frost. She started to use her key to the front door—the Reverend had given her one so she could clean his house when no one was home—and noticed that it was unlocked.

*Odd.*

She went in, called for the Reverend. Then for his wife.

When they didn't answer, she forgot about the unlocked front door and started to clean. She had cleaned nearly every other room in the house when she came to the bedroom.

She began screaming so loud that everyone on Airline Road could hear.

# CHAPTER
# 4

Harry Fletcher wiped mayonnaise off his mustache with his napkin. He had just finished a double cheeseburger with all the fixings from Mark's Burgers. Along with his new partner, he had dropped off the report on the John Tyler case, then grabbed a doughnut and a pig-in-the-blanket. They had gotten to know each other a little bit. Not much, mostly just small talk, but Fletcher was able to see the kid was all right. He wasn't ready to admit it yet, but he was starting to like the kid. He had a good, positive personality, and seemed eager to learn all he could. But there was one thing that bothered him.

The kid was a Jesus freak. Oh, sweet mother of all that is good and pure, this kid was a *serious* Jesus freak.

He was praying over his food, even saying things like 'Praise God!' after a good laugh. It was a bit much. Fletcher supposed he should be thankful that the kid wasn't wearing a giant crucifix around his neck and blessing the table with holy water.

*Small mercies.*

Not that Fletcher hated Jesus or anything. It was just that he had some serious issues with the church.

Many years before, when Fletcher had been only twenty-one years old, he'd been much the same as Benson. Deeply involved in a church. He even had a young beautiful wife and an infant daughter. They had been happy, once upon a time.

But all that had changed.

Scandal. Such an awful scandal. It had shattered Harry Fletcher's faith beyond repair. He pushed the memory away.

"Any good?" a voice asked. Fletcher snapped out of his daze and looked up at Benson, who was motioning towards Fletcher's empty plate.

"Sure," he said. The bottom of the plastic basket—it really couldn't be called a plate—his burger had come in was soaked with grease. It had tasted more than good. It was, in fact, *wonderful*. But alas, it was *not* good. Not good *for* him, anyway. He was doing nothing to stem the tide of his middle-age bulge. If he kept this up, it *would* begin to roll soon.

"So," Benson started, and trailed off. He had been *starting* all day. Question after question. Always leading back to the same damned thing. The job. The work. Fletcher found it almost exhausting.

"What's on the agenda?" Benson finally finished, wiping his face with a napkin saturated with burger gore.

They hadn't done much since breakfast. In fact, it was almost three in the afternoon and they had just finished a late lunch. All they *had* done was drive around town while

Fletcher pointed out known thugs on the streets and told Benson stories of his biggest cases. If his arm was going to be twisted into training a rookie, by God he was going to stroke his ego a bit in the process, and anybody who didn't like it could piss off.

Longview wasn't a large city by any means. In fact, it wasn't even considered a metropolis, not technically, anyway. There were less than ninety thousand persons in the population, and there were only four detectives in the entire department. All told, there was Fletcher, this new kid, Benson, and the other team of Albert Gonzalez and Ernest Johansen. Fletcher called them 'Bert and Ernie'. They weren't bad detectives, he had explained when giving Benson the rundown, they were just, well...*goofy.*

"Well, I guess we can take another drive around, show you the town," he said as he stood.

Benson grinned. "You forget, I worked these streets for seven years in the patrol car."

Fletcher frowned. "Oh, yeah."

He *had* forgot.

Benson said, "Come on. Let's go and see if we can *detect* something! Whattayasay?"

Fletcher's frown inverted to an aggravated thing which might be considered a distant cousin to a smile.

"Listen, kid, this isn't the patrol car. We don't go around catching people going five over the speed limit. We don't check doors to make sure they're locked. We're *detectives,* for Christ's sake! We *detect* things when a crime has been committed. *Real* crimes. You know, like, murder or sexual assault, sometimes robbery if the take was too big to let the uniforms deal with it. We wait on a call to come in that requires our expertise and *then* we go and be detectives."

He snorted and shook his head, as if to indicate he felt he shouldn't have to be saying this, then went on.

"This is Longview, pal. Not Dallas. Not Houston. We don't get murders every day. Hell, sometimes not even every week! And we sure as hell don't get any serial killers around here so don't get your hopes up on getting into some *big* case. Most of the stuff we deal with is real cut and dry. Some guy wants drugs, but doesn't want to pay for it so he kills his dealer and steals his stash. Or maybe some nerdy dork wants to make it with some lady and she says no. But he doesn't *listen*, if ya know what I'm saying. So how 'bout you just relax and when something comes in, I promise you, I'll let ya know."

Benson looked slightly embarrassed as Fletcher finished scolding him and Harry felt a sting of guilt.

"Look, kid, I'm sorry. I shouldn't have—" he stopped short when his cell phone rang.

It was the office.

"Well," he grinned, almost feeling embarrassed himself. "Looks like you're gonna get your wish after all."

He answered his phone just as both his and Benson's beepers started to sound. Oh, yes, Longview's finest still carried beepers. That was real life. If that wasn't proof that they were living just this side of the sticks, Fletcher didn't know what was.

"Fletcher," he answered as he snicked the button on his beeper, silencing it.

He listened intently for a moment, then said, "We're on our way."

He hung up.

"Is it time to *detect* something, detective?" Benson asked with a sly grin spreading across his face.

Fletcher nodded with a hint of admiration on his face. "Touché, kid. Touché."

---

When they arrived at the home of Reverend William Frost, there were already several patrol cars out front, their red and blue lights flashing on the roofs. Officers were walking in and out and all around the house on Airline Road. A hysterical Hispanic woman stood trembling in the front yard, howling something in her native tongue.

Fletcher guessed that it was a cry to God. His Spanish was spotty at best, but he was sure that's who she was wailing to.

*Sorry lady. God doesn't live here.*

He and Benson made their way to the front door. On their way in, Fletcher motioned an officer in uniform to come over.

"What have we got so far?"

The officer looked up at him, a young kid, maybe twenty-two or twenty-three. He had stark blonde hair, clipped short, and terrified blue eyes. Fletcher thought he could detect a touch of nausea in them.

"It's awful, sir," the young cop said, his face drained of its blood supply.

Now he was sure about the nausea. Fletcher thought the kid might throw up. His face was just this side of green.

Fletcher opened his mouth up to say something else when he looked up and saw Albert Gonzalez and Ernest Johansen approaching, donning latex gloves.

*Damnit. Bert and Ernie beat us here.*

"Harry," Bert said, a ridiculous smile stretched across his face. "What took ya?"

Bert had an olive complexion and dark eyes that matched his hair. Like Fletcher, he kept a neatly trimmed mustache, but it was miles away from achieving the thickened nuance that Fletcher had mastered. He was a thin man, and relatively tall at six feet, plus a couple.

Ernie was fair-haired and had eyes the color of ice-water. He was shorter than Bert, maybe five-feet ten, and was of a stockier build.

Both men were grinning widely and chewing gum in loud smacks, the white ball of the candy dancing in the corners of their mouths. Fletcher rolled his eyes and stepped through the doorway.

He pulled out a pair of latex gloves from his jacket pocket and put them on. He told Benson to do the same.

Benson introduced himself and exchanged pleasantries with Bert and Ernie quickly, then donned his own gloves. After that, they all headed back to the bedroom.

On the way, Bert said, "Prepare yourselves, boys." He looked at Benson. "Especially you, kid…"

He trailed off as they approached the blood-spattered bedroom.

The scene was horrific. Blood and brain matter speckled the walls. Fletcher saw Benson look to their left at the headless body of a woman on the floor. The young man's face began to green almost at once, and Fletcher saw him gag as a grotesque belch escaped his lips.

He turned to Benson, and with a low voice said, "If you can't handle it, step outta here until you can."

Benson began nodding furiously, the back of his hand in front of his mouth. He assured Fletcher that he was fine, then went to a uniformed officer in the room and started asking questions, flipping his miniature notepad out and fetching a pen from his shirt pocket to take notes.

*He's shaking it off. Maybe he'll make it yet,* Fletcher thought to himself skeptically.

*Maybe.*

There were officers taking pictures, both close and at a distance, of every possible angle of the scene, filling the room with snicks, flashes, and whirs.

"Have we found a point of entry?" Fletcher asked one of the officers snapping pictures.

The officer could only speculate. "Well, we assume it was the front door. The housekeeper said it's almost always locked, but today it wasn't. No signs of forced entry on any of the doors. And of course, there's this."

He led Fletcher and Benson—who had returned from asking a few questions of one of the other uniforms—over to the other side of the room to a door that led into a laundry room. The officer pointed at the large doggie door across the laundry.

"The doggie door?" Benson asked.

"It's possible," the officer responded with a shrug. "If the perp was thin enough, and could do a little wiggling, he might squeeze through."

Fletcher thought it unlikely, but he also didn't see a couple living in this sort of house leaving anything unlocked. In houses like this one, the occupants parked their cars in the garage and entered through the garage. It was unlikely the front door had been unlocked until the killer arrived. Or left.

He turned back to the bed. Fletcher looked over the body of the disemboweled man. Fletcher was indifferent to the horror before him, gazing up and down, peering closely at the wounds and at the deceased's face.

The wound on the torso was massive. So much blood. And then there were the bullet wounds in the man's throat and head.

*Why?*

"It looks like the guy was shot before he was cut open," Benson mentioned.

Fletcher smiled as he looked at him. "That's right."

The kid seemed to have his color back.

"So why cut him open?" Benson asked.

Fletcher erected from his stooped position, and exhaled.

*Huffed.*

"I'll show ya," he said.

He snapped his fingers at the Medical Examiner, who'd just shown up. "Come here. Take a look in there."

Even the ME was looking a little pale. Though he'd certainly seen plenty of dead bodies, Fletcher imagined he'd never seen anything this brutal.

The ME joined Fletcher by the bed. He retrieved a pair of blue latex gloves from his pocket and pulled them on, gulping as he did.

He leaned over, considering the opened man on the bed. His eyes squinted for a moment, and then widened.

"Oh, Jesus," the ME moaned.

*I doubt it,* Fletcher thought.

The Medical Examiner reached into the man's abdomen, and Benson peeked over his shoulder, shuddering.

"See it?" Fletcher asked him.

"Is that hair?" Benson asked, even though Fletcher could already see knowing in the younger man's eyes.

The ME pulled Mrs. Frost's head out of her husband's abdomen. A terrible sucking sound accompanied the extraction, and tendrils of intestine slithered off the blood-slathered face. It was still locked in a mangled look of shock, forever frozen in terror beneath its crimson glaze.

"This guy is sick!" the ME grunted.

"Why on earth would anyone do that?" Benson asked.

Fletcher frowned, disgusted at what he was seeing. "I don't know. Maybe some ritual, maybe some kind of trademark."

He paused, a pondering look passing over his face.

"What, Harry?" Benson asked.

Fletcher shrugged and issued another of his patented *huffs.* "Maybe just because he could. Who knows?"

Benson visibly shuddered.

Bert and Ernie moved towards them now, looking at the macabre scene with a new sense of wonder.

"Christ on a stick, what a sicko, huh?" Bert quipped in a conversational tone that seemed totally out of place for the setting.

One of the Forensic boys walked up to Fletcher, Benson, Bert, and Ernie. He held up a wadded piece of lead.

"Lookin' for a .25 caliber handgun, fellows."

"Find any casings?" Bert asked.

The Forensics scientist shook his head, frowning.

"Naw, guy must've picked 'em up before he left."

"What about fingerprints?" Fletcher asked, knowing the answer.

"That's another negative," the scientist responded. "I did find some powder residue that I'm all but positive will match the type on these latex gloves we're all wearing."

They nodded.

"What about shoe impressions?" Fletcher asked.

Yet again, it was a no-go. "Nope, might've been barefoot or wearing moccasins. No indentations."

Then Fletcher saw the dead dog on the floor, its head twisted around grotesquely out of true.

"He got the dog too?" he asked, disgusted.

"Oh, yeah…fucking psycho."

They spread out through the house then. They checked every nook and cranny, looking for anything at all that could point them in a meaningful direction. But meaning seemed to elude them. In typical cases, there was a motive. Usually, the motive was obvious. But not here. There seemed to be no point to any of it. And with the lack of even a hair fiber, they were searching for clues in vain.

Yet, search they did.

*Nothing.*

After they worked the immediate crime scene, they went out to the neighborhood to do a canvass. The only thing they found were some shoe impressions on the banks of the creek running through the front yard. It was determined rapidly they had come from a pair of running shoes. It wasn't much, but it was something.

The only witness was Jerry McMahon. He had seen two joggers and Mrs. Jeans driving home in her car. The first jogger had longish black hair, a gray T-shirt and some running shorts. The second was a blond man in a *white* T-shirt with running shorts.

"Didn't pay too close attention to either one of 'em, but, come to think of it, they looked like they were similar in build, I guess. About the same size. But the hair was different, that's for sure," Jerry said.

Instantly, Fletcher believed the two joggers were one, and that singular jogger was the killer.

———

Later that night at the station, Fletcher and Benson were pouring over photographs of the macabre scene from Reverend Frost's home, desperately searching for clues. Anything they might have missed. Anything that might give them a lead.

*A breadcrumb…*

Benson leaned over to Fletcher and asked in a low voice, wrought with disgust and a hint of fear, "Have you ever seen anything like this, Harry?"

Harry Fletcher shook his head. "Welcome to the Detectives Squad."

Fletcher felt a cold shiver run up his spine.

*Holy hell, what's happening?*

# CHAPTER
## 5

"Okay," Fletcher started.

It was the next morning and the faces looking back at him in the Detective's office were very tired. They had all been up very late working the crime scene, interviewing neighbors and friends of the Frosts, grasping for clues. And speaking of clues, they had virtually nothing. Worse, they were thoroughly exhausted.

"Let's go over what we got."

He snatched a file off his desk and opened it, producing pictures taken of the crime scene. Written reports of the first officers on the scene were mixed in, along with typed statements from Amelia Sanchez and Jerry McMahon. Fletcher divided all the items amongst Longview's four detectives.

"So, we got this fellow McMahon," Fletcher continued through sleepy eyes pried open by gallons of coffee, "Says he saw Mrs. Jeans coming home in her car and two different joggers, one with black hair and a gray T-shirt, the other guy with blond hair and a *white* T-shirt. Now…"

He paused, massaging his mustache and trying to stifle a yawn. He licked his thumb and flipped a page in the file.

"These two joggers were headed in opposite directions, about thirty minutes apart. Mr. McMahon says he'd never seen either of these guys before."

Fletcher looked over the file at the other detectives. They were weary-eyed, displaying their desperate need of a couple hours of precious sleep. Dark blotches plagued the skin under their eyes and deep lines creased their faces. Yet through their exhaustion, he could see dread lurking deep behind their eyes. They were facing down the most sadistic murder ever to take place in Longview, hell, in *East Texas* for that matter. Tired though they may be, there was no time to lose. Sleep would have to wait.

"I think they're the same person," Fletcher finished, scanning their faces for a trace of agreement.

He found it.

"Yeah," Bert popped in, "I think you're right. I think that's our killer."

Benson and Ernie nodded agreement.

Captain Felt walked in looking tired himself. He'd been up all night dealing with the Chief and the Mayor. A perturbed grimace painted his thick face.

"Gimme all you got," the Captain barked without looking any of them in the eye.

Fletcher obliged, telling him of their theory of the jogger—or joggers—being the killer.

"You're probably right," he said while exhaling. "Get the psycho, damnit, and yesterday!"

He turned and stormed into his office, slamming the door behind him. They winced as the glass rattled in the frame.

"Did anyone find anything on transportation for this sicko?" Benson piped in, breaking the awkward silence that had filled the room.

They all shook their heads, then Ernie leaned forward in his chair and spoke.

"No, we searched for two blocks in the direction the jogger came from and returned to." He threw his hands up. "Nothin'."

"What about the other direction?" Benson asked, an astonished sparkle in his eye.

Bert and Ernie looked at each other, then to the officer reports. "Ummm," was all either of them could mutter. Benson looked to Fletcher, bewildered.

Fletcher said, "Well, that's just great, guys!" His thinning hair revealed a reddening scalp beneath. "Did you think there was no chance he could have doubled back?"

Bert slammed the papers in his hand down on his desk. "We didn't think of it, Harry! I mean, *Jesus*, we're used to dealing with crack heads, not sadistic Reverend killers that stuff their victim's heads into someone's stomach!"

Benson stood, raising his hands in a calming gesture. "Alright, alright! Let's not freak out, okay? This guy is nuts, but he's not stupid either. He obviously has the state of mind to change his appearance to deter detection, and if he's doing that it could easily follow he would try to throw us off in other ways too."

Fletcher smiled seeing the rookie take charge, trying to keep the team calm. Then, ever so subtly, he felt his territory being invaded. *He* was the lead man here, by God, and it was going to stay that way.

"Okay!" Fletcher yelled, a little louder than he'd intended. "Let's check it out!"

He looked at Benson. "Call Forensics. Have them meet us at Frost's house."

---

Twenty minutes later they were pulling up at the home of Reverend William Frost. A few minutes after that, a small Forensics team arrived.

Fletcher directed everyone to spread out through the neighborhood and search in the opposite direction from the way the jogger had been coming and going. It didn't take them long to find tracks going into the woods. They followed the tracks and found an area large enough for a small car to get into without the possibility of anyone on the road ever noticing it.

And they found a bloodstained towel. Benson had been on the money.

Forensics worked quickly. Late that afternoon, they had determined that the blood on the towel did in fact match blood from the crime scene, not that anyone had had any real doubts about that little detail. They also determined that the tire tracks in the woods were from a small car, likely a common sedan.

The detectives began checking the DMV for all small sedans in the surrounding area, the futility of this measure not dawning in their weary minds.

They were back in the office, facing each other across their desks, clicking away on keyboards and holding telephones pinched against their shoulders. Fletcher and Benson slammed their phones into their cradles at the same time.

Fletcher asked, "Any luck with DMV?" He wasn't too hopeful.

"Yeah," Benson laughed, a frustrated twang in his voice. "We've narrowed our list of suspects down from a whole lot to just a whole bunch. There are probably more small sedans out there than any other vehicle. Even more than pickups, if you can believe that. We're getting nowhere."

He pushed away from his desk, rubbing his face. Fletcher gave him a quick pat on the shoulder.

"Don't worry," he said. "I've never lost one, I'm not about to start."

"Easier said than done," Benson said. "I did go ahead and put out an Amber Alert for any *suspicious* drivers in small or compact cars."

Fletcher chuckled. "Well, at least we'll narrow the suspect list down from a whole bunch to only quite a few!"

They shared a much-needed laugh together, the guffaws medicating their sleep-deprived spirits.

"Come on," Fletcher said, checking his watch and seeing it was nearly seven o'clock. "We're not gonna get anything new tonight. Let me buy you a drink. What do you say?"

Benson pursed his lips and nodded. "As long as it's just one."

He smiled, standing and grabbing his jacket, and they made their way out the door.

———————

Fletcher and Benson sat at a corner table at The Sportsman's Bar & Grill. Each had a tall, twenty-four-ounce glass of cold beer in front of them, sweating globs of condensation onto cardboard coasters. Fletcher's was nearly empty, while Benson's was still half full.

"Drink up, man," Fletcher said, wiping foam from his mustache. "I'm ready to buy another round!"

Benson smiled. "No thanks, I'll just have this one, if it's all the same."

Fletcher eyed him, mildly annoyed. "Fine. Just tell me this…"

He paused and leaned onto his elbows, choosing his words carefully. He genuinely didn't want to offend the kid, but wanted a straight answer just the same.

He found the words. "Is there a *religious* reason for the 'just one' thing?"

"No," Benson said, shaking his head and smiling. "I don't believe in drinking to excess-or doing *anything* to excess for that matter-but that doesn't mean a person shouldn't have a few drinks. Every person's different. It's just my choice. No way to get myself in trouble with just one beer."

He held his glass up and winked at Fletcher, then took a long swig of his amber lager.

Fletcher was shaking his head, and another of those misnamed exhales escaped his lips.

"You know I used to be just like you?"

Benson shook his head and narrowed his eyes, seeming not to know what he meant.

"I was," Fletcher continued, nodding now. "I used to go to church two, sometimes three times a week. Hot young wife, a baby daughter. I mean I was *just* like you."

He laughed, shaking his head while taking another drink. As he set the glass down, he continued.

"Don't get me wrong, I'm impressed with the way you work, I think you'll do well," he wiped more beer foam from his lips. "I'm just saying, I think you're putting a little too much stock in the whole Jesus and salvation and faith thing."

Benson nodded, still smiling, not remotely offended.

"Well, tell me why you *used* to be just like me," Benson asked. "What changed?"

"Trust me, you don't want to know."

Benson frowned. "No really, tell me. I wanna know."

"*No*," Fletcher insisted. "I don't think you do."

"Fine," Benson said. "Don't tell me. I was just curious. We *are* partners, you know, like it or not."

Fletcher sat up straight and looked Benson square in the eye.

"Alright," he said, clearing his throat. His face took on an annoyed quality, his mouth contorting into a shape whose look bordered on condescension. "I'll tell ya. But you won't like what you hear."

"I can take it," Benson assured him. "'I can handle the truth!'"

He laughed at his own spin on the famous Jack Nicholson line.

Fletcher smiled at the joke too, but there was no humor in it. An awkward pause ensued as Fletcher's mind began to ponder painful memories. It hadn't been Benson he was trying to spare by not telling his story. Not really. He was trying to spare himself. Ego had led him this far, and he regretted that now. But, here he was. Benson was waiting, and it was too late to turn back.

"A man I truly respected in our church did something terrible," he finally said. "This guy was an elder in our church, contributed so much to the congregation. He was sort of a big wig in town. Still is, I suppose. Wealthy, self-made, you know the drill. He can throw money at charity the way some people throw trash in a basket. Like I said, he was a well-respected Christian leader in the community. He was on the board of the Chamber of Commerce, heavily involved in local politics—city *and* church, that is—and he had the ear of the pastor. Well, at least his wallet did. Still does, I imagine."

Benson nodded and sipped his beer as Fletcher went on.

"So," Fletcher said, sighing, "he had cookouts and get-togethers at his house all the time." He paused to take a drink. "Any time I had a question, you know, about God or the Bible, what have you, anything to do with religion, he was the guy I went to. Hell, he was my *mentor*…"

He trailed off, shaking his head.

Benson adjusted himself in his seat across from him. "So, then what happened?"

Fletcher smiled cynically. "He began having children over to his house. Slumber parties, stuff like that. I mean, he was like, I don't know, *fifty* or something back then. I thought it was a little weird, but, this guy was my mentor. My friend, for Christ's sake. I didn't think there was any way he had any ill intentions. I guess I just thought he was trying to create a good, fun environment for the kids. They would say he held Bible studies and they would swim and play games and have a really good time."

"Sounds like a good place for kids," Benson said, optimistically.

Fletcher just looked at him, shaking his head. He took the last swig of beer, put the glass down, and ordered another from the waitress. When she walked away, he continued.

"After a few months, one of the little girls said something had happened to her. Said he had put her in his lap, reading the Bible to her, and…" He paused, disgusted. "And he touched her *privates*."

Benson's face paled. He'd been raising his glass for another drink, but it had frozen halfway to his lips. He set it back on the table.

"Oh, man, that's…*terrible*," was all Benson managed to get out.

"Yeah," Fletcher said. "And that was just the beginning. After that first girl came forward, more started to talk about what he'd done to them." He took a deep breath. "And then the boys started coming forward."

This hit Benson right between the eyes.

"Boys too?" he asked.

He was clearly awestruck, and Fletcher could understand why. Most sexual predators had a specific gender preference, and most liked little girls. There were some that favored boys, but most cops had never heard of one of these monsters going after boys *and* girls.

"My Lord, man. That's terrible."

"Yeah, it is," Fletcher responded, his voice saturated with disgust.

The waitress returned with Fletcher's beer and asked if Benson would like another. He declined and thanked her. Fletcher waited until she was gone before he continued.

"So, all that was bad enough, right? But then the bastard gets away with it." He felt sick, as if it had just happened that day.

"How?"

"Oh, our wonderful preacher along with some of the other elders in the church," Fletcher stated grimly.

"What? The preacher was in on it?" Benson sounded skeptical.

Fletcher nodded. "Yep. He and some of the other elders defended the guy publicly and had the parents of the kids over for a meeting. I don't know how, but they convinced all but two of the parents not to press charges."

He took another long swig of beer, and Benson joined him. Fletcher saw the waitress again and asked her for a shot of whiskey. There was a hint of slur in his voice.

"There were rumors that the guy paid incredible amounts of money to the families, but no one was talking. All the families who took the money left the church. And the two who didn't take the money? Well, they lost in court."

Genuine bitterness oozed from him in thick gobs. Fletcher sensed Benson might almost feel obliged to stop him, to end this horror-story that was evidently heading towards a terrible conclusion with a total absence of justice.

*No way, pal*, Fletcher thought, but did not say. *Not now. You wanted to know, well here you go! You're getting the whole thing whether either one of us like it or not!*

"How'd he get away with it?" Benson asked.

"The pervert's lawyer," he said. "He argued that all the kids had got together and made up the stories and that all the others involved had admitted it wasn't true."

He stopped as the waitress brought his whiskey.

When she was gone, he said, "That slime-ball attorney intimidated those kids on the stand. Confused them. Scared them…"

He took the shot of whiskey down in one swig and slammed the glass down hard on the table. His hand had begun to tremble.

He went on through gritted teeth.

"By the end of it, the kids didn't know what to say. They were stumbling over their words, started contradicting themselves. And the god-forsaken jury bought the defense's story."

He exhaled *(huffed)* slowly, staring aimlessly into the empty shot-glass before him.

"And that was that."

His eyes snapped up to Benson's then, and he leaned forward.

"I *know* he was guilty. I've had enough experience in this line of work to know that one or two, or maybe even three kids might make a lie up together, even one this big. But not *fourteen* kids. No chance."

Benson looked stunned.

"*Fourteen?!*" he exclaimed. "How on God's green earth did those parents take the money?"

"Greed," Fletcher said growl. "One of those *seven deadly sins*. I don't know if you've seen the movie."

Benson indicated that he had. "So, you lost your faith?"

"You might say that," Fletcher responded. "I was disgusted with the man and equally as much with the rats who helped cover it up. You know, one little girl, one of the two who had gone to trial, ended up killing herself. Twelve years old."

Benson winced. "Ah, geez!"

"Yep," Fletcher went on. "Jumped off her parent's roof. Two stories. Snapped her neck, split her skull open, the works. They found a note in her hands later, written in crayon. It said, 'I can't get Daddy D out of my nightmares. I'm sorry.'"

"Daddy D?" Benson asked quizzically.

"Daddy D is what the kids called him," Fletcher shot back.

"That's terrible."

"Yeah, and what's worse is the parents couldn't take it, so the mother swallowed like a hundred sleeping pills, and when her husband found her he went and blew his brains out in his daughter's room." He shook his head. "They also had a son."

"Ah, geez," Benson said again, "don't tell me he killed himself too."

"Oh, no," Fletcher said. "No, he didn't kill himself. He saw the whole thing, though—his sister, I mean. Watched his little sister kill herself."

Benson stared at him in shocked silence.

Fletcher continued. "After it was all said and done, he vanished into the system. Raised by foster parents in some other part of the state. No one's seen him since. It'll be a wonder if he'll ever be able to lead a normal life."

"How old was he?" Benson asked.

"Fifteen," Fletcher responded and ordered another beer. "That was twenty years ago."

Fletcher was done, or at least thought so. He stared at Benson as the young detective sat silently for a few moments, apparently unsure of what to say. Fletcher decided that maybe he wasn't quite done yet, and broke the silence.

"So anyway, I decided that if *God* was so almighty, how could he let something like this happen? Especially in his own damned house." He snorted. "If there ever was a God, he died right alongside Jesus two-thousand years ago."

Benson twitched as Fletcher ended that statement. Fletcher gulped down the rest of his beer just in time for the new one the waitress brought and he turned that one up. He drank nearly half of it before putting it down. He was thankful for the beer. If he had to tell this story, had to relive those cutting memories, at least he had some suds to dull the blade.

Finally, Benson said, "Well, no doubt that's a terrible story. And it sounds like a lot of people let you down. But that's what you should remember. *People*, not God, let you down. If we put our faith in man, we will always be disappointed. But if we trust in God, he will always come through for us. We may not understand His methods or the things that He allows to happen sometimes. The Bible tells us that we *will* go through trials and tribulations, but we'll never be given more than we can handle."

Fletcher laughed out loud now. "Really? Well, kid, I know the Bible *says* that, but trust me, that situation was more than I could handle! And *way* more than that poor girl could handle!" He threw back the rest of his beer and snapped his fingers at the waitress and ordered another shot of whiskey.

"Christians are all the same," Fletcher went on. "You spout some nice-sounding shit like that and expect people to swallow it, but the problem is it's still *shit*! If you'd seen what I've seen, *lived* it like I did, right up close and personal, maybe, just maybe you'd be singing a different tune."

Benson leaned in close, his demeanor calm. "In my honest opinion, I don't think it was more than you could handle…You just handled it all wrong."

"Sure," Fletcher snapped. "Whatever you say, cupcake."

They were silent for a moment until the waitress brought Fletcher his whiskey. He threw it all back at once.

"How 'bout you slow down there, partner," Benson said as he leaned back in his chair making a 'whoa' gesture with both hands. "I think you've had enough."

Now Fletcher was mad. "I know when I've had enough. And don't call me partner. My partner's *dead*."

Fletcher stood, threw some money down on the table, and stormed out. On his way, he heard Benson speaking to the waitress.

"Check please?"

*Check yourself, asshole,* Fletcher thought.

# CHAPTER
## 6

C harlton Fields saw the Amber Alert at eleven o'clock that night while on his way home.

He was driving along Interstate 20, heading east from Tyler to Longview. He had gone over to Tyler to buy a box of rounds for his .25 automatic and had decided to take in a movie. Contrary to what one might think, he wasn't fond of horror movies or violent thrillers. Big-screen splatter did little for him. In fact, he found it boring. Sure, he used to enjoy those types of films, but now, after years of slaughtering small animals in the most depraved ways he could imagine, and having recently upgraded to humans, the two genres had become rather trivial to him. He had an attitude of *been there, done that*. In the past few years since his appreciation for the macabre on film had been lost, he had fallen in love with another type of genre.

The romantic comedy.

Frankly, he couldn't get enough of them. Especially the ones where the lead male character was a nerdy sort, perhaps even a trifle less than good-looking. The guy will bumble around, sweetly trying and failing to win the affections of the lead girl, always a knock-out with buxom breasts, a perfect figure, and hair that makes you want to get lost within its strands. Then eventually, after some grand and ridiculous plot played out, he finally gets the girl and they live happily ever after.

His favorite.

After the movie, he had gone in search of a *working girl*, as he called them, at a little rat motel.

She was a young black girl, maybe nineteen. She wasn't beautiful by any means, likely because of too many years in this line of work—often coupled with hard drug use—but she wasn't all the way unattractive. Her eyes glowed hazel, and she had hair so perfect and flowing it simply had to be a wig.

He parked his car, spying the woman, lust in his eyes. She would do. She would do just fine.

Charlton got out of his car, locking the door as he did, and casually crossed to where she stood. She glanced back and forth down the street, no doubt looking for some shmuck to come by with a wad of bills in his pocket and an itch he just couldn't quite scratch on his own. As Charlton neared her, her eyes fell on him and she smiled.

"Hey there, mister!"

She smiled at him, exposing an overly large set of gums and teeth that were stained yellow enough to nearly blend with several gold caps. He smiled back to her, exposing his own bucked teeth in an awkward, but predatory fashion.

"Do you party?" he asked, his vocal cords betraying him in a crack.

She leaned in close, never missing a beat, and whispered seductively into his ear. "I party with anyone who can *afford* to party with me. Question is, do you got enough green, sugar?"

Charlton produced a wad of bills. "I have plenty."

He was awkward but she didn't seem to mind. He could smell her, a lingering scent thick with cigarettes and cheap perfume. And something else. Sweat maybe, but sweeter.

She had been working hard tonight.

They went into the motel. Once he'd had his way with her, depleting his libido and his funds considerably, he rose from the bed and dressed to leave. Her hazel eyes danced behind the sheets as she watched him, soft giggling escaping her full lips.

"What's so funny?" Charlton asked, a flush of heat tinging his cheeks.

"Oh, nothing," she replied, as she continued to laugh.

Charlton got angry. Was she laughing at him? Was she laughing at his performance? Or was it the way he looked? The way he talked, perhaps?

*Shut up!* he screamed at her in his mind. *Shut your cock-sucking mouth, you whore!*

He didn't know what she was laughing at, but the sound of it began to build a black rage inside him. His mind swirled with thoughts of the movie he'd watched earlier in the evening and how it had made him desire companionship. Charlton was not a good-looking fellow. He knew that. He didn't need to be reminded of it. He'd paid for the woman's talents, and with that should come some appreciation. Some respect. Some goddamned tact.

"Are you laughing at me?" he snapped, an audible edge in his voice.

She stopped laughing at him quite suddenly and glared.

"Oh, shut up, dude! Don't snap at me! Don't even be knowin' who you talkin' too, white-boy!"

She spoke as if she had authority over him. Like *she* was in charge, instead of the paying customer. He might have found it amusing if it hadn't been so infuriating. His hands started shaking, clenching into fists.

*She IS laughing at me! She thinks I'm ugly. Thinks I don't perform well!*

Her demeanor changed as her eyes drifted to his clenched fists. The smile was inverted and her eyes lost their amused light.

"Listen, dude," she said, sitting up in the bed, "I don't think I like how you lookin' at me! Do you know who you dealin' with?"

"Do *YOU?*" he screamed at her, hardly able to contain himself.

He wanted to kill her now. Wanted to pull her throat out of her neck and cram it into her mouth. He wanted to tear her open and bathe in her blood. Show her what her insides looked like between his teeth.

But he couldn't do that.She wasn't one of the devils he was after. She never did any harm to Sophie or his family.

*Neither did Reverend Frost…*

True. The Reverend hadn't done anything to his family, but he *did* represent everything that had destroyed Charlton's, world.

But none of this reasoning did anything to calm the tidal-wave of fury that was swelling within him. She most certainly did *not* know who she was dealing with.

"Johnny E's gonna kill you, man!" she said. "You best fuck off! He don't let nothin' go down on his girls, not unless they payin' and play nice, and you already had your piece!"

She said this last part with an air of confidence that made Charlton laugh.

"Who the hell is Johnny E?" he asked, mildly perplexed.

"You ain't never heard of a pimp? What is you, stupid, white-boy?"

He hadn't thought of that. He figured the girls in smaller towns like this worked for themselves. He never imagined that actual pimping took place here.

*Just walk away. If this gets out of hand, the whole reason you're back could get FUBAR. Just walk AWAY!*

But, reason was losing the day.

He could already taste that beloved metallic tang in his mouth. The same one he'd felt when he'd killed the Reverend and his wife. That primal thrill. Oh yes, friends and neighbors, Charlton had tasted blood, and by fucking Jove, he'd liked it.

"I'm not afraid of your pimp," he said with surprising calmness.

He watched her shrink back in fear as he approached her, pulling the sheets up like a shield.

"But," he finished, "you should most *definitely* be afraid of me!"

He leapt onto her then, covering her mouth before she could scream, and pummeled her in the solar-plexus. Her breath jumped out of her with a grunting wheeze. Charlton's grip on her face tightened, clamping down over her mouth and nostrils. Her eyes went wide, hazel terror staring up at him through round, open sockets. She couldn't stop him. She couldn't breathe.

Couldn't scream.

Charlton, little Charlie—oh, yes, little Charlie was back now, and with a vengeance—reached to the night table and retrieved his keys. Her face writhed under his strong hand with pain and fear. Those hazel eyes managed to grow even wider now, resembling saucers.

Charlton selected the longest key on his ring with his free hand, a snarl peeling back over his crooked teeth. He wrapped his fingers around the key, holding it jutting out between his fingers which were gnarled into a white-knuckled fist, and looked back into her panicked, suffocating eyes.

"Now it's my turn to laugh, *harlot!*" he hissed, spraying her face with spittle.

He plunged the key into the right side of her throat and pulled it to the left as far as he could drag it. Skin and arteries tore and snapped as the dull metal dredged through the soft meat of her throat. Blood sprayed out in jets, the pressure incredible, stinging his eyes with dime-sized droplets.

He yanked hard, ripping the key out of her throat, tiny pieces of flesh stuck to its blade. Then he plunged it into her throat again. And again.

Then he went to work on her eyes.

Finally, as blood spurted from her throat and slime oozed from her sockets, the life almost gone from her, he thrust the key into the side of her torso. That was when he discovered her spleen.

All the while, he was laughing.

It was quite a mess, and he had not been as careful as he had at the Reverend's. Of course, the Reverend had been planned and calculated. This whore had just pissed him off. Pissed him off good.

He stood over her butchered body, marveling at just how much damage a key could do to the human body. It was remarkable, really. But now he had a problem. Someone almost certainly had seen him come in here. It wasn't exactly a deserted place, and though he was sure this whore-shack wasn't on speed-dial basis with the cops, finding something like this was bound to draw the attention of the authorities.

Charlton yanked the gore-soaked sheets free of the bed and wrapped her in them quickly. He checked his shirt, which miraculously had only a few pin-pricks of spatter on it, and decided it would be fine under his over-shirt. Then he ran to the bathroom and washed his hands and face thoroughly, smiling as the pink water swirled down the sink.

Next, he peeked outside, making sure no one was standing around or peeking out windows. Satisfied that everyone must be on their backs, hard at work, he ran out to his car and backed it up to the door. He popped the trunk, stepped out, and went back to the room.

He stuffed the girl, linens, her clothes, and all the towels he'd used into the trunk. The only thing left with any blood on it was the mattress, but luckily for Charlton it was mostly only in the middle of the mattress.

*Small mercies.*

He flipped the mattress over. This side looked completely clean. No one would bat an eye. A place like this wasn't big on cleanliness anyway, so it was unlikely anyone would check the mattress for some time. The maid would swear a few times that someone had stolen the sheets, but would then put new ones on without another thought. No one would know. And he didn't need to worry about a registry for the room. It was probably in the girl's name, or maybe her pimp's.

*Johnny E.*

Charlton's fingerprints would be in the room, but that was no matter. There would be hundreds of prints in the room and he had no record. No criminal record, anyway. If anything happened to pop up, he would be no more suspected than anyone else.

He was in the clear.

*But now what to do about the large wadded pile of evidence in your trunk? Dead people, even dead whores, tend turn heads when they're discovered.*

That was the question. And now, to top things off, there was an Amber Alert out for a small sedan with a suspicious driver. He had a license, but a small sedan like his on I-20 outside of town with a male driver in the middle of the night *might* be enough to make a cop pull him over. Especially if it were a State Trooper. *That* was a problem. It was still unlikely that anyone would notice him, but he could afford no chances.

He got in his car and took I-20 back towards Longview. He was looking around for something, some *sign* of what to do next before getting caught on the road with a trunk full of dead hooker and bed-sheets.

And that was when he noticed a car pulling into a lonely driveway in the middle of nowhere.

It was up ahead, off the Interstate, but there was an exit just past where the car had pulled in to the driveway that mated to a lonely strip of two-way service road.

He took the exit, making a mental note of where the car had been. Then he drove to a secluded area about two miles to the north. The area was marshy and completely uninhabited for miles around. He found a branch and used it on the accelerator. The engine roared, shaking the small car in its frame. Then he shifted the car into drive. It lurched forward and soared into the marsh, splashing into the water.

He watched the car as it sunk. He wasn't sure it would be deep enough to submerge the car completely, but after a few suspenseful minutes when he was sure it wouldn't go down, it finally did.

*Out of sight, out of mind.*

He made his way back to the road. After checking and rechecking for any sign that he could be seen, and satisfying himself that he was not, he walked back toward the house he'd seen the car pull into, careful to duck into the grass whenever a car came so as not to be seen.

He chose the car because it looked like it was a few years old. It wasn't too old to stand out, and it wasn't brand new either. In addition, it was a large town car, the kind elderly people drove. Elderly people were also less likely to be missed, at least quickly, anyway. *And* the home at which it resided was secluded.

It took him nearly an hour of walking and hiding from vehicles to finally make it back to the house. Once he did, he made his way up the yard towards the car, cautiously watching his step and trying to be as silent as possible. He was sweating slightly from the walk and it stung his eyes. He wiped it away with his hand and made his way to the car. It was unlocked, but the keys were gone, which he had expected.

He quietly pushed the door closed and made his way to the front door. There was no porch, only a small cement square in front of the door like most modern houses. There was no light on outside, but he expected this would change soon.

Charlton took his shoes off, walked to the door, and knocked with the back of his hand, careful to get no fingerprints anywhere on the glass. He needed to be more careful here than at the motel. It was after midnight now, and he had to knock several times before the old people inside stirred.

As expected, a light came on.

"Who is it?" a tired voice crackled from inside.

Charlton kept quiet. He stepped back into the yard a few steps, breathing deep and even.

"Hello?" the voice inquired once more.

Charlton said nothing.

Finally, there was a *snick* as the deadbolt was released, and an old man of maybe seventy opened the door. His gray hair was disheveled and he squinted out through thick glasses into the night. An astonished look donned his face when he saw Charlton.

"What is this?" the old man demanded, his wrinkled face distorting with elderly outrage.

Charlton rushed forward, grabbed the man by the collar of his robe, and yanked him outside. He spun the man around, who was now grunting in surprise, and wrapped an arm around his neck. He squeezed tightly and quickly, then yanked hard to the right. He heard a snap and a final grunt. The man went limp and fell to the ground in a discarded heap.

A moment later, Charlton heard an old woman's voice calling out.

"Walter? Who's at the door? Do you have any idea what time it is?"

Charlton quickly stepped out of sight from the door and listened to the old woman making her way.

"I told you not to answer the door, Walter!" the old woman bellowed from inside, her footsteps echoing closer and closer. "Anyone knocking at this hour is nothing but a heathen! I told you to call the—"

The echoes of the footsteps died a moment after her words abruptly stopped. Charlton was pressed against the side of the house, just out of sight of the door, and he could hear the woman breathing heavily for several seconds.

"Oh, Lord! Walter!"

She came running out the door, right past Charlton, with no evidence of having seen him. With what seemed a great effort, she knelt by her dead husband and began shaking him, begging him to wake up.

"Walter!" she screamed. "Walter, what's happened? Walter?"

Charlton made his way up behind the old woman, silent as a snake. He grabbed her, and broke her neck the same way he'd done her husband's. The only sound was a muffled scream, a dying croak, and a soft thump as she collapsed next to her husband.

Charlton turned his head and cracked his neck. Then he went inside, wiping the dirt from his feet thoroughly on the welcome mat before entering. He touched nothing as he searched for the keys. He meant for this to look as though the old couple had merely decided to take an unexpected trip somewhere, and nothing more.

The keys—which he finally found after several minutes of searching—were upstairs, on a bedside table. He picked them up, careful not to touch the table as he lifted them, and left the house. He found a branch in the yard, and used it to shut the door. Then he dragged the bodies over to the car and put them in the trunk, retrieved his shoes, and drove out to the marsh again.

After dumping the bodies next to his car, he was finally able to drive home. He decided to park a block away just in case the car was reported stolen by a family member stopping by to check on the elderly couple. He got out quietly, looking about for any night owls with wandering eyes. He saw none, and made his way into his house.

Once inside, he stripped his dirty clothes off and threw them in the trash. He walked naked into his kitchen and opened the refrigerator and stared into it for several moments, deciding if he wanted anything.

He didn't.

He shut the door to the fridge and made his way to his bedroom. He crossed to his closet and opened the door. It swung open, revealing five pictures tacked to the inside.

The first was of Damien Smith. The second was the preacher of his church from childhood. His name was Percy Wilkes. The other three were elders from the church: John Hays, Tony White, and Morgan Jones.

These men were the ones responsible for killing his family. They had murdered them. Murder by suicide was still murder, and the time had finally come. Time to set things right.

Time for justice.

But Charlton felt a tremor in his body. As though he was getting out of control. Developing a blood lust. He'd killed three random people tonight. People wholly uninvolved with killing his family. People who didn't even *represent* what had killed his family. And he had liked it.

Oh, yes, he had liked it. In fact, he had *loved* it. It had been exhilarating, fulfilling. This was nothing like the animals, oh no, not at all. This had been on another level entirely. Almost orgasmic. Killing the whore had been a release a thousand times better than fucking her. The old couple, too.

He was suddenly struck with a worry that he was going to be unable to stop once his crusade was done. But then, did he *want* to stop? What if after he took out the bastards from the church he had to keep on killing? What then? And who?

*No bother,* he thought. *Tomorrow, the game is on.*

Yes. Tomorrow he would start. And if he needed to go on after he finished them? Well, there were plenty of churches all over the place. Plenty of *people* in the world.

He would cross that bridge when he came to it. For now, he would move through the bastards on his door quickly and get revenge for Sophie.

*Mom and Dad too.*

It was painful for him to think about his parents. After Sophie was gone, their pain had intensified astronomically, and they had been unable to take the weight of it. His mother had taken some pills and his father had redecorated the walls of his sister's room with his brains.

A shiver ran up his spine at the memory of his parents dead in the house he'd grown up in.

But even as he shook off the memories, his mind kept going back to the killings. Five dead already, and as yet, none of them had been who he was after.

This was supposed to be a specific series of slayings. The Reverend Frost had been only to prepare for the coming murders of those responsible for the deaths of Sophie and his parents. But then the man's wife had walked in and he'd had to improvise.

And then? Then he had flipped out.

Stuffing the woman's head into her husband's abdomen had not been a part of the plan at all. But when he had seen her lying there on the floor, dead, he'd felt an impulse to do something more. Dead wasn't good enough. He didn't just want death. He had realized this in that moment. He wanted *mutilation*.

So, he had mutilated.

There was no rhyme or reason to it. It was just something he had done in the moment. Almost like watching from afar. Like a movie. Only the movie had starred him.

And then there was tonight. Three *more* people. The first merely a reaction to rage. The others merely because he'd needed a car.

*Forget about it. Just focus.*

But he couldn't focus. He kept thinking of killing the people. As he relived the events in his mind, a sadistic smile spread over his face, obliterating reason. He couldn't wait to do it again. And again.

*And again.*

He shook his head, snapping out of it. He felt tired. All that fucking and killing was hard work.

*Time for bed*, he thought. *You've got a big day coming up. A very big day. The game is about to begin.*

He looked to the pictures on the door. He ran his finger over them, top to bottom, and stopped on the last one.

"See you tomorrow," he said with a grin of rage as he tapped the picture.

He was going to kill Morgan Jones.

———

Fletcher awoke with a start. Sweat beaded his face and soaked his sheets.

The same nightmare. Again, and again. Marvin Gaston arresting Natalie Jenkins. Jimmy Mitchell coming from the closet.

The single word from Gaston.

*"No."*

The shot. Gaston's head exploding.

Then, as Fletcher watched on, helpless and aghast, Gaston would sit up. Gore hung from his head in thick clumps. Dead, gleam-less eyes, filmed in a milky slime, found his own.

"Harry, why'd you let him do it? *Why?*"

Then he would collapse again.

Fletcher wiped his face with the sheets, trying to shake off the dream.

*Just a dream. Calm down. Get hold of yourself.*

He got out of bed, feeling a freight train suddenly rush through his skull, its horn blowing loudly.

*Here we go!* screamed the engineer. *How far we go, nobody knows!*

*Hoot-hooooooot!*

Fletcher stumbled to the wall, pressing his hands against his head in a futile attempt to stave off the pain.

It didn't work.

He glanced at his bedside table and saw the empty bottle of whiskey sitting there. He remembered, through the hooting of the engineer's horn, that after he'd left Benson at the bar, he'd stopped by the liquor store and picked up a bottle of the hard stuff, desperate to dull the edge of the memories that had surfaced as they'd talked. Desperate to drown those memories, to *sanitize* them, he'd figured his own personal party at home might do the trick.

He stumbled to the medicine cabinet, ripping it open and fumbling for the bottle of Aspirin. Several other bottles tumbled out and dived into the sink, rattling and spinning.

*Come on!* he thought. *Come on, work, damn you!*

He managed to grab hold of the right bottle, gripping it tightly, and popped the top off. He threw it up to his mouth, cocking his head back as he took in a couple of the pills.

*Man alive, last night was a bad idea.*

After a while, the pain in his head began to abate. He managed to fetch his clothes from the dryer, shaking them out and freeing them of the wrinkles. He dressed for work, all the while taking long drags on a generic but strong coffee he'd freshly brewed just after taking the medicine.

He had a killer to catch. A sadistic madman was on the loose in his town, and he had just wasted an entire night drowning his personal pain in a bath of numbing alcohol.

But even as he tied his shoes and sat up, taking another long draw on his coffee, he felt like he was at a wall in the investigation. They had done all they could do. They were nowhere with the case. It wasn't his fault, or anyone's fault. There just weren't any clues. None that helped, anyway. What evidence they did have simply didn't point anywhere.

All the same, he was suddenly filled with a sensation that he would catch a break soon. There was no reason for this feeling, but there it was.

*Why do I feel this way? Precognition? God?*

No. There was no such thing.

Despite his disbelief, he still felt that something was going to happen today. He didn't know what, or how significant, but something was coming. Something important.

He left his house and got into his truck. As he cranked it up, he remembered the conversation he and Benson had the night before. The memory made him grimace. His spill about what had happened twenty years ago at his old church had made him rather emotional, and those emotions weren't dealt with. Not really. He had snapped at Benson at the end there, and if he'd not been enthralled in such horrible, unresolved memories, he wouldn't have.

*And, of course, swimming in alcohol.*

Oh, yeah. Fletcher was a man who enjoyed drinking good beer, but he had let it go too far. At first, he was trying to have a good time with his new partner. Maybe even get to know him a little. But then Benson had asked him about his past. After that he wasn't drinking to have a good time anymore, he was drinking to cope.

And after he had blown up on Benson and bought the bottle of whiskey, he had been drinking to forget.

*A lot of good that did, eh, old boy? Getting cocked always makes you see things clear, doesn't it?*

Shut up.

Now, in his truck the next morning with a hangover and a headache that was only just subsiding, he was still thinking about it.

*A LOT of good!*

He pulled onto the road, ignoring the prick in his mind, and headed toward his office. It was about a fifteen-minute drive, so he decided to listen to the radio. Maybe some good rock 'n' roll would help him feel better, or a good morning show with a pair of idiots making moronic cracks would cheer him up.

But there was no such luck. He scrolled through the radio channels, frustrated at the terrible reception. He gave up quickly and shut it off, pulling out his cell phone. He had a thought of calling Benson and apologizing about the prior evening's events, then decided against it. Benson would be at the office, and he could just do it face to face. Better that way.

Instead, he swiped through his contacts and dialed a number he hadn't called in some time. He really didn't have any reason to call this number, and he couldn't explain his impulse to call it now. But all the same, he did.

It was his ex-wife. After two rings, she picked up.

"Hello?" her soft voice came on the line.

Fletcher started to say something, then paused. He hadn't called her in several weeks, since their last fight. Their daughter, Heather, still lived at home with her mom. She was twenty-one years old, and he had not had as close a relationship with her as he'd hoped, but he supposed he was mostly to blame for that. He let his job become more important than his family. When he left the church twenty years ago, his wife had gone with him willingly, being disgusted herself with what had happened. But she had not been turned off to God and religion like Harry had. She had been turned off to those individuals. Nothing more. Her faith had stayed just as strong as it ever had been, and when Harry refused to look for another church, their marriage started to spiral out of control. Within a year, Harry moved out, and filed for divorce. She had drug it out for a long time, hoping to work it out with him. Hoping he would come around.

But he never did.

"Hello?" she repeated. Her voice was still sweet, after all these years.

"Helen," he finally responded, "it's me."

"Oh, Harry," she said. She sounded nervous. Uncomfortable. "What's up?"

He took a moment to clear his throat and keep his voice from cracking. "Hey, uh, how are you?"

"I'm okay. Tired," she responded.

She sounded *exhausted*.

"Yeah," he said, and trailed off.

He felt palpable tension crawling through the airwaves, wrapping him up in invisible cords. He went on.

"Listen, I was just calling to talk to Heather. Is she around?"

"Sure. Hold on," she said.

He heard the phone laid down on the counter and Helen calling for their daughter to come to the phone.

"It's your father!" her voice squawked through the earpiece.

A few moments went by before someone finally picked up the receiver and started talking.

"Dad?" his daughter's voice came on the line, sounding excited to hear from him. He was thankful for that.

Over the years, when he had not been around very much, he expected that she would start hating him and maybe even start being resentful. Time and distance had a way of doing that. But she hadn't fallen into it. Every time he called to talk to her, she sounded happy to hear from him.

"Hey baby," he said, smiling to himself. "How's it going?"

"Okay, I guess," she said, her voice sounding to contrast her statement. "Mom's been a wreck the last few days."

Fletcher's eyes narrowed as he pressed the phone tighter to his ear.

"What's wrong? Is she okay?" He was genuinely concerned.

It wasn't like Helen to get depressed about things. He knew that much about his ex-wife. Even after their many fights, she was over it in a matter of moments. She didn't hold onto things and she didn't let anything keep her down.

Had he misinterpreted the way she sounded? He had thought she was only tired. Was it something else?

"Well, physically she's okay," Heather responded, her voice changing, sounding confused. "You don't know what happened?"

*What happened?* he thought. *What could have happened?*

"What's going on Heather?" he said, his heart beginning to race.

"Mom's—well, mine too—*our* pastor was murdered the other day."

The revelation hit him like a brick in the face.

"Reverend William Frost?" he asked, as if she could have possibly meant someone else.

"So, you do know," she said.

"Well of course, I'm the lead investigator on the case," he said. "But I had no idea that he was the pastor of your church! How come no one told me?"

He gripped the cell phone tighter.

"I don't know, Daddy," she said, sounding hurt at his tone of voice. "I just assumed you knew that."

"Good Christ," he muttered. "Listen, I didn't mean to snap at you, darling. I didn't know *who* your pastor was. Hell, I didn't even know where you two were going to church these days. Your mom and I never talked about it."

He felt nervous. This murder had hit very close to home. Close to his family. And he'd had no idea that the victims were connected to his daughter and ex-wife. The proximity of it chilled him, and pissed him off.

"Mom tried to talk to you about it several times," she said, her voice turning serious. "I asked her to try to invite you to come with us a couple of times. Thought maybe it could get you to, well, come back. To come back to us."

That last part was a kick in the balls.

"Listen," he began, and managed to catch his exhale before it became a huff. "I'm sorry I wasn't there all the time when you were growing up. Your mother and I just have too many differences that we couldn't work out. It wasn't-"

"The only problem was," she started, cutting him off, "you turned your back on God, Daddy. I love you with all my heart, but don't try to sell me on a story you don't even believe *yourself.*"

Her words hit him right in the heart. She was right, and he knew it. But he wasn't ready to deal with it. No sir, not now, maybe never. No thank you.

"Well," he said, wondering just why he had called now. "Anyway. I guess I'll go then. It was nice to talk to you baby. Tell your mom hi for me."

He stopped, about to hang up. But then something came to him and he went on.

"Come to think of it, tell your mom to come down to the station house sometime today. I need to ask her some questions about your pastor. It might help, you never know. She might have some insight that we could really use right now. Will you tell her for me?"

She sounded annoyed that he had changed the subject so quickly.

"Sure, Dad. I'll tell her." She exhaled, sounding exactly like her father. "I love you, Daddy."

He smiled to himself. "I love you too, sweetie."

He hung up, and a moment later he was pulling into the station.

Benson was already there. Fletcher exhaled *(huffed, Harry)* and made his way over to him. He made his apologies about the previous night, replete with grunts and *uhs* and eye-darting. There was even some shrugging.

Benson just smiled and clapped him on the shoulder.

"Forget about it, buddy! I already have!"

Fletcher smiled and thanked him. "Anyway, at least let me buy you some dinner sometime soon."

Benson nodded. "Dinner. Sounds good. As long as we drink *tea*."

Benson winked and they both laughed. Fletcher was really beginning to like Benson despite himself. He felt the partnership would end up a success.

Fletcher said, "Deal. And by the way, don't call me buddy. Sounds kinda...I dunno. Just don't."

"Okay," Benson said. "Then what *should* I call you?"

Fletcher wanted to say *partner* but he was going to pull the kid along a little longer before he let him in completely.

"For now, just call me Harry."

"Deal."

---

They went to work on the case, calling everyone affiliated with the church Reverend William Frost had pastored. But nothing out of the ordinary reared its head. No new members for a long while and nothing to imply that the Reverend had been threatened by anyone. No known enemies.

Nothing, nothing, *nothing*.

In fact, everyone they talked to had the utmost respect for the man. The consensus seemed to be that the Reverend was a terrific guy. Everyone loved him and said he was one of the very best people they had ever met.

After every name on the list was called—save Helen's, that was—Benson asked, "So what now?"

"Well, this, uh, lady," he was looking at his ex-wife's name, "is coming in later to talk to me personally. So, I guess we've got nothing. Again."

Benson looked at Helen's name. "Hey, same last name as you, Harry. You guys related?"

Fletcher's mouth twisted in discomfort.

*Damnit, Benson, you and your deductive skills...*

"We were," Fletcher said, "well, she's my ex-wife."

Benson eyes widened as he nodded. "Oh, okay. You think she'll know anything we don't?"

"No," Fletcher shook his head. "I don't think so."

He leaned back in his chair and rubbed his thinly covered scalp.

"Unfortunately," he went on with a patented huff, "I think we're gonna need fresh blood on this one to solve it."

"You don't think this is a one-time deal?" Benson asked, mildly perplexed.

"No way," Fletcher responded. "Everyone loved the good Reverend. No enemies. This was done by someone who obviously held some serious hate toward him and I'm willing to bet it was someone he didn't know."

Fletcher exhaled *(huffed)* again.

"I think we got a serial killer on our hands."

"Whoa, that's heavy," Benson said, his eyes wide as he leaned back in his own chair.

Fletcher checked his watch. It had been several hours since they had begun calling the church members and it was after one o'clock now. He stood up, grabbing his coat.

"Come on. Let's get some lunch."

They stood up and were on their way out when Captain Felt stuck his head out the door.

"Hold up fellas," he said. His face looked grim.

"What is it, Captain?" Benson asked.

The Captain shook his head. "We've got a serious problem on our hands."

# CHAPTER
## 7

C harlton Fields rose promptly at seven, and went about his morning rituals like a man on a mission.

And he *was* on a mission.

He took a shower, brushed his teeth, shaved, combed his hair, and dressed in a semi-fine business suit. He'd been waiting for this day, *preparing* for this day, for twenty years. He meant to savor it.

Saliva discharged in his chops.

He'd done some checking on Morgan Jones, and had a good idea of his routines. Jones would be at work today, and Charlton didn't want to run into another situation like when the Reverend's wife had walked in. No, today he would take out Jones, and *only* Jones.

*So long as no one else gets in the way...*

That was true. He would do whatever necessary to complete his task, but he didn't *intend* to deliberately kill anyone else.

Killing Jones would be sweet enough.

Yet, killing was fast becoming his most favorite past time. When he took control of another human being and ended their life, he felt more empowered than ever before. He was soaring when he'd shot the Reverend and his wife, when he'd slashed the prostitute's throat and eyes and spleen, and finally, when he'd snapped the elderly couple's necks like fragile twigs.

Oh, yes, he'd *loved* it.

It was better than the finest drugs and more intoxicating than the sweetest liquor. When he did it, he felt...

Well, he felt like a god.

Just thinking about it was making him salivate anew. Warmth flooded his mouth and made goose-flesh rise in mounds on his arms and spine. He would do quite a number on Jones. Oh, yes, friends and neighbors. Quite a number indeed.

Charlton grabbed the keys to the town car.

---

Sandy Clark answered the phone on her desk.

"Thank you for calling Jones Construction, how can I help you?" she said into the receiver.

The voice on the other end was hard and, it seemed, a bit confused.

"Um, yes. My name is..."

The caller trailed off for a moment, and Sandy leaned forward on her desk.

"I'm sorry," she said, perfect polite etiquette dripping from her voice. "Who is this?"

The voice coughed in her ear, and she had to pull the receiver away for a moment. Then she heard the awkward voice come back on.

"This is Jonathan Clark," the voice croaked. "With Clark Lumber Company. M-may I speak with Mr. Jones?"

Sandy was smiling giddily now, and she completely ignored the caller's question.

"Your name is Clark?" she asked.

The caller cleared his throat. "Um, yes."

"Oh, my gosh! That is *sooo* cool! My last name is Clark too!"

She started laughing as if it was the funniest thing that had ever occurred. And to her, it genuinely ranked up there, right alongside *Who's On First?*

"My, my. That's amazing," the voice said coldly. "May I please speak with Mr. Jones?"

"Oh," she cleared her throat, "of course. I'm sorry. Please hold."

———

There was a soft click and a rather talented saxophonist came on serenading Charlton for nearly two minutes. Finally, a gruff sounding man came on the line.

"This is Morgan Jones. What can I do for you?"

Charlton smiled.

"Mr. Jones, it's so nice to speak with you."

Within minutes, Charlton had set up an appointment to come by Jones's office at noon to discuss a possible business transaction between Jones's company and the fictional one Charlton was fronting. Charlton had insisted on meeting Jones at his mobile office to the mild disdain of Jones, who had wanted to meet for lunch, but he had finally given in.

"We'll have the place to ourselves," Jones said. "Complete privacy creates a good working environment, don't you think, Mr. Clark?"

Charlton had to contain himself from an explosion of maniacal laughter. But he allowed himself a broad, wet smile.

"Yes," he said breathily. "I do believe it does."

"Alrighty," Jones said. "See you then."

Charlton ended the call on his cell phone, a cheap throwaway he'd bought at a local store earlier in the week. He looked across the street at Morgan Jones's office. It was a construction site with a mobile office that looked like your average single-wide mobile home. A crew of maybe twenty men were behind that, building the skeleton to what would be the offices of *Graham, Woodall, and Sharp, Attorneys at Law*, according to the sign out front. Several vehicles were parked around the area, which looked like someone had taken a piece of the Sahara Desert and deposited it in Longview, Texas. Tan dirt spread across the entire lot, and there were piles of it pushed off to the edges of the property by backhoes and bulldozers.

Charlton checked his watch. It was nearly eleven in the morning. He decided he would drive around for a while until his meeting with Jones. No need to make himself conspicuous sitting across the street in his car, drumming his fingers on the steering wheel. Maybe he would go to a fast-food drive-thru, grab a bite to eat, and slowly make his way back to Jones's office.

He put the town car in drive, and pulled away from what would soon be a rather horrific crime scene.

*See you soon, asshole.*

---

Noon.

Sandy Clark was walking out the door as Charlton pulled into the dirt parking area in front of the mobile office. She smiled professionally as he stepped out of his car. He wasn't nearly as pleased to see her as she was to see him.

"Are you Mr. Clark?" she said, the cadence of her voice like a ping-pong ball flying back and forth in rapid succession.

"Yes," he replied tepidly, looking past her to the door of the office.

He had hoped that she wouldn't pay him any attention. Attention like this was a problem, and if she hadn't been standing out here in the stark daylight, he might have carved an extra smile under her chin. But alas, she was here, and he could not risk it.

"Oh, hey," she said in a rather high pitch. "I'm *Miss* Clark! Ha! Anyhoo, I won't keep you. I'm off to lunch! As you can tell, I don't miss many of those!"

An eruption of high-pitched, cackling chatter which may have been distant cousin to laughter burst from her red lips, peeled back over lip-stick-stained teeth.

*Go away, lady, please!* Charlton thought, maintaining his polite smile while the jiggling hyena before him regained control of herself.

"Mr. Jones is in his office, right through there," she pointed to the office, the dying vestiges of her laughter fading away with her words. "Just hang a left when you go in!"

"Thank you," he said.

He watched her a moment as she got into her car and started the engine. She looked up at him, smiled hugely again, and waved. He smiled and waved back, a heroic effort. When she was gone, he made his way up the stairs, reaching into his pocket, feeling the pistol and the box cutter.

Electricity filled his veins.

He took a quick look around the job site. No one else remained. All the crew members he'd seen earlier, milling around with saws and hammers and framing squares, were gone. The sounds of metal disks spinning at high RPMs and the thwacking sound of hammers were absent.

Everyone had gone to lunch.

*We'll have the place to ourselves!*

As he crossed the threshold of the mobile office, his heart began beating loudly in his ears. The bright sun vanished behind him as he entered the artificial gleam of fluorescent light fixtures and table lamps. He looked to his left, just as Ms. Clark had told him to.

There was a modest desk with a phone, some pens, a stapler, a note pad, keyboard, and computer monitor. Beyond that, there was an office window, blinds drawn, and a door next to it, cracked open. He could hear a gruff voice coming from the office. It was the voice of a man who'd been a key player in the destruction of his life. In the death of his family.

Of sweet, innocent Sophie.

Charlton walked silently towards the door, his head cocked, listening.

"No, no," he heard Jones say. "Baby, listen, just go by the motel and get us a room. I should be there…"

Jones paused, maybe to check his watch. A second later, he went on.

"Should be there about three. I got some things to tie up here at the office, then I gotta call my wife and tell her something or other. If I don't, we'll have a whole new set of problems on our shoulders."

There was another pause as Jones listened to the person on the other end of the call. His mistress, Charlton guessed.

"Yes, baby, yes! I promise, this is only for a little while longer. I mean it. I'm gonna leave her soon. Then we can be together, just like you've always wanted. Just like *I've* always wanted."

Charlton felt rage run through his veins. Jones hadn't changed at all. He was a scumbag. A cheater. But that wasn't really the great crime. The great crime was that he was all those things, yet to the rest of the world he was a fine Christian and upstanding businessman. And *everyone* loved him. Thought he was such a great guy. A great *Christian*. What a joke.

*What a lie.*

A moment later, the phone hung up and Charlton pushed the office door open with a knock. Jones's head snapped up, his hand still on the phone.

"Mr. Clark?" Jones asked, snatching his hand from the phone as though it were a snake.

Charlton nodded. Jones came around his desk smiling, and extended his hand.

"Mr. Clark, it's a pleasure!"

Their hands clasped and they shared a firm handshake. Charlton felt ill. Invisible slim coated his hand and he snatched it away as Jones gestured for a chair in front of his desk.

"Please, have a seat."

Charlton waited for Jones to return to his chair, and they sat in unison.

"You know, it's funny," Jones said, a charming, phony grin on his face, "but I feel like I've seen you before. Do I know you?"

Charlton gazed intently at Jones, then smiled.

"Perhaps. I do seem to have one of those faces everyone thinks they've seen before."

"Huh," Jones grunted. "So, you're the lumber man, eh? Tell me, why should I drop my supplier and switch to you?"

An air of arrogance surrounded him.

Charlton clenched his jaw tight. "Because of Sophie."

Morgan Jones's face went white as a sheet. Realization spilled over his face, much faster than Charlton had expected. But there it was. Live and in Technicolor.

"Oh, fuck, it's you!" Jones spat, sitting up in his chair.

Charlton pulled his .25 automatic out of his pocket and shot Jones in the left shoulder.

Blood spurted out of Jones's shoulder, and he grabbed at it with his right hand.

"Oh, God!" Jones screamed. "Oh, no, God! Why?!"

Tears spilled from the bleeding man's eyes. Charlton glared at him, fury blazing on his face.

"Why? *WHY?* My little sister! That's why!"

He shot Jones again, this time in his right shoulder. The hand that had been nursing the left shoulder jerked away as another spout of blood erupted from Jones.

"Oh, *Jesus*, I'm sorry!" he wailed. "I'm so sorry! Please! Don't do this!"

Charlton walked slowly around the desk, the gun's aim never moving from Jones's head.

"You may as well shut up, because I'm not through with you by a long shot," Charlton said. "I'm going to completely incapacitate you with bullets, then I'm going cut open your meat shirt and show you your own *black* heart, beating its final beat in my hand while you try to hold your lower intestines inside your gut!"

Morgan Jones looked terrified. His bottom lip began to quiver like a child's who's been chastised.

"I'll do anything! *Please!* ANYTHING!"

Charlton shot two more times, once into each of Jones's knees. Jones screamed some more as blood spritzed his face. He begged a while longer, even after Charlton shot each of his hands and feet, and finished up with the elbows. Blood found its way all over the walls and covered the desk and carpet.

Then Charlton put the gun away and pulled on latex gloves.

"Time to get dirty," he said, a hint of glee dancing from his tone.

Jones cried like a ten-year-old girl as Charlton reached into his pocket and retrieved the box cutter. It was stained with the blood of Reverend Frost and his wife.

Something clicked in Jones's eyes when he saw the box cutter, and his dreary, drooping eyes shot open wide.

"You," Jones said, panicked. "It was you that killed the Reverend! My, God! What're you doing, Charlie?"

The name caused extra rage to dance into Charlton's nervous system.

"Don't you dare call me that, you *shit*!"

He pushed the blade out of the box cutter with a ratcheting click.

"This is gonna hurt," Charlton said, grinning. "Bad."

---

Charlton cut off Jones's head and stuffed it into his abdomen. He'd very much enjoyed that part at the Reverend's house, and like before, as though watching from afar, he watched himself do it again.

Once done, he stuck Jones's heart on the top of his neck, right where his head had been moments before. The heart had myriad tubes and veins, severed and ripped from the removal, splaying out in several directions like a bad hairdo on a homeless man.

He thought it looked nice.

Charlton made quick work of picking up his empty casings, and then wiping down everything he'd touched with a paper towel from the bathroom. He put the gun and knife back into his pocket, along with his gloves. This time he'd worn slick-bottomed leather loafers with no impressions on the bottoms, so he'd not bothered with the hospital booties.

After one final look, satisfied that he'd gotten all the evidence he needed to get, he strolled out to the town car, got in, and drove away.

On his way down the road, about two miles from Jones's office, he saw Ms. Clark pulling out of a sandwich shop. She saw him and waved, her smile beaming.

*Great. Now the heat is gonna be intense.*

No matter.

He'd been under the radar for long enough now, it didn't matter what he did. No one had ever heard of him. He would at least have time to finish what he had to do. And after that, he didn't care what happened. All he wanted was justice. Justice for Sophie.

Charlton, little Charlie, drove straight home.

# CHAPTER
# 8

F letcher gagged as he walked into the mobile office of Morgan Jones.

Blood was everywhere. And the word *everywhere* should be taken quite literally. It spattered the walls, the desk, a computer screen. Thick, drying clots of the stuff had pooled into the thin carpeting and soaked the chair. Even the man's intestines were all over the floor in tangled knots. There was a human heart—presumably Jones's own—where the man's head should be, and the grotesque image of a face, frozen in terror, gaping out of Jones's unzipped stomach.

Fletcher turned away from the sight, pinching his eyes shut as he suppressed a wave of nausea. As he took a deep, steadying breath, Benson walked up beside him. Fletcher opened his eyes, grateful to look upon a living, breathing, all-put-together person, even if that person was a little green.

"So whatcha think? Same guy as the Reverend?" Benson said flatly, his jaw locked tight in a grimace that Fletcher presumed was either fear or anger. Maybe both.

"Yeah," Fletcher responded as he let out another breath. "Probably the same guy."

*Either him or our OTHER psycho who's opening stomachs and stuffing them with heads. Fifty-fifty. Could go either way.*

He paused and turned to take one more look at Jones. That terrible, horrified face glared out from behind a curtain of human flesh. A face he knew.

And despised.

"Elliot, I know this guy," Fletcher said, still staring at the nightmare.

Benson stiffened beside him. "You know *him*? How?"

Fletcher grabbed his arm and pulled him into a room at the opposite end of the trailer where there was a considerably smaller quotient of Forensics Specialists and Medical Examiners.

Once inside, he closed the door to a crack and spoke in a low voice.

"You remember last night at the bar?" Fletcher began, pausing to take a large gulp of saliva, "I told you about the guy who molested those children?"

"Yeah, yeah. I remember," Benson said, rocking forward on the balls of his feet.

"Well," Fletcher continued, "our DOA is one of the guys who helped the preacher cover it all up."

Benson's face drained of color and his jaw fell open in a comical parody of surprise that was altogether humorless.

"*Him!*" he exclaimed in a hissing whisper. "He's one of the scumbag hypocrites who helped a child molester walk free?"

Fletcher could see his young partner's arm trembling—it had snapped out to point towards the room at the other end of the trailer where the dead man sat—and noticed the mildest quiver in Benson's bottom lip. His face conveyed pure surprise, disgust, and something else Fletcher couldn't identify.

"Yep," Fletcher said. "He was one of the elders. Everyone in the church looked up to him. Hell, *still* do for all I know. But he tried convincing those people their children were lying to get attention. All *fourteen* of them."

"Ah, *geez!*" Benson said, clamping his hands to his waist. "Look, I think this dead guy was of the lowest caliber of people on the planet, *but*...I don't think he should have been murdered. Certainly not like this."

Benson finished and looked over Fletcher's shoulder toward the other end of the trailer. Toward the carnage.

"*Humph*," Fletcher grunted. "He got off easy as far as I'm concerned. But never mind him, the Reverend Frost never seemed to hurt anyone and his pretty little wife certainly didn't hurt anything but a few male necks. *They* didn't deserve it, fairy-tale beliefs or not."

Benson shrugged and straightened. Fletcher could see Benson didn't want to get into it again. Not now.

"Alright, well let's go talk to this hysterical secretary," Benson said as he pulled the door open and went back into the trailer proper.

They walked out of the mobile office and into the early afternoon sun. Fletcher waved at the ME along the way, miming a phone call with his hand and pointing to him as they went. The ME gave him a thumbs-up and turned back to his grizzly work.

Fletcher and Benson crossed the parking area and approached Ms. Sandy Clark. She stood by a patrol car, visibly shaking and crying profusely. Some of the men who worked for Jones's company were trying to comfort her, but there was no comfort to be had and they were bad at it anyway.

Fletcher flashed his badge to her and the others with her.

"Hey fellas, we need a few minutes alone with the lady," he said.

They looked at her, as if seeking permission to abandon her. She gave it with a nod. They made a few more pitiful condolences and ambled away.

It took longer than Fletcher would have liked—patience was a virtue he had only a nodding acquaintance with—and he had to suppress another of his patented *huffs*.

When the men were gone, Benson opened the dialogue.

"Miss, we understand this is very difficult for you, but it would really help us if you could tell us *anything* that might help us find who did this."

He was delicate. The perfect balance of empathy and professionalism. It was a way of dealing with people that made them feel safe and understood, but without becoming entangled in their feelings. Detached, yet comforting. Fletcher was impressed. Benson handled the fragile woman's emotions better than he would have been able to do himself.

*Yeah. Some great feat, Harry. You're about as emotionally gentle as a hippopotamus is graceful.*

Shut up.

The woman began to nod in quick jerks. She dabbed her tears from each eye with the palms of her hands while trying to calm herself.

"Clark," she said after a moment in a shaky voice. "He said his name was Jonathan Clark. Mr. Jones had an appointment with him at noon today. I met him as I was on my way out to lunch. He was right on time."

She smiled, looking rather silly with the streaks of mascara running down her face, and for a moment it seemed she was about to dive back into her hysterics. But then Benson smiled, more with his eyes than anything else, and she seemed to calm down to a manageable level.

"I said hi to him," she went on with a forced smile. "I joked about us having the same last name."

She stopped smiling then. Fear returned to her features, carving deep lines into her face. Her eyes suddenly seemed too big for their sockets.

"Oh, God! What if I hadn't left? What if I'd stayed in for lunch? Oh, geez, that's what I usually do! I just forgot my bag lunch this morning by accident and had to go out for lunch today!"

Her fragile calm broke. She began to cry again in big, gasping sobs.

"Poor Mr. Jones!" she wailed. "If only I'd been here! Maybe he would be okay if he hadn't been alone!"

"If you had been here," Fletcher piped in, "you'd probably be dead too."

He said it so matter-of-factly that her face turned nearly white. All remnant of color quite literally vanished.

"Oh…my," was all she could mutter in return.

Benson reached out and gave her a reassuring squeeze on the shoulder. She tensed for a moment, then Fletcher watched her muscles ease and her shoulders drop as she accepted the comfort.

"Do you think you could describe him to us?" Benson asked her in a kind, soft voice. "Maybe to a sketch artist? What did this Jonathan Clark look like?"

She was wiping her eyes clear again as she began to nod.

"Yes," she said. "I-I think so."

"Was he tall, short, fat, thin, white, black, Hispanic?" Benson trailed off, leaving the opening for her to fill in the blanks.

"He was kinda tall, I guess. A white guy. Pretty thin, too, but he didn't look *skinny*, you know, like a puny dude with no meat. No, he looked like he was in good shape, but he was wearing a business suit so it was sort of hard to tell just how built he was. His hair was long and black. Went all the way to his shoulders. Oh, and…"

She trailed off, not finishing. Her eyes looked down to the ground and she knotted her hands together at her middle.

"And, what, Miss Clark?" Benson asked, kindly and patiently.

"Well," she said, an awkward expression on her face. "He was sort of, I dunno…*ugly*. His teeth were all bucked out and his nose was sort of crooked, like maybe it had been broken before. But maybe not. It *was* crooked, though."

Fletcher had to stifle a frustrated and humorless smile that threatened to spread across his face. Aside from the teeth and the nose, she had just described more than seventy percent of males in East Texas.

"So," Fletcher stepped in, unable to contain his frustration, "he's a kinda tall white guy who's fairly thin but buff, though you're not sure how much because he was wearing a suit, had long, black hair and he was ugly? Is that what you're telling us, miss?"

His words were sharp, much sharper than he'd intended, and he could see they cut her.

"I'm sorry," she said through eyes now welling again with tears. "I'm trying to help! I just keep seeing Mr. Jones when I walked in there after lunch, and…"

She broke down again. Benson helped her to a seat in the back of the patrol car, her legs and feet hanging out the side. Once he had her situated, he glared up at Fletcher and took him by the arm, leading him away from the crying woman.

"Was that necessary?" he said through clenched teeth.

Fletcher felt a pang of remorse.

*What, you're an asshole, just not a TOTAL asshole? Is that it, Harry?*

Shut up.

"I'm sorry, lady," he said to Sandy over Benson's shoulder. "I'm just frustrated. There's a guy in *my* town doing this and I'd really like to catch him. I shouldn't have been so rude."

She looked up at him and smiled from the back of the patrol car. Fletcher noticed for the first time how elegant her eyes were. They reminded him of eyes that he'd stared into a thousand times before. Found comfort in. And lost.

Fresh remorse panged him in the ribcage.

"It's okay," she said. "I know you want to catch the guy. I hope to God you do. I'm sorry I can't be of any more help."

Benson turned and smiled to her again.

"If you could just repeat what you told us to our sketch artist down at the station, we'd be very grateful."

"Okay," she said. "And I'll pray for y'all."

It was the first time Fletcher noticed a southern drawl in her voice, though it was slight.

"Thank you, ma'am," Benson said. "The more prayers we can get, the better."

Now Fletcher rolled his eyes. He turned to walk away.

*A lot of good that'll do,* he managed to only think and not say.

He was angry. Angry about the killer. Angry about the lack of leads. But mostly he was angry because the killer had just done to Jones what Fletcher had *wanted* to do twenty years ago. Not that Fletcher agreed with vicious murder, not at all, but he was not surprised to find that he was glad Jones was dead. The man was scum, no question about it. *Church* scum, at that. *Church ELDER* scum.

But it was still wrong…*right?*

Benson caught up with Fletcher, snapping him out of his thoughts.

"So, what's our next move?" he said through clenched teeth, clearly biting his tongue about something.

"We get the phone records on Mr. Jones's home and office and see if we can't find something out. This Mr. Clark must have called to make an appointment so we'll go through each number and see what we can turn up."

"Okay," Benson said.

Fletcher could feel the disapproval oozing out of Benson.

"Alright," Fletcher said, stopping and turning to Benson, "what is it?"

Benson tensed, but wasn't backing down.

"I saw you roll your eyes when she said she would pray for us. Why do that?"

Benson's eyes had narrowed as he spoke, and Fletcher was reminded of his high school English teacher, Ms. Higgins. Fletcher had been a bit of a cut up in school, much to the chagrin of *all* his teachers, but especially Ms. Higgins. She was always glaring at him over large, horn-rimmed glasses, perched neatly on the end of her nose as though they were meant to be there, icy thin slits for eyes. The woman could issue disapproval and reproach, all in one intimidating look, as if firing daggers from her eyes.

The memory almost made Fletcher laugh. But he was too pissed off to laugh.

"You know how I feel about that crap," Fletcher said with a dismissive wave of the hand. "Those guys who covered this thing up, especially Damien Smith, mister molester himself, walked away from the worst kind of crime without so much as getting their shoes dirty!"

He paused to let that sink in. Just for a moment. It wasn't going to change Benson's mind, he knew that, but he was going to have his say, goddammit.

"I stayed on my knees through that whole time," Fletcher continued, "*begging* God to let justice befall these men. But it never happened. Ever! For twenty years now. They just walked away clean and that little girl and her family were destroyed. You tell me, what good did my prayers do? Huh?"

Fletcher was inches from Benson's face now, his hot breath pouring onto the younger man.

"They were good for shit, that's what!" Fletcher barked. "Because no one was listening, Benson! No one was there!"

He pointed to the sky with his last statement, a posture he knew was dramatic. But he didn't care. He wanted to get through to Benson. He didn't really care about changing his beliefs, but he wanted, no, *needed* Benson to get it.

But his young partner stood his ground.

"God was there, and He was listening," Benson began. "Everything happens according to His perfect plan. We may not understand why he does things, or allows certain things to occur. But justice, *God's* justice, will be done. God works on an infinitely different timeline than we do. We just have to keep faith, Harry. That's all."

He paused, apparently gathering the nerve to go on.

"And if you don't want to believe it, that's fine," Benson said, holding his hands up in surrender. "That's your choice. But don't mock those of us who choose to have faith. At least we have someone to look to."

Benson turned and walked away then. Fletcher could see his hands clenching at his sides, smacking into his hips as he went.

After Benson had gone about twenty feet, he turned suddenly, staring into Fletcher's eyes. The anger was still there, but there was something else too. Something like wonder.

Sad wonder.

"What do you put your trust in, Harry? Tell me that?"

Fletcher's face was red and bristling with anger. Anger at the case. The job. This new partner. So much more.

"I trust in my*self*!" he shouted.

Benson heeled over, laughing out loud. His brays seemed to be utterly genuine, not forced at all, and it was pushing Fletcher to a point he really didn't want to go. As much as he didn't like his job right now, it was all he had. And if this went much further, he was about to lose it.

Benson finally calmed himself, and wiped tears from his eyes.

"I see, Harry," he said, the last vestiges of laughter exiting now, stage right. "And tell me, what has that gotten you?"

That hurt. Benson could have said any number of things, and all it might have done is piss Fletcher off more. But instead, Benson decided to take a crack at the only tangible thing Fletcher could hold on to in this world.

And he made a mockery of it.

Benson turned and walked towards their unmarked, dark blue police car. He slid into the driver's seat, started the engine, and pulled up next to Fletcher, gravel crunching under the tires. Benson rolled down the window.

"You coming or what?" he asked, not seeming to care either way.

Fletcher frowned at the young cop. He wanted to slap him around, teach him some manners. But he also felt some strange sort of conviction in his heart.

*What if the kid is right, Harry? What if you're just a stubborn old prick?*

Shut up.

It wasn't possible anyway, in Fletcher's estimation. If God was such a merciful being, then why did the family of Sophie Fields suffer so much? Why did so *many* people the world over suffer so damned much?

He didn't have the answers. He wasn't even sure he *wanted* the answers.

"Yeah," he finally responded to Benson. "Yeah, I'm coming."

He walked around to the passenger side of the car and jumped in. He made sure to slam the door hard, a testament to how maturely he was handling their fight.

"Where we going?" Benson asked, ignoring the slam.

Fletcher reached up, pulled his seat belt across his chest, and snapped it into place.

"To tell Mrs. Jones that her husband has just been slaughtered."

They exited the construction site, weaving through the sea of reporters that were assembled at the edge of the property. Throngs of people were scattered about behind the police barricades, some asking questions, others snapping pictures on their cell phones.

Lust. *Blood* lust. The bane of the human condition.

*Deep down, we're all just animals,* Fletcher thought.

But his inner Harry didn't answer him this time. Maybe, for once, he actually agreed.

# CHAPTER 9

Twenty minutes later, Fletcher and Benson arrived at the home of Shannon Jones, wife of the recently disemboweled Morgan Jones. As they parked, they saw her on the front lawn, propped on her knees, wailing in grief. Her dark hair flowed down just past her shoulders where it wasn't matted to her face, and watery brown eyes, soaked with tears, gleamed behind puffy sockets.

She was a thin woman, perhaps fifty years old by the look of her. As they approached, Fletcher was struck by the woman's beauty, despite the streaks of makeup masking her face.

*She could turn heads all day long,* he thought.

Fletcher guessed she was slightly tall for a woman, maybe five foot nine or so. On her knees, though, he couldn't be sure. Her legs were long and nice.

There was a swath of reporters and cameramen surrounding her, firing their questions, oblivious to her woe. Well, maybe not oblivious, but they sure didn't seem to give a damn.

"We're too late," Benson said.

"Let's get the vultures off her," Fletcher said, shouldering his door.

They piled out of their sector car and rushed up into the yard.

"Alright, you blood-suckers, back off!" Fletcher yelled at the reporters, waving his arms at the rodents.

The reporters—neither heeding Fletcher's orders nor caring about his associating them with vampires—diverted their attention from Mrs. Jones to the officers. They were blood-suckers, alright, and they meant to have their blood no matter where they had to plunge their fangs.

Their questions came at Fletcher and Benson like machine guns set to full auto.

"Detectives, do you have any leads?" the first reporter asked.

"Is this murder connected to the murders on Airline Road?" another piped in.

"Any ideas on who's going to die next?" asked a third.

Fletcher pushed reporters off himself and Benson. There were recorders, microphones, cell phones, and cameras jutting from the mob like mechanical limbs, desperate to lap up even the tiniest fragment of information.

"Get outta here!" Fletcher boomed with another wave of his arms. "We have a job to do, and you're all obstructing!"

His words were doing little to persuade the newsmen. Hungry eyes looked back at him like tiny, black monsters preparing to feed. Fletcher was getting nowhere with them, and fast.

"Get her inside, now!" Fletcher snapped at Benson as they pushed through the crowd.

Benson moved. He managed to get past the last of the reporters, knocking one onto his back as the man blurted a grunt of either pain or indignation, and scooped Mrs. Jones up by the arms.

"Come on, miss," Fletcher heard him urge her.

She managed to get her feet under her with Benson's help, then stumbled and sobbed all the way into the house as the younger cop led her away from the blood-thirsty media. Fletcher wasn't far behind them, and he pushed his way backwards through the door, slamming it on the reporters with some satisfaction.

He turned to his partner and the beautiful crying woman. Muffled shouts of questions drifted through the door, but seemed to already be receding. The lack of fresh meat on which to dine had caused the vultures to lose interest.

"Mrs. Jones," Benson began, his voice as soft and soothing as ever, "we know this is a very difficult time for you, but we must ask…"

Fletcher could see a grimace crease Benson's face, and it was one he knew well. That grimace meant the man donning it was having serious regrets on his choice of career. Any detective who's been on the job for any amount of time is well acquainted with these feelings, but Fletcher knew it was also a fleeting thing. Time covers a multitude of sins, and it also turns a man hard.

*It'll get easier, Benson,* Fletcher thought. *Just give it some time. Now, pull it together.*

Benson did.

"Ma'am," Benson said, shedding the grimace, "we need to know if your husband had any enemies? Anyone with a grudge against him that might want to do this?"

Benson's eyes met Fletcher's for a moment, then flicked away. Fletcher could sense a lingering tinge of the anger which had flared between them back at the construction site. He knew the whole thing had been unnecessary, and his own fault to boot, but it didn't give this pretty-boy prick any justification for getting in his face either.

*Screw you, asshole. If you can't take it, find another partner.*

"No," Mrs. Jones said, breaking Fletcher away from his inner monologue. "No one. Everyone loved him! He's a...*was*...an elder in our church!"

Fletcher winced. He was already having trouble with the idea of seeing Morgan Jones as any kind of victim. Jones had been an evil hypocrite, a man who used his position in the church to manipulate people to take money rather than pursue justice for their children. Sure, those parents were no better, choosing money over the well-being of a child, but that didn't change anything about what Morgan Jones did. What he had been.

*Loved him, my ass,* Fletcher thought.

He stepped forward now, taking the lead from Benson in a single stroke.

"You're sure, Mrs. Jones?" Fletcher asked. "There's no one your husband might have pissed off? Maybe, the parent of a molested child, something like that?"

Shannon Jones looked up at Fletcher, her face streaked with black lines, her eyes wide with shock. The color drained from her face, leaving only a pair of rosy blooms on her cheeks.

"How *dare* you accuse my husband of something like that?" she screamed indignantly. "Who are you to—"

She paused a moment, looking closer at Fletcher's face. Her eyes were searching his, stripping the weathering years off his flesh, spreading wider as the endless seconds stretched out.

Fletcher's eyes blazed back at hers, his anger getting the better of him despite his inner Harry warning him to the contrary.

*Reel it in, Harry. Tone it down. You could turn this south real quick if—*

It hit her.

"You!" she screamed, spittle diving from her mouth in a spray. "You're that policeman from the church! Oh, my good Lord! You're the man who arrested Damien! I recognize you now, you terrible man!"

She rose to her feet, fingers pointed at Fletcher accusingly. Her pretty lips were snarled back over her teeth, and any semblance of beauty was now fully erased. Her dark eyes seemed to turn black, and Fletcher wouldn't have been surprised to see foam leak from the corners of her mouth.

She stumbled as she came towards him, and caught herself on a small table of knick-knacks. They rattled and rocked on the frame, a couple tumbling to the floor and shattering.

"You terrible, *awful* man!" she screamed again.

Her hand happened upon a glass ornament perched precariously on the table—some sort of elephant Fletcher deduced—and she threw it at him. He ducked, arms flailing upwards to protect his head. Benson stood aside through all of this, seeming to fade into the setting.

The ornament crashed through a window behind Fletcher, shattering it into large, sharp claws. Out front, delighted murmurings began to rise from the reporters, still lingering about, waiting for blood.

"Get out!" Mrs. Jones screamed. "Get out! Get out of my house! My husband was slaughtered and you *dare* to attack his character? GET *OUT!*"

She continued screaming as Benson emerged from the background and turned Fletcher to the door. Their heads were down, eyes adjusting to the light, and they all but stumbled right into the flock of reporters. Cameras flashed. Microphones were shoved in their faces. The questions recommenced. The vultures had found a corpse, and they meant to feed.

After about a dozen "No comment" responses to the questions, Fletcher and Benson finally made their way back to the police cruiser and dived in, muffling the caws of the news crews.

*Leeches,* Fletcher thought. *They wait until you're down, then come to suck your blood.*

Fletcher turned in the driver's seat and told Benson to call Bert and Ernie.

"Get them down here to finish up with Mrs. Jones," he said. "I think we blew it."

Fletcher dropped the car into drive and pulled onto the street. In the rear-view mirror, Fletcher could see the reporters turn like zombies and go back to the front steps of the Jones residence.

"You mean *you* blew it, Harry!" Benson said as they pulled away. "You were way out of line!"

"Maybe," Fletcher said with a shrug. "But maybe she's just painting her husband in a friendly light. She was right there twenty years ago, right by his side through the whole thing! She's as guilty as he was!"

"Gosh, Harry! You almost sound like you're glad he's dead!"

Fletcher slammed on the brakes. The car came to a screeching halt on a suburban road just North of Longview.

"Well, maybe I am!" Fletcher spat. "Justice is justice, Elliot. You need to get that through your head, get me? It's not all black and white in this god-forsaken world, and sometimes it takes a monster to stop a monster! Especially after our *justice* system screws the fucking pooch!"

He made quotation marks in the air as he said *justice*, and could feel spittle running down his chin. He quickly wiped it off with his sleeve. He was coming unglued. His heart pounded in his chest and in his ears.

*Nice outlook, Harry.*

Shut up.

Benson just glared back at him.

"Maybe it takes a monster," Benson said after a moment, "and maybe it doesn't. But I *refuse* to become one. I'm not going to let the world turn me into one. *Or* let it turn me into you!"

Fletcher could feel the fury trying to swell in him once more, but managed to get the better of it this time. He wrestled it down, took a few deep breaths, and leveled his eyes on Benson.

"That grieving widow," Fletcher said with strained restraint, "stood by and did nothing while her husband manipulated members of their congregation. And he was successful, who *knows* how, with all but *two* families! The Fields's and the Connelly's."

He turned and looked out the windshield, an idea formulating in his mind.

"I think Jack has come back for revenge," he said after a long moment.

Benson's eyes grew wide and his mouth hung open. In an instant, he seemed to have completely forgotten about their argument.

"You mean the father of one of the families who filed charges?"

Fletcher nodded, huffing loudly and not giving one solitary fuck what anyone thought about it.

"She's not going to tell me her husband didn't have any enemies. He's dead, and all she can think about is how he's going to look in the public eye. How *she* is going to look to the public eye. Why the Christ do you think she was out there in the yard when we got there, carrying on? What person would come outside and carry on in front of the cameras like that? No, she doesn't give a shit about Jones, only about his image, which by default, reflects on *her* image."

Now it was Benson's turn to nod.

"You're right," he said thoughtfully. "I didn't see that before. I still think you're a grade-A jerk for how you handled her, but...yeah. I see it."

Fletcher began driving again, and they were silent for several moments, both mulling over the situation and their confrontation in their minds. At least Fletcher assumed so.

Finally, Benson turned to him and spoke.

"Does Ms. Clark's description of the man calling himself Jonathan Clark match this Jack Connelly?"

Straight back to business. Fletcher both admired and despised his partner, at the same time and for the same reasons.

"That's the thing," Fletcher started, completing his self-soothing with a final huff. "He would be older than what she was saying. And he was blond, though that doesn't mean too much. But…"

He paused, staring ahead at the road, thinking hard. Putting things together in his mind.

"He was a smart guy," Fletcher continued. "One of the smartest I've ever known. It's possible that he could have dyed his hair and used makeup for his appearance. And one thing's for sure…"

"What's that?"

"Jack Connelly was one *ugly* dude."

———

They arrived back at the office forty-five minutes later. They had stopped and grabbed a burger before coming back in, and had employed an open avoidance to talking about their disagreements, which were myriad, instead focusing only on the case.

They had discussed Jack Connelly, and his possible connection to the murders. The more Fletcher talked about it, the more he thought it likely, and Benson had agreed.

Now, back at the office, they had fallen into another strained silence. The tension between them was real and palpable, and though Fletcher knew that this could compromise their investigation, he just couldn't bring himself to set things right with Benson. He was, after all, right. Maybe not in how he'd handled the secretary and the widow—he was honest enough with himself to see that—but it didn't make him wrong in what he believed.

So, no, he wouldn't apologize. At least not first, anyway. He'd put in too many years on the job and seen too many things to lower himself to such humility. Benson could apologize, and maybe Fletcher would reciprocate.

*Well, after all, that's how mature adults deal with things. Right, Harry?*

Eat my cock, jerkoff.

*I rest my case.*

Finally, Benson *did* make the first effort.

"Look, about earlier, I just wanted to say I'm sorry."

Fletcher nodded, coming out of his internal turd-tossing contest with his inner Harry, and exhaled.

*Huff, jack-ass.*

Christ, would you shut up?

*You believe in Christ now? Hmm...*

Turd toss won.

"So am I," Harry said, flipping the bird to his inner self. "I *was* out of line back there, even if she was lying. I shouldn't have acted the way I did. I'm just all knotted up about this thing. The only thing I can think of that might have provoked Jones's murder is what happened twenty years ago, but it doesn't explain Frost and his wife. That's the one thing that doesn't add up. I dunno, I guess I'm wound up too tight."

Benson smiled, that sparkling sheen Fletcher despised dancing off his teeth as he did.

"We're gonna make a habit of all this apologizing stuff if we don't watch out," said Benson. "Let's just forget about it. You know, I was thinking the same thing about the Reverend. That just doesn't seem to fit. The wife, that part I get. The guy is doing the deed on Frost, she comes in, he improvises. But why Frost to begin with? That is, if we're even on the right track at all, with the connection from twenty years ago."

"Yeah," Harry said, sighing. "It sounded good to me at first, but who knows, maybe my judgement is getting clouded with all that. Jones is the only connection to it. I think you're right, it doesn't fit. But I'm still going to follow up on Jack Connelly. Prudence, and all that."

Benson nodded, agreeing.

They were walking up the steps of the police station when a rather striking forty-something woman with blond hair stormed out of the building. She was obviously flustered—people leaving police stations often were—and she fumbled with her purse.

Then she saw Fletcher and shot icy daggers from her eyes.

"I've been waiting up here for hours!" the woman barked.

Her eyes were slits and her lips were pressed tightly together, reducing them to little more than a white line, and rose blossoms flushed high on her cheeks.

"Hi, Helen," Fletcher said in a friendly tone, stroking his mustache.

But Helen wasn't in a friendly mood.

"Our daughter says you needed me to come in to discuss your case on my pastor. So, of course, I drop everything and come right down here. Right away! And then I get here and I'm told you took off, wouldn't say what for! So, I waste my time—believe it or not I *am* a busy woman—and all for—"

"Helen," Fletcher started, cutting her off and raising a hand, "I'm sorry. Something came up. I completely forgot."

"Yeah, I'll bet!" she said with a sardonic laugh. "You're good at that! Real good, Harry!"

She started storming past him when he reached out and grabbed her arm to stop her.

"Helen, wait," he said, his voice instantly switching to diplomacy. "Listen. Someone else was murdered."

Her face went white. She had started to pull away from his grasp at once, but his words had rendered her frozen in place. Her bottom lip began to tremble and her eyes clouded, seeming to release the steam that had been trapped in them before.

"Oh, my Lord, Harry," she croaked, covering her mouth. "I'm so sorry. I—I didn't—oh, God, I'm such a fool!"

She smiled now, trying to regain her poise, her cheeks more flushed than ever.

"Just like a woman, eh, Harry?" She attempted to smile at the last part and looked to the ground.

"It's okay," Fletcher said, releasing her arm. "I should have called. No excuses."

Benson stepped forward then, extending his hand and shattering the tension at once.

"Hi," he said, his customized, gleaming smile beaming. "I'm Elliot Benson, Harry's new partner."

She wrenched her eyes free of the ground and met Benson's gaze, smiling. She accepted his hand.

"Helen," she said. "Helen Fletcher. So, your Marvin's replacement?"

The words kicked Fletcher in the stomach. No, it was more like a kick in the balls. A hard kick. He immediately looked to the ground, shoving his hands into his pockets, almost feeling as if the wind had been knocked out of him.

Helen noticed his body language—it wasn't exactly covert—and put a hand over her mouth.

"Oh, my," she groaned. "I'm sorry. That was a stupid thing to say!"

Fletcher looked at her. His eyes stung with tears, but he was smiling.

*Bury it, old-buddy-old-pal. Bury it, and kick dirt over that grave.*

"It's okay," Harry managed. "I know you didn't mean to."

Obviously looking for a way to change the subject, Helen's eyes darted back and forth between he and Benson.

"So," she said. "Who was killed? Was it the same perp who killed my pastor?"

Benson grinned when she said that, and Fletcher did too. She was trying to mend a fence now. Speak his language, so to speak.

"Looks like it," Fletcher said. "And, uh, you're not gonna believe who it was."

Her eyes narrowed and took on a perplexed quality. "Who?"

"Morgan Jones," he said, matter-of-factly.

Helen Fletcher's mouth fell open.

# CHAPTER
# 10

Johnny E was angry.

Born John Michael Elk, he was a tall, muscular African American, and his build lived up to his last name. His head was shaved to a buzz and his eyes were an interesting shade of green. A scar started just above his left eye, and traveled downward to the rise of his cheekbone, the scar-tissue standing out much lighter than his chocolate skin. His nostrils flared as he tried to calm himself with even, deep breaths.

*Just relax, E.*

One of his girls, Shari, was missing. No one had seen or heard from here since last night. It wasn't like her to vanish like this. She knew her place. Johnny E himself had put her in it more than once, and like a good little doggie, she had trained quickly.

The sun was on its way down. It was creeping up on twenty-four hours that Shari had been missing now, and he wanted to find her. *Needed* to find her. A decent shepherd went after his lost sheep, right? At least that was something he'd heard as a child when his grandmother had taken him to her Holy Ghost church.

*Gotta keep the herd together. Can't make no money if the herd starts driftin' off.*

And that was the crux of the matter. He needed her to be generating some income. *His* income.

*Just relax.*

Shari was his best girl, bar none. She made more money for him in a week than all his other girls combined made for him in a month. She was his star. His bankroll. His ticket to the big time.

*My sparklin' flower.*

But she was missing. A good little trained doggie, and she was just gone. Poof. Over and out. See you on the other side, buster. He could see himself searching for her, like any good shepherd, and then finding her. Finding her hiding in some hole in the rocks, thinking she didn't need a shepherd anymore, *no sir, thank you ma'am.* Then this delightful vision would close on Johnny E. placing his gigantic hands around her defecting little neck, and then, *oh, brother,* then he would teach that old dog a new trick.

*Yassuh, boss!* she would croak. *I so sorry boss! I come back wit choo!*

Just like a good little sheep. And sheep need a shepherd. Without your shepherd, who would fight off the wolves?

Johnny E would fight off the wolves. Because Johnny E. was a good shepherd.

*You damn right.*

She wasn't answering her cell phone. That was another thing that didn't add up. She *always* answered her cell phone. He'd bought it for her himself. He told her it was a gift, but of course, as far as Johnny E was concerned, it was a way to generate more income. A good doggie needed to be called. A good doggie *answered* the call, especially the call of her master.

And this good master had tried to call her four times in the last hour. Nothing. He unlocked his phone, tapped and swiped to the dialer, punched in her number. It began to ring.

Once.

Twice.

*Three times*.

After another two rings, her voice mail came on and informed him that if he could just leave her a sexy message after that tone, Shari would call him back as soon as she could and make his dreams come true.

He slammed his thumb hard on the end icon, cursing bitterly. He missed the days of flip-phones when you could angrily snap your phone shut, releasing fury and aggravation.

*Where IS she?*

He had asked the other girls if they had seen her with anyone the night before. A good shepherd investigates, and brother, Johnny E was a good shepherd. He had found through his inquiries that she had been with some ugly-ass white dude—the other girls had said *ugly* with heightened disgust as if balling anyone below a seven on the looks chart were utterly beneath them, which was why Shari brought in so much more money than they did—at around nine-thirty. They told him that it had sounded somewhat rough in her room, but that wasn't unusual. She often took in some wild Johns and she knew how to handle them.

"Grab hold that crank and twist," one girl had said. "He either gonna stop what he doin' or he gonna finish the session early! Either way, all good. Shari know the tricks."

But one girl, a pale little white girl by the name of Brandi, said she had seen the dude leave, and no one had heard from Shari since. She had noticed him just as he pulled out of the lot. Hard to miss an ugly dude like him, she'd told E.

"What was he drivin'?" Johnny E asked, perturbed.

If he found out some *punk*-ass white boy had come in and taken his best girl...

*Oh, Lord Jesus, cracka goan meet his maker!*

Brandi shrugged and dug into her bag, producing a pack of cigarettes.

"I dunno," she said and coughed as she lit a cigarette.

When she dispelled the smoke from her lungs, a fresh fit of wet coughs ensued, followed by a grotesque hocking which produced a lunger most high-school boys would be proud of. She spat it into the trash can, then took another drag, holding it together a little better this time.

"I think it was like a little car or something," she said. "Can't be sure, though. It was dark as shit."

Johnny wanted to smash her puny face to a pulp, then keep on smashing until the pulp turned to a watery mush. But, like a good shepherd, he resisted the urge.

"Did you see her with him?" he asked. "She maybe in the back? Leaned over the front in his lap? Some dudes is into that."

She shrugged, maddeningly aloof.

"How should I know? I was just lookin' out my window and happened to notice the guy leave. If he was gettin' road head from Shari, I couldn't tell. One thing, though…"

Johnny was leaning forward on the balls of his feet, his flesh tingling.

"One thing? One thing what?"

She smiled. "He was calm. I mean like *really* calm. A John comes and gets his jollies off with one of us, he's usually nervous as hell when he leaves, lookin' all around, making sure he isn't seen. You know."

"Yeah, yeah."

She began laughing aloud, and this led into another coughing fit and a few more drags on her cigarette.

Johnny glared down at her, the disgust on his face all too apparent. "The hell is so funny, Brandi?"

She settled her laugh into chuckle and shook her head. Then she shrugged again, her greatest talent outside the sheets.

"We get a lot of weirdo's around here, but Jesus. I dunno why it strikes me funny. Maybe 'cause it was so weird. Creepy even. Dude was calm. Way too calm."

Johnny slapped her across the face hard. That had been quite enough for him. A calm John leaving the motel meant nothing to him, but her laughing indifference was pissing him off.

The cigarette in her mouth flew from her lips in a spray of sparks and she stumbled back into the wall of the rat motel. Blood started streaming out of her nose and her jaw hung open in shock surprise.

"Ah, Christ, Johnny!" she yelped. "The hell was that for?"

"You ain't told me sooner!" he yelled and smacked her again. "A too-calm dude don't mean shit, not normally, but a too-calm dude taking off, who been with Shari—who's missing—*might* mean shit!"

Her lip was busted and bleeding now, joining her nose.

"I'm sorry, Johnny!" she whimpered. "I'm sorry. I didn't think!"

"When have you ever thought?" he said, then spat in her face.

She shrunk to the ground, crying. Blood and spittle ran down her face, obscuring her tears as she sobbed.

Johnny walked away, unlocking his cell phone, again longing for the good old days when you could dramatically flip them open. He dialed a number and after a few rings a man answered.

"Hello?"

Johnny spoke quietly.

"J.R.," he said. "It's Johnny. We got a problem."

The man called J.R. spoke rashly.

"Don't call me with your problems. They aren't mine and I'll have nothing to do with them. Do you know how stupid you are to call here?"

Johnny ignored him and went on. "It's about Shari."

There was silence on the line for a few seconds.

"What's happened?" J.R. finally responded.

"She's missing," Johnny went on. "Since last night. I've done some checking. She was with a John last night about nine-thirty. Then that dude took off and she ain't been seen since. We checked the room, too. No sheets on the bed and no towels in the bathroom."

"Do you think she's dead?" J.R. finally asked coolly.

"I don't know, man," Johnny said. "I don't think so. I think this punk came in and snatched her, then took the sheets and towels to tie her up with. I seen it happen before."

"And the mattress? Was it cool?"

"Yeah, nothin' on it."

"You were thorough? You know how important it is to be thorough."

"Yeah, yeah. I was thorough, brah! Nuttin' on it, man. It was clean!"

J.R. breathed deeply a few times.

"I don't need to tell you how much money we could both loose because of this," J.R. said evenly. "My clients like Shari. In fact, the only reason they will even go to someone else is if she's busy, and even then only if they simply can't wait. Some men's…appetites must be satiated. Do you understand me?"

"Yeah, I know, bruh! That's why I done called you! You think I'm stupid?"

There was quiet laughter on the other end of the line which caused Johnny E to grip his phone tighter and made his nostrils flare.

"Do you really want me to answer that?" J.R. asked.

"Man, fuck you!" Johnny said. "We need to find this girl and waste this punk-ass, and quick. I gots bills to pay, and you gots dudes to get laid. Ya feelin' me, bruh?"

"Yeah," J.R. said, exhaling into the receiver. "I'm feelin' ya. What do you need?"

"I'll need a car, a nice one, some firepower and…"

He paused.

"And *what?*" J.R. asked impatiently.

"And a couple of your best bloodhounds," Johnny said, his jaw clenched.

"Oh, I see," J.R. responded blandly. "You mean Alexander and Douglas."

"Hey-hey, my man," Johnny said smiling. "You *are* feelin' me!"

---

Two hours later, Alexander and Douglas pulled their car—a beautiful, black Mercedes Benz—up the drive of the rat motel. The falling light sheened off the reflective paint and sent dancing prisms in every direction.

Johnny, unaware of their presence, was in his office watching the news. There was a report about a possible serial killer on the loose in Longview. A police sketch drawing of the perpetrator appeared in the top right corner of the screen, next to the news anchor.

While the anchor went on about the killings, Brandi walked into the office of the motel, her face bruised and puffy, but clean of blood. She'd even put some make-up on, perhaps in hopes of luring some undiscriminating John for an evening of her services.

She glanced up at the screen, peering at it like it was some ancient relic she had heard of, but never actually seen.

Then her eyes lit up.

"I can't believe it!" she exclaimed.

Johnny glanced over at her, annoyed.

"Man, what choo goin' on 'bout, girl?"

She began to point at the screen, her shaky finger bouncing from her excited hand.

"That's the guy, Johnny! That's the guy who was with Shari!"

Johnny's jaw fell open as his gaze followed her finger back to the TV.

"Naw, you lyin', girl!"

"No I ain't, Johnny!" she exclaimed, shaking her head and continuing to point at the television screen. "That's the guy! I'm tellin' ya, that's him!"

Johnny spun around to his computer and looked up the news channel's website. After a few clicks and whirs from the CPU's internals, he was printing out the picture of a man the police were calling Jonathan Clark.

As the picture fell onto the tray, Alexander and Douglas walked in, and Johnny E met their eyes, beaming.

"Alex, Doug, 'bout time y'all got here!" Johnny exclaimed and held up the sketch of the serial killer.

"This the dude we lookin' for!" Johnny said. "And we gotta find his punk-ass before the Five-O do!"

The two men, dressed in fine designer suits, took a good look at the drawing, then nodded.

# CHAPTER
## 11

J.R. Hays hung up the phone. He'd just spoken to Alexander Spears. He and Douglas Weir were now with Johnny Elk and there had been a very favorable development.

They had a picture of the last man to see Shari alive. But not all was favorable. The picture of the man had come from the police sketches of the maniac who had allegedly slaughtered Morgan Jones that very day. Whoever the man was, he was fucking with J.R.'s chi from every angle.

J.R. sat down at his desk. He was in his home office, a large study with an oak desk, and shelves and shelves of books on various subjects, both fictional and non-fictional. His chair was a large, black leather thing with a tall back that emphasized the epitome of expensive taste. There was a computer to the left side of the desk with a picture of him and another man, shaking hands and smiling.

J.R. was an older man, sixty-three, but was in reasonably good health. His hair was short and wiry, peppered with dark patches here and there that stood out against the gray of the majority. His face was weathered, the look a man gets by spending too many years out in the elements, but it gave him a hard look. An intimidating look. It matched perfectly with his icy gray eyes and his six-foot two-inch stature.

He was not someone people wanted to cross.

*Percy's gonna freak out,* he thought.

Percy was the other man in the picture. J.R. had just recently been informed about the death of Morgan Jones. They'd served as elders together at Glorious Rising Church for decades, and had been friends even longer. Together with the others on the Elder Board and the pastor, they had made a small fortune raising money for various organizations, all of which were founded and run by them. The five of them had been defrauding people for a long time and they had the system down pat. Each of them got a share of it and each had his own part to play.

*And Damien nearly ruined it for us all, the filthy pervert...*

Oh, yeah. Damien. The liability. But a very wealthy liability. A liability worth keeping around, as it turned out. The man had more money than he knew what to do with. Millions. *Tens* of millions.

And that had been their saving grace.

*Thank God for greedy people.*

Incredibly greedy, as it had turned out. Those people had sold out their children's welfare for a stack of cash, and the Elder Board had been happy to provide the stacks.

J.R. reached across the table to a small chest atop his desk. He opened it, revealing a stash of large cigars. He took one, closed the chest, and opened his drawer. After rummaging around for a few seconds, he produced a cigar cutter, and he clipped off the end of the stogie. He placed the cigar between his lips and reached again across his desk, this time just to the right of his cigar box. He picked up a rather nice, gold plated lighter, struck it, and fired up the cigar. After it was lit, he watched the flame on the lighter for a couple of moments, thinking deeply.

Finally, he clicked the lid of the lighter shut, sighing as he did so, and replaced it where he'd found it. He took a couple of long drags off the cigar and leaned his head back as he released the smoke. It danced out of his mouth and rolled into the air above.

*We have such a problem.*

He pulled an ashtray up and placed the cigar delicately on the lip. He turned to his computer and powered it on. It whirred and moaned as it booted up. After a few moments, he was at the login screen. He typed a password, the screen redrew, and he was suddenly staring at his computer desktop in Windows. He then logged on to the internet and looked up the same website that Johnny Elk had. He wanted to see the picture of the man the police were calling Jonathan Clark. He hadn't been following the story on the news. The news—all of it—would be easily accessible on the internet, and he needed to think first. J.R. was a man who thought a lot, and he liked to get his mind serene before diving into a problem.

But now the time had come to dive in, and he needed information. He studied the picture for several moments. It had a strikingly familiar quality, but he couldn't place why.

*Do I know this man?*

No. Certainly not.

Whether he knew the man in the picture or not, the man posed a problem for him, and in more ways than one.

First, of course, there was the disappearance of Shari. J.R. and Johnny had a good deal going. Had for years now, in fact. J.R. would bring some wealthy businessmen, tired of their wives and mundane routines, to Johnny's establishment. Those men would pick out a girl and pay Johnny for time with her. It was a different deal than what any old Joe off the street would have to do. Most guys would just come up, find a girl outside her room, and pay her directly.

But not wealthy men. J.R. and Johnny knew it, and had thus made the new deal for them and them alone.

J.R. received a fee for delivering the men, and Johnny took a large cut after paying the girls their pittance. It was quite the arrangement, and the two of them were making a killing at it. Shari was the group favorite among the rich guys, and her disappearance could prove devastating to their income. She had to be found, *if* she was still alive. And if she wasn't, well…

Well, then they were due some justice. Which brought him to the second problem.

*Morgan.*

Morgan's murder and the link between his killer and Shari disturbed him. Morgan had been an intricate part of their dealings through the church. And if this Jonathan Clark did such horrible things to Morgan, the logical assumption was that Shari had met a similar end.

However, that was not certain. The whole thing could be coincidence, as much as his gut told him it wasn't. If she was alive, they needed to get her back—*on* her back—so she could make them money. If she was dead, they needed to find the guy responsible. They needed to make an example of him. And if he turned out to really be the guy who'd done in Morgan, well, all the better.

He picked up his cigar and took another few puffs. He was thinking, that thing he was best at, his stomach in knots.

Mr. Spears was his most efficient employee, and Douglas was certainly no slouch. He had no doubt they would find this Jonathan Clark and dispose of him properly. But the link to the serial killer was eating at him.

*Who IS this guy? And what does he want?*

His head had begun to ache at the news of Shari's disappearance and Morgan's death. He had some Vicodin in his medicine cabinet, and strode toward the bathroom to retrieve it. He had been taking the sedative for a couple of years. He'd first gotten started on it when his severe migraines had gotten out of control and nothing else would work. His doctor prescribed it to him, and in return, he received a discount on Johnny E's girls.

He opened the cabinet, found the Vicodin, and popped one. Then he retired again to his study to await the high and the pain relief. He decided to call Percy. He needed to know what was happening. He probably already knew about Morgan, but likely not about Shari. The preacher and the other remaining elders would want to know about this. After all, it affected them too.

J.R. picked up his phone, dialed a number. After a few rings, a man answered.

"Hello?"

J.R. took another drag off his cigar before speaking.

"Percy," he said, exhaling the smoke, "it's J.R. We've got a problem."

Percy's voice came through frantic.

"Yeah, I know there's a problem!" he squawked. "Morgan's been fucking murdered!"

"That's not what I'm talking about, Percy," J.R. said, sighing. "It's Shari. She's missing."

Percy cursed a few times, tainting the line with profanity.

"Do you have Spears on this?" Percy finally said.

"Yes. Of course."

"Any leads?"

"Just one," J.R. said. "You watched the news on Morgan's death, I assume?"

"Of course! Why?"

"You remember the sketch drawing of the man they call Jonathan Clark?"

"Yes! Yes! What are you driving at?" Percy said, panic in his voice.

J.R. took in one more hit off his cigar and proceeded to mash it out in the ashtray.

"What I'm driving at," he began, obvious contempt in his voice, "is this Jonathan Clark is the last person seen with Shari."

There was a thump on the other end of the line and another eruption of profanity.

"Hello?" J.R. said. "Percy? You there?"

Nothing.

"Hello? Percy, pick up the phone!"

There were some fumbling noises and finally Percy was back on the line, hissing through the receiver.

"I don't need to tell you what kind of shit will fall in our laps if this Clark isn't stopped. You know he also did the murders on Airline Road?"

"Yeah," J.R. said. "I know."

"This psycho is targeting church leaders and apparently hookers too," he panted. "If he decides to continue in on our eldership, we've all got to watch our backs!"

J.R. nodded, pinching his eyes shut in frustration.

"Yeah, I know, but he didn't touch anyone else from Reverend Frost's church. No reason to think he'll do any different with us."

"True," Percy said, a little calmer now. "It's a shame too. Frost was a problem I'm glad to be rid of. He was getting too close to, well, you know. Nonetheless, make sure Spears and Weir have all the resources they need. Damien has offered any funds necessary to get this done."

"Damien's there?" J.R. asked, perturbed at this new information.

"Yes, he is. We were just finishing a nightcap when you called."

"Okay," J.R. said. "I'll pass the offer along."

"Very good," Percy said, then added, "Make this go away, J.R."

"Don't worry," J.R. smiled to himself. "It's gone."

# CHAPTER
# 12

Charlton Fields awoke the next morning, exhilarated.

He was smiling as he went to his bathroom and showered. He was still smiling as he dressed for the day. Yesterday had been one of the best experiences of his life. The first kill of the five had given him a new zeal for life. He savored every breath of air, every bite of food, every minute of the day.

Every second of Morgan Jones's weeping, pathetic death.

Ah, yes. Killing Jones had been wonderful, alright. Charlton could feel Sophie and his parents with him, cheering him on, helping him carve out the man's heart.

*No, not man. Monster.*

Yes, Jones had been a monster. A man willing to bribe and lie about little children just to save face with a community of imbeciles who couldn't see—or *refused* to see—what the leadership of their church was up to. That they were raking in thousands of dollars a week, even *tens* of thousands of dollars a week after a while with the wealthy membership they attracted, was a foreign idea to these dolts. If they even knew, they didn't seem to care.

*No matter.*

Charlton, little Charlie, would show them. He would show them all. He no longer simply wanted to kill off the people responsible for his family's death. No sir, that just wouldn't do. That was only the beginning. Beyond that, he meant to humiliate them. Expose them.

*Stop them.*

Yes. He would stop them. They could not be allowed to continue. If they did, there would be no end to their reign of terror. Their reign of lies.

Oh, that made Charlton cringe. The lies. The spreading of their lying Gospel.

When Charlton's mind went to God, he felt that he might puke. Could taste it in his mouth. What idiot would believe such trash? His parents—may they rest in peace—were obviously manipulated into believing in a Sovereign and Holy God. But what God would allow such atrocities to *happen*, much less go unpunished? Was this supposed to be how an all-loving God operated? An all-*merciful* God?

*Too merciful, if you ask me.*

No. No *true* God would allow such things to occur, especially in His own house. It was an insane idea, this one of God and Jesus and the Holy Spirit. All a bunch of horseshit.

But it hadn't been God who'd killed Charlton's family. God's *followers* had done that. And now he would destroy them. Expose them. Humiliate them.

End them.

The one thing in the Bible Charlton agreed with came to his mind. The Old Testament's take on justice.

*An eye for an eye.*

Charlton, little Charlie, smiled again. Even a broken clock was right twice a day, he supposed.

He was all ready for his day. He walked to his closet and opened the door, exposing the hit-list within. Charlton grabbed a pen and marked through Morgan Jones' picture.

*One down, four to go.*

Four to go. Next on the list was Tony White.

Tony had been harder to locate than the other four. He was still involved in the church with the others, but he had moved to the country several miles out of town and lived a rather private life.

But not private enough.

Charlton had found him and mapped out his plan. Since he lived in the country, in a small mansion in the woods, he felt more comfortable striking at night. After all, the closest neighbor was more than a mile away through the woods, so there would be no chance of anyone hearing *anyone* scream.

*And oh yes, friends and neighbors, there would be screaming.*

Little Charlie savored the thought. The anticipation surged adrenaline through his veins. A primal, metallic taste flooded the back of his mouth.

Ready.

He watched the news later that morning and saw there was a seventy percent chance of thunderstorms for the evening.

*How fitting.*

Then he saw a rough drawing of himself and a story about a manhunt for a man named Jonathan Clark. Irritating as it was—he now wished he'd spent just a few more minutes to take out Sandy Clark—it was of little importance. No matter. He could change his appearance and simply not make the same mistake again.

*No more mistakes!*

He looked in the mirror. The resemblance on television was shaky at best, but still too close for comfort.

He ran his fingers through his long, thick black hair. It was a shame, but it would have to go. It was the most prominent thing in the sketch and its disappearance would change his look significantly.

He shaved his head with a pair of trimmers, then lathered his scalp with shaving cream. He took a straight razor to it. Within a few minutes, the hair was all gone.

After drying off his head, he beheld the results. It was almost shocking how different he looked.

Sure, he still had the bucked teeth and crooked nose, but anyone who didn't know him would never recognize him.

And *no one* knew Charlton Fields. *No one at all.*

His boss had hardly looked at him the entire three years he worked at the firm. This wasn't surprising. After all, he was only a janitor. He'd quit nearly two months ago and moved. The address the firm had was no longer where he lived and he'd left no forwarding address. It would be some time before anyone found him.

*Unless...*

Old Miss Blalock was unless. She lived next door and she'd tried to introduce herself when he moved in, though Charlton had resisted. He soon realized her habit of staring out her window all day and night, noticing when he came and went. Not that she was watching for him specifically, just an old broad who did a lot of looking out the window. Nothing uncommon, really, but under the right circumstances it could prove to be a problem.

He'd also noticed that when she wasn't watching him, he could hear her TV blaring through the windows at phenomenal levels of volume, usually tuned into the local news channel. He had little doubt she had seen his picture. Poor eyesight might be his saving grace, but he couldn't be sure just how sharp her eyes were.

And he'd almost forgotten his landlord.

Mr. Shepard, his crotchety old landlord, was even older than Ms. Blalock. But he didn't have a TV. Charlton was sure of that. The man had gone on and on and on about the moral decay of society at the hands of television when Charlton had been signing his papers on the lease. He was no worry.

*But Miss Blalock...*

Best to grab a few things and disappear. He had his spot in the country he could go stay, a little cabin in the woods. It was only about ten miles out of town. He had run into it while wandering aimlessly one afternoon about six months back, beating trees with sticks and gutting a couple of squirrels he happened to incapacitate with a pellet gun. His typical therapy.

The cabin looked as though it was never used, except perhaps during hunting season. He had a good month or so before that and he would be long finished and gone by then.

He gathered a few clothes, toiletries, and his weapons. He stuffed them into a bag, then stood, rubbing his newly shaved scalp. He smiled broadly.

*Ready or not, Tony, here I come.*

# CHAPTER
## 13

Fletcher arrived at work hung over for the second day in a row. His head ached, only just starting to ease as the Ibuprofen he'd taken with his coffee kicked in, and his stomach felt like it may be planning a revolt, though for now all was quiet on the front.

Dan Felt apparently deduced his state at once—and why not, the man was a detective after all—and issued a disapproving shake of the head, accompanied with a distasteful scowl.

*Yeah, whatever,* Fletcher thought. *Get bent.*

The nightmares had returned with a vengeance after Fletcher finally found sleep the previous night, following a bottle of Jackie D and some worship at the porcelain altar.

In his dreams, Marvin Gaston had asked Fletcher why he had allowed his partner to get killed, Marvin all the while donning a red bullet hole in the center of his forehead. Then, a new dimension to his nightmares joined the first. This one featured Reverend Frost and his wife, live and in technicolor. In it, Fletcher was leaning over Reverend Frost's body when the man's wife's head popped out of the abdomen, glazed in thick blood and spitting out sausages of intestine, snarling all the while.

*"You getting anywhere, Fletcher?"* the head asked, blood running out of the corners of its mouth.

Fletcher had recoiled. Terror beat in his chest and temples, blurred his vision, and clutched his spine with icy fingers.

*"What's the matter, Harry? Never seen a talking head before?"*

The gore-drenched head had begun laughing maniacally, cackling with madness and delight.

Fletcher had run out of the house screaming, but when he exited the front door, he was in his daughter's bedroom. Not her bedroom as it was now, with a college girl's touch, but a little girl's, the room of a girl yet to hit puberty and who still played with dolls.

He took a moment, trying to process what he was seeing, where he'd come from, and how he'd gotten here, when he saw a man with long, black hair standing over his little girl, Heather, no more than ten years old here.

The man was holding a box cutter.

"No!" Fletcher screamed.

The killer just smiled at him and raised the knife above his head. A terrible ratcheting sound seemed to boom in the small room as the blade was pushed out of its housing and gleamed in the gloom.

*Cl-click-click-click-cha!*

That had been when Fletcher awoke, covered in sweat, screaming into the darkness of his bedroom.

Fletcher shuddered at the memories, shoving them aside as he arrived at his desk, as far from himself as he could manage. He tried focusing on the work at hand.

Atop a pile of paper work on his desk was a fresh stack of papers, stapled together. They hadn't been there the night before when he'd gone home. He picked them up, thumbed through a few pages, and realized they were the phone records from Morgan Jones's home and office.

*Back into the grind. You just bury that shit and kick dirt over the grave.*

Good advice.

He sat down and started going through the numbers. Some were already identified as businesses, but others were private and unlisted numbers. Benson came in, holding two cups of coffee and sipping from one. He sat down across from Fletcher.

"Good morning," Benson said with a smile and handed Fletcher a Styrofoam cup with steam rising from the brim.

Fletcher accepted with a nod.

"Morning," he said. "Got the phone records in on Jones. I was just about to go through them. Want half?"

Benson sat his coffee to the side, then got situated in his seat. He twisted his neck one way, then the other, and a haunting, almost ratcheting sound seemed to issue from him as the bones popped.

Fletcher, in his mind's eye, saw the extruding blade of the gleaming box cutter.

*Cl-click-click-click-cha!*

"Sure," Benson said, snapping Fletcher back into the moment. "I've been thinking this through. This guy is pretty calculating. I bet you he called from a pay phone or a throwaway cell phone."

Fletcher nodded.

"Probably so, but we have to run through these and hope he didn't think of that."

Benson nodded in return and grabbed half the stack of numbers from Fletcher.

They began going through the numbers one by one, calling and annoying people who'd had the simple misfortune of knowing Morgan Jones. After an hour, all the numbers had been called and they were again no closer to the elusive *Jonathan Clark*—or so he was called—than they had been before.

"Nothing," Benson said, hanging up the phone on his last call. "The only thing I could dig up on this guy is that he had a lady on the side."

"Oh," Fletcher said. "You talked to her too? That explains her attitude when *I* called!"

They looked at each other a moment, then burst out laughing together. It felt good to laugh, and neither of them did anything to squelch it. They just let it out.

"Yeah," Benson said, wiping an errant tear from the corner of his eye, settling from his laughter. "It's a shame, too. Guy was an elder at his church."

"Since when did *that* ever keep anyone sinless?" Fletcher popped off. "In my years on the force, I've arrested or come across more scumbags that were selling drugs, sleeping around on their wives, even a couple of guys who were stealing, all proud members of their respective local churches."

"No one ever said church made people good." Benson said. "It's your personal walk that defines who you are, not where you go on Sundays."

Fletcher raised his eyebrows, then lowered them in quick succession while sighing.

"Seems a lot of folks just keep falling outta step."

Benson slammed his stack of papers down suddenly, startling Fletcher.

"And what about you, Harry?" Benson snapped. "Huh? You go home and get hammered every night or is that just a new thing you're trying out?"

Fire blazed behind Fletcher's eyes, threatening to burst through his sockets and consume his young partner.

"You mind your own damn business, Elliot!" Fletcher growled, pointing a finger in his face.

"Then how about you quit deliberately stepping on my toes! I'm not gonna change your mind. I accept that. You hate God, hate the church, whatever. It's a shame, but I accept it. But you need to wise up on something yourself, partner! You're not gonna change *my* mind either!"

He sat back in his chair and rubbed his eyes. Fletcher considered what he'd just heard and nodded.

"You're right," Fletcher said. "I'll keep my opinions to myself. But don't you call me *partner* again, you hear me? Not until I say you can. Fair enough?"

"Fair enough," Benson replied, the blaze in his own eyes diminishing.

The phone on Fletcher's desk rang, jolting them both. Their eyes shot to the phone, and Fletcher picked up the receiver.

"Detective Fletcher here," he said into the phone.

There was a pause as he listened to his caller. After nearly a minute, he was scribbling down an address and reading it back to make sure he got it right.

"Thank you, ma'am. We're on our way."

He hung up.

"What's going on?" Benson asked.

"A break, that's what," Fletcher said, grabbing his coat. "That was a Ms. Blalock. She claims to be living next door to our Jonathan Clark!"

Benson sucked down another sip of coffee and grabbed his own coat.

"Sweet."

# CHAPTER
## 14

Twenty minutes later—Fletcher marveled how nearly every place he went in Longview seemed to be
twenty minutes away—they arrived at the home of
Ms. Blalock. She instantly began telling them about a man
living next door whom she recognized as Jonathan Clark
from the police sketch drawing on the news. No hellos, no
introductions. They didn't even have a chance to pull their
badges out. The old lady just dove right in.

She was an elderly woman, probably in her early
eighties. She had the whitest hair Fletcher had ever seen,
almost glowing in the sunlight, and her skin was loose,
sagged and wrinkled, as though the contents within had
shrunk over the years. Her glasses were thick, looking like
the bottoms of glass soda bottles, which made her eyes
look fifty percent larger than they really were. She wore an
old gown or dress, or something like that. It buttoned up
the middle from top to bottom, and a faded floral pattern in
pastel hues of blue and pink splashed its surface. To
Fletcher it looked like a tent with arm holes.

Yet, she had the sort of spunk common to many elderly Southern ladies, a marriage of a know-it-all attitude and utter humility. It was a strange mixture, but there was simply no other way to describe it.

She had a walker, a thin-walled aluminum thing with four legs and three walls, and her arms propped her on it. There were punctured tennis balls on the bottom of each leg, scuffed and bald around the bottom, the yellows dulled to a dirty lime.

"Oh, yes, it was him alright! I'm sure of it," Ms. Blalock said, her eyes floating in the soda bottle glasses. "I don't get around much these days, what with my bad hip and all, so I usually sit by my window and just watch everyone in the neighborhood. Watch the news, too, when it suits me. Most evenings, that is."

Fletcher nodded, taking notes.

"You're *positive* it was him?" he asked.

"Absolutely," she said with a grunt of indignation. "Not a doubt in my mind. I'm old, but I ain't blind yet, son! Eyes may be wearin' a bit, but my spectacles fix that just fine. I could tell ya just how many hairs you got on your lip there if you sit still long enough!"

"That won't be necessary, ma'am," Fletcher said with a laugh.

"He left just a little while ago, too," she went on as though she'd never stopped. "Shame I couldn't reach you sooner. Damn shame, it is."

"Thank you for calling, ma'am," Fletcher said.

They left Ms. Blalock's home through the front door and walked out to the sidewalk. They turned to go to the killer's house when Ms. Blalock called to them once more through her still open door.

"Also, I don't know if it means anything or not, but I'll tell ya anyhow, when he left earlier, he was blond."

Benson's eyes leaped skyward.

"Blond?" he asked.

"Yep!" she quipped, nodding. "Just as blond as he could be. Must've colored his hair or somethin', I dunno. Boy's usually got that long, dark hair, like the TV shown. T'wern't today, though. Yella as bright piss! If I'm lyin', I'm dyin'!"

She punctuated this with a stern, singular nod.

They thanked her and headed on their way. When they were far enough away from her so that she couldn't hear them, Benson spoke to Fletcher.

"Jerry McMahon, that neighbor of Reverend Frost, he said he saw *two* joggers that day, one with longish black hair, the other *blond*. Ms. Clark said—"

"Ms. Clark said that the man called Jonathan Clark had long black hair," Fletcher said, finishing his sentence. "Now we've got a neighbor saying without a doubt the drawing of Clark is her neighbor, but this morning when he left, he was blond."

"Yep," Benson said.

"So, our guy wears wigs, eh?"

"Looks like it," Benson said. "I'm gonna call and get us a warrant. We need to get in there."

Fletcher nodded. "Good idea."

An hour and a half later, they were entering the front door to the home of Longview's first serial killer. The name the house was registered to was Ronald Shepard, but the house wasn't Mr. Shepard's primary residence. He rented it out. Benson had called him to come to the house with everything he had on the renter.

As they went through the house, they found various dead animals in Ziploc bags in the freezer. Most were in several pieces and in varying stages of decay.

*This guy is sick,* Fletcher thought as he shut the freezer door on the corpses.

There were clothes and shoes still in the bedroom closet. The bed was messy, hadn't been made in while it seemed. Old rotting food had fused with paper plates strewn here and there about the house. In the closet, they saw several spots on the door where several things had been for some time, but were now removed.

*Photos, maybe?*

Finding nothing of real interest, they went outside to wait on Mr. Shepard, allowing Forensics—newly arrived in their shiny van—to do their job.

Benson said, "You think this is our guy's house or is Ms. Blalock over there just seeing things?"

Fletcher considered it for a moment, but he already knew.

"I betcha this is his place, alright. Lots of serial killers get started on animals, or so they say in the documentaries. Yeah, this is his place. And hopefully Mr. Shepard will be able to give us a name to go on, always assuming he didn't use an alias, which is a real possibility. But if he didn't, we'll get this guy."

"Yeah," Benson said. "I kind of doubt his name is really Jonathan Clark. By the way, Harry, you ever find anything on Jack Connelly? Think there's a chance this is him?"

"Naw," Fletcher said, shaking his head. "I looked into that. It's not him."

"How are you sure?"

"Because," Harry said, letting loose another huffing sigh, "Jack Connelly died of a heart attack three years ago."

A moment later, an old, beat-to-hell pickup truck pulled to the curb, and a man that looked as old as time stepped out, grabbed a cane, and slowly shuffled up to them. In the eon that passed from the time the old man began dismounting his ancient steed to when he finally stood before them, they got a good look at him.

His head was completely bald, and he was slightly heavy-set. He didn't appear to have always been, but it looked as though age had finally killed his metabolism—merciless bastard that age was—and he'd sprouted love handles, as old men often do. He was about five feet ten inches tall, wearing blue slacks and a white polo shirt with a small alligator etched in over the chest. His shirt was stained with the colors common to battle with various condiments; ketchup, mustard, etcetera.

Under his arm he carried a manila folder, tucked up high to his chest. When he spoke, it was loud and gravelly, like he had swallowed a box of rocks and thought the detectives were a mile away.

"You the fellas I'm supposed to deliver this too?" he shouted.

"Yes sir," Benson said, reaching out to him.

Fletcher thought Benson had meant to shake the man's hand, but instead, the old man offered only the folder. Benson recovered quickly, taking the folder from the man, and flipping it open.

A second later, his mouth fell open.

Mr. Shepard said, "Well, I hope he ain't done nothin' too bad! Sumbitch owes me a month's rent!"

The salty old man turned then, without another word, and shuffled back to his truck.

Fletcher turned to see the expression on Benson's face.

"What is it?" he asked.

"You're not going to believe this," Benson responded, handing over the folder, his jaw still slack.

Fletcher took it in his hands, opened it, and peered in at the name on the renter's agreement.

His heart stopped and his jaw joined Benson's somewhere near the ground.

*Charlton Fields.*

"Isn't that the name of the kid whose family was involved in all that mess twenty years ago?" Benson asked, eyes wide.

The folder fell from Fletcher's hands and tumbled to the grass.

"Yes," Fletcher said. "Little Charlie Fields has come home."

# CHAPTER
## 15

"Just lock up tight, Tony," J.R. Hays was saying on the other end of the line.

Tony White was an aging man with platinum hair and the belly that seemed customary to the elderly, if not quite a legal requirement. He had a salt and pepper beard—much more salt in it than pepper—and the most perfect looking porcelain veneers you ever saw. He was a tallish man, a little over six feet, and he wore blue jeans with a button-down denim shirt.

He stood by a small table in the foyer of his mansion in the woods, a cord swaying gently between himself and the console, the receiver pressed tightly against his ear.

"Yeah, yeah," he said. "I'll lock up so tight it'll make his balls ache. And maybe I'll turn George and Mack loose on the property. Let 'em stretch their legs a bit."

George and Mack were Tony's personal bodyguards, but they weren't human. Tony never fully trusted humans—they could be swayed so damned easily—but dogs were another matter. Dogs understood loyalty. Or maybe it wasn't that they understood it, so much as it was the only thing of which they were capable. Betrayal wasn't in their nature, not these dogs anyway. No, his pair of Doberman Pinchers—his attack dogs, and well trained at that—didn't have a disloyal bone in their bodies.

"That's a good idea," J.R. said. "Like I said before, we don't know if this guy is even coming after the rest of us, in fact it's probably all coincidence and we're up in a scare over nothing, but it would be foolish not to take precautions."

"I agree."

"Also," J.R. began again, "I've put Spears and Weir on this. They should be making headway. They'll report in soon."

"Good," Tony said. "Is it possible to have one of them put on my place tonight?"

While his trust in humans was dubious compared to that which he put in his dogs, he also understood that money bought loyalty in people the way a treat does in dogs. And Spears and Weir were being paid very handsomely.

*Can't be too careful, right?*

There was silence on the line for a few moments as J.R. presumably pondered the idea. Tony could almost see the man holding the idea in his hands, turning it over and over, inspecting it from every angle. J.R. was like that.

Finally, J.R. came back on the line.

"Perhaps Weir," he said. "I don't want to slow Spears down. He's invaluable in a situation like this."

"Fair enough," Tony said with a sigh. "Have him here by six o'clock. He can spend the night here."

"Very well. Six o'clock then."

Tony grunted a modest farewell and hung up the phone. He made his way through his illustrious home to the kitchen and fetched a beer from the refrigerator. Despite his immense wealth, he still had a poor man's taste for alcohol. A cheap, domestic beer quenched his pallet better than fine wine or bourbon. As far as he was concerned, you could keep the cocktails and the fancy drinks. He'd be just fine with a taste of the Rockies.

He took a long swig of beer and ended with an over dramatized 'ahhh!'. The micro-brewed beverage really hit the spot.

He shuddered then, unsure if it was the cold beer chilling his core, or the situation at hand, then decided it was the latter. For more than twenty years, he and his cohorts in the church leadership had been skimming money from the congregation. They were running several 'business endeavors' on the side in both Longview and Tyler, and he'd earned a fortune through it, coupled with his successful career in law.

*Who says the bad guys don't win?*

Oh, yes. Tony White *was* a bad guy. He knew it. Hell, he relished it, never mind being at peace with it.

*Takes a big man to admit what he really is,* Tony thought, putting the beer to his lips for another swig. *Takes an even bigger one to enjoy it.*

And what was there not to enjoy?

He had a life of luxury, a gorgeous young wife, and no less than *three* mistresses. That's right, *three*. Not to mention the girls that Johnny E. managed. Keeping an extra piece or six of ass within arm's reach at all times had almost become a rule. The parties he had with the ladies on his quiet estate, the ones that always ended with he and sometimes two or three of the girls together in his bed.

Sometimes with Shari.

Yes, Shari. She was worth any three of the others on her own, and that, friends and neighbors, was a bona fide fact. That girl was…well…

*Was.*

He winced at the thought of Shari being gone forever. She really was quite something.

*Oh, well,* he thought. *All good things must come to an end.*

But why?

That question had risen in him since the news of Morgan's demise. It was gruesome, and the police were sure that it was the same culprit that killed Frost and his wife, not that anyone with a single, operational brain-cell between their ears thought otherwise. The only real connection between Frost and Jones, so far as Tony could see, was that they were both churchgoers. *But,* Frost had been a straight arrow preacher and Morgan had been a crooked elder.

But no one knew what Morgan really was. In the eyes of the public, Morgan Jones was a saint. Shit, they all were.

*What if someone found out the truth?*

Now therein laid a serious problem, assuming the answer was valid. Of course, that would mean that Frost was as well, if he was to assume this killer was targeting hypocrites in churches.

But that didn't make sense. Frost had been on to the leadership of Glorious Rising Church. He'd been dangerously close to exposing them and ruining everything they had built in their more than twenty-year reign. So the killer going after Frost just didn't add up.

*Unless…*

Unless Frost was trying to get in on it, take a cut for himself. Tony supposed it was possible, but still extremely unlikely.

He returned to his living room, beer in hand, and sat down on his couch. He turned on the TV and switched the channel to a local news station. Once again, they were showing the police sketch drawing of a man they were calling Jonathan Clark.

*And he looked so damned familiar…*

Tony took another long gulp of beer and set the bottle on the table next to him. He had one of those Digital Video Recorders that could pause live television, and he made use of the feature now. He leaned in close, studying the picture. He'd seen this person at some point, he knew it, but he just couldn't place the where or the who. Probably because the artist who had drawn the sketch had accentuated the long, black hair so much that it stood out more than the facial features, which Tony could tell had been skimmed over. Perhaps the witness describing the man hadn't caught a good look.

*But that nose…*

The nose disturbed him. He was certain he'd seen it before, and not just one like it. No, he had seen the bastard on the TV, and now it was going to drive him mad trying to place who it was. If he *did* know the person in the picture, then the threat to him became more real. More than just a *precaution*, and all the more reason to remember.

He turned the TV off with a sigh, his brain spent from searching, but not finding the information he wanted. He went into his study and logged onto the Internet. His computer was already on and idling at the Google search site. With a few clicks, he was looking at a screen where a young girl, maybe eighteen, was looking back at him via web cam. She was completely nude and she smiled broadly at him. It was forced, he could tell, but she earned an A for effort.

"Hello, Mr. White," she said in a sultry voice. "What do want me to do for you today?"

Tony smiled, sickeningly, his perfect dentures slimed with spittle.

"Lola, sweet girl…you know what I want, baby."

Again, she forced a smile. She began to do what he wanted and Tony leaned back in his chair, watching her. He started doing what *he* wanted, but about five minutes into it, his phone rang, interrupting this little exchange.

He swore loudly and told her to hold on. He minimized the window and looked at the caller ID on his phone.

It was J.R.

He swore again, louder and more profanely than before. He snatched the phone up and hissed into the receiver as his penis, an exclamation point only moments before, now drew down to a wrinkled cord in his lap.

"This had better be good!"

There was a momentary silence on the other end, then J.R. said, "Tony, this problem just got more serious than we anticipated!"

There was a definite panicked staccato in the man's voice, yet Tony—still on the verge of rage for having his time with Lola interrupted—hardly registered the gravity of J.R.'s tone.

"What *is* it, J.R.?" he nearly screamed.

"It's about this Jonathan Clark."

"Yeah, yeah," Tony said with a dismissive wave of the hand. "The serial killer we're all shitting our pants about. What about him?"

J.R. cleared his throat, clearly rattled by what he was about to relay to Tony. Thoughts of Lola and what he wanted to finish doing with her began to fade. It wasn't like J.R. to be flustered. Not about anything. The fact that he was caused goose-flesh to sprout all over Tony's skin. His anger turned towards panic.

"Well speak, damnit!"

J.R. cleared his throat once more, and managed to croak out the words.

"Well, his name isn't Jonathan Clark, Tony..."

His voice trailed off again. As though the man simply could *not* relay the information that apparently was important enough to interrupt his hanky-spank time. Hanky-spank time was important, for Christ's sake, and J.R. needed to spit whatever the fuck it was the hell out!

Anger had led to panic, and now panic was leading to frustrated pandemonium in Tony's mind.

"Are you going to tell me, or what? I don't know how many ways to say *spit it out*!"

His statement dripped with sarcasm, but it also dripped with fear.

"I—I'm sorry Tony," J.R. said, gulping audibly. "It's just such a shock. A shock to all of us. It's so…well, it's just crazy is what—"

*"Would you just get to the goddamned point?"* Tony exploded.

And that, *finally*, broke through.

"The killer," J.R. said with a final clearing of his throat, "this Jonathan Clark on the news…well, it's actually Charlton Fields."

The words struck home like an atom bomb.

"Oh, my…" Tony managed, and that was all.

He knew he had recognized the face in the drawing, but he hadn't even considered little Charlie. Little Charlie, whose whole family had committed suicide twenty years ago.

*You killed them, and you know it,* he thought, and didn't disagree.

"*Oh, my* is right," J.R. finally said, some of the strength returning to his voice. "There's now little doubt he's coming after all of us."

Tony finally got his head back on and said, "Yes, but that doesn't explain Frost and his wife!"

"Or Shari," J.R. added.

"You're right. Does Spears have any leads yet?"

"Not yet, but he's working."

"Well you tell him to hurry up, or he's going to be fresh out of employers!" Tony yelled.

Panic was seeping back into his voice now.

"He's on it," J.R. said. "I'll send Weir out to your place now. You're the only one that lives in the country, so you're at the greatest risk."

*That was reassuring. Thank you, J.R., thank you for that!*

"Well he hit Morgan and Frost in the middle of the day *in* town! Who's safe?" Tony asked, as if searching for reassurance.

"No one's safe," J.R. said. "That's my point. No one is safe, least of all you."

Tony realized that his knuckles were aching and turning white around the receiver.

"Get Weir over here, *NOW!*"

He slammed the receiver down on the cradle, his hands trembling. He grabbed his beer and downed the whole thing in a single gulp. His mind thought of Shari. The girls. The money. His business partner, Johnny E.

And it was Johnny E's voice that drifted to him, taunting him, though it was only the voice. The user of the voice was something much darker than Johnny.

*Done messed up now, bruh!* his gigantic, black friend—that wasn't his gigantic, black friend at all—said. *Done shit where you eat, now them flies is coming!*

Tony rushed to the kitchen for another beer, stuffing his flaccid member clumsily into his jeans as he went.

# CHAPTER 16

Alexander Spears, Douglas Weir, and John Elk, a.k.a Johnny E, were driving out of Tyler towards Longview on Interstate 20. They'd seen the news report, as well as received a phone call from J.R. Hays informing them of the killer's identity. Spears had wanted them all to go over to Fields's house right away to go over it with a fine-toothed comb. Find something the police missed.

They always missed something.

Yes, the police, for all their thoroughness, were incapable of catching every detail. Sure, they found clues and got leads as to how to proceed, but they rarely caught that one little detail that could bring them straight to their suspect.

And the reason they always missed that little important detail was they themselves weren't killers. Oh, they say they *get into the mind of the killers*. They *think the way the killer thinks*.

But it just wasn't the same.

Nope. One couldn't merely *think* like a killer to bring one down. It was true that eventually the cops caught most killers, but that was because they went through days and days of questioning and fingerprints and forensics. All that.

But Spears, he had a different approach. He could catch a killer in no time at all because he *was* a killer. He had killed countless people over many years. And he was good at it. Oh, yes, he was *very* good at it. All he needed was a few minutes to poke around, and he would have them. Always had. He had a *nose* for it.

But then J.R. had called back and told them to drop Weir at Tony White's house for protection. Apparently, Tony was scared. Scared he would meet a similar fate to Mr. Jones.

No matter. They would drop Weir at Tony's, then he would take Elk to the home of Charlton Fields that night to execute a search. Spears wished he could have Weir with him at the search, but Elk would do. Elk wasn't *stupid*, he just wasn't precisely smart. This was of little consequence however, as the absence of Weir and the presence of Elk would simply make things take slightly longer. They had plenty of time, so this did not concern Spears.

They arrived at Tony White's home in the country about forty minutes later. As they pulled up, Tony walked out to greet them, his two Doberman Pinchers practically dragging him down the walkway, snarling. White foam oozed from their jowls and their dark eyes were precise and focused.

Spears rose from the vehicle, a sinister grin splitting his face. He had little fondness for his employers, at least on a personal level, but this scene had almost struck him as funny. The old man with his dogs, looking for extra protection.

"Expecting trouble, Mr. White?" Spears said, looking at the dogs.

Tony didn't look amused. Didn't look amused at all. His eyes were wide, and his cheeks were flushed. Spears automatically knew the man had been drinking, even without smelling any alcohol. That was probably a good thing, he presumed. Weir would be alert, and the dogs would too. And anything that kept the scared old man calm was a welcome addition to the recipe.

"I'm trying to deter trouble, thank you," Tony said, a scowl on his face. "Nothing wrong with taking a few precautions."

"Absolutely not," Weir said, stepping out of the vehicle.

Weir strode over to Tony, keeping just out of reach of the dogs' lustful grasp, and smiled. His smile was slightly more sincere than Spears's had been, but was equally detached.

"Don't worry Mr. White," Weir said, "things are under control. Spears and Mr. Elk here will be dealing with your problem this evening. They will have him shortly."

Weir's smile broadened.

"Good," Tony said, visibly gulping.

Johnny E. stepped out of the car and looked at the mansion before him.

"Damn, dawg!" he said, his eyes alight. "This pad is tight! Shit! How much you pay for this joint?"

Tony glared at Johnny E with contempt. "Mr. Spears, can you put a muzzle on him? Why is he even here?"

"Muzzle?!" Johnny E protested, the light in his eyes darkening. "Ain't nobody puttin' no muzzle on me, mah-fah, bess believe!"

"He's here because of Shari, Mr. White," Spears began. "She's gone missing, as you've heard. Mr. Elk here is coming along to assist us because of his, uh, *personal* involvement."

"Muzzle?" Johnny E said again, stuck on the subject. "Man, who you think you talkin' to? I will *cut* yo punk-ass!"

He stepped forward reaching into his pocket.

The Dobermans bowed up to him and growled. The deep, monstrous sound that came from them seemed to cause Johnny to reconsider his course of action. He shrunk back to the car.

"You betta watch yo back makin' noise at *me* like that! Cracka betta recognize! Bitch, I thought we was friends!"

Now there was an almost hurt quality to Elk's face.

"We are," Tony said, pulling again against the dogs straining towards the car. "Just find this guy, okay?"

Spears and Jonny nodded and climbed into the car. They pulled away, leaving Tony, Weir, and the two dogs behind.

They were going to Charlton Fields's house.

# CHAPTER
## 17

The night was intense. Actually, it was beyond intense. Dark clouds shrouded the moon, casting black ink on the world beneath it, and the air rumbled.

The night would be *brutal.*

Charlton Fields crept in the woods near Tony White's estate. He was wearing an all-black outfit he'd picked up at the surplus store. Black BDUs and a black beanie hat. It was all a bit dramatic—he admitted this to himself—but he needed all the stealth he could get. His pistol and his knife were stuffed into his belt, their weight reassuring as he approached the perimeter wall.

Cameras perched all around the estate wall like watchful birds, but Charlton had already scoped them out. There was one at each corner of the perimeter wall and one in the center of each wall as well. In addition to these, there were another six cameras around the house itself, and possibly more inside. Those were of little consequence. The police already knew who he was, as he'd heard on the radio earlier in the evening, so the point of being careful in concealing his identity was now a moot one. He only wore the black because he knew Tony had two Dobermans, and though it was almost laughable the thought of outsmarting a couple of highly trained dogs by wearing black, he'd decided on it because of the rain.

Ah, yes. The rain.

It was already starting to come down, only a light drizzle now, but within minutes it would be coming down in torrents. That would help with getting around the estate unnoticed.

The pair of Pinchers would have little problem seeing him in the rain, even dressed in all black, but the rain would conceal his scent. That was a welcome coincidence.

Charlton strode up to the wall and looked both ways down its length. By his best guess, he was roughly in the center of the east wall, below the camera stationed there. He leapt up, caught on to the edge of the wall, and hoisted himself to the top. Once up, he scanned the area. He realized that he was indeed directly in the center of the wall and was sitting right next to the camera. It stood on a small stand about eighteen inches atop the wall, and its eye was pointed straight forward and down, toward the house. This was good because that meant that the camera on the west wall, directly opposite him, was likely positioned the same way and therefore would be unable to see him where he was.

He pulled his knife out and reached behind him toward a pine tree limb. He flipped the knife over in his hand to utilize the serrated edge.

He began to saw the limb.

"What the hell is that?" Tony White asked aloud.

Weir rose from the couch, strolled toward Mr. White's office, and peeked his head inside. There was an area of bookshelves to one side of the room. Instead of books, however, the shelves were lined with hi-tech surveillance equipment. There were more than a dozen TV monitors, all revealing a different part of the property or house. Red and green lights gleamed from various electrical boxes, reminding Weir of the arcade hangouts he used to frequent as a child.

Tony was standing close to the monitors, leaning in close to one.

"That's never been there before," Tony said.

"What hasn't?" Weir asked, stepping into the room and crossing to Tony and the monitors.

"This branch," Tony said pointing to the monitor in question, his voice as shaky as his hand. "It's never blocked this camera before."

Weir stiffened. It wasn't likely that Fields was already here, but it wasn't impossible either. The camera's view was completely obscured by the pine branch, but that wasn't what caused Weir's brow to moisten. In fact, it was entirely possible that the storm outside could have knocked the branch into this position. *Entirely* possible.

But tonight, he knew better than to assume.

"Which camera is that?" he asked.

"Um," Tony thought aloud for a moment. "Th-the center one on the east wall!"

"Stay put," Weir said, pulling his gun from his shoulder holster. "I'll check it out. Are the dogs outside?"

Tony nodded, fear painting his face in clumsy streaks.

Weir turned and made his way to the east side of the house. He peered out a glass door into the night.

He saw nothing. Not a single thing seemed out of place. Streaks of rain were pelting the earth and drumming on the roof now, creating a loud and ominous drone. It wasn't deafening, but it was the forefront sound and he could hear nothing else. There was little visibility in the gloom, and he could make out almost nothing beyond the porch. A few bushes swaying in the deluge, but virtually nothing else.

Then the sky lit up like daytime as a bolt of lightning streaked the heavens. In that brief moment, Weir thought he saw something by the wall. As the lightning faded instantly to darkness, and the after-effects of the flash danced across his vision, he was struck by disbelief and shock.

He thought he had seen a person jumping to the ground.

Thunder cracked loudly a moment later in a deafening boom. Weir's throat tightened. There was no hoping against it now. It was happening. He was here. It could have been his eyes playing tricks on him. Hell, it could have been one of the dogs he'd seen, it had happened so damned fast. But he knew better. His training told him better.

*Fields is coming.*

Another streak of lightning split the sky, and this time he saw the figure clearly, coming across the yard. A second later, the shape vanished into darkness as thunder rolled in, dominating the drumming rain.

Weir called down the hall to Tony. Told him to hide. To get under a damn bed if he had to, but fucking hide. And now. Then he slipped out into the pouring rain.

A second later, the bottom *really* fell out.

---

The rain came down in sheets seconds after Charlton hit the ground.

He had looked up as he was falling and saw one of the dogs over by the corner of the house as lightning had slain the dark.

And the dog had seen him.

The sky went black again and Charlton scrambled for a nearby bush. It wasn't much cover, but it was something. He didn't think anyone inside knew he was here yet, but he couldn't be sure. He pulled his pistol out, cocked the hammer, and double-checked that the silencer was on firmly.

It was.

Then he heard the *splish-splash* of a dog's sprinting footsteps somewhere under the pelting sound of the rain and thunder.

The Pincher was coming.

He rolled out on his belly and aimed the gun at the darkness. The darkness was absolute where he was, the lights from the house stopping some thirty feet away from him. He was engulfed in pitch.

*Splish-splash-splish.*

Though he could see nothing, he was relatively sure he was aiming in the general direction of the dog. He held his pistol level, waiting for another streak of lightning. *Willing* the sky to flash for him.

*Splish-splash-splish.*

*Come on...*

He waited. Then he waited some more. The snarls of the animal were audible now, getting louder, but still he could see nothing. The barrel threatened to tremble in his hands and he took a quick, rasping, but steadying breath. The suspense was excruciating as he listened to the Pincher get closer and closer. The sound of its snarls. Its feet splashing the perfectly kept grass. The steady staccato of its paws.

*Splish-splash-splish.*

In his mind's eye, Charlton could see what the dog looked like. Its lips would be peeled back over its teeth now, revealing the menacingly jagged incisors. Foam dripping from its sopping jowls, its eyes wild with anticipation. He was sure the dog could see him, but Charlton couldn't see the dog at all. Hear it, yes, but there were just no visuals. It was coming, and oh, it was so close now! Right on top of him!

His heart pounded in his chest, drummed in his ears, but still he lay unmoving, holding his gun steady.

*Wait for it. Come on...*

The dog was so close now, he thought he would soon feel its breath on his face. He could hear it, mere feet away, growling the hound's chant of death. He was tempted to jump to his feet, make a break for it, scale the wall. To run away.

But he didn't have that option. He was too close to Tony now to back off. He knew that if he left now, he might not have another chance. The others were all scheduled for the next few days and the police were already closing in. No, he had to deal with this, and now.

*Give me some light, damn you! I need some light! Come on...*

It finally did.

Another streak of lightning ripped through the sky like a knife through the heavens, illuminating the yard in front of Charlton. It was only a moment, but he could see the Pincher, only about five feet away, in a full charge, its eyes maniacally wide with anticipation and its teeth nearly leaping off its face at him, foam and drool slapping from its jowls in the rain.

It was only a moment, but it was all he needed.

He squeezed off two rounds at the dog and saw it collapse into a heap before him in the flashes of the barrel. The corpse slid the rest of the distance to Charlton, bumping to a stop at his hands.

The Pincher was dead.

A half second later, thunder clapped across the sky and filled his ears. It followed the lightning quicker than it had in the last flash, meaning the storm was moving right over them. At least that was what he remembered from science class.

He jumped to his knees and looked around. Except for the house, everything was dark and he couldn't see anything.

Total blackness surrounded him.

He decided to make a run for the house. He knew there was another dog somewhere, but he couldn't see it or hear now, so he decided to ignore its existence until reality dictated otherwise. To deal with only one thing at a time.

He had made it a few feet toward the house when the sky lit up again. As it did, he saw the other dog coming at him from the left. Like its dead companion had been, it too was in a full sprint. He whipped up his pistol and fired one round in the direction of the dog just as the sky went black again and his ears were filled with the boom of thunder. He heard a loud yelp of pain from the dog and then it began to whine.

He had hit it, but it wasn't dead.

At the same time the thunder had deafened him, he'd felt a stinging, burning sensation in his upper left arm. He ignored it at first but it persisted, getting worse with every passing nano-second. He reached up and touched his arm with his other hand. Something warm and wet like gel oozed from a small hole in his arm.

*What?*

Pain exploded in his arm then and he spilled to the ground.

Lightning flashed again, and in that moment, he saw two things: the injured dog still lumbering in his direction, and a man in the bushes firing a gun at him.

He hadn't heard the shot because of the thunder clap, but with the sky now dark again, he saw the muzzle flashes.

A bullet whizzed over his head as he hit the ground in a splash. He rolled over to his side and shot three times in the direction he'd seen the shot come from.

The rain was coming down so hard that it felt like needles puncturing into Charlton's skin and eyes. He was half on his side and half on his back now, the gun aimed towards the bushes. He struggled to see through the dark pouring rain, but to no avail. He could see nothing. The darkness was like ink.

The dog howled.

It was closer now, relentlessly pursuing him. Its howls were riddled with pain, but there was also another sound behind it.

*Fury.*

Charlton struggled a moment and began to push with his legs towards the house, always aiming the gun in the same place he had before.

Then he could hear *two* sets of footsteps in the rain.

One set he quickly identified as the dog's, but the other he hadn't heard before now. They were much farther apart and sounded heavier. They were moving slower and in a different direction. He quickly moved the gun back and forth between the two sounds, not sure what to do, unable to see a thing.

*I need light, goddammit! LIGHT!*

As if hearing his plea, the sky lit up yet again, revealing the limping dog a few feet away to his left and the man from the bushes running toward the house, gun in hand.

Charlton acted quick.

First, he squeezed off another round at the dog. It fell dead in a furry heap with a final yelp. Next, he swung the gun over to the man running for the house and shot twice more. One of the rounds found its way into the man's leg and Charlton could just see a spray of blood and the man beginning to fall when the lights went out and the audio returned.

*Who in hell is that?*

---

Weir grabbed his leg and let out a yelp of pain as he toppled to the rain-soaked earth. He hit with a splash—hearing it, though he couldn't see it—and slid several feet. He reached down, grabbing his leg, quickly finding the bullet hole.

*Son of a bitch, this guy can shoot!* he thought bitterly.

The wound was extremely small, indicating that a rather small caliber had been the culprit. However, small or not, pain surged through his leg, and he could feel the warm ooze of his blood against his hand.

The sky boomed with thunder in a deafening roar. Weir looked around, unable to see a thing except for a few dim lights coming from the house.

He cursed bitterly, crawling a few feet, wishing he had more light. He looked to the door, knowing he needed to get back into the house and hide Tony.

He started to get up and pain shrieked up his thigh in a high C note. He gritted his teeth against the pain and limped towards the house, his leg singing a song of agony.

He made it inside the house. After a few lumbering steps, he whirled around as lightening flashed again. He saw Fields, just a few yards from the door, sprinting towards him. Weir raised his gun and fired a few rounds. The first went through the window next to the door, shattering it. Fields stumbled backwards, hands raised, warding off bullets and shattering glass, then turned to run around the side of the house. Weir fired three more shots which chipped harmlessly at the lawn.

Then the sky went dark again.

Weir turned back into the hall behind him. Limping to the office trying to find Tony.

"Tony!" he screamed. "Tony, you in here?"

There was silence. *Not a creature stirring.*

Nope. Only the mouse.

The mouse was Tony, hiding under his desk, whimpering like a lost child.

"Is he dead?" Tony's voice quivered.

Weir shook his head as he hurled himself into the room.

"No. I hit him, but only winged him. He's still out there."

Tony shook and looked up and down Weir. His eyes fell on Weir's leg, then tripled in size.

"Holy *shit*!" Tony hissed. "You've been hit!"

Weir had almost forgotten about his wound, but with fresh awareness came the pulsing pain.

"I need a towel or something to wrap around this, quick!" Weir said, the words spitting from his mouth in strings.

Tony sprinted from the room, returning a few moments later with a dish towel.

"Here," Tony uttered. "Did the dogs get to him?"

Weir shook his head. "No. They're down."

Tears welled in the corners of Tony's eyes.

"Oh, fu—"

"Quiet!" Weir began, cutting him off. "We've got to get out of here. With the storm outside, I can't see a thing and we're sitting ducks in here. If he finds a way in, we're fucked! You understand?"

Tony's pale face began to nod absently.

"So," Weir went on, "we need to get to your garage, get a vehicle, and get the hell outta here before he gets inside!"

Tony nodded, shaky, but holding it together.

"Okay! Follow me!"

Then the lights went out in the house.

---

Charlton fired three rounds into the two-hundred-amp main breaker in the circuit panel on the side of the house, and the house went dark.

He fumbled in his pocket and produced another full magazine of ammo, swapping it for the empty one inside the gun. He racked the slide, sending a round home in the chamber, then made his way towards the back door, willing his eyes to adjust to the dark surrounding him.

When he got to the back door, he peeked up over the crest of the windowsill, whose glass had been shattered from the shot from the mystery man.

Nothing inside. Not that he could *see* anything.

He reached through and groped for the lock on the door. After a moment, his hand found purchase, and he freed the door from the frame with one quick movement. Then he was inside the house.

There were hushed, terrified voices coming from somewhere inside the house.

"Oh, *shit!*" one voice hissed. "Get me out of here! Now!"

Charlton quickly identified the voice as Tony White's.

*That's right Tony. Be very afraid.*

Another voice, frustrated, yet calmer, said, "Calm down. First things first. Where are your keys?"

*They're going for the car.*

Charlton had seen the garage whilst outside and knew it was closer to where he was than the voices were. He crawled silently through the house towards the garage and found the door.

"Is that them? Let's go!" the protector's voice chimed in a whisper.

Charlton slipped into the garage and closed the door behind him, quick and silent. Once inside, he could see absolutely nothing. Blackness. Outside had been dark, but this was the absolute absence of all light, and he could hardly tell if his eyes were open or shut.

Then lightening flashed through the windows on the garage door, confirming that his eyes were indeed open. He got a quick sense of the things inside.

Car. Nice one too. Bicycles. Gas cans. A lawn mower.

Farther to the north wall, there hung a long metal shelf that held many random items.

Paint. Oil cans. Tools. Flashlights.

Charlton smiled.

*Flashlights.*

He crawled over to the place where the flashlights had been before the darkness returned and felt for one. From inside the house he could hear Tony and his protector coming. He fumbled for the flashlight in the darkness. He needed to have it in hand before they got in here with him.

He suddenly became aware of the wound in his left arm again as he groped for the flashlights. The pain began to swell and pulse. Tony and his protector were getting closer, just outside the door now, and he could hear muffled voices. He could almost hear what they were saying.

The pain became more intense.

*Come on...*

There was a loud thump on the wall between the garage and the hallway inside. Charlton's heart leaped into his throat. His arm began to throb.

No. That wasn't the right word.

It was *pounding.*

*Come on...*

Just then, he found the flashlights. He snatched one off the shelf, flicked it on and back off quickly to make sure it worked.

It did.

The door flung open.

---

Tony was behind Weir, following close and keeping his head down. They had gotten the keys and were now stumbling through the dark toward the garage.

"What are we going to do?" Tony asked, moaning with fear.

He was beginning to regret his years of lies and cover-ups. The fraud. The phoniness of it all. It had all lead to this. A madman in his house, dead dogs, and running around in the dark!

*Was it worth it? Huh?* his mind taunted him.

"We're going to get in the car and drive out of here. Then we're going to get Spears and Elk on the phone and we are going to lock this place down. He isn't getting out of here alive."

His words were spoken with sincerity and command.

"We'll gut this ugly son of a whore before the sun rises," Weir finished.

Though the sentiment was nice, his words did little to comfort Tony. Charlton had already gotten past his Dobermans *and* had wounded Mr. Weir. He was *here*, for Christ's sake. In his house. Somewhere with them in the dark.

*My God...what have I done?*

They were nearing the garage door when Tony's foot hit something and he fell against the wall hard, making a loud *thump*.

Weir turned around wincing, the look on his face conveying this was both from pain and the audible confirmation that had just been made to their whereabouts. Tony looked back at him apologetically. Weir put his forefinger vertically across his mouth.

*"Shhhh!"*

Tony nodded, then they continued to creep slowly the rest of the way to the door. When they got there, Weir grabbed the knob and opened the door, quickly stepped in, and pulled Tony in behind him. Then he shut the door.

Weir turned to Tony in the pitch of the garage. Tony could feel him do this rather than see it.

"Okay," Weir said, "you go get in the back seat and lay down on the floor board. I'll drive and—"

Suddenly, a beam of light shone on Weir's face. His eyes closed involuntarily as he was momentarily blinded.

"What the—"

Then there was a quiet pop and the back of Weir's head opened, vomiting blood, brains, and chips of bone. A healthy mixture of all these speckled Tony's face, the rest spattering the door behind him and attaching like slugs. The slugs began to slide downward and clump to the floor in audible *splats*.

Then the lights went back out.

Tony stood there, trembling, unable to move. He became aware of something soft and slimy in his mouth. He spat it out and heard the same *splat* as it hit the ground that he'd heard a moment before.

*Brains? Oh, Christ, were his brains in my mouth?*

A moment later, he heard the sound of Weir's body collapsing to the floor, and a violent wretch began to swell in the pit of his stomach. Just before he spewed his dinner all over the body before him in the dark, he heard a voice. One that he immediately recognized. One that immobilized him.

*"Remember me, Tony?"*

*Oh, my God!*

He turned to rush the door and the light came back on.

"Oh, no you don't," Charlton Fields said.

Tony fell back against the wall, facing the light. He was shaking, another man's blood all over him, and the boogeyman was here to finish him.

"Please!" Tony screamed. "I'll give you money! Anything you want, it's yours!"

"I don't want your money, you *fuck*!" Charlton growled. "I want your *heart!*"

Tony's eyes squinted against the light. He could see nothing beyond it but a swaying shadow.

Then he remembered what had happened to Morgan.

"Oh, dear God…"

There were two more pops as Tony's shoulders spat blood and erupted in a symphony of pain. He wailed, crying like a scolded child as he slid to the ground.

*"God is dead!"* Charlton's voice boomed.

Then Tony watched Charlton's silhouette place the flashlight on the floor and step in front of it, transforming him into a towering shadow.

The lightening flashed again outside, revealing a sinister grin on a face only a mother could love. An ugly face with a crooked nose and bucked teeth. A face Tony had not seen in twenty years.

Little Charlie Fields.

The lightening was still flashing when Charlton put the gun in his waistband and pulled out the box cutter.

Thunder boomed, but Tony could still hear Charlton, little Charlie, very clearly.

"Now, how 'bout that heart?"

He came toward Tony, pushing out the blade.

Tony screamed.

# CHAPTER 18

*N*othing.

Spears tossed a notebook onto the coffee table in Charlton Fields's living room. Or what *had been* his living room, until recently. It contained pen drawn sketches of dead animals, of people, of what looked like broken crosses and a burning church, but no clue as to where he might be. None at all.

This was frustrating. Perhaps the police *had* been thorough for once. Taken a clue to his whereabouts. Something.

And then there was Elk.

Elk was not helping the process. At all. The man—if you could even call him that—was a lumbering fool. Tossing and cursing his way through everything, with little or no regard for the fact that they were trespassing on a police crime scene. A police *homicide* scene at that, something Longview saw very little of. There was absolutely no concept of stealth within this man. No finesse. And it all made Spears's head ache.

*Calm down...*

Spears felt a rage come up within him, one that could only be quenched with blood, and he was dangerously close to demanding that soothing blood from John Michael Elk himself. But not right now.

*Not yet...*

He could hear Elk in the back room.

"Stupid cracker," he muttered. "Mah-fah don't even clean his damn house!"

Then a sound of something falling over. Crashing into something metallic.

*Clang!*

Spears's blood began to boil. Literal ripples of flesh began to bubble over his veins as the temperature inside them began to reach a fever-pitch.

*I'll kill him,* he thought, pinching his eyes shut. *I'll cut his damned throat and bathe in his blood, I swear to Go—*

"How we supposed to find nothin' in here? Huh? This is some bullsh—"

Something else fell over. Something else crashed and *clanged.*

That was it. The last draw. The whole search was a bust anyway, but dealing with this imbecile had become intolerable. It had to end.

Spears made his way to the back, where Elk was, his teeth grit to the point of shattering in his gums.

"We're leaving," he said through clenched incisors.

"What choo mean we leavin'? We ain't found nuthin' yet!"

The obvious lack of reasoning in the huge pimp was wearing thin on Spears, and he was struck as to how he ever thought this idiot was *not* an idiot. He was a first-rate imbecile.

"And we *won't* find anything!" Spears spat and growled. "There's nothing here. We are leaving!"

"How you know they ain't nuthin' here?"

White dots of fury speckled Spears's vision. He felt his head ache again, not from the lights, but the man's stupidity. It was insatiable.

"Because I know these things, okay? Let's *go*!"

Elk looked at him with moronic contempt. In that moment, Spears could see the man's eyes cross, though he was sure this was an apparition. It was the visual representation of the man's idiocy manifesting in his own mind's eye. He knew then that he would kill him. Not right then, but soon, and with pleasure.

"Whatever," the idiot continued. "I just wanna know how we goan find Shari if all we do is piss around with our dicks in our hands?"

He stormed out the back door past Spears and into the night. The short time they had been investigating *had* seemed to produce little in the way of a lead, and sure, this was frustrating, but not uncommon. It came with the territory. Weir would understand this, but Spears had the misfortune of having to work with Elk instead. And Elk, for all his faults, *did* want to find Fields; he just had no clue as to how to go about accomplishing that. Perhaps he should cut him a little slack. Perhaps he should—

Another crash, this time from outside. Elk cursing loudly and profanely.

Fury welled inside Spears. There would be no slack. Fuck that! There would be no damned *mercy*! Elk's end would be apocalyptic, and merely for the joy it would bring Spears for having had to tolerate the fool this long.

*I'll kill him!*

Yes. Yes, he would. But not now. Not *yet*.

Spears turned and headed out of the house. With all the noise Elk was making, there would certainly be authorities on the way soon. They had to leave, and immediately.

Miraculously, Elk followed him out without further incident. They got to the car and were driving off when Spears's cell phone rang.

"Hello?" he answered.

There was no voice on the other end at first, only breathing. And something else…

*Crying?*

No. More like a pathetic whimpering. Then a wail of pain. The only thing he knew for sure was the voice belonged to a male.

"Who is this?" Spears spat into his phone, his eyes wide.

More breathing. More wails and whimpering.

It dawned on Spears that he hadn't checked the caller ID. He pulled the phone away from his ear and looked at the screen.

*Weir.*

A lump formed in his throat as he slowly replaced the phone to his ear.

"Weir?" he managed.

Then the breathing began to laugh. Insane cackles rose into his ear in a crescendo, then went silent all at once. Several seconds went by, and Spears began to wonder if the call had dropped when finally, someone spoke.

"No, I'm afraid he can't talk," the voice said. "Not now, not ever again."

More laughing.

"Who is this?" Spears roared, his teeth bared at nothing more than the windshield. "Fields? Charlton Fields? Is that you, you son-of-a-bit—"

"Why, as a matter of fact, yes," the voice cut him off. "This is Little Charlie. Just called to let you know your associate will no longer be of any consequence to my…my little crusade. And unless you back off, you will meet a similar fate."

Spears felt the casing of the phone begin to crack in his hand as he gripped it tighter, fury rising in him like a splitting atom.

"Now," Fields cleared his throat and went on, "if you don't mind, I need to get back to Mr. White. He seems to be struggling to hold…to hold his…"

Another eruption of laughter overtook Fields on the other end as Spears's hand actually cracked the glass on his phone.

"Tries to hold his shit together!"

Fresh guffaws of laughter boomed through the speaker for a few seconds, then the line went dead.

Spears cursed and threw the phone onto the seat. Then he pounded the steering wheel with his fist, repeatedly.

"Man! What choo flippin' out about?" Elk asked, bewildered.

"Weir and White are dead." Spears said flatly after hitting the wheel a final time.

Realization—*astonishingly*—spread across Elk's face.

"Oh, man!" the giant idiot said. "Is the dude still there at White's place?"

Spears nodded, a cold, distant stare in his eyes.

"Yep."

Spears slammed on the brakes and jerked the wheel to the left. The car started to spin around, and about halfway through, he gunned the accelerator. The car spun all the way around and straitened up in the opposite direction after a quick fish-tail.

"We gonna git 'em!" Elk proclaimed, not really a question.

Knowing it wasn't a question, and despite this, Spears nodded.

"Yep."

# CHAPTER 19

Fletcher was still at work, standing by the window on the east side of the office, staring out into the storm. His mind was on his ex-wife. His daughter, too. Even on his long-lost faith, of all things. His head swirled with thoughts of the past. He thought about the ignorant bliss he'd lived in up to the time when he learned what Damien Smith really was. What the church really was. The phoniness, the hypocrisy, his own stupidity, all of it. He fancied himself to a be a reasonably smart man, and reckoned he'd been so even twenty years ago. But, boy, had he been fooled. So terribly fooled. And now…

*And now Charlie. Oh, Christ, what a nightmare.*

"Whatcha thinking about?" Benson asked walking up to him, holding out a cup of coffee with one hand while sipping on another.

Fletcher's mind snapped back to reality as he grabbed the cup. He took a long sip. Then another. He'd heard the question, and meant to answer. He just didn't know how. What exactly *was* he thinking about? Everything that made him angry? What made him bitter at the very thought of religion? Or was it really all about Charlton Fields?

"Thinking about a lot of things," he finally said, feeling his way through his thoughts. "Been thinking about my daughter. My ex-wife. Thinking about the church and all the shit it created with little Charlie. Thinking that none of this, none of what Charlie seems to be trying to do is gonna change the hypocrisy in the church..."

He trailed off and took another sip. It stung his lip and he winced.

"In short," Fletcher went on, nursing his burned mouth, "I guess I've been thinking about everything."

Benson grinned and took a sip of his own coffee.

"Yep," Benson said. "Know the feeling. Brain's on a bit of an information overload, trying to sort it all out. Been there."

"Yeah, but the one thing I don't get is..." Fletcher said, pausing a moment, searching how to proceed. "The thing is, I don't understand how you can see everything now, see what that church did, and still buy into this Jesus crap. Now, I said I would live and let live, and I'm not coming down on your beliefs this time, really, I...I just honestly don't get it."

Benson laughed softly.

"Harry," Benson said, "I don't believe in people. Now don't get me wrong, I love people, even trust a few of them, but believe in them? Nah. I believe in God. I've said it before, I'll say it again, *God* didn't have anything to do with all of this. This was evil men doing evil things, plain and simple."

He sat his coffee cup down and faced Fletcher, who did likewise.

Benson continued. "The devil's best defense is misdirection. Getting your mind and trust off what it *should* be on, and getting it on something else. This preacher, the elders at your old church, they did some *very* evil things. They have a lot of people deceived. Heck, even the newspapers are calling Morgan Jones a freaking *saint*! But it's all misdirection. It's all lies. And most importantly, it's all *man's* doing."

Fletcher cut in nodding. "Okay, okay, but if God is all powerful, then how could He let something like this happen? How could He allow what happened twenty years ago to happen?"

"I don't have all the answers, my friend. I wish I did, truly I do. I just don't. But I'll tell you what I *do* have."

"Yeah? What's that?"

Benson leaned in close and smiled.

"Faith," he said. "I have faith."

Fletcher opened his mouth to say something when Dan Felt stuck his head out of his office.

"Fletcher, Benson, get in here!"

Then he vanished back into his cave as quickly as he had appeared.They crossed over to the office and stepped inside.

"Yes sir?" Fletcher asked.

Dan Felt rubbed his head and then his eyes, tired and frustrated. The man hadn't slept much in the last few days, that was obvious. There were bags under his eyes and said eyes were bloodshot.

"So," Felt started with a sigh, "Harry, I understand that you went to church with this Charlton Fields character years ago?"

Fletcher nodded.

"So," Felt went on, nodding himself, "do you have any reason to believe that there will be more people on this psycho's hit list, and if so do you know who those folks may be?"

Captain Felt pursed his lips while waiting for Fletcher to answer. His impatience was apparent on his face, but his virtue held it in check. After a few moments, Fletcher finally answered.

"Yes sir, I have a pretty good idea who will be next," he cleared his throat, "if, that is, there *is* a next."

"Oh, you can bet there'll be a next," Felt said. "This fella *likes* killing. You can tell that by what he does to their corpses. So, who's it gonna be?"

"Well, sir," he continued, "there was Morgan Jones of course…"

Dan Felt rolled his eyes and his tone became sharp.

"Okay, tell me something I don't know, smart-ass."

Fletcher stifled a snotty response and went on. "Then J.R. Hays, Tony White, Percy Wilkes, and, um, Damien Smith."

Captain Felt nodded. "Okay, here's how we proceed. Get on your way out to one of these boy's places, and on your way, wake up Bert and Ernie, get them to go out to another one, I don't care which, and then get them to send a couple uniforms to the others. When you get there, question them, and talk them into getting the hell out of there, so we can protect them and maybe lure this Charlton Fields out into the open. Okay?"

They nodded and turned to leave. When they were nearly out of the office, Captain Felt called to them once more.

"And just in case…"

He paused, obviously not wanting to admit the possibility.

"Just in case *he's* at wherever you go, you might want to wear a vest."

They looked at each other and nodded.

---

Ten minutes later, they were out of the station and on their way to Tony White's house. They had roused Bert and Ernie, who were going to J.R. Hays' house, and some uniforms would be stationed at the houses of Percy Wilkes and Damien Smith.

They had gone about five miles when Fletcher finally broke the awkward, crippling silence.

"Can I tell you something?" he asked.

Benson glanced over to him, an almost shocked expression on his face.

"Of course, you can," he said. "We *are* partners."

Fletcher nodded, taking a deep breath.

"Yeah, about partners," he said. "My old partner, the one who died? He and I were pretty close. I watched him die, right in front of me."

"Yeah, I read about it in the papers when it happened…" Benson said cautiously and with a gentle tone.

"Anyway," Fletcher went on with a wave of his hand. "He was wearing his vest, just like we are now. But it didn't do him any good. Perp got him in the head. Blew it off, really. Just…just watch out. I doubt we'll see anything tonight, but if we *do*, be alert. Keep your gun up, and your eyes open. And the most important thing…"

He stopped, choking back tears.

"What is it, Harry?"

"Don't be a hero," Fletcher said, his voice quivering.

A solemn look fell on Benson's face, and they rode on in silence once again.

# CHAPTER
## 20

S pears and Elk pulled up to Tony White's front gate.
Spears punched in a four-digit security code on the
small key pad that leapt out at them from a thin metal arm anchored to the ground. A moment later, the big,
black iron gate in front of them opened inward. Large, iron
hands granting access.

They pulled in.

Spears was alert, his eyes darting this way and that,
looking for any sign of Fields or White or Weir.

*Weir.*

If Spears had been capable of feeling emotion—*real*
human emotion—he might have felt something over
Weir's death. He had been the closest person to Spears
since his long-forgotten childhood. Weir had been very
young for the job when Spears had taken him in and taught
him what he knew. Taught him *everything* he knew. And
Weir had been a good pupil.

A *very* good pupil.

This was bothering Spears. Weir had been more than capable of taking care of himself and White. The fact that he'd been overrun by this Fields character was evidence they were dealing with someone far more formidable than they had first assessed. Someone who'd trained for this. For years, perhaps. Someone driven. Driven by a sense of justice. By pride. By pain.

By vengeance.

He shook his head almost imperceptibly and put all his thoughts of Fields's motivation and training aside. There would be time for that later. For now, he needed to focus on the task at hand. He looked sharply at the dark landscape around them.

"Keep your eyes peeled," Spears said to Elk.

Johnny E was wide-eyed and alert, but looked more like a deer caught in headlights than a hunter searching out its prey.

"I ain't missin' nuthin', man!" Elk pontificated with an arrogance that would have been amusing had it not been so idiotic. "This dude out here, I goan see 'im!"

Spears nodded and grimaced. Spears was a man who exercised extreme patience, but this intolerable fool was pressing his limits. Elk was sure to be more trouble than he was worth in the end. And oh, the end…yes, that couldn't come soon enough. Elk's end, a therapeutic execution that Spears would relish.

*But first things first…*

He pulled the car around to the front of the house, parked it, and the two men stepped out. Spears reached into his jacket and removed his weapon. Lightning flashed, and a *boom* of thunder rolled over them almost simultaneously. The rain seemed to thicken on them as they moved, like falling gobs of gel rather than water, and they were instantly soaked. Their clothes fused to their bodies like oversized skin. The drone of the rain was nearly deafening, all but eradicating the sound of their feet sloshing through the muck.

Spears had to shout to be heard over the roar.

"Be aware of your target, Elk!" he said. "On the off chance White or Weir are still alive, we don't want to take *them* out, got it?"

Johnny E smiled nervously and nodded his head as he blinked the pelting rain out of his eyes.

"Gotcha boss!"

They moved through the deluge to the front door. Spears checked the knob with his free hand. It was locked. He motioned Elk to remedy the problem.

A moment later Johnny E crashed the door in with a crushing kick. Elk was expert at little in this world, but beating women and knocking in doors were areas in which he had a great deal of experience and efficiency. The huge black man hurled himself three paces across the porch, then heaved his massive leg in to the air and planted his foot squarely next to the deadbolt. The deadbolt was relatively new and made of high quality steel, but the frame of the door was older, softer, and far more willing to yield.

It did.

Wood splintered and cracked as the door gave way to the thunderous kick of John Michael Elk. The door crashed inward and slammed in to the sheetrock of the wall adjacent to the door, causing a plum of white dust to glide into the entryway. Shards of shattered wood clattered ahead of them into the house, scraping and spinning across the floor before finally coming to a stop.

They moved in quickly, guns raised.

Spears took the lead. He held his gun up with two hands, his trigger finger outside the trigger guard, pointing forward. He was a professional. Elk, on the other hand, was holding his gun with one hand, lazily aiming it in front of him cocked sideways. Spears thought he looked like a stereotypical thug. The absolute *opposite* of a professional. A brief but intense urge to turn and shoot the man, right then and there, to put him out of *both* of their misery, rose in Spears. There was even one moment where he felt the urge would overtake him, that his calm and collected constitution would crumble and rage would get the better of him. But he managed to wrangle the impulse, and stop short of evacuating the man's skull.

A sound.

A quiet, barely audible sound against the roar of rain and thunder outside, but it was definitely from a separate source. He paused to listen, straining his ears.

The rain drummed on the roof, making an ever-present *rap-a-ta, rap-a-ta, rap-a-ta* sound, accompanied every few moments by a *crack* of thunder.

There it was again. That other sound. Coming from his left.

He swung his weapon around in the direction of the sound and paused once again to listen.

*RIP! RIP!*

Soft, faint under the cacophony of the storm, and grotesque. The sound was fleshy and wet. Like someone skinning and gutting a deer.

*Or gutting a human.*

Spears stretched his neck to the right and left, bones in his vertebrae popping, relieving pent up tension and strain. He moved forward.

He was now fully aware of what was happening down the hall. He'd heard what happened to Jones and the couple on Airline Road. The way Fields finished his victims was sickening, even for Spears. But only hearing, especially in the dark with the storm raging, it was somehow worse.

They were coming down the hallway in pitch darkness. With a flash of lightening, Spears saw a light switch and flipped it on with blinding speed.

Nothing happened.

He tried it several times, but to no avail.

*He's cut the power,* Spears thought bitterly.

Spears looked over his shoulder to check on Elk. Elk was still there—*unfortunately*—looking like the dumb thug he was, his gun raised and sideways.

Spears peered back around to his twelve o'clock, his eyes coming to rest on a door that gave on the garage. He tiptoed towards it. After several agonizingly cautious moments, he arrived at the door. The grotesque sounds of shredding flesh on the other side continued, louder now.

*RIP! RIP! SPLAT!*

He motioned Elk to get on the other side of the door. He silently explained with hand signals how they would enter the room. Well, he *tried* to explain, anyway.

Spears's plan was that Elk would throw the door open, Spears would rush in, hopefully take out Fields, and then Elk would follow, providing cover. But as Spears expertly expressed his intentions with his hands, Johnny E became expertly confused with the sign language. Spears's jaw clenched, fighting back frustration. Having to deal with such an incompetent fool in such a dangerous situation was stupid on an epic scale, and he couldn't fathom how he'd allowed this to occur. Yet here he was, right in the middle of the epic stupidity.

But then, an amazing thing happened. Elk actually nodded. It was as if he seemed to finally understand, even though his mind had taken precious moments away from them to formulate this understanding. But, by Christ, there it was. He got it.

Spears sighed with relief.

He gave him the signal to proceed and accompanied it with a vertical finger across the horizontal plane of his tightly pressed lips.

*Be quiet!*

Again, Elk nodded that he understood and reached for the doorknob slowly, silently. He grasped the handle.

*RIP! RIP!*

Then suddenly: *BUZZZZZ! BUZZ! BU-BUZZ! BUZZZZZZZZZZ!*

Johnny E jerked his hand back, startled. Spears was still trying to wrestle his own heart back down into his chest when he looked down the hallway to the opposite end and noticed that there was a glow coming from the somewhere in White's office, even though the power was off in the house.

*The security monitors.*

The whole security system was still on. Connected to its own power source, it was unaffected by Fields's disconnecting of the power. That was why he'd been able to get in through the gate with the keypad.

Then another realization dawned on Spears that made his skin go the color of milk. If the security system was working, and there was buzzing coming from the gate, that meant…

*Someone's here!*

———————

"No one's answering the bell," Fletcher said, pushing the red button on the keypad in front of Tony White's gated estate.

He tried the buzzer a few more times and cursed, pulling his now soaking arm back into the car and rolling up the window.

"Hang on a sec," Benson said and opened his door.

He stepped out into the rain and ran to the gate. There was a small metal box, located near the ground, attached to the robotic arm which opened and closed the gate.

Fletcher peered through the rain and windshield wipers as Benson fumbled underneath the box for a moment with his hands. Then a moment later, the gate magically began to open. Benson ran back to the car and hopped in.

"How'd you do that?" Fletcher asked as he pulled the car into the estate.

Benson smiled, tousling water from his hair.

"There's an override switch on the box there," he pointed to the arm as they drove through. "It lets you open the gate without a pass code. Not all these kinds of gates have them, but a lot do. It was worth checking."

Benson smiled again, thoroughly proud of himself.

"Most people don't know it's there, so a lot of people have them put in, in case they forget the code or the keypad gets damaged."

"Fascinating," Fletcher said, actually impressed, but refusing to let on to the fact.

They pulled the car into the driveway in front of the house and noticed another car sitting there.

*Odd. I would have figured Tony White to have a much nicer car than that...and why isn't it parked in the garage?*

Then Benson was pointing to the front door.

"Crap, Harry!" he said. "Look!"

Fletcher followed his finger to the entryway and saw the busted door hanging ajar.

"Looks like we may be too late," Benson said.

*No shit, Sherlock,* Fletcher thought.

---

Spears and Elk saw the lights from the car spill in through the chasm of the front door. The ripping and splashing sounds from the garage had ceased and everything had fallen into a painfully suspenseful state of limbo. Fields was on the other side of the door. Spears knew it. The madman was probably staring up at the closed door, just as he and Elk were staring out the front door at the oncoming vehicle. Spears imagined him in there, his hands holding a bloody knife, sweat dripping from his forehead, his pulse visibly pounding in his throat, deciding what to do.

There was no time.

Seeing no other course of action, Spears took the initiative. He turned in one, quick motion and kicked the door to the garage. It flew open with a loud *crack*, and he rushed in, gun raised.

There was no Charlton Fields. That was the first thing he determined. There was, however, Weir. The man was dead on the floor, a bullet hole in the middle of his forehead and a glazed, disconnected look in his eyes.

The second thing Spears determined was that Tony White was also in here, and Fields had gotten a good start on the man. His body was *very* mutilated, his shocked face staring out at Spears from his abdominal cavity. Intestines were spread across his lap and on the dirty floor of the garage like thick spaghetti noodles doused in marinara sauce.

Blood was everywhere.

Elk rushed in and then vomited at once.

"Oh, man! That's sick!" he muttered, wiping wet chunks off his chin.

Spears ignored Elk. Ignored the ripe stench of vomit and blood. He was scanning the room, looking for any sign of Fields, ready to put lead into him. All he needed was movement. A shadow would do.

But there was no killer to be seen. He hadn't escaped through the garage door, Spears was sure of that. The power was out. But all the same, the garage was empty.

*Where did he go?*

Spears thought he could hear car doors shutting outside. Voices shouting, frantic ones.

*Come on! Where could he have gone?* Spears thought, his pulse rising faster and faster.

Then Spears noticed the rope to the attic door. A thin string, hanging down from the ceiling and ending a few inches above his head.

It was swinging.

It was slight, and the dark of the garage had kept him from noticing it right away. But there it was. Swaying in the dark.

There was a bump from within the ceiling.

Spears raised his gun toward the attic door.

---

"Be careful!" Fletcher hissed as he and Benson made their way to the front door. "If Fields is still here, he'll have the drop on us!"

"Gotcha!" Benson said.

The rain was a torrential downpour. Within seconds of stepping out of the car, they both had been soaked through.

They stepped slowly up the embankment to the gaping front door, eyes darting this way and that, looking for a killer.

As they neared the entrance, Fletcher motioned to Benson. Benson nodded and they each spun their backs to the wall on either side of the door, guns raised. Another nod, and Fletcher swung in through the door, his pistol leveled and ready. He was followed closely by Benson in a like manner.

Blackness. Sheer, unadulterated blackness. They could see nothing. A foot in front of his eyes the world seemed to vanish into ink. Then lightning flashed and lit up the room for a moment.

There really was nothing.

Nothing seemed out of place, broken, or moved, except for the door. The wall in the adjoining hall had an area that had caved in when the door had slammed open and a picture that had fallen and busted. Aside from that, Fletcher saw some shattered glass. Yet the home still looked immaculate otherwise.

Just before the lightning went out, they reached into their pockets, produced small flashlights, and clicked them on. Now, with illumination, they could see what they were doing and signal to each other.

Fletcher nodded at the picture and they moved forward slowly. Upon reaching the mouth of the hall, Fletcher paused, taking notice of everything in front of him. Beside and just behind him, Benson did the same, keeping a close on eye out for any movement.

Fletcher glanced around. The hallway was a typical one, with pictures, ornaments, and a couple of small tables with flowers and knick-knacks on them. Three-quarters of the way down the hall on the left was a door that he guessed must lead to a garage.

His eyes scanned all this, and had started coming back to the busted picture on the floor in front of him when he suddenly froze. He had noticed something in his scan, but his mind had taken several seconds to register what it had seen, and his brain hadn't processed the information immediately. But now it was.

His eyes moved back in the direction they had before and stopped. He was looking at the door. The one that he had thought must lead to the garage. There was no reason for him to think this, not knowing the layout of the house. But now he realized why his mind had made that association when his eyes had passed over the door.

It was open.

———————

Spears's body tensed when he saw the flashlights. He tensed even more when he heard the footsteps in the hallway.

*Cops.*

He was still aiming up at the attic. The bumping sounds coming from the ceiling had moved on to a different part of the house. Away from him.

Time was running out. There had to be some action occur soon or everything would be completely FUBAR, and he didn't mean that in the Southern Baptist rewording of the term either. Fields was starting to get away. If he succeeded, they would have to go back to J.R. Hays with nothing to report but their failure and Tony White's blood-bath.

He had to do *something*.

His eyes darted back to the ceiling, and he reached up, yanking the cord to the attic door and pulling the folding stairs out to the floor.

"What you doin', man?" Elk muttered in a hoarse whisper.

His eyes were bulging from their sockets and he was trembling with fear.

Spears looked at him grimly.

"Taking action."

---

Charlton heard the attic door squeal open and his pulse quickened.

*They've found me!*

He had fled to the attic the moment he heard the buzzing from the gate. The security system must not have been on the same power source as the rest of the house.

*Or it's on a backup generator.*

Yes. That was quite possible. But this was no time to worry with that. He'd had barely enough time to begin to enjoy himself with White's corpse before the shit hit the fan. People were in the house, had almost stumbled right on top of him.

*And now someone's coming after you in the attic!*

He thought he'd been silent enough getting in, but it was so damned dark in here he'd bumped into a few things while crawling over the rafter boards. There was only a small area that was covered by plywood and the rest was only rafters and insulation. If he fell into the insulation, he would go right through to the floor below, crashing through the ceiling.

He had to get to the farthest end of the house. Once that was complete he could get the fuck out of there. The evening had turned into a nightmare. A nightmare that threatened to end his crusade before he'd finished it. And that simply couldn't be allow—

*Voices.*

Two people. Hushed tones back by the attic door. And, was that...*footsteps?*

Yes. Footsteps. But from a different part of the house than the voices.

*Who the hell else is here?* he thought with wild-eyed panic. *The cops?*

No matter. He had one mission now: Get out. Get out and regroup.

Three more devils remained, and he meant to see them all into their graves before his crusade was done. That was priority number one. The crusade. Kill them. Those responsible for Sophie. For mom and dad. Kill them. *Kill them.*

*Kill them all!*

As he scrambled towards the end of the attic, he thought about priority number two.

*And anyone who stands in my way.*

———

Fletcher and Benson were just outside the door to the garage. They had heard a sound like wood clunking together and metal springs stretching. Then a moment later, someone's voice. No. Not voice. Voices. *Plural.*

*Is Fields in cahoots with someone else?* Fletcher wondered to himself.

It was doubtful. This was too personal. No, something else was going on. Someone else *was* here, but not *with* Fields.

*But...who?*

Benson made the nod this time and they both rushed into the garage, guns raised.

It was clear.

They scanned the area quickly at eye level and noticed only the attic door hanging down. They immediately moved their attention to that and circled around it, pointing their guns at the ceiling.

Then Benson's flashlight caught something on the floor.

They whirled towards it, the cone of light from their torches flooding over the scene before them, shadows retreating like rats in a sewer.

Two dead bodies. One had been shot in the head, but that seemed to be all. The other one didn't have a head. Well, that wasn't quite right. There it was, in the corpse's abdomen.

They shuddered.

"This is definitely our guy," Fletcher whispered.

Then there was noise behind them.

They spun around, wielding their weapons in front of them, and they caught sight of a rather large black man standing in front of them like a deer in the headlights. He looked almost as startled as they were.

"Freeze!" Benson screamed.

The big black man's hands went up. That was when they noticed the gun in his right hand.

"Drop it!" Fletcher yelled, his breath panting out of him. "Drop it now or I'll blow a hole through ya, so help me!"

The black man looked at his gun as though he had forgotten it was there.

"Man," he muttered, "I ain't did this!"

"Just drop it now!" Benson bellowed.

"I ain't done nuthin'! Y'all motherfu—"

"I don't care if you did or not," Fletcher said, trying to remain calm, "but if you don't drop that gun within the next three seconds, I *will* do something to you. Something permanent!"

The black man glared at him, his fright instantly morphing into menace.

"Oh, yeah?"

Then the black man moved with a speed Fletcher would not have thought possible. He pointed the gun at Fletcher and fired. A bullet whizzed by his head and thudded into the wall behind him.

"No!" Fletcher screamed.

He began to dive to the ground, firing once at the black guy on the way, and hitting him in the arm. Fletcher saw blood spritz out in a thin mist as he collided with the garage floor, and the black man's teeth clenched as his eyes went wide.

Unfortunately, Fletcher had hit him in the wrong arm.

The black guy yelped in pain a second later. As he wheeled around, he brought his right arm up and pointed it at Fletcher again.

Three quick shots rang out, and three spurts of blood erupted out of the black man's gun arm. The gun fell to the ground with a chatter of metal on concrete, and a moment later the big man did too with a more muffled sound. He was grumbling and cursing in pain.

"Ah!" he screamed. "Spears! What you waitin' fo man? Waste these bitches!"

Fletcher was pushing himself up from the floor, his gun still pointing at the black man, and Benson was moving toward the gun on the floor. Benson kicked it away.

"Who's Spears?" Benson asked as he and Fletcher came and stood over the big black man.

The black man laughed and winced in pain.

"He goan kill you honkey mah-fahs!"

Fletcher heard the hammer cock before the shot rang out.

There was a sudden, horrible pain in his lower back. He went reeling to the floor past the black guy, and rolled onto his back.

Benson had just enough time to spin around before a bullet slammed into his chest and he was thrown into the wall.

---

Spears lowered his smoking pistol. That had been too close.

He turned his eyes to Elk, who was on his knees and bleeding like a stuck pig. The giant man seemed to be trying to laugh instead of cry from the pain, but failing at the effort.

"You got them honkeys!" Elk said, then cried from the pain. "Damn five-o didn't even know what hit 'em!"

"They sure didn't," Spears said coldly, looking Elk over.

The man was in a truly bad state. His arms were useless hulks of meat and he was losing a lot of blood, though not quite enough to be life threatening, Spears estimated. But that was no matter.

*No matter at all.*

"Hep me up, man," Elk muttered.

His eyes met Spears's and went flat. Spears made no move to extend a hand of help. Instead, he gave a sinister grin.

"What?" Elk mumbled, his eyes seeming to widen and narrow at the same time.

"You've outlived your usefulness," Spears said coldly.

He raised the gun up to Elks head.

"What you doin', man?" Elk pleaded. "I been heppin' you, dawg! You can't do this! You need me!"

Spears laughed at this.

"I've never needed anyone less."

Elk's bewildered eyes grew furious in the second before Spears blew his brains out all over the cop that lay behind him.

Then Spears sniffed.

He turned away from the large black man, listening with glee to the sound of his corpse thumping to the floor. He felt exhilarated. And free. *That* had felt *good*.

He smiled and then shook his head to clear it. His eyes went back to the attic.

*Back to business.*

———

*Gunshots?*

Charlton heard the shots and quickened his pace over the rafters, careful not the put a foot or a hand down into the insulation.

Something bad was going on back there. Something *very* bad. He needed to get *out*, and now. It couldn't be much further to the end of the house and—

*Shit!*

Despite his caution, he kept bumping into the rafters and making noise. Whoever it was that was after him had most certainly heard him and would be coming. They would have a homing beacon directly to his location.

*Shit! Gotta move!*

He scrambled over a few more rafters and then he ran into something, creating another loud *thump*. He reached out in the dark and felt something hard and flat.

*The wall! Okay, time to get out of this attic!*

He positioned himself over a rectangular area of insulation and prepared to drop through. He was just about to go when he heard something that caused him to freeze.

*More footsteps?*

Most definitely. And they were almost right under him. Just a few feet beneath him, maybe six feet behind him. And they were getting closer.

Then someone spoke to him from beneath the insulation and drywall.

"Charlton Fields?" the voice said. "Is that you I hear up there?"

Charlton's jaw clenched tight.

"It is, isn't it?"

Charlton heard the voice laugh, then say, "Guess what?"

There was a pause while the orator chuckled some more. Charlton did not answer. Charlton did not move. He was completely and utterly frozen in place. But as the voice's next words rang up from below, he knew that none of that mattered. He was cornered.

"I know where you are!"

---

Spears was just aiming his gun up at the ceiling, ready to fire, when the ceiling itself fired at him a few times.

There were some very muffled pops from the attic and things began to zing past him. He dived to the floor and began to crawl away, chips from the tiled floor leaping up all around him.

He got a safe distance away and rolled onto his back. He fired his gun seven times at the approximate area of the ceiling the shots had come from. His shots sounded like cannon-fire compared to the ones issued from the ceiling.

And then, aside from the ringing in his ears, there was silence.

Spears held his aim at the ceiling for an eon, watching, listening for any movement from above.

Nothing.

He got up slowly, never averting his aim, his eyes sharp. He willed the ringing in his ears to cease, and eventually, it obeyed.

He still heard nothing as he rose to his full height. He waited. Maybe a body would fall through the ceiling and crash to the floor. Maybe blood would trickle through the bullet holes in the ceiling. Maybe *something* would happen.

But nothing moved. Nothing crashed or bled or did anything at all. He lowered his gun and decided he would have to crawl into the attic to make sure of his kill.

He turned to walk away, then he heard something. Something moving.

Directly above him.

He jerked his head up and tried to get his gun aimed but it was too late.

Charlton Fields was crashing down on top of him, along with the ceiling.

# CHAPTER
# 21

Fletcher's left eye opened grudgingly. Horrible pain coursed through his back and trickled into his arm. Little dots of light danced in his vision for a moment like fireflies.

He looked around the room with his eye only, careful not to move his head or body, for fear that his assailant was still nearby. He saw the two dead, mutilated bodies of Tony White and the unidentified person. Blood smeared on the wall. Spread across the floor.

His senses were becoming clearer now. He had taken quite a wallop, but it seemed he would live to fight another day. He continued his scan of the room with his eye.

Beside the bodies were an old bicycle and a rather nice car. There was a large rack of shelves holding oil, rags, and other typical garage items. Directly next to the rack was the body of the black guy. Most of his head was gone.

That was when Fletcher became aware of the bloody brain tissue that was all over his own face and clothes, and his stomach threatened revolt.

*Fuck!*

Benson was on the other side of the black guy, against the wall. He wasn't moving.

*Oh, no.*

He was about to whisper to him, try to get him to move *(please don't be dead!)* and he drew in breath to do just that.

Gunshots went off in the hallway and Fletcher stiffened.

*Pop! Pop! Pop!*

Then there were the *booms* of another gun, significantly louder than the first.

He heard Benson moan. Fletcher's eye darted over to Benson who was just regaining consciousness. His eyes were opened and he seemed acutely aware of the agonizing opera singing out from his chest. He reached up with his hand and began rubbing the hole in his shirt.

Fletcher was rushed with relief, but also knew they were still in a great deal of danger. They needed to keep quiet.

He lifted his head and whispered to Benson.

"Be quiet! They're still here!"

Benson looked at him, still dazed, but nodded his head. He gritted his teeth.

Fletcher began scanning for his gun. Now, he allowed his head to stand up and swivel on his neck to assist in his search.

He finally found it about three and a half feet from where he was. He reached out with his left hand—the one not experiencing horrific pain—and grasped it. He was right handed, so handling it was a bit awkward, but he felt better with it than without, regardless of how steady he could hold it.

Then there was a guttural, *primal* scream and a crashing sound coming from down the hallway.

The screaming in the hallway was accompanied by another eruption of gunfire, consisting of both *Booms!* and *Pops!* There was a scraping noise in the direction of Benson and Fletcher noticed Benson was moving now, slowly getting up and grabbing his own pistol.

They made eye contact and Fletcher spoke.

"Be careful, keep your head down, and follow me!"

Benson nodded, still wincing with pain. They made their way to the door and placed themselves on either side of it. They knew the drill: one would go left, the other would go right, and they would take down any threats that came their way.

Fletcher held his hand up.

"One."

Benson gripped his gun tighter, awaiting the signal.

"Two."

Benson now aimed his gun forward and down, entirely ready.

"*Three!*"

They both went into the hall, their backs to each other, facing opposite ends of the hallway, guns raised.

There was a split second of blackness, and then the lightning struck again, returning in glory, lighting up the hallway.

Directly in front of Fletcher was a face that he instantly recognized. It was smeared with blood and perspiration, but the crooked nose and bucked teeth were unmistakable. It was a face he'd not seen in twenty years, but in that moment, he instantly knew who it was.

Little Charlie Fields.

Charlton had his gun pointed right at Fletcher, but looked utterly surprised to see him.

---

There had been a moment of blackness between the lightning flashes. One moment Charlton had been looking at the phantom gunman, the next he was staring at a face that he recognized at once.

Fletcher.

*Where the fuck did you come from?*

---

At the same exact moment, Benson saw yet another man. This man looked confused as well. They stared at each other, guns aimed, bewilderment seizing them in the moment.

*Who is this guy?* Benson thought.

---

There was an eruption of gunfire.

Fields and Spears began firing at the same time, and each seemed intent on unloading their weapon. Fields hit Fletcher square in the chest four times. Fletcher went down, wincing in pain, and discharged his pistol three times. The first two shots went wide, but the last shot blasted through Fields's right cheek. Blood spattered the wall next to Charlton and he screamed and gurgled, furiously roaring, falling himself.

---

Spears instantly knew that the cops must've been wearing their Kevlar vests. Another shot to the torso would be pointless. He quickly aimed for the head and was about to squeeze off a round when the cop in front of him got a round off into the outer edge of Spears's left arm. This threw off his aim and his own round nicked through the outer edge of the cop's left shoulder. The cop yelped and went down.

*Shit, this is bad!* thought Spears. *This is very bad! I've got to get out of here!*

He quickly decided not to worry with killing the police officers as he looked past them and noticed Charlton Fields crawling out of the hallway, towards the front door.

*No time! NO TIME!*

He leaped over the moaning officers and bounded out of the hallway, his gun raised and ready to kill Fields.

Only Fields was nowhere to be seen.

*"Fuck!"* he barked.

The lightning flashed again. Thunder boomed. Then Spears heard car tires squeal over wet driveway.

*Fields.*

Spears rushed out the front door and saw Fields driving away in the policemen's vehicle. He fired a few times, blew out the back windshield. But the car kept speeding away, and finally cleared the gate.

*"Freeze!"* came a shout from behind him.

*Cops!* Spears's mind roared. *These relentless assholes! No time for this!*

Spears spun around in a flash and fired five times, not aiming at all, just trying to buy some cover.

It worked.

He ran out the front door and back into the storm. He rushed to his car, slammed the door, and fired up the engine. Spears managed to drop the transmission into gear and flick on the headlights at the same moment, then he sped away into the night, baring his teeth furiously.

*Fields!*

---

Fletcher and Benson stumbled out of the hallway, gasping for breath and limping. They were both hurt, and had little to show for it except for three dead bodies. Their wounds were completely superficial, and for that Fletcher was thankful. But the mystery man was speeding away, the one the black guy had called Spears. Fields was gone too.

As they neared the front door, they noticed that their own car was gone.

*This is no good,* Fletcher thought.

He turned to Benson.

"You okay?" he said, sounding slightly frantic.

Benson began to check himself over as though he hadn't really thought about it, wincing in pain every time he moved his left arm.

"I think I'm alright," he said, "but my arm hurts like crazy!"

Fletcher limped to him and inspected the wound.

"I think you'll be okay. Looks like a flesh wound."

Benson nodded, trying out a weak smile.

"Well, that doesn't make it hurt any less."

Fletcher managed a smile in return.

"Nope, it sure doesn't."

Suddenly, the reality of what had just transpired hit Fletcher like tidal wave, and he began to tremble. He turned away from Benson as tears rushed to his eyes, stinging them. His mind instantly went to Marvin Gaston.

Benson placed a hand on his shoulder.

"You okay, partner?" he said.

Fletcher waved him off and took a few deep breaths.

"I'm fine, I'm fine," he said, his voice wavering on the edge of control. "Just call this in."

Benson nodded. "You got it."

As Benson walked away, Fletcher sank to his knees and wept.

*Get it together!* he hissed to himself. *Get it together, you weak shit!*

But then he saw a vision of Marvin Gaston's exploded head staring at him with dead eyes. Marvin's dead face haunted him like a ghost.

He shook it away while he cried.

*Not again,* he thought. *We're okay. It was close, but we're okay!*

Emotion overwhelmed him then, and he put his head between his knees and sobbed until there were no more tears left in him.

# CHAPTER 22

Heather Fletcher awoke to the phone beside her bed announcing an incoming call. Groggily, she felt across the nightstand and grasped the phone.

"Hello?" she muttered, a bitter tinge seeping into her voice.

She was still asleep for the most part. Somewhere in her mind a voice was asking her what time it was. This seemed like an excellent question, and she looked at the clock next to the phone to retrieve an answer.

*4:33 A.M.*

That was odd. In fact, that was a *really* odd time for anyone to be calling. And how rude was it to call at such a time? Who would be so thoughtless as to call so incredibly early—or incredibly late, depending on how you looked at it—rousting her from slumber, especially a slumber that was so deep and restful? This was *crap,* that's what it was! Whoever it was had better have a darn good reason for disturbing her in the middle of the night, or they were going to get a piece of her mind!

She was awake now, and mad.

"Who is this? Do you have any idea what time it is? Huh? I'll tell you what time it is! It's four-thirty-three in the morning! Why are you calling? Huh? Huh? Why aren't you answering me?"

She finished this sentence with the realization that the still unidentified caller had yet to answer her string of questions because from the moment she first said 'Hello', she had yet to stop for half a second, denying the caller any word in edgewise.

She took a breath. Calmed herself down.

*Come on, Heather. Cool it.*

She tightened her lips and spoke more softly and controlled her tone.

"I'm sorry," she said. "Hello? How can I help you?"

As she mentally chastised herself first for losing her temper and then sounding like a retail salesman on acid, she heard a voice on the phone. It was a male, she could decipher that much, and he was bumbling through his first sentence in this conversation.

"Ah, yes, uh, hmm, I, uh, I'm sorry to call in the middle of the, uh, the night like this, but…"

The caller trailed off. He sounded as though he were nervous, and more so than her little scolding should've warranted.

"My name is Albert Gonzalez," the caller continued finally. "Detective Albert Gonzalez. I work with Harry Fletcher."

Heather sat up straight in bed, her heart pounding all at once.

"Is daddy ok?" she asked sharply. "What's going on?"

She felt her pulse quicken. Police officers didn't call you in the middle of the night just to have a little chit-chat, especially officers that worked with your father.

"Has something happened?" she asked again, the blade of her tone razor-sharp now.

Albert Gonzalez took his time to answer, and it was excruciating. She was on the verge of losing it again when he finally spoke.

"Well, this is Heather Fletcher then, I'm assuming?"

"Yes! Yes, I'm Heather! *What is going on?*" she demanded, the strain in her voice obvious.

"I'm sorry," he said. "Your father Harry, well he was involved in a shooting tonight…"

Her heart exploded inside her, shattering her nerves. There were footsteps coming down the hallway and a voice called out to her.

"Heather?"

Heather tried to answer, she even opened her mouth to tell her mother, *hey daddy's been in a shooting and I think he's dead,* but her throat had swollen shut and she couldn't utter a single word.

Then the door to her bedroom opened and her mother stepped in. Helen's face was streaked with concern, and that concern seemed to intensify as her eyes met Heather's.

"Darling, what is it?" Helen said.

Heather reached deep inside herself, found her voice, began to wrench it free. She finally pulled it from its prison and was about to speak, when Gonzalez came back on the line.

"Now, your father is hurt..." he said, again trailing off—something that was sheer murder to Heather's heart.

*Just spit it out already!* her mind roared.

"...but he's gonna be okay," Gonzalez finally managed to get out. "He was wearing his Kevlar vest. That's what saved him."

Relief rushed into her like a tidal wave.

"Oh, thank God! Thank God!"

Her mother was trembling with anticipation now. "What, dear? What's happened?"

Heather held up a finger, the universal signal for *hold on a moment,* and then wiped tears of relief from her face. She listened for a few moments, nodding along and saying things like 'Yes sir' and 'Yes, I know where it is'. Then she hung up.

Helen Fletcher's face was boiling red.

"*What is going on, Heather?*" she screamed.

Heather looked up at her mother and said, "Daddy's been shot."

Helen's hand leapt to her face and clutched her mouth. Tears glistened in the corners of her eyes.

"He's okay, though," Heather went on. "He was wearing his vest, so he's just *hurt.* They told me what hospital he's at, so I've got to get up and go."

"I'm coming with you," her mother said without a moment's hesitation. "Just let me get ready. Five minutes."

"K," Heather said, leaping out of her bed. She rushed to the closet and flung it open.

*Oh, thank God, thank God, thank God!*

She found a shirt and snatched it off the hanger. She had it on and was pulling her shoes over her heels when she heard her mother from down the hall.

"I'm ready when you are!"

"Okay," Heather said, pulling a jean jacket on. "Let's go."

The hospital was twenty minutes away. They made it in ten.

# CHAPTER
## 23

Charlton Fields kicked in the door to the shack with a growl. He made his way in and threw his gun down on the cot, clutching his right cheek with his right hand, pressing firmly against the gaping wound. It wasn't doing much good. Splashes of blood were pouring between his fingers. His hand was slick with the stuff. Flaps of skin dangled between his fingers and jagged shards of shattered teeth poked his hand.

*That damn COP!* he thought. *That fucking PIG!*

He made his way to the sink, located in the back of the shack, and started the water. He first rinsed his hand, watching as the sink bowl turned red. His lips trembled with fury.

*I'll get you, cop! You're gonna pay!*

Finally, he looked at himself in the mirror, something he'd managed to avoid doing in the car, and took a good look at the wound, so as to assess the damage. It wasn't good.

A hole, about one and three-quarters inches in jagged diameter, was torn out of the side of his face. He could see shards of his teeth through it, a couple still mostly intact. They were stained crimson. Chunks of dark, almost black flesh were speckled about his teeth and gums.

And there were empty spaces where some of his teeth *should* be.

*There. Right there.*

There were two teeth, one on top, one on bottom, that were still in there, but shattered horribly, leaving jagged, sharp spikes jutting out from his gums.

His breathing became labored. His pulse quickened. Every breath was a deep, quick rush of air.

*In-out. In-out.*

A voice began to rumble deep inside of him. Only, it wasn't really a voice at all, but a primal roar bellowing up inside of him, thrashing, clawing its way out.

Then he screamed like a madman and put his fist through the mirror. His disfigured image broke away and crumbled to the floor, clinking on the wooden surface with a glassy sound. His entire body shook now. Not from pain, though there was plenty. Not from shock either, though that was setting in.

It was *rage.*

*I'll kill you, Fletcher,* he relished in his mind. *I remember you. I remember how pretty your wife was. How pretty your daughter was...*

*...is.*

That was it. That would be his revenge. And oh, how *sweet* it would be.

Then a voice came to him.

*Don't forget what you're doing here. Why we're doing this in the first place. Forget the cop. He's nothing. A minor inconvenience.*

*Minor?* he thought. *Minor?! Have you seen my fucking face?*

No. He would not forget the cop. That *minor inconvenience* had just ruined his face. Maimed him. This was *not* something he could just let go.

*So what? Like your face could be much worse. In fact, it might even be an improvement!*

Charlton uttered that primal roar again, this time accompanying it with a fist through the wall over the toilet. His hand rang out with pain, and he noticed blood running down his knuckles even as he pulled his fist from the splinters. He turned his head away quickly and felt a flap of skin flop against his face. This enraged him even more.

*"You're a dead man, Fletcher!"* he screamed out the shack.

His voice was slurred and lisped from the wound. He felt saliva dripping out of the hole in his face and tried to suck it back in, creating a wet, gurgling sound.

He stumbled out through the front room of the shack and into the open air outside. He was miles from anyone. From anything. He cried out again.

"I'll kill you, Harry Fletcher! I'm gonna burn your life to the ground! And everyone in it!"

He dropped to his knees in the tall grass.

*And I mean everyone.*

He began to laugh then. At first, it was little more than a snickering giggle, but it developed into guffaws of maniacal, bellowing chatter that chilled the air itself.

A quarter of a mile away, at the tree line of the clearing, two yellow eyes watched with murderous glee.

---

*Good. Very, very good, my dear boy. Embrace it. Cling to it. Bask in it. Hate leads to vindication. Vindication leads to triumph. And triumph leads to redemption...*

The two yellow eyes blinked and a grotesquely misshapen mouth beneath them peeled back over brownish, dripping fangs. Its body was humanoid, though it had horrible, crookedly set wings on its back. The wings spread and fluttered, easing the creature to the ground with silent grace. Then it dropped to all fours and began sprinting like a leopard. Its hind legs bent in the opposite direction as a human's would, and there were long, black claws on all its 'fingers'. Its nose was more of a tusk. Or *two* tusks rather. A black, forked tongue slithered in and out of its fangs, lapping up the slime that was its saliva.

*Finally,* it thought. *Finally, it is time! This wretched soul has finally opened to us and he is ours! Oh, thank you, dear leader! Thank you for this one! His sin is rich, and oh, so sweet! Oh, this will be glorious!*

The thing charged closer to Charlton, relishing every moment of the attack. He had been assigned plenty of bodies to acquire in the past, but none so sweet as this one. None with such festering hate. Hate was the sweetest of sins. It was the catalyst for all the great multitude of evil, and it was sweeter than honey to the thing's lips.

*So sweet...*

The thing leaped into the air and dived inside the laughing madman.

It was a perfect fit.

---

Charlton felt the thing come into him, though he hadn't known what the *thing* was. He hadn't seen it. But he *had* felt it.

All he really knew was he was suddenly filled with a power he'd only dreamed of in the past. Every cell in his body tingled with electricity.

*What is this?*

He knew, whatever the thing was, it was filling him with power, feeding off his hate.

Charlton's body rose from its knees, not standing, but *lifting* from the ground. And it didn't stop when his feet were level beneath him. He rose into the air a foot, then two. He leaned his head back and arched his spine. His feet dangled freely beneath him.

Again he let out a cry, not out of anger this time, but sheer adrenaline. He wasn't afraid. He was mesmerized.

Charlton had found the strength, the *power,* to kill the ones who murdered his family.

Oh, yes, it *was* murder. He was convinced of it. Murder by suicide. They had terrified his little sister, his sweet Sophie, into jumping off his family's roof. They ruined his parent's lives in the process. *That's* what killed them. Suicide was merely the tool the brutes used.

*But now…now they'll pay!*

Two already had. Well, quite a few more than two, actually, and most had had nothing to do with his family's massacre. But, oh well. Every war had collateral damage.

There was one more jolt of energy that surged through him, yanking his thoughts back to the present. He began to sink back to the ground. He'd never felt better. He'd never felt more *alive*. He tingled all over and felt stronger than ever. He rushed back into the shack and walked to the wall. After a moment of staring at it, he put his fist through it, the same fist as in the bathroom earlier. He was amazed.

Not only did it not hurt this time, but as he pulled his hand from the splintered wall, he noticed there was no blood. No scratches.

*No cuts.*

And he didn't feel his cheek flapping. He was breathing hard, but didn't hear—didn't *feel*—the wet, gurgling slops.

Shaking with anticipation, he rushed back to the bathroom and grabbed up a large shard of the mirror from the floor.

He held it out in front of him.

*The wound on his face was gone.*

He giggled crazily as he touched at the spot where it had been, pinching at it to be sure he wasn't dreaming.

He wasn't. It was really gone.

In a near crazed state, he sliced his hand open deliberately on the shard of mirror. There was no pain. He looked at his hand. A long ravine of pink flesh stood out on his hand, but there was no blood. A moment later, the wound sealed itself up like a plastic sandwich bag.

*Oh, boy...*

Then he saw something in the shard of mirror. Two yellow eyes gleaming out of his own.

*What?*

Then he heard a voice. It was one he was well acquainted with, though he'd always thought it his own.

Tonight, he would learn that it was not.

*Hello, Charlton. My dear little Charlie.*

"Who-who are you?" Charlton asked, slightly afraid for the first time since he'd felt the power surge into his body outside the cabin. He had been on such a high from adrenaline that he'd not been capable of any significant fear.

*A friend,* the voice answered in his mind. *I've been around for years. Now you've let me in.*

"What?"

*Hush now,* it went on. *I've been around for a long, long time. I've been many men. I've lived in many hearts.*

Charlton was beginning to see what the spirit inside him was. He didn't believe it. How could there be demons? Especially if there was no God?

*Oh, don't be fooled,* the thing laughed. *There is a God. But He hates you. He wants you to do nothing. To live with your loss. To go on and on and on, never feeling avenged. Never feeling vindicated. He is the one who killed your family. And me? I'm here to help you kill 'em all.*

"Kill 'em all..." Charlton said, smiling.

Charlton grinned ear to ear. When he did, he could feel the vanished wound on his face open again. The flesh merely separated and folded back, dribbling blood. It was like stretching a plastic bag too far and causing it to tear.

He quickly rejected his smile, and the wound vanished.

"Okay," Charlton said aloud. "No smiling. That'll be easy enough. There's nothing left to smile about anyway. Nothing at all."

*That's right,* his new friend mused. *Not a single thing. So, down to business. Pleased to meet you. My name is Trocephus.*

"Hello Trocephus," Charlton said aloud. He couldn't help feeling a bit ridiculous about the whole situation. But this *power*... it was so incredible.

He grinned again, uncontrollably, causing the wound on his cheek to open. Blood oozed out of his face, ran down his jawline, and dripped off his chin in thick, crimson globs. This time he let it run.

"So, Mr. Trocephus, what now?"

# CHAPTER
## 24

"Where's my father?" Heather Fletcher asked the nurse at the desk in the ER. "I want to see him right now!"

The nurse nodded to her, holding up a finger, and retrieved the phone from its cradle. She punched in a number, and a moment later was speaking in hushed tones to someone on the other end.

Heather threw up her hands in frustration and turned to her mother.

"What is *with* these people?" she hissed.

Helen Fletcher gave her daughter a reassuring look, though it had little soothing effect.

"Honey," her mother said in a sweet voice, "they're just doing their job. They have certain procedures to follow when there has been an officer-involved shooting."

Heather nodded and turned back to the nurse's desk. As she did, she noticed a tear trying to dive down her mother's face, which Helen quickly wiped away.

The nurse set the phone down and was about to open her mouth to speak when Heather cut her off.

"So now that you've chopped through all the red tape, can I please see my father? Like now!"

The nurse forced a smile, obviously biting back her own comments, and pointed to the left of her desk.

"Go to the third curtain on the right. He's in there."

Heather didn't even bother to say thank you, but rather stormed away towards the curtain that contained her father.

She flung the curtain open and saw her father lying on the bed. His shirt was gone, but his chest was wrapped tightly with what appeared to be Ace bandages.

He smiled at her as she entered.

"Hey baby!" he said. "I thought I heard you out there!"

She grinned, choking up all at once. Her lips quivered and moved to the side, and her eyes welled with tears.

"Daddy!"

She ran to him and threw her arms around his neck. She squeezed as he tried to reach an arm up around her, and he winced audibly.

"Ooh! Be careful!" he said. "I kinda got shot right there."

She pulled back and apologized at least forty-five times within four seconds.

"It's okay, darling," he said, trying to sit up and stifle a laugh at the same time.

She said, "Are you okay? How do you feel?"

He looked around at himself and shrugged.

"I've been better, but for a guy who just got blown away twice, I'm not too bad!"

She giggled at that and he started laughing with her. His eyes looked past her, the humor leaving them, and Heather turned to see her mother standing there.

Fletcher's tone turned somber at once. His smile vanished, but Heather didn't think it was because he was unhappy to see her. He seemed surprised. Almost reverent.

"Helen," he said.

Helen forced a smile through her teary eyes. "Hello Harry."

She walked into the room and stood beside their daughter. "The nurse says you'll be fine. That's good news!"

She cleared her throat, probably to keep her voice from cracking.

"I'm glad you're okay."

Fletcher smiled mildly, and looked a little choked himself.

"Thank you. It means a lot."

He then cleared his throat awkwardly.

"You know," he said, "you didn't have to come, I'll be alright."

"I wanted to come, Harry," she said quickly and sharply. "I wanted to."

"Oh," he mumbled, and shut up.

The main problem they had nowadays, in Heather's mind, was knowing when to shut their mouths. But somehow Heather knew, at that moment, her father would say no more about her mother coming to see him in the wee hours of the morning. He seemed glad to see her, and it was evidenced all over his face.

He turned his attention back to Heather, who was feeling the tension between her parents all too well.

"So, how's school?" he asked, seeming unsure of what to say, perhaps dying for the opportunity to change the subject.

The question disarmed her.

"Oh, uh, well," she began, and paused for a moment. She hadn't been expecting to talk about her scholastic standing, not with her father bandaged up in the hospital, but she set her mind and went on.

"I'm, uh," she continued to stutter, "I'm doing well. Just took a pretty important test the other day. Did well on it."

'Did well on it' meant she had aced it, and she had, but she was far too modest to ever say so. But she could see father knew better.

He smiled.

She changed the subject back to his ailment.

"So, does it hurt?"

*What a question,* she thought. *Knocking them out of the park tonight, aren't you, Heather?*

"Yeah, baby, it hurts," he said with a grin. "It hurts pretty bad, but it's just bruising. It'll go away."

They talked for a while and finally, when the sun was coming up, Heather and Helen decided to go. Heather kissed her father on the cheek.

"I love you," she said as she turned to leave.

Helen came to his bedside and grasped his hand.

"I'm glad you're okay," she said.

There was a moment where they stared into each other's eyes with a look that bordered on longing. Heather saw it, and saw her mother was caressing her father's hand with her thumb until he looked down at it. When he did, Helen quickly pulled her hand away and said good bye.

As they walked out, Heather heard her father begin to cry.

---

In the parking lot, Heather grabbed her mother by the arm.

"What was that, mom?"

She was talking about the way her mother and father had parted just then.

"I don't know what you mean?" her mother said, overtly fibbing.

She sucked at fibbing. She didn't do it enough. Heather wasn't buying.

"Oh, yes you do! You're still in love with him, aren't you?"

Helen began shaking her head much too vigorously.

"I don't know where you get your ideas from but you're way off, young lady!"

Helen paused for a moment, looking her over.

"Besides, it's none of your business!"

"Excuse me?" Heather said vehemently. "My mother and my father and *any* feelings the two of you have for each other are most certainly my business!"

She paused for a second, mulling over what she'd just said.

"Or maybe it isn't my business, but that doesn't matter to me because I'm butting in and there isn't a thing in the world you can do about it, mom!"

Her mother shook her head, rolled her eyes, and turned away, walking towards her car. She began digging in her purse, presumably for her keys.

"Sometimes, I think you need professional help!" Helen said.

Heather saw her pulling her keys out of her purse when someone grabbed her from behind. Panic rose in her, and she had just enough time to get out a single word.

"*MOM!*"

She saw her mother turn quickly, horror showering her face as she did. Helen's mouth opened as if to scream when everything went black.

———

Fletcher was wiping away the rest of his tears when Benson wheeled himself into his room. It was actually more of a *space,* seeing as the walls were made of curtains.

"How you doing?" Benson asked, himself bandaged to the hilt.

Fletcher shrugged and sniffed away the final remnants of his cry.

"I'm alright," he muttered. "Did you give your description to the sketch artist?"

"Yeah, he's got it. It looks really close."

"Well, that's good," Fletcher said. "So, how are you?"

Benson shrugged, then winced.

Fletcher chuckled. "Never mind, it's obvious!"

They both shared a painful, but much needed laugh.

When it had ceased, Benson said, "I couldn't help overhearing you and your family talking."

"It's only my daughter," he said. "The other woman is my ex-wife."

Benson shrugged, wincing once more.

"Sounded to me like she still cares about you."

Fletcher grunted.

"Maybe. I don't know," he said, then shook his head after a moment. "But no. We've just got too many differences."

Benson opened his mouth to say something else when Bert and Ernie came bustling in. They both looked flustered and out of breath. Fletcher forgot all about the conversation he'd been having with Benson.

"What's going on, guys?" he said.

Bert caught his breath. "Someone just came in and said something happened in the parking lot!"

Fletcher's heart firmly lodged itself in his throat.

"Who? What happened?"

Ernie said, "Just calm down Harry, everything is gonna be okay!"

"Don't tell me to calm down!" he said, raising his voice and crawling painfully out of the bed. The pain was becoming a distant discomfort.

"Tell me what happened!" Fletcher barked.

Ernie looked at Bert and Bert took over.

"It's Helen and Heather," he said. "Someone's taken them!"

# CHAPTER
## 25

Helen opened her eyes and saw black.

She could feel something over her eyes. Some sort of fabric. She tried to reach up to remove it, but couldn't. Her hands wouldn't move. Then she realized her hands were tied behind her. Throbbing pain pounded in her head. She tried screaming, but found she couldn't do this either. Everything she tried to do, every movement she tried to make, something was stopping her. Something was stuffed in her mouth, held there by some other piece of rope or fabric. The soggy mess in her mouth then began to make her gag, but even her gag was held in place by her restraints.

*Oh, sweet Jesus, what's happening?*

Next, she tried to move her feet, but, you guessed it, no soap. They were tied too, and she could tell this tie was connected to the one on her hands, and virtually every movement she tried made her restraints tighter and tighter.

She was hog-tied.

The ground beneath her bounced and she was thrown upwards into some metal roof that couldn't have been more than a foot or two above her head. A small space. A small *bouncing* space...

*I'm in a car! In the trunk of a car!*

She came back down with enough force to knock the wind out of her. Terror stole through her as the wind blew out of her lungs and she found that she could not suck air back in. The gag was in the way. That blasted gag that was stopping her from screaming or even gagging—*Ha-Ha*—and she couldn't breathe! No air was coming back into her lungs. She knew that soon she would see spots, then she would be thrashing about helplessly for several moments while the ties about her feet and hands bound tighter against her skin, burning it and digging in, but not letting go! No, they wouldn't let go, they would never let go, and she would not get to breathe. Never breathe again, oh God!

*Oh, help me!*

Amid her panic, she felt air rush into her nostrils and begin the slow work of refilling her depleted and shocked lungs. She had been so frightened that she hadn't even thought of her nose. She supposed she should feel foolish, and perhaps under different circumstances she might. But not now. Now, trapped in her small, metal prison, tied back on herself like a farm animal going to the slaughter, she felt no foolishness at all. All she felt was relief and thanks to God for the sweet, precious sips of air she was getting in through her snot-caked nostrils.

Once her breath was back and the panic had been quelled, she began trying to feel around the floor of the trunk for something that might help her free herself. She groped and groped for something, anything, but found nothing. Then her hands came across something. Something soft. Something like…

*Flesh.*

Again, the idea that she should feel foolish swept over her. It was her leg she was feeling. Merely the skin on her leg that was bound up behind her and tied to her hands. The skin that she had covered just a few hours before with a pair of jeans and…

A pair of jeans.

She had felt flesh, alright. But it was not *her* flesh.

She recoiled in horror.

*Oh, sweet Lord Jesus, help me!*

Then she realized something she'd forgotten. Something that now, even now in her tiny moving dungeon, actually *did* make her feel foolish.

*Heather!*

She reached backward again, as far as her restraints would allow her, and found the flesh again. She scooted her body closer and as she did she could feel more and more.

*A hand. An arm. A breast.*

*Heather?*

She worked backwards now, feeling again for the hand, and found it. She felt about the hand, finding the fingers, and started to fondle them. She was looking for the ring she had given her daughter on the night of her High School graduation. It was a large, golden ring with a three-quarter karat diamond as its centerpiece.

*Where is it?*

As she groped more and more for it, dread overcame her with the thought that it may not be her daughter lying next to her in this dark abyss.

*Oh, God!* she thought. *They aren't moving! Who is this?*

Then her hands came across some rope that was binding the wrists of whoever's hands these were.

*Okay, find the ring Helen. This must be Heather. You know it's her. JUST FIND THE RING!*

Heather wore it on her right ring finger so as not to confuse potential suitors about her marital status. It was her prized possession. As ever-present as her hair.

She *never* took it off.

Helen worked her way back down the hand to the fingers and started checking each one. She finished with one hand and was getting at the next one, when another bump in the road threw her into the lid of the trunk again. She banged her head on the way down and felt fresh pain pulsating through her skull. White dots of light danced in her vision, and for just a moment, she thought she would pass out.

*Focus!*

Her voice screaming at her yanked her back to the moment, and the dancing light diminished. She scooted her body back over toward the other person.

*Heather*, she prayed.

Again, she found the hands and got back to the work of checking for the ring. She felt quickly, dismissing the hand she'd already checked, and moved on to the other one. She began pulling the fingers apart, checking each one individually with panicked speed.

And then she found it.

Tears poured from her eyes as she was overcome with joy and dread at the same moment, knowing she'd found what she was looking for, but also now knowing it was her daughter. She didn't know if she was alright. In fact, Heather had not moved since Helen regained consciousness.

*Okay, time to get out of here. First rule, Harry always said, if you're trapped, free yourself first. You can't help anyone else if you can't move.*

She positioned the ring in a way that she could get her ropes over the top of it. She thanked God that the ropes, while very sturdy and tight, were at least not very wide in diameter.

She began to move her ropes back and forth over the diamond. It was difficult work, trying to hold the ring steady and scrape the ropes over it. It was wearing her arms out quickly.

*Oh, please God! PLEASE!*

She felt a thread of the rope pop and give way. There was a rush of exhilaration as she felt freedom inching its way towards her.

Another pop. It was working.

She found new strength as she sawed herself loose, and she kept praying, harder and harder as she went on.

*Thank you, God! Thank you! I can do this! Just a little more!*

There was another pop. Helen smiled and then shrieked mutedly into her gag as Heather's body suddenly tensed and began to jerk about behind her.

*She's awake!*

Helen tried to finish the work on her ropes, but Heather's flailing made it impossible. The ringed hand jerked away and she could hear her daughter screaming into her own gag. She wanted desperately to grab her, hold her, tell her everything was okay, tell her not to worry.

But she couldn't. It wasn't possible. She couldn't move.

*Oh, please, God! Help me here!*

She prayed this prayer repeatedly, all the while making new attempts to get her ropes over the ring. Finally, whether hearing God herself or simply realizing what Helen was trying to do, Heather lay still. Helen moved herself back again, and reached for her daughter's hands. They found each other and clasped tightly for several moments. Her thumb caressed her daughter's hand, and she felt Heather's hand squeeze back, as if in understanding. Knowing it was her mother.

After a moment of this, Helen grabbed her daughter's restraints, shook them, and then grabbed the ring and shook it. Heather then positioned the ring just so for her mother, and more rigidly than it had been before.

*She knows what I'm doing! My smart baby girl! She knows!*

Helen began cutting her ropes again and in a few moments, her hands were free. She quickly untied her feet and pulled the gag out of her mouth.

"I'm here baby!" she said, not too loudly for fear their captor might hear her.

She still couldn't see anything in the trunk, but soon her eyes adjusted and she could just make out Heather's shape from the light dripping in from the trunk lid. It was little more than a silhouette, but it was her. Her baby.

She began to untie her daughter when she felt the terrain under them go from smooth to rough.

*We're in a driveway.*

She quickly freed her daughter, and began putting her blindfold back on.

"What are you doing, mom?" Heather asked, spitting out the last remnants of her gag.

"We're about to stop," Helen said. "I'm gonna catch him off-guard."

"Oh…"

"It'd be nice to have a weapon," Helen said as she picked up her gag.

Heather reached up to the cab end of the trunk and produced a tire-iron.

"Will this do?" she asked.

Helen peeked through her blindfold, which she had deliberately put on a bit too high so she could peer underneath it.

Helen smiled broadly.

"That'll do just fine!"

Heather handed it to her mother and began to put her own gag and blind fold back on.

A moment later, the car stopped.

Heather reached for her mother's hand and squeezed.

# CHAPTER 26

*C*aution...
    That one word. Nothing else. Over and over again.

*Caution...*

*Is Trocephus trying to warn me?* Charlton wondered.

He didn't know what the word was referring to, but he felt a heightened sense of anxiety. Anticipation.

Fear.

But of what? What exactly should he be afraid of out here, in the middle of nowhere? He didn't know.

Charlton was just pulling up to the cabin. There was not another person around for miles in any direction. The women were bound and gagged so tight they would never get loose, and on top of that, he'd smashed a billy-club into their faces. They wouldn't be moving around much.

Yet that one word kept ringing in his mind.

*Caution…*

"Of what?" he asked his internal friend aloud. "What am I watching out for?"

*I'm not sure. There is something wrong, but I can't quite see it. I think He is meddling!*

"HIM?" Charlton piped. "What does *He* have to do with this?"

*I'm not sure,* Trocephus repeated amiably in Charlton's mind. *He's done this before. Sometimes I can't see Him right off the bat. But something is definitely amiss, mark my words. Be alert.*

"Great," Charlton said, and sighed.

He shifted the car into park, swung his door open, and stepped out. He had already begun to shut the door when he remembered the club. He reached back into the cab and grabbed it.

*Keep it close.*

"Yeah," Charlton said with a grunt. "But I still don't know how you can know something is wrong and not know *what* it is. I would think those things would be mutually exclusive. Am I being watched?"

---

Trocephus giggled within Charlton, which translated to his host's face and vocal chords. Whatever Trocephus said or did, was mimicked involuntarily through Charlton.

Unless, of course, Trocephus detached himself from the man's soul momentarily. But as of that moment, he wanted to stay close. It was so sweet. The sweetest of the sweets. A flavor he could not get enough of.

The nectar of hate.

Ah, yes, that sugary-sweet core of loathing inside his host was indeed grand, but he couldn't dine on that now.

Right now, he had to focus his attention on the problem at hand. Something was happening, that was for sure, only he didn't know what it was. Hell, he didn't even know if it was significant. Might only be the eons old paranoia his kind was now bred with. Being at odds with the Creator did that to a spirit.

But was this significant? Was there a genuine threat here? And even if it *was* significant, *how* significant could it be? He was keeping a keen eye out, you can bet your balls on that, but he was still coming up with nothing solid. Only that building, relentless dread.

*Caution…*

---

Charlton made his way to the trunk of the car. He began thinking about the two beautiful ladies he'd taken hostage. Not only were they beautiful, but they were *Fletcher's* beautiful ladies, and that shit was the real cat's meow.

This made him smile. And smiling made blood ooze from his face.

He noticed the open, warm flow almost at once, and stopped smiling. As he did, he noticed his arm had bled as well when he'd smiled.

*Don't smile. Don't even grin. Happiness isn't what's going to free you. Only hate will bring vindication. Only hate can set you free.*

"And what's there to smile about anyway?" Charlton asked aloud to his new guest.

*That's right,* Trocephus replied. *There's nothing left to smile about.*

Charlton didn't know why, but he had another urge to smile at that moment. Maybe it was knowing he had Fletcher hurting. Maybe it was the powerful presence of his new, mysterious friend. He didn't know, but what he *did* know was smiling brought blood. And that was bad.

*Push it away! Now, damn you!*

Charlton pushed it away with a startle. Trocephus had been nothing but cordial up to now, but his tone just now had sent chills down his spine. No matter. His friend seemed to be looking out for him. Making sure he didn't hurt himself. After all, they were on a mission. A crusade. If they didn't look out for each other, they would surely fail. And failure, friends and neighbors, was not an option.

He came back to himself and focused again on the trunk. He fumbled through the keys until he found one that would open the trunk. Upon finding it, he plunged it deep into the heart of the lock. He could feel the tumblers shift obediently into position.

He twisted.

Then the trunk lid was coming up, slowly, peeling away from the portrait of the two bound and gagged women. It was a delightful sight. One filled with vengeance. With blood.

A sense of pride cascaded over Charlton like a waterfall.

But then the portrait began to move as the lid came to rest in its raised position. The older woman's hands were moving. They weren't bound together. They should have been. He'd tied the knots himself, he knew good and damned well they were tight. Yet here were her hands, free and in motion, coming out from the dark well of the trunk.

Her body was rising swiftly. One hand went to her blindfold, while the other wielded a weapon of some sort. A tire-iron, maybe? He wasn't sure. It was moving too fast.

Then she was almost upright. The hand holding the weapon was moving at an alarming rate towards his face. He needed to move. To react. To do *something*, for shit's sake, and quick!

*Caution! Caution! Move! You've got to react!*

Charlton could hear Trocephus screaming at him, but the choice of words failed to have the desired effect. Instead of moving, as he knew deep down he ought, it made him laugh. Cackling laughter burst forth from him in a gale for about three-quarters of a second.

But then he saw the younger woman begin to move behind the elder. She too was not bound at the wrists as he'd originally thought. How? How the fu—

The weapon struck the side of his face like a locomotive. His face spun away, ejecting a few teeth in a bright crimson spray. The spray and his teeth seemed to hang in the air for a moment. Not quite suspended, but in an eerie ultra-slow motion. He saw blood-stained teeth tumbling end over end through the air in a wide arc, a stream of blood dancing about them, separated here and there as resistance in the atmosphere made the blood pull apart into smaller globs. He stumbled backward a few feet, sure he would fall.

But amazingly, he didn't fall. He was very dazed, staring at the ground in what could only be described as a stupefied daze as his dumbfounded eyes followed the dripping rubies pooling on the ground, soaking into the dirt and becoming a dark, biological mud with teeth standing in it like stumps.

*Pay attention!*

And then, time resumed at normal speed.

His eyes darted back to the trunk, snapping back with cold rage. The older woman—the one who had struck him—was tumbling out of the trunk. She'd swung the tire-iron with such force that, after it had struck him, the momentum of the blow had literally thrown her out of the trunk. She was headed for the ground, face first.

He began to stumble toward her, his head throbbing and spinning like a violent tornado. The pain was intense, but incredibly, it seemed to already be diminishing.

As he reached the woman on the ground, he snatched her hair, yanking her head back.

"That was a very stupid thing to do, bitch!" he spat.

Her face was speckled with blood. He reared back to pummel her face to a pulp, perhaps then on to a soup, and *then* go to work on her. She was going to pay, friends and neighbors, and Little Charlie had the bill.

*Caution!*

But before Charlton had a chance to ask what Trocephus was screaming about this time, something hard and sharp buried into his eye. There was a horrible *pop*, then searing pain shot through his skull and snaked down his entire body.

Blood and slime oozed out of his face as he screamed like a cartoon villain who'd just stubbed his toe. He forgot all about the older woman and what he'd planned to do to her face. In fact, for a moment, nothing else in Charlton's world existed. An opera of agony boomed through his face as he tumbled backward. And this time, he *did* fall. He collapsed to the ground in a lurching heap, grasping at his eye.

And he screamed.

———————

Heather gagged as she pulled her hand away from the man's face. Her diamond ring had sunk into and then burst his eye. Blood was oozing out of his face along with some other horrible liquid. It was on her hand, sliming her fingers and turning her stomach.

He was screaming.

She barreled out of the trunk and scrambled to help her mother to her feet.

"We've got to go, mom!" she yelled at her as she pulled her up. *"Right now!"*

They began to run away from the car, like screaming madwomen, toward the wood line of the forest. They didn't know where else to go. They didn't have a clue where they were. But none of that mattered right now. Right now, getting the—God forgive her—*hell* out of here was the only thing that mattered.

Helen grabbed her daughter's hand, gripping it tighter as they ran.

"Come on!" she screamed.

Someone would hear them. Someone would find them. Someone had to—

Something struck Helen in the back of the head with a loud *crack* and enough force to drive her to the ground.

Heather turned and saw some sort of club—a billy-club she thought she had heard her dad call them—lying on the ground next to her mother. She screamed.

*"Mom!"*

"Run!" Helen managed to say in a shaky voice. *"Run!"*

Heather had no intentions of leaving her mother to the whim of the madman. She ran to her mother, grabbed her by the arms, and started pulling on her. She noticed the psycho marching toward her with mad, frightening purpose. She looked back and saw the club.

She dropped her mother and grabbed it.

She came up to her full height again and raised the club over her head as the man neared her. She was just about to let out a primal scream and pummel the man's skull to mush when his hand fired out like a rocket and snatched her wrist. His grip was so forceful that when he twisted her arm, she went to her knees in a screaming heap. Pain shot through her arm and into her shoulder like a thunder-clap.

He relieved her of the club.

She looked to his face through tear-soaked eyes. What she saw caused the breath to catch in her throat.

*It can't be,* she thought with horror. *It just can't be!*

The eye she'd just destroyed with her ring only moments before was back to normal. Well, *almost* normal. It was a pale grayish color, but it was intact and it was not oozing blood and slime anymore. She looked at her own hand and saw the blood and slime was still there, crusting on her flesh like a cocoon.

She began to tremble.

*"He has failed,"* a terrifying voice rumbled and growled out of him.

It was not a human voice.

*"He has failed you, young lady. And now, you will pay the price!"*

The madman raised the club over his head and smashed Heather into unconsciousness.

# CHAPTER 27

Fletcher was unable to rest. He'd been up for over twenty-four hours by this point. Intensely fatigued, his body wanted little more than to close its eyes and shut down, to rest, to recharge. But he simply couldn't do it. Every time he tried to shut his eyes, to merely rest them for a few precious seconds, he could see his daughter and ex-wife walking out of the hospital room he'd been in, waving goodbye. Smiling as they turned to leave.

Then he saw blood.

It was haunting him. No, there would be no sleep for him. Not now, anyway, and likely not in the foreseeable future. At least not until his body simply gave out and he collapsed to the floor from sheer exhaustion.

*No,* his inner Harry said. *You can sleep when you're dead, but not before. Not until this business is finished.*

Fletcher nodded absently to the voice in response. The inner him was right. He would not stop until he found them.

There had been some speculation about who might have taken his daughter and ex-wife amongst the police force, but he knew exactly who had done it.

Little Charlie Fields.

Fletcher crossed the length of his bedroom in his house. It was nearly noon. Dan Felt had taken him home after several hours of questions and speculations about Helen and Heather: who might have taken them, Fletcher and Benson telling them exactly who it had to be, and the bureaucrats in the department not wanting to 'jump to conclusions'. Fletcher was exhausted, in pain, and he was desperate. Captain Felt had insisted Fletcher go home and get some rest. They would be in touch the moment there were any developments.

He reached his chest-of-drawers, picked his pistol up off the top, and put his shoulder holster on. Then he threw his sports coat on over it.

He wasn't going to wait for *developments*. He was going to create some. He wasn't going to sit by and let other people—good people to be sure, but people who really didn't understand what was going on and didn't have anything at stake in the issue—do his job for him. Heather was *his* daughter, damnit, and she was *his* responsibility. His little girl. He'd failed her at holding together the family she'd been born into, but he'd be damned before he failed her now. Not now. Not ever again.

But not without eating first.

He went into the kitchen and thought about what he wanted to eat. After several moments of salivation over juicy steaks and steamed vegetables, his mind then went to more realistic things he might actually *have*. A sandwich, maybe. Some turkey, ham, olive loaf, a few vegetables, all wedged between two slices of wheat bread slathered in mayonnaise and spicy mustard. That would really hit the spot right about now. That would put some energy back in his tiring body.

He opened the fridge door...

*...and saw Marvin Gaston's head on a plate.*

He yelped in a pitch he'd been unable to attain since he had first started noticing hair sprouting around his pubescent stump and roots, then fell backwards onto his ass, the door to the fridge still hanging open. Marvin's head still had the red hole where Jimmy Mitchell's bullet had gone, the skin all over pasty like old wax. It looked completely dead. Absolutely no life. As if someone had severed the head of his dead partner's corpse and preserved it in a jar of formaldehyde for all this time, then prepared it neatly on this plate for just this moment. His dead partner, the gleam totally gone from his eyes, stared blankly at him from the ominous glow of the refrigerator's light.

But then, of course, it spoke.

"Got your baby girl mixed up in all this shit, huh Harry?" the head said to him in a windy, swollen voice, as if its tongue were three times too large. "Couldn't even take care of your own? I'm not exactly surprised, of course, I mean, *look at me!*"

The reanimated severed head then burst out in a series of wet, gurgling chatters that might have been laughter, the dead, glazed eyes bulging forward and back in their sockets as if they were ready to pop out.

Fletcher was dumbfounded and realized he had lost his breath at some point in the moments since he'd opened the door thinking of turkey sandwiches.

"What?" he blubbered, unable to say much else.

"Your ex too, that's a gas, Harry my boy!" the wretched thing that had been his partner gasped through continued laughter. "All because you couldn't hold it together after that child-rapist pulled his diddly out with those kiddies! What a waste!"

More gasping laughter.

But Fletcher's fear had diminished now, and he had become angry.

"*I don't know who the fuck you are, but you're not Gaston!*" Fletcher screamed at his refrigerator. "*I'm a failure? Well how about this? I am! God damn you, I AM a failure! Alright? Is that what you want to hear? Fine then, you son of a bitch! I am a failure! I failed my family! I failed my wife! I failed my little girl! But most of all, I failed myself because I let a bad man define who I was and what I believe for twenty years, and I was too arrogant to let it slide! Instead I let...I let...*"

He trailed off then, his bottom lip trembling. He licked his lips as he thought about the words he was going to finish the sentence with. Words that had haunted him for two decades. Words he'd tried to drown in gallons of alcohol and macho attitude, but was just never quite able to kill. Words he knew he needed to say, to himself if no one else.

"*I let my family slide...*"

He put his hands over his face and began to weep. Great, heaving sobs escaped him, punctuated by giant, uncontrollable gulps of air. His body shook. Stinging tears lurched from the glands on either side of his nose and streamed down his face. Sweat beaded across his brow even though it wasn't warm in the house, least of all with the frigid air blowing across him from the refrigerator.

He sat there like that, on the floor of his kitchen, for a long while. At last, the tears began to dry up, and his sobs softened to whimpers. He'd gotten it out. He'd said it. Said it out loud. He had failed his family, and let them slide, all because he was too bitter and too angry to hold onto his faith, a faith that, if he was truly honest with himself, had brought his family to him in the first place. And all of it because of what a bad man did, who had nothing to do—not really—with his own faith.

He took a few moments to compose himself. He wiped the tears away and the sweat from his brow. Sniffed a couple of times to clear his nose.

When at last he looked up again, the head was gone. His partner wasn't there. He'd never been there at all, he knew. But in a way, maybe he had been. Maybe his dead partner had shown up to give him the swift kick in the ass he needed to pull it together. To pull it together for his family.

He got off the floor and checked through the refrigerator thoroughly anyway, however, and satisfied himself that the corpse head was truly absent. Then he shut the door without making a sandwich.

He'd lost his appetite.

Fletcher walked out of his house and turned to lock the door. As he did, he felt someone walking up behind him. He couldn't really hear it, but every hair on his neck stood on end, the way you feel when you know someone is watching. In his fatigued state—and certainly after the ordeal with his refrigerator—he wasn't willing to take any chances.

He whipped around, drawing his pistol as he did in a fluid motion, his finger curled around the trigger and his thumb snatching the hammer back.

He leveled it on Benson's face.

"You," Fletcher said, releasing the tension on the trigger and sighing.

*That's another huff, Harry.*

He pulled the gun away from Benson's face, aiming it straight up. He eased the hammer back down gently, and re-holstered his weapon.

"What are you doing here?"

"I, uh," Benson started, then gulped. "I'm here because, well, I don't exactly know why. I just felt I'm supposed to be here with you. With whatever you're planning. Something just told me to go with you."

Fletcher nodded slowly. "I, uh…I'm glad you came," he said. "I could use a, well…"

"You don't have to say it, Harry," Benson said, holding up his hand.

"Yes, I do," Fletcher said, and set his face. "I could use a friend right now. A partner. Jesus freak or not."

He said this last part with a sly grin, and Benson gave him one in return.

"Listen," Benson said, "I'm not here to brow beat you with anymore talk about God. I'm sorry I ever did that. I was wrong to push it on you. You know us Jesus freaks."

Now they shared a laugh.

"Okay," Fletcher said nodding. "Apology accepted. But listen, we've got to get going."

"Okay."

Fletcher headed for his car, and Benson fell in beside him.

"Elliot," Fletcher said as they went, "I need to know that you understand what you're getting into here. I may get fired for the things I'm about to do. Hell, I may get *killed* for the things I'm about to do. I'm off the case, I'm supposed to stay out of the way. But I can't do that. And that's okay. I'm single, I have no one to answer to. But that isn't you. You've got a future. A *family*, for Christ's sake. I don't want to take anyone else down with me."

"Like I said, Harry," Benson said, swelling his chest, "something told me to go with you, wherever you go, whatever you do. I mean to do that, Harry. You're right, I've got a family, but I also have a friend. A *partner*. And I know if it were my family…"

He trailed off and they stopped walking for a moment. Fletcher looked him up and down, contemplating the whole idea for a moment.

Finally, Fletcher sighed—a genuine sigh this time, no huffing involved—and smiled faintly at Benson.

"I appreciate that, Elliot. I really do. You do what I say, when I say it, and you keep yourself alive. You got that? Consider it an order from a superior officer."

"Loud and clear!" Benson said as he grinned and gave a mock salute.

"Alright, let's go."

"Where we going?"

Now it was Fletcher's turn to grin. "We're going to get in front of this psycho."

They marched to his car, got in, and drove away. There were three more people Fields was going to hit, if Fletcher's guess was right. And of course, he knew he was.

They were going to be waiting for Little Charlie.

# CHAPTER 28

Charlton Fields tied the gag firmly around Helen's mouth just as she was returning to consciousness.

Fields smiled. He was amused by the woman's spunk, even if it had been infuriating. She certainly had some fire in her, he had to give her that. But it was no match for what was inside of him. Especially now.

Warmth cascaded down his face as he dwelled on these things, and he quickly removed his smile. The blood was thick and hot.

He looked over the bound women before him. He'd done quite a number on them.

The older one's hair was matted with blood on the back where the club had struck and broke the skin. Her head would throb, he had little doubt of that, and she might even develop a scar under the carpet of her hair, but that was about the extent of her damages.

The younger woman, however, was in much worse shape.

Both of her eyes were swollen shut. Her upper lip bulged and seemed to quiver with swelling. It was split in two just below her left nostril, and Charlton could see bloodied teeth underneath, peeking through the macabre curtain of her lips. Her entire face was a tapestry of blues and blacks, spattered with drying blood. If he hadn't known better, he might have thought she was a corpse.

She was still unconscious.

Charlton had had to stop himself short from killing her. This was no easy feat either. It had felt so good! Perhaps even better than beating Fletcher himself. And he supposed, in a way, he was. This was flesh of Fletcher's flesh, blood of Fletcher's blood. Smashed and sprayed over a face that only hours before had been vibrant and beautiful. Not now, though. Now it was a nightmare landscape of pain and suffering. And that, friends and neighbors, made Charlton Fields salivate.

Fletcher's time would come, and soon. Charlton would relish the sight of Fletcher's torment when he showed him just what he'd done to his precious baby girl. Let Fletcher scream and wail, raging inside with desire to tear Fields apart. But he would be unable to do anything. Fields would see to that, you can bet your ass. He would sit there and have to watch his own flesh and blood get pulled apart before him, and then Fields would start in on him.

Yes sir, that would be sweet. That payoff would certainly come. And he wouldn't let Fletcher die until he was sure the man understood just what he was capable of.

*This* would hurt him.

*Back to business.*

There were still three people on his list. Still three people that needed to die. A preacher, an elder, and a monster.

*They're all monsters.*

Indeed, they were. All three were an absolute menace to the earth. Murderers of families. Slayers of little girls. Perverts.

*Sophie.*

His thoughts went to her and tears found their way to his eyes as he fell into a trance.

He was standing atop his childhood home, looking out over the landscape of their neighborhood. Peace and tranquility seemed to be etched into every detail. As his eyes scanned, they fell upon her. His sweet Sophie. She was there too, standing atop the roof, and looking at him with a faint smile. Her arm was outstretched toward him, as if beckoning him, and her hair flowed in some phantom breeze. She was so beautiful. So sweet. So innocent.

*"Kill them Charlie,"* she said, and he could see she was crying too. *"Kill them all..."*

Then she jumped.

She dropped out of sight, and Charlie ran, he ran like he'd never run before, across the pitched roof of the house, his feet slipping and sliding across the gravelly shingles. But even as he ran with all his might, he could hardly gain any ground. It was as if he was running under water, or perhaps in a tar pit. Yet he *was* gaining ground, ever so slowly. He pushed and struggled, fought his way to the edge. Finally, he made it. He peered over, knowing he would see her there, there on the driveway below, surrounded in a pool of blood, her body twisted and disjoint-ed. He drew in breath, ready to see the inevitable.

But when he looked over the edge, he didn't see the grassy yard or the cement driveway Sophie had cracked her skull on. He didn't see his sister's twisted corpse. In fact, his home, his neighborhood, wasn't there at all.

What he saw was a fiery abyss.

An endless oblivion of torment and angst stretched out beneath him like a ghastly pit. Beastly beings, some with severed limbs and torn flesh, others without skin on their faces or bodies at all, merely bloody muscle with eyeballs that seemed ready to pop out, their teeth bared with nothing to cover them, tendons and sinew popping and stretching with the relentless straining and flexing of the bare muscles. He saw still others, with no face at all. All of them reaching with whatever limbs they had, stumped or full, bloody and shredded, screaming. Wailing. *Writhing.*

A hum rose from the pit, an almost electric buzz, the sound of billions of tortured souls crying out all at once, out of unison with one another, their cries all forming into one solitary, indecipherable hiss, crawling upward labori-ously, never getting anywhere. The sight of monsters, beasts of the pit, horns and ragged wings, slimy skin the color of blood, laughing at their pain, beating them, tor-menting them, *torturing* them.

And the stench. It rose from the horror below and stung the nostrils, bringing bile leaping up the throat in uncontrollable wretches. A stench of death. Of rot. The stink of forgotten corpses, unearthed after centuries. The stench of separation from the world. Of uncleanness.

What Charlton saw was hell.

He snapped out of it. All at once the aberration was gone and he found himself staring at the two women he'd taken hostage once again. The older woman was fully awake now, pulling at her restraints in a futile attempt. Tears streaked her red face.

"Maybe you should pull a little harder," Charlton said. "Really snug those ropes into place."

He snickered as he said this last part. Then he turned to walk out. He was just past the door when Trocephus began to speak to him, and he stopped.

*We're on a mission,* Trocephus said. *Our father below knows best. His law is higher than this land's, and higher than that Big Bastard in the sky's. Our father below has sent us on a mission. To kill the rest of these monsters and expose them for what they are. And when we are done, all the world will know the true nature of those who follow that Big Bastard in the sky. The world will know them for what they are.*

Yes. Back to business.

*That's right. Back to business.*

Do we leave them here unsupervised? The women, I mean?

*Don't worry about that. I've got someone coming. He will be here after dark.*

Who is he?

*A very close friend. But worry about that later. For now, you must sleep.*

Yes. I'm so very tired...

Charlton walked across the room and laid down on his cot. He closed his eyes.

*Sleep well. Rest up. You have a very big night ahead of you.*

Fields began to drift off to sleep. But Little Charlie did not rest well.

# CHAPTER
## 29

S pears stood before J.R. Hays. They were in Hays' mansion, and J.R. was *not* happy.

His brow was furrowed into folds and his upper lip was positioned in a faint, but noticeable snarl that quivered every so often. His eyes squinted and burned into Spears.

"You have been a disappointment thus far, Alex," J.R. said, coldly. "Morgan and Tony are dead. Weir is dead. And now you tell me you killed Elk *yourself!*"

J.R. slammed his palm down on his desk with a thunderous clap.

Spears didn't like the situation he was in. He didn't like it at all. Mr. Hays was a powerful man, and powerful men had machines in place to eliminate problems. Still, he didn't flinch at J.R.'s theatrics. J.R. was blowing off steam. He was angry, and Spears could understand why. But though J.R. was a powerful man with machines in place to eliminate problems, Spears knew something else.

Something that allowed him to keep his calm, and dismiss the threatening nature of J.R.'s dramatic tirade.

Spears *was* the machine.

"That's right," Spears replied without emotion.

"And *why*, might I ask, did you kill him?"

Spears exhaled, frustration in his voice. His demeanor was like it might be if he was having to explain the simplest of issues to a retarded person. Like he was talking to a four-year-old. With Down Syndrome.

"He was a problem," Spears said. "He had been shot up pretty bad. But that wasn't the problem. The problem was Fields was there too, and in the moment, I realized getting Elk out while staying alive against the police *and* Fields would be a futile attempt. The option of leaving him there alive was no option at all. He would surely have given us up. Certainly, you can appreciate that."

Spears did his best to keep a cool and collected demeanor. He had done well under J.R.'s employment, and he had no interest in dissolving their mutually beneficial arrangement over this ordeal, but there was a distinct desire within him to pluck the man's eye out just then. His right eye, specifically. Dig his thumb and forefinger around behind the eyeball, and yank it free of its cords. Being spoken to as though he were beneath J.R. made Spears's skin crawl, and it demanded the utmost of his restraint to endure.

"Well, what's done is done," J.R. said, waving his hand. "This is going to cost me a great deal of money until I can find a replacement for him. Those whores of his bring in a lot of money. A lot of influence too. The pricks that come in for pastor's conferences are a cash-cow for us, and the reason is those whores. Or did you forget about that?"

J.R. paused and pinched his eyes shut tight. Spears could see him forcing his frustration to subside. Forcing himself calm.

His eyes popped back open to controlled, angry slits.

"But forget that for now..." he said, trailing off.

A smoldering cigar sat poised in the ashtray on J.R.'s desk. The man snatched it up and shoved it into his mouth. Took a long drag. Blew out the smoke.

Spears reached into his pocket and pulled out a pack of cigarettes. He retrieved one, put it to his mouth, and lit it, relishing the sweet relief it provided his frayed nerves.

"Tonight," J.R. started again after several monstrous drags on his stogie, "Percy is throwing a party at his house. I can't figure out why, in the wake of Tony and Morgan's deaths and with all the problems we have right now, but he's doing it, the goddamn fool. Damien will not be there. At least I hope not. I told them to stay separate, but Christ knows what they'll do. Everyone's acting like fucking idiots lately! But I certainly won't be there, because I haven't got a death wish. There *will* be over fifty people at Percy's tonight, complete with a police detail and all, watching the house. They're even sending an officer to my house tonight to keep an eye on things with me. But no one will be with Damien. That's where you come in."

Spears nodded and gulped back acid which had formed in his throat. Damien Smith made him ill. Spears was not a moral man, nor did he even *believe* in morals for that matter, but something about men who wanted to have sex with young children just didn't sit right with him. It was about the only hint of humanity in him, and he knew it. Sitting with Damien would be torture, but he would have to endure it. Guarding the disgusting child rapist would be awful, to say the least, but it was better than being fed to the dogs.

"You need to get cleaned up, geared up, and get over there," J.R. said. "And don't screw up this time! Damien gives more money to the church than anyone else, hell, more than all the rest of the congregation *combined*, and we need him to continue our…"

He trailed off, his eyes straying to the right, his lips pursing, trying to think of the right word.

He found it.

*"…Operations."*

Spears nodded.

"Alright, get to it," J.R. popped at him.

Spears turned and walked out of the room, wincing from his wounds. He'd had zero sleep now going on thirty-six hours, and he'd had to doctor himself after the incident at White's house. He was exhausted.

But that was no matter. He would have plenty of time to rest when Fields was dead. And Fields *would* be dead by the end of the night. He was sure of that. There was no way he would hit Percy's tonight with all the party-goers there and J.R. would be ready for him as well, with or without a police detail. Damien would be the one he would strike tonight. Spears was sure of it.

And Spears would be ready for him.

*You come on, you little shit! You come and get some! We've got a score to settle, you and me, and I mean to settle it good!*

Spears got to his home an hour later. He showered, changed clothes, and then went into his basement to make a few selections from his arsenal.

The walls of his basement were lined with shotguns, rifles, pistols, machine guns, knives. It was a regular gun show down there, and without the inconvenience of background checks.

There were silencers and magazines—fully loaded, of course—for virtually all his weapons. Spears looked them all over carefully and made his selections. He put them into a large duffle-bag and carried them to his trunk. He slammed the lid.

*Tonight! Tonight, you motherfucker! I'll be waiting for you! And this time, you'll be the one running! I'm gonna rip you apart and bathe in your blood!*

Spears got into his car, threw it into drive, and headed for Damien Smith's house, spitting gravel all over his front porch.

# CHAPTER 30

"*Reports have come in that people from all areas of the state are traveling to East Texas today to hold a candlelight vigil for the losses of Morgan Jones and Tony White, elders of the Glorious Rising Church of Longview. Many lives have been touched by these men and their church, ranging from the homeless on the streets to the wealthiest of businessmen and women, many of whom contribute to their cause. The pastor of their church, Percy Wilkes, was noted as saying the loss of these two 'saints' will hit not only this town, but the entire county—and quite possibly the entire state—very, very hard. Back to you John.*"

Fletcher twisted the knob of the radio in his car to the off position, cursing as he did so.

"Saints my *ass*!" he growled.

"Saints or not, that's how people saw them," Benson said. "Can't change that."

"If people only knew. Hell, if they just *wanted* to know! These men would have a very different reputation.

Do you realize just how many kid's lives were impacted by these guys? And *not* impacted for the better, I might add. No siree, uh-uh! These sons-of-bitches are *monsters!*"

"True, but do you believe they deserve to die?"

"Yes," Fletcher said, without hesitation.

"Well, that's where you and I disagree. They will get what's coming to them, but that will be in God's time, not ours."

"Perhaps."

Benson eyes lit up as if he was stunned.

"No arguments this time?"

Fletcher grit his teeth and curled his lips back, a way of showing his frustration. Another customary *huff* threatened to escape his lips, but he managed to hold it in.

"I don't know. I just don't know anymore..."

"Well, I gotta say, that's the best news I've heard in a while!" Benson quipped, happily. "It's certainly better than *no way, not possible!*"

He chuckled.

Fletcher said, "Yeah, don't get your hopes up. I just, well," he was searching for words. "With Heather and Helen involved now, I feel like I need something to turn to. Something to provide strength. I'm not saying God is who I'm turning to, I'm just saying that *maybe* He does exist. Still doesn't explain His absence in all this." He trailed off momentarily. "Twenty years ago, *and* now."

"Why do you think He's absent?"

"Well, what's He doing? My daughter and my wife are missing, in the hands of some psycho who's doing God knows what to them, and I haven't got a clue as to where to start looking, except that I'm pretty sure he's gonna try to hit one of these other three scumbags soon, if not to-night."

"Your *ex*-wife."

"What?" Fletcher said, not understanding Benson's statement.

"Helen. You called her your wife. Last I checked, you two were divorced."

"Oh," Fletcher said, his face flushing red. "Well, that's what I meant."

He looked over at Benson who was grinning ever so slightly.

"Shut up."

"Sorry, man, sorry!" Benson said, throwing his hands up in mock surrender. "But seriously, I'm glad to hear that you're not shutting out the very *idea* of God."

"Whatever."

Benson laughed again.

They were parked in front of Percy Wilkes' house. It was coming on dusk, and there were several cars pulling into the preacher's driveway. The man was having a party. All that was happening, and the asshole was having a *party*.

*Unbelievable.*

The man was acting completely unconcerned with what had happened to his parishioners. Well, almost. He *had* given a press statement, in which he'd called the two dead men "saints". Pretended to look sad for a while. Talked them up. Said everyone would miss them a lot. Blah, blah, blah…

*Scumbag.*

That he was. Truly and to the core. But there was an even bigger scumbag that they were out to catch. Little Charlie Fields.

*Or big Charlie Fields, the psychopathic, serial-killing maniac.*

Yeah, that fit better. Much better.

The communications radio under the dash squawked.

*"Fletcher, you there? This is Gonzalez."*

Fletcher stared at the receiver for a long moment before picking it up. He pressed the transmitter button.

"Yeah, I'm here Bert, what's up?"

*"The Captain called. He wants to know why he can't reach you or Benson at home?"*

There was silence for a long moment as Fletcher held the mic, thinking of how to respond. Eventually, Gonzalez broke the silence for him.

*"Should I tell him you're out of town or something?"*

Fletcher thought about it for a moment, then said, "No. Tell him where I'm at and that if he wants to talk to me about it, he needs to come down to Wilkes's place and talk. And tell him the preacher's throwing a party."

*"He's throwing a party?"* Bert said over the radio. *"After all this? Is he nuts?"*

"My guess is he thinks Fields won't come after him if there are lots of people around him. Probably makes him feel invincible."

*"Huh, I guess that makes sense…sort of. Anyway, I'll let the Captain know. Give us a call if anything happens. We'll be over here at Hays's place tonight."*

"Will do, talk to ya later."

He put the receiver back in its cradle and leaned back in his seat. It was going to be a long night.

Fletcher and Benson sat in silence for a whole ten minutes. There was tension in the air. Dancing in the invisible world around them. Taunting them.

Finally, Benson broke the silence.

"Harry?"

"Yeah?"

"Why did you tell him to let the Captain know what we're doing? I thought you wanted this to be under his radar?"

He was looking at the patrol cruiser already parked up the road a bit and the two officers who were inside, watching the preacher's house.

"I dunno," Fletcher responded with a sigh. "What's he gonna do? Come stop us?"

"Maybe so."

Fletcher shook his head.

"I don't think so. He'll be mad, he'll throw a fit, but he won't make us stop."

Fletcher's tone grew serious.

"It's what we're gonna do when we find Fields that's going to be sketchy."

Benson looked over at him, concern in his eyes. "What exactly are we going to do?"

Fletcher cocked his head to the side and his neck made an audible *crack*.

"Whatever it takes."

# CHAPTER
# 31

Charlton Fields's eyes popped open.

"What was that?"

There had been a rumbling noise coming from outside the cabin. His eyes darted about the room, looking for any indication as to what had made the sound.

*What's happening?*

He crossed the room and looked out the window. It was dark. The last shards of sunlight had vanished over the treetops and night had set in. The air outside was swirling, creating hi-pitched *swooshes*, and making little tornadoes of leaves spin through the field, no doubt picked up from the forest floor. Charlton had no idea how long he had been out.

*He's here,* Trocephus said, and began to chuckle.

There was a flash of lightning outside. A boom of thunder.

The ground shook.

Charlton jumped, then ran to the door frantically. He looked back at his hostages as he went. The older one was wide eyed and frightened. The younger one was obviously awake, judging by her trembling and weeping, but her eyes were swollen almost completely shut. Two tiny slits where her eyelids puffed up like a balloon were leaking tears.

She was awake alright. And she was mortified. Something was happening.

Something was *coming*.

"What is this?" cried Fields.

He was talking to Trocephus aloud and in a panicked tone.

*My friend is here. He's come to take care of the women.*

"Who is he?"

*I just told you. A friend.*

Fields stepped out onto the porch. There were absolutely no clouds in the sky, yet there were no stars either. Only a bright, shining moon.

And bolts of lightning.

They cracked and streaked through the sky, chasing unknown targets. Booming thunder roared seconds later, the sound chasing the light with all it had, incapable of keeping up with its speed.

It was downright eerie.

"When will I meet him?" Charlton asked, a tremble in his voice.

*Soon. Oh, so very soon.*

One of the women emitted a muffled scream into her gag. More weeping.

*Isn't that sound wonderful?*

"What sound?" Charlton asked, perplexed.

He listened close. He heard the women moaning and sobbing. And there was another sound. Like rock on a chalkboard.

*The weeping and gnashing of teeth.*

Ah, that was what he heard. And a moment later there was an open scream, one not muffled by a gag. One of the women had managed to spit out the gag!

He turned from the front door just as another flash of lightning erupted behind him, accompanied simultaneously by ear-shattering thunder.

*He's getting closer.*

The younger woman had spit out her gag. She was screaming, nearly incomprehensible at first, but when her puffy eyes fell on Fields, she started saying one phrase over and over again.

*"Oh, God! Oh God, oh God, oh God!"*

*Shut that bitch up!* Trocephus demanded.

"*Shut up!*" Charlton screamed.

Another bolt of lightning. Another crack of thunder. One of the front windows cracked from the force of the tremoring sound.

"Oh, God!" Heather screamed out again. "Oh, God please *HELP US!*"

*Not another word out of her!*

Charlton sprinted over to her and shoved the gag back into her mouth, deep, and heard her wretch. He tied the bandanna back in place and peered into the slits in her puffy eyes.

"Don't you *dare* bring Him into this!" he said, and backhanded her.

She turned her head to the side and wept, still scream-ing that same phrase, over and over again, into her gag.

Charlton stood and turned back to the door. He crossed the room quickly. He was just about to exit the door when a bolt of lightning struck the ground out front of the cabin and there was an explosion of blinding light.

Thunder boomed.

A blast wave emitted from the explosion and it threw Charlton back into the house, hard. He landed on his back a foot away from the women.

He locked eyes with the older woman, who was star-ing at the area of the explosion through the open front door, horrified.

Charlton jumped up and bolted for the door, stumbled onto the porch, and fell down the steps. He landed face first in the dirt, mere feet from ground zero of the explo-sion, his heart pounding.

The ground moved. He could feel it rippling beneath his body like water.

*He's here.*

There was a rumbling noise, and the earth began to bulge upward where the lightning had struck. It went back down, then up again, as if breathing.

Or as if something was breaking through.

It bulged again, this time a much larger area. Then the ground began to break and open before him. Cracks in the earth ripped open, and shards of red light glowed from beneath.

Charlton felt panic brewing inside him. Whatever this thing was, this friend of the demon inside of him, he had a feeling it was something far bigger, and far more powerful than he'd ever imagined.

Trocephus was laughing maniacally somewhere in the recesses of Charlton's mind. A bellowing sound, deep and ominous, like a maniac in an asylum, laughing in the corner of the room as he cut his own flesh.

Charlton's blood went cold.

The ground broke free and something began to rise out of it. And some*thing* was the only way to classify the beast that rose from the earth.

It rose slowly, one foot, then two, as if it were unrolling from the fetal position.

And it was *big*.

The thing had what looked like black ram's horns coming out of its head, though they weren't quite ram's horns. They curled first forward, then down, and finally around to the back of the beast. Its skin was a bloody color, akin to rubber in texture. Slim coated its body from head to toe.

Or *hoof*, if you will.

Yellow eyes glowed in the dark, peering this way and that, taking in its surroundings. Fangs, black as pitch, lashed out of a horribly distorted mouth. A black, forked tongue snaked in and out between them, lapping slime. Its nose was like two miniature horns pointing out and up at rough forty-five degree angles.

It had long, black talons, sharp as razors from the look of them, jutting from its fingertips, and slime dripped from them as well.

Charlton wanted to run. He wanted to forget all about Percy Wilkes, J.R. Hays, and Damien Smith. He wanted to flee into the woods, screaming like a ten-year-old girl. Only he couldn't move. His hands and knees were fused with the ground, white knuckles griping the grass at their roots. He was petrified. All he could do was look at the thing.

And then the thing looked at him.

*"Hello, Charlton,"* it said. *"Or should I say Charlie? I've heard much about you. We are very pleased with your, hmmm, how shall I say this?"*

The thing trailed off for a moment. Its voice was deeper than the other demon's, if that was possible. An incredible bass sound, otherworldly, because it was most certainly *not* of this world. The thing was looking for the right words to finish its sentence. It found the words it was looking for, and continued.

*"Work ethic!"*

It smiled grotesquely at him. A shiver crawled up Charlton's spine.

Then he felt something happen in his own body. Suddenly, he was lifting off the ground, as if floating up through water from the bottom of a pool. In moments, he hovered a couple feet in the air, his legs dangling, eye to eye with the creature.

Trocephus was taking over.

Charlton listened to them talk, Trocephus talking *through* him. Oddly, they exchanged pleasantries. Trocephus asked about home.

*"All is well below. We have been eager to see where this human would take our cause. Thus far, we are very pleased. The Enemy is surely squirming in that wretched throne of His!"*

*"Surely,"* Trocephus said. *"I must warn you though, to be cautious. There are two female hostages inside."*

The larger beast laughed. *"What concern have I with these pitiful women?"*

Trocephus's voice was deadly serious. *"They pray to Him!"*

He finished the sentence by pointing up to the sky with Charlton's finger.

The massive demon's eyes flashed with anger and desire at the same time. Then the thing smiled.

*"Good. Let them pray. I receive no greater pleasure than to turn one of His into a trembling bag of fear! And perhaps dining on their hearts!"*

They both erupted in laughter at that. Trocephus lowered Charlton to the ground and they both headed for the door to the cabin. They could see the women inside weeping and trembling, the older one's eyes so wide he thought they might pop out. He wished they would. It would have been a beautiful sight.

And such a delicacy.

*"These are the two pitiful souls we've saved for you. I know how much you enjoy taking one of His."*

The huge demon licked its lips with its black tongue, making a smacking sound.

*"I'm sure they will be simply...divine!"*

More octaves of laughter.

*"We must be on our way,"* Trocephus said. *"We have souls to claim."*

*"Fare-thee-well, dear Trocephus,"* the large beast said.

*"Before I forget,"* Trocephus said, almost as an afterthought, *"I believe our boy here wanted to meet you formally."*

Trocephus relinquished control of Charlton and the big demon seemed to know it when he did. Its whole demeanor changed to that of a classy gentleman meeting an admirer for the first time.

*"Well then,"* it said, extending its dripping hand, talons extended. *"It's nice to meet you!"*

It began to laugh evilly. The laugh was layered in octaves of psychotic cackles.

Charlton took the bladed hand in his own shaky one.

"Hello, I—I'm Charlton. Or Charlie if you like."

His voice was quivering.

The beast gripped his hand and pulled him face to face with it, it's black, dripping fangs only inches from his nose. It uttered an evil giggle.

*"Hello Charlie. My name is Raktah."*

# CHAPTER
## 32

Percy Wilkes opened the door to his luxurious home and smiled at the couple standing on his stoop.

"Welcome!"

He ushered them inside, exchanged pleasantries with them, and then they joined the others. There were over thirty people at his house that night. Most were parishioners of his church, others were business associates of Damien Smith's, the one man not present at his party.

*Coward.*

The spineless insect had refused to come to Percy's party that night, saying he was likely safer to stay at home, what with all this business with Charlton Fields going on.

"I'm a target, Percy!" he had said.

Percy had scoffed.

"And do you suggest that I am any less a target? In case you've forgotten, Morgan and Tony are dead as well!"

He had huffed.

"We have got to get out here in front of this," Percy had continued. "Make ourselves look like caring members of society. If Fields's motives ever come out, we won't have a snowball's chance in hell at coming out clean on this to the public. Not this time. I think you know that."

"Can we please talk about something else?" Damien had pleaded.

"Something else?" Percy laughed out loud, mockingly. "What the fuck else is there to talk about? You're the reason we're in this situation!"

"We don't know that."

"As a matter of fact, *yes we do!* If you could keep your philandering cock out of *children*, we wouldn't have a psychopathic murderer named Charlton Fields out there picking us off one by one!"

He had then growled something unintelligible to himself, then said, "You know something?"

Damien's voice was smug. "What?"

"We should have let them crucify you twenty years ago."

There was a palpable tension oozing out of the phone.

"You watch your tongue!" Damien piped.

Percy said, "Or what, Damien? Hmm? What exactly are you going to do?"

Damien had hung the phone up then. All for the best, Percy had gathered.

Percy had decided to throw this get-together for his parishioners on the basis that they would be doing it in honor of the lives of Morgan Jones and Tony White. And then, somehow, Damien's rich-suit friends had caught wind of it and showed up.

*Why? What purpose did they have for showing up? Most of them were either agnostic or outright atheists. What did they want at a preacher's party?*

Contacts. That's what they were after. As many people as they could find to pass a business card to and try to exploit. They were lawyers. Judges. IRS agents. The slime was almost tangible.

Percy made his way to the back bedroom, dismissing the memories of his conversation with Damien as he went. He set down his drink, a diet cola. He never drank alcohol in front of members of his congregation. Certainly not after his sermon on alcoholism and the horrors it can create.

Ah, what a sermon that had been.

The pews had been full that day, and he'd delivered the message perfectly. At the end, he, Morgan Jones, J.R. Hays, Tony White, and Damien Smith had all gathered on the stage, the leaders of the church, prayed for God's will, and then told the congregation that the Lord's will was to start a half-way house for victims of alcoholism. They would not reveal the location of the half-way house, to protect the privacy of those who came for help, of course. God had apparently said that the church needed to raise a substantial amount of money *on top of* the normal tithes, so such an endeavor could occur.

The sheep had given generously. For several months.

Of course, all that money had gone into their pockets. Not one cent went to purchasing a building, or hiring a staff, and people who came to ask for help were told that the program was packed and could accept no new people.

All for the money.

Percy smiled to himself as he knelt next to his bed, reminiscing about the event. It had made them more money than most of their false institutions. And everyone had bought into it! The five of them were revered as such *saints* that no one questioned a thing they did.

*Like lambs to the slaughter.*

He chuckled to himself and opened a cabinet on his nightstand. There were several bottles of liquor, some full, others partaken of, most in yellow and amber hues, some clear.

He reached in and found a one, a bottle of scotch about twelve years old. He opened it, dropped a bit into his soda, and began to replace the cap.

*I'm a target.*

The thought came to him like a bullet, out of nowhere, totally devastating. He yanked the cap off the scotch and threw the bottle back, draining a large, burning gulp down his throat. His body shivered as he pulled the bottle from his lips and swallowed. It felt like jet fuel going down his throat and sent chills through his body. He replaced the cap and put the bottle back in its hiding place.

He rose and fetched his drink, feeling unnerved about the events unfolding with Fields.

The party he was throwing actually served *two* purposes. First, it would appear to look as though a good man was celebrating the lives of two of the church's saints, which helped his image. And secondly, it would surround him with people.

The latter was his main motivation.

If people stayed close by his side, Fields wouldn't dare try to make a move on him. Right? He wasn't *that* insane. Especially with the police watching the house.

For the first time in eons, Percy Wilkes found the thought of police watching his house comforting. He lived in a nice neighborhood, at the end of a cul-de-sac. To his front were million dollar homes and police. To his rear was a large, open back yard full of people enjoying the party. Beyond that, there was forest.

*He won't try a thing with this many people and police around. He wouldn't dare!*

But even as the thought crossed through his mind, he doubted its surety.

He took a long drink.

———

Fletcher stepped out of the car. Benson followed suit.

"What is it?" Benson asked.

"I'm not sure," Fletcher said. He was staring into the home of Percy Wilkes. "Something just seems wrong about all of this."

Benson looked around cautiously, seeming to sense it too.

"Yeah."

Fletcher turned and faced him.

"I mean, who throws a party the day after a couple of your closest friends are murdered? It never ceases to amaze me, the balls of this guy Wilkes!"

"Yeah," Benson said again. "He's ballsy, but I think he's scared. He wouldn't be doing this if he wasn't absolutely petrified by Fields. He knows he's a target. And he's trying to hide behind all these people. He's scared out of his mind."

"That's what I figure," Fletcher said. "He thinks Fields won't strike if he has lots of people around. Thinks Fields will think it to be too risky. That he won't expose himself to get at him."

"And what do you think?" Benson asked.

"Me?" Fletcher grunted a laugh. "I don't think Fields *thinks* about exposure. I think all he *thinks* about is getting even with these guys. And *I* think he's got the balls to try just about anything."

# CHAPTER
## 33

*T*hey *don't think you have it in you. They think you're a coward. They think you won't make a move in the open.*

"They're wrong."

*Are they? Look at those people down there. They're all laughing and smiling, having a grand old time! They're laughing at you! You, Charlie!*

"Why?"

*Why?* Trocephus chuckled. *Because that's what they do. People who follow Him always laugh and mock those who see things differently.*

"They're evil."

*I agree! They want a monopoly on beliefs in this world. If anyone believes another way, that person is going to hell! No questions! Do not pass go, do not collect two-hundred dollars! That's how they get people, Charlie. Fear. Pure, concentrated fear. Nothing more. Do you think there's any real substance to what they say? Of course not! It's all fear tactics. Hitler did the same thing to Eu-*

*rope in World War II. He told a lie big enough, loud enough, and long enough, and the people believed it. Then fear kept them in place.*

Charlton nodded, agreeing.

*Do we want these Christians to do the same thing here? Will we allow them to continue forcing down everyone's throats these lies and hostilities against other institutions of faith? Or no faith, for that matter? No! We will not! We will meet force with force. We will shut them up tight! And then we will expose them for what they truly are. Do you know what they are, Charlie? Liars. Bigots. Cheats. Thieves. Pedophiles. The world will see them for what they are, and the world will know that their Holy God is nothing more than a jealous beast. They will know that He will strip all happiness from their lives like the skin off their flesh!*

Charlton's face threatened to smile, but he thought better of it. He needed blood flowing through his veins, not out of his body.

*And how do we know they will be exposed? Because they'll be dead. And when they're dead, the authorities will investigate. And when they investigate, they will find what these liars have been doing for all these years. They will no longer be revered as saints. They will be shunned as devils.*

"Devils is precisely what they are," Charlton said.

*Indeed! So, tell me, Charlie, these Christians, these 'Holy Rollers', what exactly are they?*

"They're dead."

Charlton was in the woods a quarter of a mile up the hill behind Percy Wilkes's house. He was dressed in all black, and he carried a large black duffle-bag on his shoulder. He set it down, unzipped it, and pulled out a rifle with a scope. He leaned it against a tree, then pulled out a rather large caliber pistol. After this, he retrieved a sound suppressor from the bag for the rifle. He screwed it onto the weapon, stuffed the pistol in the back of his waist band, and slung the rifle over his shoulder. Then he reached into the bag and removed a large black knife. It was in a nice black sheath, strings dangling from the top and bottom. He fitted the top of the sheath to his belt and tied the strings to his right leg.

He was ready.

It was a short jog down the hill to the edge of the woods near Wilkes's place. The yard was open in front the wood's edge for nearly a hundred and fifty feet before it met the house. It was packed with people. All laughing and having a good time.

*Laughing at you! At Sophie!*

Charlton set his jaw. They would pay. They would pay for empowering the people who killed Sophie. For throwing her off the roof of his family's once happy home. For killing his mother. For his father. His entire family.

His entire world.

He lay down on the amber leaves that carpeted the forest floor. He found a nearby log to use as a support for the rifle and dragged it over to a spot positioned directly behind the house. He slid up behind the log. He could see perfectly into the yard and beyond it, into the house. There was a large window that looked right into the living area of Percy Wilkes's home. He cradled the stock of the weapon in the groove of his shoulder. Lined up his sights.

He was staring at several people. He didn't recognize them, but that didn't matter. They would likely die anyway. It made little difference to him who *all* died, so long as Wilkes went down tonight.

He continued to scan the crowd of people looking for Percy Wilkes.

And then he found him.

He was past a cluster of people, *inside* the house, but by a large, single-pane window.

Charlton had a clear shot.

He started smiling. Within seconds, his cheek, arm, and eye began oozing blood and other muck. He quickly removed the smirk.

*Nothing to be happy about.*

"Nope. Not a thing."

He centered his cross hairs on Wilkes's head.

"Well, maybe this one thing."

He smiled again. This time, he let the blood flow.

It was killing time.

# CHAPTER
# 34

Helen looked at her daughter. The swelling was beginning to subside, but there was still spattered blood on her daughter's face and her split lip looked extremely painful. It pained Helen to see her own flesh and blood in such a state.

And then there was this...this *demon* which had been left with them. So far it hadn't done much, just paced back and forth in front of them, a deep, throaty growl emanating from its grotesque mouth. She was truly terrified of this monster. Its stares were petrifying. Every time it looked into her eyes, she felt icy hands gripping her throat, clamping it shut. Pure, unadulterated fear unlike any she'd ever experienced before in her life. It overwhelmed her.

The whites of her eyes stayed visible as she watched it pace.

*"You're wondering why I'm here?"* the beast said to her. *"What I'm doing? What I'm going to do?"*

It paused, both in speech and motion, and peered right into her eyes.

Into her soul.

*"Isn't that right?"*

Helen began to tremble. Dread was taking over like a deluge. The thing was beginning to win.

*I can't let it take my daughter!* Helen thought in a panic. *But how can I stop it? What can I do? I'm all tied up and it's so big. So dreadfully big!*

In the depths of her mind, a familiar voice came to her. A comforting voice that pierced through all the horror and pain.

*Be still,* the voice said.

What?

*"Forgive me,"* the beast said in an aberration of chivalry. *"I'd almost forgotten the restriction in your mouth! Allow me..."*

It crossed the room in one gargantuan step and knelt before her, its knees buckling in the opposite direction of a human's. It reached out with its terrible fingers and plucked the gag from her mouth. Helen began to cough and heave.

*"There now,"* it said. *"We can talk. Exchange dialogue, if you will."*

She coughed a final time and clamped her mouth shut. She was trembling from head to toe and her mind raced with horror. What could she do? What should she say?

*Be still.*

That voice again. She knew the voice. It was the voice of God, speaking to her, telling her to control herself. To allow *Him* to control her.

But so far, she couldn't.

*"I say, my dear,"* Raktah continued, *"for such a* Spirit-*filled person, you haven't much faith. Why do you tremble so?"*

"Shut up!" she managed to spit weakly.

Fear gripped her entire body. Every cell quivered in terror. She glanced at Heather, still wearing her gag. Heather's barely opened eyes transmitted the same fear Helen felt within her, and it made her nearly launch into convulsions. Every muscle in her body twitched violently.

*"That's not very Christian of you!"* it mocked her. *"Your God will not be pleased!"*

He was right. She was in a dire situation, face to face with pure evil, and she was alone. All alone with her daughter, whom she'd failed to protect. She had failed her. She had failed the precious gift she believed God had given her.

She had failed God.

Helen began to cry.

"Why are you doing this?" she sobbed uncontrollably.

Raktah smiled broadly, exposing black, slime-dripping fangs.

*"Because you are His."*

It began to laugh deeply and terrifyingly. She was surprised to find it was much the way one might expect a demon to laugh. Not without humor, but totally without joy.

*"And I love to take what is His!"*

It continued to laugh as Helen screamed as loud as she could. She had never been so afraid in her life. The demon screamed with her, mockingly.

"Please leave us alone! Please!" she pleaded with the devil. "I'm begging you!"

Raktah shushed her, wagging its head back and forth while holding a bloody colored finger and black talon in front of its mouth.

*"Hushhhhh, hushhh. No need to carry on this way, child. And no, I'll not be leaving you alone. The rest of your miserably short lives will be spent with me. And when I've had my fun, I will bring your lives to a screeching and bloody halt. Maybe I'll make you watch your daughter die as I strangle her with your lower intestine. Wouldn't that be a sight?"*

It laughed again. Octaves of terror bellowing out of its mouth and invading her ears like an army of the dead.

Helen glanced at her daughter again, whose swollen eyes were now pressed open so wide that she thought they might pop out of her head.

*I'm here.*

That voice. Faint, quiet, still.

*Where?* she thought. *Where are you?*

But there was no answer. All the same, the voice had managed to inject her with comfort, even if it was slight. A minute amount of Helen's trembling subsided.

*He's here with me,* she thought. *I have to trust that. He will never forsake me. Yea, though I walk through the valley of the shadow of death, I will fear no evil.*

But she did fear. Evil was right in front of her, mere feet away. Pure, filthy, disgusting, rotten evil. Forget about the shadow. She was practically touching it.

Raktah leaned over to Heather and snatched her face into its hands. She moaned audibly through her gag and looked frantically at her mother with saucer-sized swollen eyes.

Raktah began to laugh.

"You leave her alone!" Helen screamed. "You hear me? You get away from her! Take me! Do whatever you want to me, but you let her go!"

Helen was losing any cool she may have retained. That small ease she had felt was slipping away.

The fear was gripping her again.

*"Tell me, why would I do whatever I want to do to you and let her go when I could just keep her here and do whatever I want to both of you?"*

Another disgusting laugh. Another moan from Heather. Tears streamed down her daughter's face and Helen followed suit.

Raktah continued to laugh, then snaked out a black, forked tongue. The slimed horror slid up the side of Heather's face.

Another muffled scream from Heather.

Another open scream from Helen.

Another throaty chuckle from Raktah.

*"Where is He, Helen? Hmm? Can you tell me where He is? He isn't protecting you now, is He? Has He sent an angel down to protect you? A person, maybe? No? Hmm…I wonder where He could be?"*

In that moment, Helen wished she could die. She wanted to just lie down and give up. But despite that, even more than she wanted to give up and die, she wanted to be strong for her daughter. She couldn't deny the urge in her to protect her family.

*"Harry gave up on Him a long time ago, Helen. A very long time ago. He realized the hypocrisy in His house, by His own followers. He saw what He really leads to. Crying children. Broken families. Death."*

*I can't give up!* Helen screamed inside her own mind. *He's a liar, a thief, and a destroyer! These are all lies!*

A morsel of strength rose within her and she managed to speak.

"You are a liar! Do your worst to us, but we will not be afraid!"

It rose to its full height of eight feet and smiled.

*"One thing you can count on, my dear,"* it chuckled, *"I* will *do my worst."*

Raktah grabbed Heather by the hair and threw her across the room. She slammed into the wall, and Helen could hear the air *whoosh* out of her. Then she thudded to the floor. Her swollen eyes were wide and she was gasping for air through her gag.

Helen screamed at her.

"Baby, hang on! It's going to be okay! I promise! You are not alone! We are *never* alone! Remember that! I'm here and I—"

She was cut off by a backhand with the power of a lightning bolt. Her own body spun like a top into the air and collided with the wall several feet behind her. She crashed to the floor, her face throbbing, her lungs gasping for breath.

Fear was winning again.

"Oh, my God," she prayed in a whisper once she found her breath. "Oh, God, *help us!*"

Then Harry came to mind. She felt a strong, urgent need for him at that very moment in a way she hadn't felt in years.

Raktah laughed at her. *"He can't hear you my dear! He's too busy with Himself to hear you! He isn't sending help, and you* will *die alone!"*

The thing roared like a lion and pushed out its chest, flexing its arms like a gorilla. Then it laughed again.

Helen wept.

*Be still,* the voice returned to Helen's mind.

Where are you?

*I'm here.*

But I don't see You!

*I'm here.*

Show me!

*You are not forgotten. Be not afraid.*

How?

*By being still.*

I don't understand!

Helen looked around at their dire situation. Heather was across the room on the floor, gasping for breath through a gag, her face beaten to a pulp. Raktah towered over them both, laughing at them, *mocking* them. No one was there but them. No one was coming.

"Oh, Harry," she said as she shivered. "Please come, Harry!"

She whispered the last part and shut her eyes.

*Be still.*

# CHAPTER
## 35

Charlton Fields put the cross hairs on the back of Percy Wilkes's head.

*If you hit it just right it'll pop like a balloon!*

A hint of humor crossed Fields's face and he felt warm blood flow from his eye, cheek, and arm. There was some distant pain, but he ignored it.

*Stop smiling.*

"Why?"

The question popped into his head from nowhere. He'd not been terribly prone to arguing with Trocephus since his arrival the previous night. With all the power he'd given him, Charlton didn't think it prudent to do so. But out of some deep place in his mind came this question.

*Why?*

He could feel Trocephus become anxious at the question.

*What do you mean, why? Because there's nothing to be happy about!*

"Nothing? Even the fact that I'm about to blow away one of the men responsible for my family's deaths is no reason for even a slight bit of jubilee? Some small amount of joy?"

This puzzled Charlton. In his twisted and distorted mind, he wanted to dance with glee over the moment which was upon him. Just as he'd been happy and joyful when he handed Morgan Jones and Tony White their demise. This was vengeance, damnit! Why not be happy about it? If it didn't bring joy, then why do it in the first place?

*Because it leads to bad things,* Trocephus answered. *No one likes you. They all hate you. They all want you dead. Why do you think they sent that man to White's house? Because you pose a problem to their whole religion. You could blow the lid right off their racket and expose them! And when their rather sizable congregation sees what they've been up to these past twenty years, they will finally know the truth.*

"And what is the truth?" Charlton said out loud.

*The truth is those who follow Him bring death. He says in His own Word that death was brought on by disobedience to Him. Really? Would a father murder his son just because the boy did something he was told not to? No! A spanking, a grounding maybe, but certainly not death! But He says you all must die because of something that one man and one woman did eons ago. That is why your family died. Because it was what He wanted. They dared to go against His church, and He killed them.*

The words rang in Charlton's mind.

*Because they dared to go against Him.*

Percy Wilkes was His representative. And Percy Wilkes had to die.

Blood was all over Charlton's face and hands, and now on his rifle as well. He quickly removed his smile and trained his eye back on Wilkes's head. There was, of course, the practical reasoning that whatever power Trocephus was giving him was keeping him from bleeding to death so long as he didn't smile. He supposed that was reason enough not to show joy.

There would be no more joy in his vengeance. Hate had consumed him to the point that there would be no pleasure in what he was doing anymore; it was simply a duty now. He had a duty to rid the world of these hypocrites. To end their reign of holy terror. And, good person or bad, straight arrow or criminal, these were bad people. Worse, they were bad people who had the public so deceived that they were looked upon as saints. They were revered by the public as spiritual authorities.

It was madness.

The thoughts made Charlton ill. How could people receive what these men had to say in church and *actually* be touched by it? How could that work?

*Pull the trigger! Kill the fucker now!*

Charlton zeroed in on Wilkes's head again. He appeared to be giving a speech of some kind to his guests. People were standing all around him, inside and out on the patio watching him through the window, their eyes and attention solely on him.

*Pull the trigger! PULL THE TRIGGER NOW!*

Charlton wrapped his finger around the trigger and held his breath.

---

Fletcher heard the sound of a window shattering, then blood-curdling screams coming from inside the house.

*Fields.*

Fletcher and Benson looked at each other frantically. Fletcher leaned into the car and hit the trunk release. Then they rushed to the back of the car and flung the trunk lid into the air. They grabbed a shotgun each from the carpeted floor of the trunk. A moment later, they were sprinting for the house, racking a round into their weapons.

# CHAPTER
## 36

"I just want to say again," Percy Wilkes said in conclusion of a speech he'd begun a few minutes earlier, "I appreciate you all being here. Morgan and Tony were good men, *godly* men, and they will be missed. I know even now they are looking down on us from above, smiling to themselves at what wonderful friends they had here on this earth, and I know they look forward to seeing us all again, just as much as we look forward to seeing them again in glory!"

There were a few sad chuckles amongst the crowd of people in front of him as a slow, soft applause began. Some were just smiling reminiscently, others were dabbing the corners of their eyes with napkins or handkerchiefs. But all were nodding in admonishment.

"So, raise your cups," Wilkes continued, holding a plastic drinking cup over his own head, "and let us remember these two great men, these two *saints,* as the good people in the news media have so appropriately titled them as of late."

Then he prayed.

"Father, into your hands, we commend their spirits."

There was a murmur of 'amen' throughout the crowd as all took a long swig of their drinks, mostly punch, a few sodas, and one spiked cola.

Jerry Locke, a parishioner of the church, stepped up next to Percy and slightly behind him. His smooth, freshly shaved face was tight with what appeared to be heartfelt grief and appreciation, taut over straining facial muscles that were fighting to keep back the tears trying to escape his eyes.

"Thank you pastor," he said.

And then it happened.

Jerry clapped Percy on the shoulder, and a millisecond later the window behind them exploded. Percy half ducked from surprise, his hands coming up beside him in involuntary reaction and sloshing his spiked cola over the rim of his plastic cup. As he did this, he turned toward the falling glitters of glass, and got a speckling of blood in the face.

It was gushing from Jerry's throat.

Women started screaming. People began to scatter. A chunk of sheetrock exploded from the wall and peppered the floor with white, chalky powder.

Percy hit the ground and started scrambling for the hallway that led to his bedroom. Over his head, a chandelier shattered, and florescent lights exploded with a loud pop, raining razor-sharp shards of bulb down all around him.

*Fields!* Percy's mind screamed.

He had absolutely no doubt who was doing this. Why would he? He'd known well and good what was going on, especially after getting the reports from the news and J.R. Hays on what had happened at Tony White's house. And he'd been sure that his safest bet was surrounding himself with people. There was no chance Fields would do *anything* with all these people around, yet his current circumstance was proving this notion to be nothing more than a pipe dream draining into the sewers of bullshit.

But where the fuck was he? Percy looked about the area, not seeing Fields anywhere. In fact, he didn't see a gunman at all.

*Where's he shooting from?*

White-hot panic was setting in and a burst of adrenaline flushed his system. Dread exploded from his eyes like a visualization of internal horror. He could feel his pulse beating against his throat, in his chest, all over his body. His limbs were trembling and his breathing had become a pant. Sweat burst forth all over his body as he was struck with a heat-wave of sheer terror. He scrambled on across the floor like a mortified slug on speed.

Just as he was making it to the mouth of the hallway, he turned and looked back through the shattered window. Jerry Locke was lying on the floor just in front of the window, clutching his gushing throat. Bob Jacks, another churchgoer, was dragging Jerry out of the line of fire, ducking his head and throwing his free hand up every few seconds when new bullets would splinter the wood of the windowsill or chip away more glass from the surrounding windows.

Percy turned, crawled into the hallway, and peeked his head out to look again. Powdered sheetrock rained on his head from a bullet striking inches above him. That's when he saw the muzzle flash from the woods beyond his back yard. The gun made no sound, none that he could tell, but the bullets striking wood and glass and lights did.

*Thunk! Crash! Pop!*

*Oh, my God!* Percy's mind screamed again.

He turned back into the hallway and scrambled for his bedroom. He was going for his .38 snub nose revolver, which he kept in his chest-of-drawers.

Somewhere behind him, he heard the front door smash. He could hear splinters of wood falling and skidding across the tiled floor at the entryway.

*Oh, God!*

---

Fletcher and Benson rushed up the front steps. Fletcher reached the door first. Without missing a step, he threw his right leg up and kicked the door inward, mid-stride. His foot landed just beneath the door knob, and the wood of the frame succumbed to the strength of the steel locking mechanism under the force of the blow.

The door flew open and they rushed in. People were scrambling this way and that, frantic, frightened looks on their faces. Women screamed. Men screamed.

Fletcher and Benson leveled their shotguns and tore through the living room in a half crouch as fast as they could. When they rounded a corner which fed into the dining room, they were met with a showering of fresh splinters and sheetrock. They both ducked down and fell back. Fletcher dared a peek and saw Percy Wilkes crawling briskly down the opposite hallway. He was moving so quickly and frantically that his butt was wiggling in the air in a comical fashion.

*A slug on speed,* he thought.

Benson pulled his radio off his hip and keyed the mic.

"We need back up here, *now*! Paramedics and police! We have an active shooter and people wounded!"

Fletcher dared a second peek around the corner, saw nothing, and bolted across the open living room. Three bullets zipped by him, two lodging in the wall to his side, the third striking and destroying a lamp. The lamp exploded with a glassy *pop*, and shards of ceramic housing flew through the air, skittering to the floor. The bullets hit so close that Fletcher could feel the wind as they passed.

He dived into the hallway, landing on his stomach just in time to look up and see Percy crawling through the door to a bedroom at the end of the hall. Fletcher looked back across the room to where Benson was crouched.

"I'm going for Wilkes!" Fletcher yelled. "Cover us!"

Benson nodded and peered around the corner toward the direction of the gunfire, his shotgun leveled and pressed firmly against his shoulder.

Then his face went white.

Fletcher noticed this and peeked around his own corner.

Through the shattered window in the dining room, he could see Charlton Fields jogging across the large back yard, coming directly for the house. There was a large gun in his hand and he used it on a woman who was screaming and running across the yard toward safety. Crimson jetted from her shoulder and she fell to the ground, screams turning more panicked.

Charlton never veered off course. He was coming straight for the house.

Fletcher saw Benson aim the shotgun, and fire. But Fields was too far away for an accurate shot and he missed. It was, however, enough to deflect Fields's charge. He turned and ran toward the side of the house, out of sight.

*Shit.*

Fletcher turned and bolted down the hallway. He burst through the door that Wilkes had gone through moments earlier, finding him there with his hand in a drawer. When Percy saw him, his face chalky and lined with terror, he whipped a revolver up and fired a round at Fletcher in fear.

Fletcher ducked and through his hands up instinctively. A split-second later he looked up at Percy Wilkes, whose eyes were wide as saucers, the gun in his hand shaking with the tremble of his panicked limbs. Fletcher looked at the door frame next to him and saw the shattered wood. Luckily, Wilkes's fear had been greater than his aim and the bullet had lodged itself in the door jamb *next to* Fletcher's head instead of *in* his head.

"Oh, my God!" Percy yelped in a voice that sounded adolescent.

"Get down and follow me, now!" Fletcher yelled, both desperation and anger in his voice.

As soon had he said it, the bedroom window behind Percy erupted into a thousand tiny fragments. A bullet tore through the flesh of Percy's upper left arm. He fell to the ground with a howl of pain, blood streaming the air in fine arcs.

Fletcher could see Fields through the now glassless window. He raised his shotgun and fired it from his hip, just as Percy fell past him to the ground. The window-sill was peppered with pellets and Fletcher saw Fields turn his face away as even more pellets dug into his skin.

Not enough to seriously injure him, but better than a complete miss. It would slow him down. It had to.

Fletcher chambered another round.

*Crunch-crunch.*

He grabbed Percy by the collar.

"Move your ass!"

Fletcher pulled him into the hallway as several more bullets tore through the walls.

# CHAPTER
## 37

Charlton Fields felt the pain from the shotgun pellets pulsating through his body. They had struck the right side of his face and his right arm. To put it lightly, it stung.

It stung like hell.

Then, in the next moment, the pain vanished and the wounds sealed up. He turned back to the window and fired a few shots at Wilkes, who was fleeing into the hallway with the assistance of Harry Fletcher.

*You're dead, Harry!* Charlton thought, venomously. *You're so fucking dead!*

Then there was movement in the peripheral vision of his left eye. He turned, pointing his gun, and saw two uniformed officers running towards him, drawing their guns as they ran.

*Fools.*

He threw two rounds at them. One struck the first officer in the head. He spun and hit the ground, a pink mist hovering over him. The second hit the other officer in the side of the neck, just above where the shoulder started. He also emitted a pink spray and collapsed.

They didn't move again.

Fields then bolted towards the front of the house in a full sprint. Moisture peppered his skin and instantly cooled as he ran. He kept his breathing even as he moved, not huffing for breath at all. He'd trained for this kind of thing. In all the years he'd been preparing, he kept himself in perfect shape, and it was showing now.

And, of course, there was Trocephus there to help.

He reached the corner of the porch, jumped up on it, and peeked through a window. Inside he saw Fletcher, Wilkes, and another man holding a shotgun, probably Fletcher's partner. They were all crouched, discussing something quietly and quickly. He aimed his gun at them. Wrapped his finger around the trigger.

*Do it! Do it now!* Trocephus screamed inside him lustily.

He was just about to squeeze off a round when the trio inside quickly got up and ran for the door.

Fields pressed his back against the wall and leveled his gun at the area just in front of the door, his pulse deafening in his ears.

*Wait for it…*

———

"He's outside the house, close," Harry was saying to Benson and Wilkes. "We have to get out of here, and fast!"

They were huddled next to the corner that Benson had been crouching behind.

"I say we bolt out the door, keep our heads low, and make for the cruiser," Benson said. "But we gotta move now!"

Fletcher nodded in agreement. Wilkes did nothing but shudder and moan under his breath, his eyes still wide and full of fright.

"Alright, let's do it!" Fletcher said.

Fletcher grabbed Percy again by the collar and they rushed for the door. It was still hanging open from when he'd kicked it in just a few moments earlier. Benson followed in the rear. Other than a bleeding man on the carpet, the house was now deserted, Wilkes's guests having fled the scene.

"Keep your heads down, both of you! And do *not* stop moving!" Fletcher yelled at them both.

He ducked his head down, and Benson and Wilkes followed suit in identical fashion.

"You have to get me out of here!" Wilkes cried as they neared the door.

"Shut your fucking mouth and keep you head down!" Fletcher piped back at him.

"You don't understand," Wilkes began again. They were just coming through the front door out onto the porch, when he raised his head up.

"He's going to—"

Blood sprayed out of the side of his head and splattered Fletcher and the wall next to him. A thunderclap of gunfire erupted in the same moment. Wilkes fell down the steps of the porch from momentum, his body a lifeless rag doll of flesh. He took Fletcher with him.

Percy Wilkes was dead before his face struck the concrete pathway.

Fletcher knocked his head against the pathway, causing specks of light to dance in his vision. Through the daze, he looked up at the porch and saw Fields jumping over the side railing to the ground beneath. Benson, who had pulled up just before going through the doorway when he saw Wilkes's head explode, rolled out of the doorway and blasted the shotgun at the side railing Fields was leaping over. Wood splintered and broke apart, but Fields continued to flee.

He had missed.

Fletcher shook the daze off and looked quickly at Wilkes. The man was dead. Half his head had opened up and his eyes were open, vacant, and cocked at unnatural angles.

*Damn you, Charlie Fields!*

Fletcher cursed audibly, and forced himself to his feet. He ran for the side of the house.

"Get the car," he yelled at Benson as he was rounding the corner. "Meet me on the other side of the woods!"

Then Fletcher went after little Charlie on foot.

---

Benson jumped into the side of the cruiser, tossing his shotgun into the passenger seat as he did, and dropped the transmission into drive. He floored the accelerator. White smoke billowed from the wheel wells as the car slid sideways a bit. A couple of seconds later, the tires bit down, found traction, and the car sped on to the road. He looked in his rear-view mirror as he barreled away. People were still scrambling to their cars and running down the streets in hysteria from the nightmare party.

He turned hard to the right, fishtailing out into a connecting street. He jammed the gas pedal to the floor again and the engine roared, eight cylinders pushing the car to maximum acceleration. After a small correction with the steering wheel, he was heading straight again, the woods to his right.

Benson silently offered up a prayer, then pressed the accelerator to the floor again.

---

Fields ran into the woods at full speed. Branches and twigs slapped his arms and face, pelting his skin with stinging welts that dissipated and vanished as soon as they came on.

He ignored them. He was too preoccupied with getting away.

*You got him! Didn't that feel good, Charlie? Wasn't that orgasmic?*

Yes.

*Now run, boy. Run like you've never run before!*

He did.

He ran at a full sprint through the thick brush. He threw his arms up to shield his face from some low hanging branches, reaching out like wooded arms trying to stop him.

He felt exhilarated and furious all at the same time. His blood was pumping with glee as he replayed Wilkes going down over and over. But fury reared its ugly head when he thought about Fletcher. He hadn't got him yet, and that was not only upsetting, but very dangerous. He knew Fletcher was chasing him on foot, but it was no matter. He had several years of youth on his side, not to mention impeccable stamina. He would put it to full use as he barreled through the woods.

*They're wishing they'd never messed with your family now, Charlie! They're shaking in their boots! Now, off to J.R.'s. It won't be much easier, especially if you don't shake this son-of-a-bitch on your tail. He is a serious problem! You need to kill—*

Something stopped Trocephus short.

Charlton felt a chill as he considered his visitor's emotions. Was this fear he felt coming from Trocephus? Surely not. What could make Trocephus scared?

*Run.*

What's wrong?

*Just run! He's close. Fletcher's right on your ass, and He has sent help.*

He? He who?

*The Enemy!* Trocephus boomed. *Fletcher isn't alone! That big fucker in the sky has sent him help!*

But why are you afraid? I thought we were more powerful—

*JUST RUN!*

Charlton ducked his head, and ran.

# CHAPTER
## 38

Fletcher entered the woods approximately ten seconds after Fields. He ducked his head and put his hands up in front of himself to block the onslaught of branches, swinging and slapping their merry way at his face with every intention of disabling an eye.

Once he crossed the main threshold of branches, the woods thinned out a bit. The trees were slightly more spaced here than at the edge of the woods. Fletcher looked around and found no sign of Fields. Nothing.

He pushed on.

He ran straight ahead for nearly fifty yards, then he noticed the ground starting to take an upward slant. The grade was enough to make his legs—which, like the rest of him, were in fairly good shape, but still over forty years old—ache. They began to burn with the extra strain. He tried to ignore it, but they would not be ignored. His breathing was also becoming labored.

Somewhere ahead of him, wood snapped in two with an audible *crack!*

*Fields.*

Fletcher reached deep inside himself and found the necessary resolve to force his flaming legs to move faster and his collapsing lungs to inflate. He pushed forward.

*Move it, Harry!*

The anxiety in him lifted slightly. Not completely, but enough that he noticed the fact right off. It was a strange phenomenon. He was closing in on a killer, in the dark woods, and instead of becoming *more* anxious, he was becoming *less* anxious. What could do that? Why did he feel this...*peace*?

The answer came soon enough.

Fletcher leaped over a log, and when he landed, he saw Fields not more than thirty yards in front of him. Even the darkened woods seemed to have brightened. Was the moon coming out from behind some clouds? He looked up.

There wasn't a moon or a star in the sky.

*Strange.*

He brought his gaze back down level and pushed harder, moving himself closer and closer toward Fields. He was closing the distance between them, and fast. He didn't know where his speed was coming from. Fields had several years of youth on him, was in far more fit condition, yet Fletcher was closing on him all the same. He couldn't seem to wrap his mind around it, but he wasn't about to argue with results.

*You don't bite a gift horse in the mouth.*

Another log leered up in front of him. He leaped over it and saw that he had closed the distance between himself and Fields to a mere fifteen yards. He could clearly see now the frantic movements Fields was making. By all accounts, Fields should have been leaving Fletcher in a trail of dust and dead leaves, yet Fletcher was steadily barreling down on him. Fields's arms began to flail about in fear. He was making frightened leaps from left to right. He began zig-zagging a bit, which slowed him down even more.

Fields wasn't a stupid man.

*He must know that will slow him down,* Fletcher thought. *Why is he doing that?*

Once again, Fletcher decided *not* to argue with results. And then he felt that peace again. Even more than before. Confidence grew inside him. His limbs tingled with electricity.

*You're gonna get him. And you're gonna get your family back.*

Fletcher smiled broadly and ran faster.

---

Benson fishtailed around another corner, corrected, and barked into the radio again.

"I'm on Airline Road heading north! Destination is Hemingway! I'm gonna cut him off there, hopefully! I need every available unit, now!"

He gunned the engine and felt the entire car shake with the force of the torque. There were two more streets he had to take before he would reach Hemingway. His mind was racing.

And then, from nowhere, peace fell on him. Somehow, he knew they would get this guy. They would bring his blood lust to end. His reign of terror. His killing spree.

He didn't know how or when *exactly*, but he knew it *would* happen.

One of his streets was coming up to the left and he slowed slightly before taking it. When he did turn, he gunned the engine and slid the car into perfect line with the street and sped forward, his eyes darting to and fro, watching for pedestrians.

*Come on, come on, come on!*

———

*You must run faster!*

Trocephus's frantic words were bouncing around in his head like a rubber ball. Charlton was giving his all to running faster, but Fletcher continued to gain on him. He knew himself to be in peak physical condition, but the older man was closing on him with great ease.

*Move it! He can't catch you! We still have to get to J.R. and Damien TONIGHT, damn you!*

He pushed ahead with as much strength as he could muster, but it wasn't enough. He glanced behind himself to see Fletcher now mere feet away.

And what about the light in the forest? Where the hell was that coming from?

"*Stop!*" Fletcher demanded.

Fletcher was only a few feet behind him. Fletcher was right on top of him. Fletcher was going to *catch* him!

*Kill him! Kill him you motherfu—*

Charlton whipped his gun around behind him and fired three shots without looking or slowing down. When he glanced back again, eyes wide and panicked, he didn't see Fletcher anywhere. That was good.

That was oh, so *very* good.

---

Fletcher was within ten feet of Fields when the psychopath aimed his gun behind him and fired three shots.

Fletcher saw the gun coming around and immediately dived for the ground. The shots were like thunderclaps, booming over his head. He could feel the rounds whipping the air above him.

As he was diving, Fletcher looked to the ground and saw a jagged branch coming up at him.

Right for his eye.

He closed his eyes, waiting for the puncturing impact that would certainly destroy his vision, and quite likely end his life.

*Oh, shit,* Fletcher thought. *Oh, my sweet—*

Then he was hitting the ground and air was whooshing from his lungs. He'd missed the branch. He would have sworn he was headed straight for it, but somehow, he had missed it. As he shoved himself back to his feet, he once again decided not to argue with results.

---

Benson rounded the corner onto Hemingway and finally let the engine come to a lull. In his headlights, he could see a car parked on the side of the road, next to the woods, about a hundred yards ahead. He killed his headlights so as not to draw attention to himself. Two seconds after he did this, he saw Fields come out of the woods.

*"What the..."* Benson started, then trailed off.

Benson could have sworn the woods were glowing.

But there was no time to contemplate glowing forests. There was a murderer right in front of him, and he had to be stopped.

Benson floored the accelerator and the car lurched forward, gaining speed fast.

Fields must have heard the noise. He had been half-way around his own car when he turned and fired several shots at Benson. The windshield turned into a montage of holes and spider webs. Benson ducked his head down to avoid the bullets.

Then he felt the car jerk to the right.

He grabbed the steering wheel and tried to correct, but, in the excitement of the moment, he'd forgotten to take his foot off the accelerator.

It was still on the floor. He was going too fast and the force of the pull was too strong.

Fields had hit the right front tire, and the event had caused the vehicle to lose control. Benson was going much too fast by then, and his attempt to correct the steering did more harm than good.

The car came fully sideways, then jumped into the air and began to flip sideways, like a barrel rolling down a hill.

It flipped over and over and over again. Glass shattered and seat belts locked. Benson's internal organs felt like a tennis ball in a match between the greatest players who ever lived.

He was sure he would die.

*This is it! Oh, sweet Jesus, it's all over!*

The car tumbled ferociously several more times before sliding upside down on the hood for several yards. It came to a rest only eight feet from Fields's car. Benson's vision was blurred and dazed, but he could see Fields smiling maliciously as he made his way around the side of his car.

Fields jumped into his car. White smoke erupted from the tires and the car sped away. Then everything went black.

# CHAPTER
## 39

F letcher heard the crunching. He heard the smashing. He heard the sound of metal being battered. He heard the shattering sound of exploding glass. The screeching fingernails over chalkboard as metal scraped across pavement.

*Oh, my God...*

The worst part of the chorus of sounds was the bridge leading up to them.

*Gunshots.*

He erupted from the forest just as a ball of white smoke roared down the street. He knew it was Fields. The fuck was getting away. But there were more pressing matters at hand.

*Benson...*

Fletcher saw the wreckage. The cruiser was mangled. Torn pieces of sheet metal were reaching out like battered arms from the corpse of a horribly disfigured car. Pebbles of shattered glass littered the street, creating little sparkles of dancing light as the street lamps illuminated them.

Blood was spattered on the interior of the car. It didn't look good.

Not good at all.

His cell phone was in his hand and latched to his ear even as he sprinted to the twisted pile of metal. He could see gas leaking from the tank near the back. It had been punctured during the wreck.

*At least there isn't a fire.*

But then there *was* a fire. That's what he got for thinking too soon. Tempting Murphey could prove to be a real bitch.

A small flame *flumped* from the engine. It wasn't much. A rather small flame, really. But Fletcher knew it only took a spark.

"Dispatch."

Fletcher was too mortified by the sight of the leaking gas and the flame to respond to the young lady on the phone. She would have to use sterner tones. And she did.

"*Dispatch!*" she spit, apparently just tickled pink about her job. Answering phones with lunatics on the line and speaking into radios all day must be rather rewarding.

Fletcher snapped out of it.

"Ah, yes," he began, "this is Detective Harry Fletcher. We have an officer involved shooting and vehicle accident on Hemingway! We need Paramedics, Fire, and Police on site now!"

The lady on the line was starting to say something like 'okay' when he ended the call. He got on the ground and looked inside the wrecked vehicle.

His heart sank.

Benson was unconscious, hanging upside down in his seat belt. Blood was dripping from a nasty gash in his head. His arms dangled limp from the sockets in his shoulders. The seatbelt was taut with his weight. It had done its job. He hadn't moved from the seat or been ejected from the car.

But there was no movement.

"Elliot!" Fletcher hissed, whispering.

He didn't know why he whispered. It just came out that way. Some subconscious predisposition on how a person is supposed to speak to someone whose eyes were shut and who wasn't moving. Like they were asleep. But Benson *wasn't* sleeping.

Fletcher decided whispering wasn't necessary. He spoke louder.

"Benson!" he barked. "Wake up, Benson! Come on! We gotta get you outta here!"

He reached in and slapped Benson in the face a couple of times. He brought back a bloodied hand, and a groggy, disoriented Benson started coming around. His eyes fluttered open.

"What happened?" Benson muttered, completely confused.

"You were in an accident," Fletcher said in a calm, stern voice. "But don't think about that now. We have to get you out of there, and fast!"

That's when Fletcher heard the tell-tale *flump!*

It was unmistakable. Almost as universal as the sound of a pump action shotgun racking a round into the chamber. It was every bit as identifiable.

It was the sound of fire. *Spreading* fire.

He jumped up from his squat and his guess was confirmed. He saw the flame spreading to the rear of the car from the engine compartment. Little yellow, red, and blue arms snaked, slowly but persistently, towards the back of the car. The back of the car held the gas tank. The gas tank was leaking fuel. And the fuel was getting dangerously close to the flames.

They had to move, and fast.

Fletcher got back on his knees and peered in through the shattered window.

"Alright, Elliot, you are about to explode! Can you undo your seat belt?"

Fletcher could see the fear in Benson's eyes as the severity of his situation sunk in to his understanding. He only hesitated a millisecond and then began working at his belt.

After several tries, he realized that it wouldn't budge. The weight of his body pulling down on the mechanism which latched the belt into place was more than he could displace pushing with all his fingers, much less only one.

"I can't get it!" he screamed. "Oh, Jesus help me, I *can't get it!*"

Panic was seeping into his eyes and vocal chords. Fletcher crawled in and past Benson and tried the latch himself, but to no avail. Above them, new *flump* sounds flew into their ears.

*Unmistakable.*

No doubt the fire was catching on old grease and oil in the undercarriage, aided along freely by its uninhibited access to the fresh air.

*Getting closer.*

Not good. Not good at all.

The fire began roaring above them now. Any second it would ignite the gasoline and…

Fletcher didn't want to think about that right now. No point. It would only slow him down. It *was* slowing him down. He had to focus on getting Benson out of the seat belt and then out of the car. No time to worry about the inevitable if he couldn't accomplish those two tasks.

*Focus.*

"Hang on," Fletcher said as he rolled out again on his knees and thrust his hand into his pocket. A moment later, he produced a folding knife. He flipped the blade out and slid it between Benson and the seat belt strap.

"*Attention all cars, Officer involved shooting and vehicle accident on Hemingway. All available units respond.*"

The young lady dispatcher was just getting around to putting the call out. Luckily, Fletcher knew several cars were within two miles at Wilkes's house. They would be there shortly.

*But not soon enough to keep this thing from blowing us sky high!*

He blinked the thought away, yanked hard once with the knife, and then the seat belt was in two pieces. Benson fell to the roof of the car and uttered an "*Oomph!*" as his head thumped into bent metal.

"Let's go!" Fletcher yelled.

He reached in and grabbed Benson. He began to pull him out.

Another *flump* of fire over his head.

*Come on…*

He was moving Benson, but slowly. The almost dead weight was more than Fletcher's body was used to dealing with, especially in this tight of a situation. His mind was racing. Sweat beaded on his brow. Stung his eyes. He dug in and flexed his muscles. All of them, just one giant pulsating flex.

He grit his teeth.

*Come on!*

From somewhere deep within him, new strength flooded his veins. He heaved Benson with gritted teeth and an audible yell, and he got the man out of the car. As more *flumps* of flame announced themselves behind them, he got Benson on his shoulder and ran for the other side of the street.

The car exploded behind them in a white-hot ball of flame.

The blast picked Fletcher and Benson up and threw them ten feet, where they landed on the sidewalk.

Fletcher looked up in pain and saw one of the doors to the car flying down at him, engulfed in flame. After a nanosecond of disoriented hesitation, he rolled out of the way. It slammed into the street where he had been a moment before with a loud *clank* and scraped to a stop a couple of feet away from him.

He could hear sirens in the background coupled with squealing tires. Out of the corner of his eye, he could see red and blue lights flashing in the distance as the boys in blue rounded the corner onto Hemingway and sped towards them. Help had arrived.

Just a moment too late.

———————

Charlton saw the ball of fire erupt into the sky in the rear-view mirror. He was nearly a mile down the street at the time, and couldn't see details, but it was still a glorious sight.

*Definitely, one cop down.*

At the thought, Fields allowed a quick, blood-oozing smile.

———————

Fletcher had Benson on his feet and they were making their way to the first police cruiser that had pulled up. The man stepping out was a fit looking black man with a bald head that gleaned in the fire-light. He was tall and lean, perhaps in his late thirties, based on his shape, but Fletcher guessed he was more likely in his mid-forties, judging by the lines on his face.

"Good Christ, guys! What happened?" the black man said.

Concern was etched all over his face. The black cop's partner was stepping out of the other side of the car. He was shorter, fatter, and white. He was almost certainly younger than his partner, but looked older. He didn't take care of himself like his partner did.

"We need your car," Fletcher said as he made his way to the driver's side door. Benson was already rounding the front of the car to the passenger side and shoving the fat white man out of the way.

The black man seemed taken aback. "Whoa, whoa, hold on now! You can't just take our car! We have to fill out a report, and he looks like he could use some immediate medical attention! Besides that, this car was issued to *me,* not you, so I can't just let you take—"

Fletcher reached out, grabbed the man and slammed him against the side of the car. His patience was gone.

"Listen, dude, I don't particularly care who this car was issued to or why, but I'm taking it, right now, and you will do *nothing* to stop me! There's a murdering psychopath on a rampage, and we are too close to him right now to follow your by-the-book protocol bullshit! Get me?"

The black man was wide-eyed and submissive at that point. He threw his hands up.

"Alright, man, shit! I give! Uncle! Take the damn thing!"

"Thanks," Fletcher said, releasing the man roughly. "I will."

Fletcher grabbed the door, opened it, slid in behind the wheel, and slammed the door shut. Benson slid into the passenger seat and slammed his door as well. Fletcher grabbed the key and turned the engine over. It roared to life.

Benson grabbed the shotgun in between them and removed it from its holder.

Fletcher paused just long enough to look Benson square in the eye.

"You ready for this?" he asked.

Benson met his eyes as he racked the pump on the shotgun, chambering a round. His face was strained, but resolved. It told Fletcher all he needed to know.

They peeled away from their wrecked car in ball of smoke.

# CHAPTER
# 40

lbert Gonzalez was shoving his phone into his pocket when he shouted at Ernest Johansen.

"Quick!" he cried. "Turn on the news. Fields just hit Wilkes's place!"

Ernie grabbed a remote off the couch in J.R. Hays's home and punched the power button. The screen flickered and then went still for a few moments as it warmed up. Then it began to glow, and Bert could hear the field of static electricity building around the set. A moment later, a news reporter was on the TV going over what had happened only moments earlier at the home of Percy Wilkes.

"Holy shit, man!" Bert said as he rounded the couch. "He got Wilkes!"

Ernie just stood there, mouth agape, staring at the grim scene on the television.

"This is out of control," he said. "This guy just walked through a house full of people, which was *surrounded* by cops, whacks the guy, and takes off…"

*"And we still didn't get him!"* Bert finished for him.

They both shook their heads, awestruck.

———

In the next room, J.R. Hays was watching, through a crack in the door, the carnage on TV. A chill slithered up and down his spine, coiling its viscous, serpentine being around his nervous system. And *squeezing*.

Ever so tightly.

———

Helen screamed at the beast once again. Once again, the beast laughed at her.

Raktah was puncturing Heather's leg with one of its talons, delighting in the torture. Heather would scream and wail, then Helen would too.

*"How does it feel, sweet child?"* Raktah said with a throaty, delighted hiss. *"Where is He? Hmm? Too busy for you, I gather. He simply hasn't the time. You're on your own. All alone."*

Its words dripped off his tongue like vomit. The beast was foul. It was cruel.

It was evil incarnate.

*"So sad, His absence,"* the thing went on. *"That He might leave His children in such,"* it held up its bony, bloody, taloned hands, *"hands!"*

It erupted into bone-chilling laughter. It was something straight out of a horror movie, only it was worse. By a factor of roughly a billion.

Helen, terrified, somehow found the strength to sit up right. She quaked with fear in the thing's presence. How it had manifested itself was beyond her, but she knew Fields had opened some frightening doors when he began thinking about revenge.

*Vengeance is mine saith the Lord.*

This scripture rang through her mind over and over. She had been praying almost nonstop, when she wasn't screaming in horror that was, but the situation was draining the reserves of her faith tank rapidly, and she wasn't sure how long she could hold on to it. Dread was winning the battle, and soundly. When the demon had begun physically torturing her daughter, her prayers had been replaced with pure panic.

*Oh, God, Harry! Please find us!*

Then the screams returned.

Raktah watched with glee as Helen whimpered and wailed. Her dread, her *pain*, they were like sweet candy. The sweetest of the sweets. Pure decadence.

The ageless horror smiled, leering into her sobbing, fear-lined face, and thought of a wonderfully ironic spin on the scriptures the bitch was so fond of.

*Perfect fear drives out love.*

Raktah snickered to himself in three octaves, and twisted his talon in the open wound of the younger woman. More screams. More writhing. More gnashing of teeth.

*And if perfect fear drives out love, then hate fills the vacuum. When hate fills the vacuum, doubt sets in.*

The thing beheld the woman, whose head was now bowing to the floor, strings of snot and saliva dripping from her face in slimy gobs. Heaves of air wrenched in and out in terrified gasps as her body trembled all over. Was there anything sweeter? Was there anything more satisfying than human despair? It didn't think so. And the thought made its nightmare face spread wider in that black grin.

*She's beginning to doubt! How divine!*

---

Fletcher rounded a corner, white smoke leaping from the tires as the car fishtailed into the curve. Benson was trying to stop the bleeding from his head with his jacket while speaking into the radio with exasperated tones.

"Everyone in the vicinity of the Hays and Smith homes, be on the alert! Subject is armed and extremely dangerous! We are in pursuit! Report in with updates!"

Fletcher's mind raced with equal parts precision and panic. Helen and Heather were on his mind, holed up somewhere, maybe alive, maybe not, and the one man who knew where they were had been right in front of him. Right *fucking* there!

But he'd lost him. His only hope now was that the psycho was crazy enough to keep going. However, on further reflection, he supposed it may be the sanest thing Fields could do at this point. Holing up again and coming in for a new strike wouldn't pan out. Not with this much heat on his ass. No, he would keep going. Tonight. And he wasn't going to stop until—

*Oh, God, help us Harry!*

Benson was still barking into the microphone, but Harry had heard the wailing cry of his ex-wife as though she were right in his ear. The panic started to creep back in.

*They're alive!* he thought. *They're alive!*

But his inner Harry reared his negative head then.

*You don't know that, Harry,* he said. *For all you know they're in forty-seven pieces, each providing a prime buffet meal to all the white-collar creepy-crawlies in East Texas! And you let this son-of-a-bitch get—*

"NO!" Fletcher cried and slammed his fist on the wheel hard enough to leave a permanent dent in the leather.

Benson hung the microphone back on the radio, looking at Harry and holding his jacket against his bleeding head. He said nothing.

He didn't need to.

---

Fields weaved in and out of traffic. His blood was pumping so hard he thought his arteries might burst.

"Time to make it back to the shack," he said aloud to himself.

*I think not...*

"What?"

Trocephus had mentioned finishing it tonight, but now, with all this heat, it seemed foolish to try. Charlton had risked too much already. It was time to head back. Regroup.

*Not tonight,* Trocephus said. *Take them all out! All the shits! Do it now, while you have the chance!*

"Too much heat!"

*Heat? This is nothing, Charlie-boy! I can show you what real heat is!*

But Fields resisted his guest. He insisted that he head back now and strike again, maybe in a night or two. Maybe it wasn't wise, maybe it was downright stupid, but it was what he was going to do, and he'd be goddamned if he was going to—

Then, Charlton Fields no longer had control.

He was thrown into complete blackness, and could feel claustrophobia set in. He was locked away. One minute he'd been driving the car, the next, here.

*Where the hell is here, anyway?*

He didn't know. All he knew was there was very little light, and not much room to move around. He was in some sort of tiny box, and the only light came around a small door which was, of course, locked up tight.

He peered through the keyhole, and could see the steering wheel he'd just been gripping. Saw his hands on it. The road beyond the windshield.

He watched Trocephus, using his body, whip the car around and head the opposite direction.

---

J.R. Hays washed down a strong martini. Ate the olive. Smashed the glass against the wall.

*Where are you, Spears? Why haven't you fixed this yet? I swear to God, the next time I see you-*

"Mr. Hays?"

It was one of the cops.

J.R. took a deep breath and exhaled it slowly. He turned around, stretching and popping the bones in his neck as he did. They made an audible *crack*.

"What is it?"

"You okay? Sounded like something smashed in here."

He glanced down at the shattered martini glass.

"There," he said, pointing to the shattered remains of the glass.

"Oh," the cop said, and shuffled out of the room without another word.

Hays turned back to the wall he'd thrown the glass against. His jaws were clamped tight, his teeth creaking under the strain. Too much of this business with Fields had transpired. It had to stop. Soon.

Immediately.

He crossed the room to his desk and pulled the top drawer open. He reached in and removed a revolver.

He cocked the hammer.

*I'll handle this myself. And then I'll handle you, Spears!*

Squealing tires outside his home.

His head jerked up and his wide, panicked eyes ached with strain as he looked out the window. Then he made his way to the door.

He saw the cops pull their weapons and make their way to the front door and window respectively. There was a loud smashing sound outside.

Adrenaline flooded J.R.'s veins.

*He's here! He's here, you old shit! He's come to take you out!*

He clutched the pistol tight in his hand.

*"Not me!"* he whispered under his breath. *"You're not taking me!*

"It's him," Ernie said in what could only be described as a high-pitched squeal, and turned from the window.

And then the glass in the window shattered and a thin stream of blood fountained out of Ernie's throat. His eyes grew wide.

Yeah. It was him, alright.

# CHAPTER
# 41

Trocephus ran the car into the yard and through the trash cans. They made a loud crashing sound as crinkled wrappers and banana peels plowed into the windshield.

He grabbed the door handle and threw the door open with enough force that it bent the door past it's halting point and slammed into the front fender of the vehicle.

His strength was incredible.

Fields's body was doing everything, but Fields was not in control of any part of it. Trocephus was calling the shots.

And Trocephus was *strong*.

As he stepped out of the car, he pulled the pistol out in a fluid movement. He had reloaded it during his getaway from the cops. Demons were surprisingly coordinated.

*And those cops!* Trocephus thought with hellish glee. *Oh, how they had burned!*

The memory of the ball of fire in the rear-view mirror was sheer delight. It made his host's body salivate.

As he rose from the car, he saw the curtains to the front window pull back, revealing a wide-eyed man peering out at him, obviously alerted from the sound of the trashcans.

*That's right, fucker!* he thought. *I'm here!*

The man in the window vanished and the curtain danced shut.

Trocephus swung the pistol up and fired in the exact place he'd just seen the man's face. The window exploded into fragments and a moment later the curtains were dyed a deep crimson in splotches and ropes.

Demons were surprisingly good shots.

Fields was screaming somewhere inside the human's mind. Screaming for release. Screaming that they would surely be caught. That he'd trusted him. Why was he doing this? Why was he taking his revenge away from him? Yada, yada, yada, and some blah, blah, blahs.

Trocephus tuned him out. He was in control now. He was going to finish what Fields had started. He was happy to. After all, what were demons for?

He smiled and let the blood flow freely. A little pleasure never hurt anyone.

---

Ernie spun, clutching at his neck. Blood sprayed onto the still dancing curtains before he collapsed to the ground, wide-eyed and gargling.

Bert ran to his side.

"Oh, shit!" he exclaimed. "Oh, shit, shit, *shit!* You're gonna be fine, Ernie, you're gonna be just fine! Hang in there!"

Ernie looked up at him with unconvinced eyes. Eyes that screamed, frantic for help. Bert grabbed his radio.

*"I need help!"* he screamed. *"Officer down! Officer DOWN! One twenty-eight, south Johnson! Need ambulance and backup right away! I repeat-"*

Suddenly, the radio in his hand exploded into a million pieces of plastic and sparks. His mind wasn't registering what was happening. Sheer confusion clouded his brain. Even as he realized that blood was flowing from where his middle and ring finger ought to have been on his left hand, he was having trouble getting his brain to react.

*This should hurt like a bitch,* he thought. *Why doesn't it hurt like a bi—*

Then it did.

All at once, pain exploded into his hand as blood jetted from his middle stump in strings that looked black against the dim light of the house. A scream threatened to rise from his throat, the pain pulsating up his arm in waves. His brain was moving from alert to shock, no longer thinking. No longer focusing on anything but this pain and the horror of his ruined hand.

Luckily, even though his brain wasn't reacting, his right hand was. It was drawing his gun from its holster and raising it up to eye level, sweeping in the direction of the window.

Training was a wonderful thing.

He leveled the gun on the window, and what he saw there chilled him to the bone.

He saw the maniac, Charlton Fields, standing with his foot propped in the windowsill, his left arm holding back the curtains, and his right hand holding a smoking gun. Maniacal laughter boomed from the killer in a voice that seemed to come out in several octaves at once. Blood flowed in gouts from wounds on his face, arm, and hand. His eye oozed some sort of milky goo that spilled on top of the blood. So much blood.

It was horrifying, indeed.

Then the gun in Bert's hand went off. And off. And off again.

He was shooting Charlton Fields in the chest. Every bullet landing home, right in the torso, right where his training had taught him to put the rounds.

Three times. Four.

Fields stumbled out of the windowsill, the curtain falling shut, swaying gently to and fro as if from a delightful autumn breeze.

Bert screamed then. Rage, fear, adrenaline, and pain all at once exploding out of him. He jumped to his feet, curling his wounded left hand to his side, ran to the window, pulled the curtains back.

Fields was stumbling and swaying, moving backwards into the yard. Blood pumped from four holes in his chest. Bert had hit him directly where he'd aimed.

And Fields collapsed.

He became nothing more than a heap on the ground.

*Oh, Jesus H. Christ!* Bert thought. *Oh, fuck, I got him!*

Bert's heart was pumping faster than it ever had in his life. With every beat, his vision bounced. He heard his partner Ernie's radio squawk to life.

*"This is Fletcher,"* he heard the familiar voice. *"We will be there in two minutes! Copy?"*

Bert made his way to the radio, holstered his weapon, and picked the radio up. While doing so, he reassured Ernie that help was on the way, to hang in there. He pushed the talk button.

"Copy, that!" he shouted, not meaning to but unable to help it. "Suspect has been terminated! I repeat, suspect has been terminated!"

There was a moment of hissing radio silence, then: *"Copy that."*

Fletcher's voice sounded bewildered.

Bert was making his way to the window when he began talking into the radio again.

"Ernie's hurt really bad. Shit, *I'm* hurt really bad. But I got him. I got him in the chest four times. He's dead. He's as dead as—"

He had just pulled the curtain back when he stopped mid-sentence. He was looking out into the yard where Fields had collapsed. His eyes grew wide with fear.

*"What was that, Bert? I didn't get that."*

Still squawking with questions, the radio dropped from Bert's hands and clattered on the floor. A second later, his gun was drawn again. Pain continued to explode through his left hand and arm. His eyes were so wide and strained he thought they may fall out of their sockets, but there was no controlling it. He began to tremble. He moved backward into the room, his gun swaying back and forth and back again.

Charlton Fields's body was gone.

---

Trocephus dragged his battered and bloodied host around the side of the house. He had managed to close the wounds up and seal the ruptured arteries on the inside, but the body he'd been using was wearing out. He'd have to be more careful next time. He could keep a body going for quite a long time after it should have expired, but it would only take so much. It was too much work to use an already dead body. A demon would have to manipulate the entire body to its whim, whereas in a living body a demon only needed to manipulate the mind and certain movements of the limbs where a human could not issue the same strength as the demon.

And that meant no more smiling. No more letting the blood flow freely. Sure, it was great for effect, but practicality dictated it had to stop.

He made his way to the back of the house quickly and looked close for an access point.

The door would be it. It opened inward, so it would just be a matter of kicking it in and taking out the target and the cops.

*For good.*

Trocephus made his way to the door and was getting ready to kick it in when the dirt in front of his right foot jumped up at him. A nano-second later, there was boom.

Someone was shooting.

He looked up and saw glass still falling from a newly busted window, and there, behind the glittering, tumbling shards, was J.R. Hays. Fear was etched across the man's face, and his trembling hand held a smoking revolver.

Trocephus fired a few shots at the window and J.R. rolled out of the way.

*"Enough of this!"* Trocephus roared.

Trocephus charged the door, broke it out of the frame on his way through, and stepped over it as it clunked to the ground.

Demons were surprisingly ill-tempered.

# CHAPTER
## 42

Sweat seemed to be diving into J.R.'s eyes.

He'd gotten a shot off at Fields, but he'd missed. His terror was overwhelming, to the point that he was near convulsions. He had rolled into the room just as several bullets smashed through the wall and window, tearing fresh holes in the sheetrock of the walls.

Then the back door came off the hinges and slammed into the floor. Frantic, pounding steps clunked over it.

*He's in the house!* J.R.'s mind whined.

J.R. slipped into the closet and slid the door shut on its tracks. His heart boomed in his ears and all the blood in his body seemed to be going to his face. His lungs tightened.

*Be cool. Just be cool!*

Suddenly, he had an incredible urge to smoke a cigar. He had no idea why this should come to mind, especially now, but it did. And quite intensely. The smell of the burning tobacco, the sensation of the smoke as it filled his mouth. Typically, most people didn't inhale smoke from cigars, but J.R. did. Just a little. He liked how it burned his lungs. The way it caressed his nasal passages as he exhaled it out through his nose. The scent it left in his nostrils.

He wanted a smoke.

This and other anxieties skittered through his veins as he stood utterly still in the blackness of the closet. There was a crack between the door and the frame through which he could see, and he watched closely as the moonlight trickled in through the crack, dancing across his eye.

Nothing. Nothing was there. And there was no sound. No footsteps. No gunshots. No breathing. No movement. No human vibrations that he could detect.

No screams of death.

He found himself wondering what had become of the two officers in his living room. He knew the one had been shot in the throat, he'd seen that much before retreating to the back room. But there had been other shots as well and a primal, chilling scream. The other cop, he assumed. All pumped up with rage and aggression and adrenaline.

Or maybe it had been Fields himself. He just didn't know.

And then he'd seen a blood-soaked Charlton Fields in the back yard and missed his shot at blowing the shitter's head off.

Now he was sitting in this black, hellish hole, waiting to be executed. For all he knew, Fields was just outside the door to the room, deciding whether to shoot him in the head, or to blast him through the heart. Probably was planning to—

A footstep interrupted his train of thought.

It *was* just outside the door to the room. And a moment later there was the sound of sirens.

*Close sirens.*

He'd never been more thankful for the ear-shattering sound that was, that very moment, beating his ear-drums like a conga.

He heard a muffled curse.

---

Bert heard the door collapse and the footsteps and the curse in the hallway near the back bedroom. With his good hand, he aimed his gun and crept cautiously down the hallway. He was nearing a ninety degree turn in the hallway where he knew he would encounter the killer.

He got to the corner, pulled a small crucifix on a chain out of his shirt with the finger and thumb of his wounded hand. He kissed it, and rolled around the corner.

---

Trocephus was furious with the sound of the sirens. They were always in the worst places at the worst times. Why couldn't they just leave him be?

*You're going to get us caught. You're going to get us killed!*

That troublesome human's spirit was at it again. He went inside himself, cursing, and whipped the spirit across the face. Then he slammed the door to the mind-cell Fields was imprisoned in and went back to the forefront.

When he returned, he focused back on the job at hand: killing J.R. Hays.

Then there was a faint sound from behind him. If he wasn't mistaken, it had come from just around the corner of the hallway. A strange sound. Like a wet, fleshy smack.

*Like a kiss.*

Trocephus turned and aimed his pistol at the corner just as the cop with the missing fingers rounded it. Shock and fear exploded on the cop's face. The cop fired.

And missed.

The bullet zipped by his host's temple and thudded harmlessly into the wall behind him, powdering the air with dust. Then it was Trocephus's turn.

He fired twice, hitting the cop on either side of his chest. The cop lurched back into the wall, grunting, but there was no blood.

*Vests.*

He aimed up a little and fired again. This time a spurt of blood spat out of the collarbone on the cop's shoulder and splashed the wall. The officer fell back into the wall and smeared red life in a sort of arch all the way to the ground where he finally lay still.

Trocephus turned back to the bedroom.

*Back to business.*

---

J.R. jumped with each shot. New fear ran through his veins like a tidal wave.

*I've got to get out of here!*

He peeked through the crack. The sirens were nearly deafening now. They had to be right outside. He could hear tires squealing.

And then he saw Fields peek his head into the room.

J.R. acted.

He burst out of the closet, gun aimed high, and began firing. Two shots whizzed by Fields before he ducked back into the hallway.

But J.R. just kept right on shooting.

A moment later, the gunshots were replaced with *click-click-click* sounds. The gun was empty.

*Did I hit him?* he thought with ponderous hope. *Oh, sweet Jesus, tell me I hit him!*

A peek into the hallway confirmed that he had indeed missed Fields with every piece of lead slung.

An evil, demonic glare was staring back at him as he continued to pull the trigger on his revolver uselessly.

*Click-click-click*

Fields raised his pistol and put the muzzle on the tip of J.R.'s nose.

*"No!"*

J.R. heard the sirens outside shut off and car doors slamming.

*Boom! Boom! Boom!*

# CHAPTER
## 43

Fletcher and Benson raised their guns and rushed the house, both deftly aware of the absence of a dead Fields in the front yard. Shots were booming inside the house, flashes of light shining through the windows.

*I got him,* Bert had said. *He's as dead as—*

They rushed in the front door and saw Ernie struggling for life on the floor. His hand was clutched over his throat and blood oozed in strings through his soaked fingers. The paramedics were only seconds behind Fletcher and Benson, and they immediately went to Ernie. They had a rolling oxygen tank and put a mask on him. That seemed to calm him. Slightly.

"Bert?" Benson called out.

There was silence in the house now. The only sounds were the quiet rustling of the paramedics behind them. Fletcher and Benson were on high alert.

After several agonizingly quiet moments, Fletcher said, "Fields? Charlie? Are you here?"

A foolish question. He knew Fields was here, somewhere. But he'd asked it anyway.

"Answer me, Charlie!" he belted.

"*He's gone,*" a voice that sounded like several voices, all in different octaves, said. "*He was a good boy, but it was time for a man to finish the work.*"

"What?"

Benson looked over at Fletcher wide-eyed. The color was draining from his face.

"Oh, my—" Benson started to say.

There were two shots. They whizzed by Fletcher's head and he rolled out of the way, pinning his back against the wall. The shots had come from somewhere down the black hallway in front of them.

One of the paramedics, the one crouched behind the oxygen tank, shouted, "Whoa! Hey, we gotta get outta here, man! I didn't sign up for this!"

Fletcher looked back at the paramedics and said, "Get out of here, but you get Ernie out with you, goddamnit!"

Another shot boomed. Fletcher watched in horror as the bullet struck the side of the oxygen tank.

It exploded.

The young paramedic was thrown violently up, back, and straight out of the already shattered window behind him. His body was enveloped in the drapes and he disappeared into the yard like a flying ghost. A second later, the other paramedic grabbed Ernie by the collar and began to drag him as fast as he could.

"You son-of-a-bitch!" Fletcher screamed.

Several more shots thundered down the hallway, and Fletcher and Benson ducked to the floor.

Then there was silence for several moments.

Fletcher and Benson made eye contact, nodded at each other, and began to move forward through the house, clearing it as they progressed. They held their guns out in front of them, ready, keeping them as steady as they could manage. They glanced in rooms with their pistols and heads, swept them back and forth, and then were back in the hallway. Only one of them would perform the tactic at a time while the other kept their eyes and gun pointed down the dark abyss of the hallway.

After several moments, they rounded a corner in the hallway and found an unconscious Bert. He was bleeding from his hand and collarbone.

"*Medic!*" Benson screamed back at the front of the house. He knelt beside Bert, holstered his weapon, and began rendering aid.

Fletcher continued down the hall and made out a heap lying on the floor in the room at the end.

It was Hays. Or at least what was left of him. His head had just about been blown completely off. Only about one-fourth of his face remained, the lower left quadrant. Blood and bone and brain matter were spread across the room and the wall behind his body in pulpy, wet gobs.

Fletcher cleared the room and returned to the body. There was no sign of Fields, and Fletcher assumed he had fled. He holstered his weapon.

"What are you doing, Charlie?" he grumbled out loud to himself, his emotions overwhelming him. "You can't possibly get away forever."

He left the remains of J.R. Hays and made his way back to the hallway to help Benson with Bert. Benson saw him coming, his face dotted with sweat. He was holding pressure on Bert's shoulder with his jacket.

"Hays?" he asked.

Fletcher nodded his head. "He's gone. Almost headless."

"Oh, sweet Jesus," Benson huffed. "Like the others?"

"No, not like the others. Just blown off. He didn't have time with Wilkes or Hays. He's just running around town wasting them now. Getting it done."

A paramedic arrived a moment later and took over for Benson, who stepped out of the way and approached Fletcher.

"This is getting crazier by the minute, Harry," he said.

Fletcher nodded. "You think? And did you hear that voice? It wasn't human."

Benson shook his head. "No, it wasn't."

Fletcher pulled his weapon from its holster and proceeded to load it with a fresh magazine. "Well, whatever happens, he dies tonight."

He chambered a round.

# CHAPTER
# 44

The phone rang violently in the cradle. An old, weathered hand reached out and snatched it up, fumbling slightly with it.

"Hello?" said Damien Smith.

His voice quivered and shook, much like his hands. Eyes wide as saucers leaped out of his wrinkle-covered skull, and cold sweat ran down his face beneath ancient, white hair, frantically racing towards an unseen finish line.

Spears looked over with a wide eye himself and stared at Damien as he spoke. They had been watching the news. There was a madman on the loose, slaughtering all in his path. And it had become grimly obvious where that path led.

*Right here.*

He had been wrong about where Fields would strike first. He'd also been wrong about how many he would come after in a single night. The inevitable truth was, even as they lived and breathed, Charlton Fields was heading their way, blood-soaked and thirsty for more.

"Are you seeing this?" Damien asked someone on the phone. "I know, I know! This is out of control!"

*"It's out of control, alright!"* Spears spat bitterly. *"You degenerate fucking pervert! You created this monster! Get off the goddamn phone, Damien!"*

Damien merely looked at him for a moment and then went on panicking telephonically as though he'd not heard a word.

"Get off the phone!" Spears repeated, raising his voice.

Damien looked at him again, his cloudy eyes spewing aggravation, then grumbled something to the person on the phone Spears didn't quite understand. As Damien hung up, the old man locked eyes with Spears.

"What the fuck is your problem? You need to remember who you work for!"

His voice was old and deep and full of arrogance. It pissed Spears off.

He wasted no more time. He crossed the room and snatched the phone off the cradle. Then he whipped it across Smith's face, not too hard, but enough to get the geezer's attention.

"Don't you *ever* presume to have sway over me!" he said, and slammed the phone in to its cradle. Then he ripped the cord out of the wall and then threw the phone at the television, which was broadcasting the blood-drenched news about Charlton Fields's killing spree. The television screen shattered and the phone blew into a million pieces. Both toppled to the floor with a loud crash. Spears turned and looked at Damien.

Damien nursed his bruising face with one hand, and looked up at Spears with eyes that ached with pain and fear.

*Good,* Spears thought.

Spears took two deep breaths, then said, "When I say get off the phone, I mean get *off* the fucking phone! We're leaving."

"But I—" Damien began.

Spears snatched him up by his collar and pulled his face within an inch of his own. His lips peeled back over tobacco stained teeth in a sadistic display of rage.

"He's coming," he said. "He's coming here. Now, *right now*, while we're arguing about who's in charge. And *you* got us all in this mess to begin with. So, *you* are going to listen to *me* now. J.R. is dead. Percy is dead. Tony is dead. *Morgan* is dead. Do you get that? This guy isn't playing games! He's killed all of them and many more who've been unfortunate enough to get in his way. Understand that he will certainly have no special pity for you!"

Spears shoved Damien back into the couch.

"You're the one he really wants," Spears went on. "The one he's *really* after. Now get your coat. We're leaving."

Damien got up, grabbed his coat, and together they made their way towards the garage.

Moments later they were pulling out onto the street and racing away from the home of Damien Smith. They went two blocks and came to a four-way stop sign.

That was when all hell broke loose.

Trocephus was speeding down a street in a suburban neighborhood. He'd managed to give the cops the slip and grabbed another car two streets over. Another sedan. An older man, in the latter part of middle-age but still shy of elderly, standing by the door, keys in his hand. His mouth was agape at the sight of the man he'd no doubt seen plastered all over the news the past few days. Right in front of him.

*Live and in person, cocksucker.*

Trocephus smiled at the thought. And oozed everywhere.

He turned around and looked behind the seat at the middle-aged man lying in the floorboard with his head twisted around backwards, mouth agape, tongue hanging out.

*Off to Damien's we go!*

Yes. Damien's house. The final piece of the puzzle. The man respected by so many adults in the community. The one feared by so many children. The self-serving pedophile.

*Oh, what a glorious day!*

He pressed the accelerator down hard.

---

"I need all units available at five-zero-four South Montgomery, *now*!" Fletcher bellowed into the radio microphone.

He dropped the receiver to the floor and slid the car onto another street, the tires smoking beneath them. He floored the accelerator.

They were heading to Damien Smith's home. Benson grabbed the handle above his head and hung on for dear life, uttering a brief prayer under his breath.

Fletcher slid onto another street and jammed the gas pedal down again, hard. There was a four-way stop up ahead, about six blocks from them.

*We're getting close.*

Another car was pulling up to the four-way in the distance. And then another car. The first was facing Fletcher, the other was perpendicular and to his right. They sat there for a very long time, it seemed, without moving.

*What the hell?* he thought.

And then there were bright yellow flashes. Some distant pops. Someone was running from the second car, shooting.

Then a body was pulled from the car, drug to the other. It sped off. A moment later, the first car came to life with a gust of white smoke and took chase.

*It's him!*

The accelerator was digging into the floor.

# CHAPTER
## 45

Trocephus pulled onto another street.

*We're getting close! What do you think of that?*

He was mocking the tortured soul he was controlling. He laughed sadistically in his mind, careful to keep his host's face free of joy, and sped forward to Damien's home.

He came to a four-way stop, roughly the same time as another car to his right. First, he looked left and saw a car coming, still a good way off.

Then he looked to his right.

There was Damien Smith and that pesky hired gun that had plagued Fields's mission at Tony White's house. He was so stunned to see them that he sat motionless for quite some time.

Then he saw *they* were noticing *him*.

Trocephus saw a gun coming into sight from the gunman in the driver's seat.

*Not this time, fucker!*

Trocephus pulled his gun up and fired several shots at the car, spider-webbing his own windshield as he did. The bullets sparked and ricocheted off the hood of Damien's car.

After a moment of this, Trocephus got out of his car and made his way towards Damien. He kept firing at the gunman as he strode confidently onward.

One of his bullets went through the windshield and into the gunman's face. The side of the man's cheek burst into a shower of red and white, smattering the driver's window next to him. The man's head kicked back, and then went still.

*Good riddance, shit-bag!*

Damien's face was mortified in the passenger seat. Behind Trocephus, the car that was coming from the opposite direction revved its engine.

*No matter.*

Then he yanked Damien out of the car and roughly escorted him to his own.

He sped away, chuckling as he went. Smoke blew up behind them from burning rubber and exhaust. The glass of the windshield buckled in the wind and tiny chunks cluttered to the foot wells.

The demon sped on.

Damien cowered next to him, eyes wide and afraid.

---

Spears's eyes snapped open. Horrible pain was pulsating through his right cheek. He looked up just as a car containing Fields and Damien sped away to his right.

Then he saw himself in the rear-view mirror.

His entire right cheek was gone. Teeth were missing. Blood was pouring.

*I'll kill him!* he screamed internally. *I'll rip his fucking balls off!*

"*AAAARRRRRRGGGGGGGGHHHHH!*" he screamed with primal rage.

He was trembling. Some of it from pain, some of it from fury. All of it feeding his adrenaline.

The few teeth left in his head bit tightly together, creaking and cracking. He could feel the grit and grind of them, slimed with his own blood. His face hurt. Bad. He knew that. But somehow it was in the back part of his mind. He was subconsciously pushing it away. Dismissing it. Burying it.

He had no time for pain.

*I'll kill you, Fields!* his mind roared. *I'll tear the flesh off your bones and bar-b-que your liver, motherfucker!*

He was vaguely aware of another car speeding after him. Coming straight at him. Coming on fast. Fletcher, probably, that tiresome cop.

His eyes set hard at Fields's taillights.

He dropped his car into drive and sped after the man who'd destroyed his face. His awareness of the car coming at them both at a high rate of speed became irrelevant.

He was going to do the cop's job for him. With pleasure.

*You're not getting away again!* Fletcher thought as he took chase.

The two vehicles he was chasing held the man he was after, a sick pervert, and a third person, most likely the gunman they'd encountered at Tony White's house.

Benson was next to him praying. Helen and Heather were somewhere, wailing in the dark of a madman's lair, *if* they were even still alive.

*Don't think that way,* he rasped to himself. *They're alive.*

Of course. But doubt flooded his brain like a stream of molten lava, obliterating all other thought in his mind.

He swerved to miss a dog in the street. He'd been too caught up in his doubt and fear to notice the two vehicles in front of him doing the same thing a moment earlier.

*Focus, damn you!*

Yes, it was time to focus. It was time to put everything else out of his mind. It was time to zone in on the killer, Charlton Fields, and whatever it was pushing him forward. It was time to save his family.

Sweat beaded on his head.

*I'm coming girls!*

# CHAPTER
## 46

*Why, God? Why?* Helen thought hopelessly through a sea of tears and anguish.

They had been trapped in the cabin for such a long time that rescue seemed like an obsolete thought. As obsolete as a six-month-old computer.

*Why us?*

Raktah circled them in the main room of the cabin. It had drug the girls to the center of the cabin and had been pacing around them for over five minutes now. Helen had no idea what the beast was thinking. No idea what was going through its head.

*Is it going to kill us? Finally kill us and get it over with?*

The beast smiled and uttered a soft chuckle. It must have heard her thoughts again. That was most unfortunate, for even if she came up with a plan of escape, the thing would know it before she could do anything.

*"Be still."*

A voice.

It came to her so absolutely audible that it must have been from someone inside the room. She glanced around, fearful of what she might see, but there was nothing. No one.

Helen was frozen with fear. Surely Raktah had heard the voice, that phantom voice from no one.

*Not no one, Helen...*

No, it wasn't no one. She knew it was someone sent to help, perhaps God Himself, but he was invisible.

She looked at Raktah. The only thing she could see on the horrible face of the monster was confusion. It was still pacing around, looking at them, but seemed agitated. As if something was wrong. But the beast didn't know what it was.

*"Who's here?"* it asked with a roar. *"I can feel you! You have no right here! None, you hear me! Flee!"*

Helen's eyes darted about the room, then back to the demon for a moment.

Nothing. Just more frantic confusion. She smiled through her gag.

Suddenly Raktah was right in her face.

*"What is going on?"* it spat. *"Who's here?"*

Helen smiled at the demon who had caused so much torment, so much *pain*. The thing was now deathly afraid. Her smile broadened and became a laugh.

Raktah stood fully erect. The beast did it slowly, its lip quivering with fury. Little flaps of mangled skin, the color of blood, curled up to one side in a furious snarl. It reared its hand back and brought it down on her face to slap her. Just as it was about to strike her, to crush her nose and split her lip, the blow glanced off.

---

The demon, however, didn't know it.

To the monster, it appeared to have smashed her in the face, throwing her back.

*"Bitch!"* Raktah cried at her, and moved in again.

---

Helen looked at Heather. Her daughter's face was swollen and bruised. There was blood on her everywhere, a gag tight in her mouth.

But Heather was looking at her. Helen could feel from her look that she had heard the voice too, and peace was falling on her, despite the horror they were enduring, despite all they had gone through...

*There was hope!*

---

Raktah paced away from them angrily. It punched a hand through the north wall and ripped it back through causing splinters and sharp stakes to clank to the floor in front of the women.

Sharp, jagged stakes.

Helen saw it and was hit with another thought. She smiled as it came to her. As if God was speaking directly to her, telling her what to do, right in that moment.

*Thank you!* she thought.

That voice came to her again, as audible as anything she'd ever heard.

*"Be still. You've got everything you need."*

# CHAPTER
## 47

Fields pounded again on the small door of his cell. He'd been trapped in the dark room ever since Trocephus took over, in almost pitch blackness, unable to escape.

Trocephus was a liar.

He had promised him so much. How they would take out the elders and the preacher together, and anyone who got in their way. They would get away with it. They would make them pay.

*Together.*

But nothing of what Trocephus was doing was *together* with Fields. It was all on his own. And Fields was being held prisoner within himself, unable to partake in any of the goings on. His vengeance was being stolen from him. Right out from under him.

He pounded the door again. Nothing. And he had a feeling there would continue to *be* nothing. Nothing at all. Just inky blackness sprawling on before him with tiny tendrils of mocking light. Unending. Forever.

*Nothing.*
He screamed.

---

Trocephus swerved to miss a minivan. Horns blared and sign language poured from the receding van's windows.

Trocephus smiled, the body bled, and he stopped smiling.

Behind him, the two cars were still there, right on his tail. Never giving up, never backing off. Relentless.

*No matter,* he thought. *I'll just bring them home to Raktah. That'll teach 'em! They don't know what horror is. But they will! Oh, friends and neighbors, they will!*

They would indeed. Raktah would tear them limb from limb and pick his teeth with their blood-slimed bones. They just didn't know who they were messing with.

*Oh, you're gonna be so damn sorry.*

But there was that pesky matter of Fields, trapped in the back of his mind. Trocephus had packed him away neatly, but somehow, his screams were coming through. He didn't know how he'd done it, but his host was actually jarring the door Trocephus had hid him behind. That could prove a problem, *if* Fields happened to get out.

But no one had ever broken out. No one had ever penetrated Trocephus's self-induced firewall.

On the other hand, no one had ever been Charlton Fields.

---

Raktah grumbled, looking at the two women. Something wasn't right. The demon couldn't put its finger on it just yet, but it was definitely something. Something *off*.

They were there, bound and bruised and bleeding on the floor. Just as they should be. Everything *seemed* right, but that pesky *something* was gnawing at him.

Raktah couldn't deny there had been some... *presence*. It hadn't seen anyone, but it *had* felt it. And the women were too quiet. Abnormally quiet. They should be wailing and weeping and losing hope. Only they weren't. They were just lying there. Not moving, except for the rise and fall of their chest in rhythm with their breathing. In perfect sync with each other.

*They were perfectly still.*

---

Fields kicked at the door with all his might. He felt pain leap up his leg. He winced and knelt to nurse his sore foot. He could see it there, in the dim light, and could see his hands rubbing over it—

He could see it.

Suddenly, the pain drained from his mind and he looked up to the door. It still stood, resolutely in the doorway, but it was no longer square. The thin shards of light that had poured in around it were wider now in places, and he thought he could see splintering in the frame itself.

It had budged.

He rose to his feet, ignoring all traces of pain now, and kicked at the door again with every ounce of strength he could muster. It splintered a little more.

He was filled with unmaintainable delight. New energy surged through him, bathing him in renewal. He was getting through. The sprawling nothingness before him began to reel in towards him. A faint horizon. A fixed place.

A destination.

*I'm coming through!*

He kicked again. Again, he felt the door give. Ever so slightly. He smiled broadly.

*I'm coming for you, Trocephus!*

---

Trocephus was now sure Fields was trying to come through and regain control of the body. He couldn't let that happen. Not now. They were too close to have some pitiful, bitter human screw everything up for them now.

Trocephus focused more of his power on holding Fields in. This took from his control of the body's containment. Little streams of blood began to flow.

From several places at once.

---

Fields felt his being weaken. It wasn't much, at least not at first, but he could feel his strength beginning to trickle out of him.

*He's letting me bleed,* Fields knew suddenly.

All at once he was feeling very drained physically. Another kick proved to him that he was certainly losing strength, as the door only gave a little. Though it *did* give.

He retreated to the back of the abysmal room, the room black as pitch with the mocking tendrils of light, and collapsed to the floor. The horizon was fading again. He was losing focus on his fixed place. He began to doubt again that he would get through. His destination was slipping away. His vengeance was disappearing.

He barred his teeth.

———

Trocephus waited a while as blood filled the floorboard of the quickly speeding vehicle. When he was sure Fields had backed off, he moved his focus back to containment of the body.

*Now, where was I?*

Damien Smith sat curled in horror, obviously observing the sight of the opening and closing of wounds all over the blood-soaked body of Trocephus's host, and he cowered in his seat. He was shaking and crying.

*Very good!* Trocephus thought, and began to laugh in octaves.

———

The cars in front of Fletcher were swerving in and out of traffic, both oncoming and with the flow.

*Someone's gonna get killed, goddamnit!*

He lightly pressed the accelerator to keep with them. He wrapped and re-wrapped his fingers around the steering wheel.

His knuckles were white.

*Just stay with him! Don't lose them!*

———————

*"Filthy, wretched fuck!"*

Spears was grumbling through his splattered cheek. Blood was freely diving off his chin into his lap and all over the car's seats.

*"I'm gonna kill you sons of whores!"*

They had begun to get out of town some ways now. They were winding down a dark highway. Yellow and white stripes snaked through the darkness, gleaming from the headlights passing over them.

*"I'm gonna kill you all!"*

# CHAPTER
## 48

Helen's eyes focused in on one of the wooden stakes. She found she was no longer capable of focusing on anything else. They were calling out to her, singing a song of deliverance just for her. A tear came to her eye.

*I'm ready,* she thought. *I'm ready, and I'm going to bury that stake in this thing's head a thousand times!*

The demon was boiling mad. It knocked a hole in the wall next to where it had just knocked the previous one. It's glare, those terrible, yellow eyes, focused on her.

It started for her.

*Okay, Helen,* she thought to herself. *This is it! Wait for it!*

Then terror seized her heart as another thought struck her.

*How do you kill a monster like this? A demon? Oh, God, what could kill this thing?*

Then that still, small voice came to her again. The one which had told her to be still.

*You leave that part to me,* it said. *You just worry about burying that stake to the base.*

She nodded imperceptibly to herself, though she didn't feel much relief. Sure, she would do it. She would go for the stake and make every effort to make it disappear into the thing's horrible throat. It's head. It's chest. *Anywhere* she could stab it. At least until the thing slapped it out of her hand and ripped her larynx out and dined on it as she bled to death, spraying her daughter with her blood.

But none of that mattered now. She had to try. She had to *trust*. Trust that it would work. After all, what else was there?

Raktah reached her and grabbed her arm. Then it grabbed Heather.

Helen shuddered.

---

Raktah was beyond furious. It'd had more than enough of this. It knew the *Enemy* was close. And it didn't like it. Not one bit.

Raktah was a powerful demon. One of the most powerful in existence, as a matter of fact. But with that came wisdom. Wisdom to know one's limits. And there *were* limits for demons, no question about it. If the Enemy was involved, the demon was finished. It knew it. Next to the Enemy, it was a weakling. It was nothing. *An insect.*

But it had seen no party to the Enemy here. Only the woman's pitiful prayers, as yet unanswered. But if they were…

Raktah had to kill these women before the chance was lost. No time to wait. No time left for fun. Time to end it.

The ancient beast stormed over to the women and grabbed them. Then it threw them through the splinters and shards of wood and watched them slam into the wall beneath the two holes it had created. They slammed into it with a grunt of pain.

*Maybe just a little more fun*, it thought.

It stalked malevolently towards them.

*"Well, ladies,"* Raktah said, *"I believe it is time for us to part company!"*

It began to laugh. In octaves.

---

Trocephus slid the car onto an old dirt road out of town. After checking the rear-view mirror, he had noticed—with absolutely no surprise—the two cars following him were not far behind him.

*"Fuck!"* he shouted into the cab.

He'd done all he could do to lose them, but to no avail. They just weren't going to be lost. Like parasites leeching on a pair of juicy testicles.

They just wouldn't let go.

No matter. He was mere seconds away from the cabin now. He'd led them out of town, down some old back roads, then to dirt roads. He was miles from anyone and he doubted even Fletcher knew where to tell the dispatchers at the police department where to go.

They were in the middle of nowhere.

Then he felt Fields, stronger than ever, trying to break through again.

*"No!"*

There was no time for this. No time to deal with this lost soul. There was too much at stake. He was too close. He was almost there. Almost to Raktah.

Almost to victory.

Damien Smith wept in the foot well, clutching himself in fear and breathing heavily. Trocephus spat on him.

*"Coward..."* he said.

He pushed the accelerator to the floor.

---

Fletcher shouted into the mic.

"I'm not sure exactly where we are! Just follow the directions as best you can and get some back-up down here, now!"

He was furious with himself for not being able to tell them better how to find him. How to find his family.

He'd not been on the radio while in town because there was too much risk of crashing, and Benson had been too busy praying. The thought pissed him off, but he dismissed it quickly. Now wasn't the time to be turning on each other.

"Just..."

He paused for a moment. He didn't know what to say. He was wasting his breath talking to them. There was no more information he could give them. He'd been so focused on keeping up with the cars in front of him that he had been unable to keep track of where exactly they were.

Which roads. He had a general idea of where they were. He *had* lived in Longview most of his life, after all. But getting anyone right to him was going to be imposs—

"You have an iPhone?" Fletcher suddenly asked Benson.

Benson blinked at him, confused.

"An iPhone," Fletcher snapped again. "Is that what you carry?"

Benson fumbled in his pocket for a moment and produced a small slab of metal and glass, and held it up.

"Yeah," Benson said. "Why?"

Fletcher ignored him and spat into the mic once more.

"Dispatch, does someone there have an iPhone?"

There were squawks and confused voices for a moment, then he received an affirmative.

"Give me the number!" Fletcher barked, then looked to Benson again. "Type this into your messages."

Benson, still confused, did as he was told as the number came through.

"Good," Fletcher said into the mic. "We're going to share our location with you. You get us back-up, you hear?"

Now Benson's eyes were widening with understanding.

"Crap!" Benson said. "Why didn't I think of that?"

"Why the hell *I* thought of it is beyond me, but there it is," Fletcher replied as he lay the mic in its cradle. "Now share it!"

But Fletcher *did* know why he'd thought of it. It had been one of the things his daughter had shown him when he first got an iPhone. A way they could find each other if something ever happened.

The radio squealed.

*"We've got you!"* the dispatcher said. *"Sending every available unit!"*

Fletcher grunted.

"Be ready, Benson," he said. "Wherever we're headed, it's secluded. And we will need a lot of luck. How 'bout you pray for some of that, eh?"

Benson pursed his lips and nodded.

"Alright."

---

Spears growled in his car.

The pain in his face was overwhelming. He continued to push the pain from his mind, but it was coming back stronger every time.

*Throbbing.*

He slammed his fists on the steering wheel and the roof several times, growling and spitting as he did. Then he willed the pain away again. He breathed out, air coming from his nose, mouth, and gaping wound. It flapped and spat blood. He extended his fingers and then gripped the steering wheel again.

Tight.

The car in front of him suddenly pulled into a rough dirt driveway and ran through a tin gate. Metal groaned and sparks flew into the air as the car rumbled past the twisted metal.

Spears jerked the wheel to follow them and felt the gyrations as his car trampled the gate. After a quick glance in his rear view, he saw the car behind him was following suit.

*"That's right, you cop fucks!"* he hissed to himself. *"Come on and join the party! I'll rip your lungs out and drink your fucking blood!"*

He swerved down a very narrow path, tree limbs slapping and scraping the car as it barreled on. It was dark, except for the lights of the cars, causing dancing shadows to bob and weave all around him. Thick forest growth was leaning in after him, reaching with wooden arms and leafy fingers out from the black night into the small path as though they were trying to reclaim what was once theirs. The small slot in the earth they had lost.

After about a minute of this, the car came into a clearing. Ahead of them loomed a small hunting cabin in a cleared area of the woods. It was surrounded by forest, with only the one trail they'd just traversed to enter and exit. Lush, tall grass carpeted this small meadow of horrors.

Finally, it was time to end things, once and for all. Full stop.

Spears gave a repugnant, clown-grin smile through his shredded face.

*Time for a showdown.*

# CHAPTER 49

The stake was right in front of her face.

Helen's eyes were focused on the stake. It was sharp. Tiny splinters spanned out in frayed chaos all around the outer edges of the spike. She could feel it calling to her.

*Take me,* it said.

Blood ran down her face. It streamed in narrow lines, some of it trailing into her eyes, causing her to see red.

She glanced up. A few feet beyond the stake the demon was standing over them, drooling some horrible black tar. It dripped and pooled on the floor. It slid down its chin. It slimed its way over the thing's nightmare body.

It was horrific.

*"Prepare to meet your eternity!"* the creature screamed at them.

Its eyes were wide and glowing. It'd never looked more fearsome. It'd never looked more terrifying.

*Are you ready?*

The voice again. The calm, comforting voice. The voice that had promised never to leave her. Never to forsake her.

To always provide everything she ever needed.

Helen's eyes flicked back down. She saw the stake again. Her eyes narrowed. Somewhere behind the demon were lights. Swirling, almost sparkling shades of blue and red and white. But she was only vaguely aware of them. She was focusing on the stake. The only thing that mattered now.

And it was everything she needed.

*I'm ready.*

---

Trocephus slid the car sideways in front of the cabin. Within him, Fields was beating his way out of his spiritual prison. More and more of Trocephus's energy was being focused inward on containing Fields. But he was losing. The door was crumbling. Coming free of its frame. Splintering.

And more and more blood was gushing from the multiple wounds in Fields's body. He was struggling to keep the body upright. The flesh he was wearing trembled and shook.

*Bleeding.*

Trocephus felt weak. Trying to contain the body was taxing him beyond what he could manage. He had no idea how much longer he could keep it up, but he knew it wouldn't be much longer. He would power through to the last minute. It had to be this body which did the deed.

Which finished the job. Even if it wasn't Fields doing it, it had to be his flesh. That's what the world needed to see. Not some demon beast, but the human monster. The one the Christians had created. That was how it had to be.

And it didn't matter. It was almost over and he had Smith. Only a few more minutes and it would be done. It would all be over. And victory was within reach.

He just had to deal with his company.

Spears slid his car up behind Fields.

The blood-soaked maniac was rising out of the car, bleeding. Insane eyes seemed almost to glow from his sockets.

He threw the car in park and started to climb out of the vehicle. He drew his pistol and pulled a second, smaller one from a holster on his ankle.

He aimed at the car.

A second later, he had his sights lined up on Fields.

Spears fired three times.

The bullets tore through Fields's torso and he fell to the ground.

*"Fuck you, psycho!"* he screamed, spraying blood and tiny bits of flesh as he did.

Then he heard the car behind him sliding over the grass to a stop. His celebration was cut short.

Spears spun around, his gaping facial wound flapping in the wind like a ruined wing, and aimed his guns. He began firing at the car. The windshield spider webbed into an unrecognizable mess.

And there was a spray of crimson from inside.

———————

Fletcher saw Fields go down. He slid the car to a stop, while he and Benson were pulling their guns out, getting ready for a battle. Or a bloodbath.

Then the gunman was firing on them.

Fletcher ducked down as he heard bullets thudding into the seat over his head. He felt something warm spray him in the chaos. His face was covered. He wiped it frantically and pulled his hand back to see.

Blood. Black in the dim light, but it *was* blood. He could smell the metallic stink of it.

*"Benson!"*

Fletcher looked up and saw Benson lurching with each new gunshot.

*"NO!"* Fletcher screamed.

He reached out, grabbed Benson, and pulled him down out of the line of fire. More bullets tore in through the windshield and smashed through the fabric of the car seat. Blood was everywhere. He'd been hit at least seven times.

Visions of Gaston flashed into Fletcher's mind. The gleam in the eye. The reckless abandon as his partner bounded up the stairs. Into the room. The resigned look of defeat on his face.

The bullet bursting out the back of his head.

*"Not again!"*

Benson was shaking. Blood was lurching out of his mouth and his numerous bullet wounds. He was coughing and gurgling. He was in bad shape.

"You hang in there!" Fletcher said, and rolled out of his door onto the ground.

He didn't aim. He just began firing at the area he thought the gunman was.

And he hit him.

The gunman's right thigh blew apart with a spray of blood and meat. Blood splashed on to the car behind him and the man screamed as he fell to the ground.

Fletcher began to stand up when he felt a bullet whizz by his head. He heard the crack of the shot a moment later.

He looked and saw the gunman was pulling himself up on the car to stand. He was holding one of his guns out, smoke billowing from its barrel.

Something in the man's eyes. The eyes of a maniac, a man pushed over the edge by anxiety and pain. Fletcher saw the man's whole face then. It was blown apart. Fragments of pulverized meat and shattered teeth were showing through. There was pain in the man's eyes. How could there not be? But there was something else too. Rage. Blind fury. Relentless, unstoppable, uncontrollable anger.

*He isn't going to stop,* Fletcher thought.

Then Fletcher noticed the gasoline flowing out of a bullet hole near the gas intake port of the man's car.

He narrowed his eyes and aimed. The man's hand which held the gun was shaking, focusing in on him. About to shoot. Fletcher exhaled. Closed one eye. Lined the sights up.

He fired three times at the tank. The gunman was leaning up against the car. A spark flew off the metal and ignited the gas.

The car blew into a million pieces.

The gunman was launched into the air, screaming and on fire. He flew backwards and came crashing down, hard, through the roof over the porch on the cabin.

Then he went still. Flames were still lapping into the air off his body.

Fletcher jumped to his feet.

*"I'm coming girls!"* he bellowed.

He began to run for the cabin. He thought of Benson in the car.

*God, if you're real, save his life! Please!*

He leaped over the body of Fields, still lying on the ground, even as he ended his prayer.

Inside the cabin, there was a horrible scream. But it wasn't a human scream. It was layered with treble and bass. Octaves. It was a nightmare sound, the kind of thing you expected to hear in a horror movie, but never in real life.

He burst through the door.

# CHAPTER
## 50

Helen's hand came to rest on one of the sharp wooden stakes. Her fingers curled around it. She could feel the splinters digging in to her palms. They cut her. Her hand bled, but she barely noticed.

Raktah didn't seem to notice any of it. His yellow eyes were wild with fury and excitement, maybe even fear. Tar-like slime dripped from his fangs. A terrifying maniacal laugh coming out of him in octaves.

Gun shots.

They erupted outside the cabin and Helen thought she heard a man scream.

It sounded like Harry.

*Oh God, Harry, no! What's happened?*

She gulped and immediately pushed all the fear and hope welling up within her as far away as she could. She had to focus. Later she would have time to break down, to weep, to let it all out. But not now. Not in this moment.

Not yet.

This was *her* moment. The *only* moment she might have. If she missed this, there were likely no more chances. Almost certainly no more chances. It would be over. For all of them.

*Just one more moment...*

She breathed in deep.

Raktah looked back down at them and raised his taloned hand over his head, preparing to shred the flesh of her and her daughter. Heather moaned momentarily behind her. There was fear in the moan. Defeat. Resignation.

The demon's eyes were wild like a feral cat.

Just then, another eruption of gunfire popped and an explosion boomed outside. Bright yellow light spilled in through the windows. Raktah's eyes darted to the door, but he didn't move.

*Almost...*

Helen could feel her arm trembling. Her fingers gripped the stake tighter. Her palms were streaming blood now, and it oozed through her fingers. Pooling around her hand and the hard, wooden floor. She took in another deep breath.

There was a crashing sound on the porch and she saw from the corner of her eye through the doorway and adjacent window a flaming heap come crashing down. It thudded loudly on the porch. After that, all she could here was the lapping and crackling of flames.

Raktah finally turned to see what was happening. It had been just enough to distract the thing's focus.

It was what Helen had been waiting for. Her knuckles went white under the blood as she clenched the stake with all her might.

*Now!*

Just as the word rang in her mind, she jumped to her feet, wielding the stake in her bleeding hand, knuckles white as sheets. She stood erect, raising the wooden spike over her head, clutching it in both hands as she did.

Raktah began noticing her and its widening, hideous eyes came back to her.

But not soon enough.

*"Burn in HELL!"* Helen hissed at the demon.

The beast's face seemed to spread into pure terror in that moment. All its menace disappeared like water vanishing down a drain.

Its blood-colored skin paled.

Helen buried the stake in the thing's chest, about where a heart ought to be. The beast screamed in horror, horrifying melodies leaping from its mortified and distorted mouth. Black, slimy tar spat from its lips and its eyes widened still in mounting terror.

She twisted the stake as Raktah fell backwards to the planks of the floor. A moment after they hit the floor with a fleshy *thump*, Raktah began to writhe beneath her, squirming, trying desperately to get free.

She pulled the stake out, slinging a kind of slime that might have been blood through the air in arcs, and began stabbing the thing over, and over, and over again.

*"Jesus, Jesus, JESUS!"* she screamed as she perforated the demon's chest.

Blood and slime were slinging through the air. Tears were flowing from Helen's eyes, but she kept on stabbing, relentlessly, all the time screaming the name of Jesus over and over and over again. Louder. Louder. Higher. Louder. Again, and again. Louder still. Over and over.

It was the only word she could think of, the only word that would come to her in the moment, and it seemed fitting.

The monster's resistance began to lessen, its fight leaving it as the slime that served as its blood dumped out of it by the gallon.

After a while, it finally went still.

But Helen continued stabbing the thing for several moments longer. She had no intention of stopping. No intention of leaving any possibility for the thing to get back up in some horror-movie finale, leaping back at her for one more chance. Oh no, thank you very much, she would have none of that.

She continued to stab.

*You're safe,* the voice within her said. The one that had told her to use the stake. The one that had told her to be still. To wait for the just the right moment.

She raised the stake a final time and buried it the monster's face. A splash of crimson and tar marked the end of the outburst of violence, and the end of Raktah on earth.

Helen scooted backwards off the beast as her body began to shiver and quake. Tears showered her blood-soaked face. Her hands came to her mouth in trembling gyrations.

She thought again of Heather. Her sweet, beaten little girl. Her baby. She turned and rushed to her, crawling on her hands and knees frantically. Heather was crying and injured, but otherwise seemed alright. Helen held her tight in her arms as they both began to heave and weep with relief.

A moment later, Harry leaped into the cabin through the door, gun in hand, his face speckled with blood. His eyes were wide and frantic, and his face filled with horrified confusion as he saw the dead demon on the floor.

He shook his head and made his way around the monster to his daughter and ex-wife. Panic seemed to spread on his face as his eyes fell on his daughter's battered face, the hole in her leg, the blood all over both of them.

*"My God..."* was all he said, and it came out in a croak.

Helen reached her arm around him and pulled him close.

"Thank God you're ok," she said to him. "Heather looks worse than she is, she'll be ok! We'll all be ok!"

Fletcher hugged her, then turned to his daughter, holstering his weapon.

"Baby girl," he said, tears welling in his eyes and his lips quivering, "I love you so much! I thought I'd lost you!"

He turned to Helen, tears streaking his face.

"Thought I'd lost you both…"

Helen smiled and hugged him again.

"We're here, Harry. We've always been here."

They're embrace tightened and they each reached an arm out to Heather and pulled her in.

They all began to cry.

---

Damien Smith had crawled from the car when the explosion happened.

He'd been curled up in the fetal position in the floorboard of the car with Fields and watched the whole thing go down.

Fields was dead. Spears had been turned into a flaming ball of fire. One of the cops looked dead in his car.

Then there had been the horrible scream. The terrible octaves. It had sent chills up his spine.

Not that he had much of a spine to be chilled, but whatever, it was the thing which had allowed him to walk upright since he had begun doing so as a child. Whatever the thing was, it tingled now.

He could hear sirens in the not-so-distant woods. They would be here soon, no doubt having seen the explosion from the road. He had to get out of here. Everyone else was dead. Percy, Morgan, Tony, J.R. All of them. Gone. And the killer Fields was here. He couldn't be here. He had to get out. To flee.

There was no way he would survive the questioning which was surely coming. He needed to vanish, to disappear. There was little to stay around for now with the pastor and the others gone anyway, and far too much liability if he stayed.

He began to make his way towards the wood line.

───────────

Trocephus was weak.

He could feel Raktah's presence was gone, and another presence was all too thick in the area. It was a presence he was not prepared to battle. Not then. Not in the shape he was in. Never mind his host.

Not that he'd have much success if he did anyway. His kind never did. Their best bet was to destroy the faith of the humans, not go to war with the Enemy head on.

No, the cause was lost, and he'd failed. All that was left to do now was to move on. Find the next willing vessel. The next hate-filled vagrant.

Time to leave.

He could feel Fields pounding again at the door. It was splintering more and more. He no longer had the strength or resolve to hold him in, and there was little point in trying to contain the body at this point. It was battered far beyond repair and could be of almost no use.

Trocephus leaped out of Charlton Fields's body and into the air. The presence of the Enemy was thick, but he also knew there was at least one thing he could walk away with in the midst of all the chaos and failure.

Charlton Fields's soul.

He darted to the field, noticing Damien Smith moving towards the tree line as he did.

*Perhaps two souls, if we're lucky.*

He grinned horrifically.

---

Fields kicked the door again and it gave way from its hinges.

He grabbed the door by its side, pulled it free of the frame, and stepped into the void beyond.

His body began to open immediately in several areas. His cheek came open, his eye oozed, and his body began to bleed from multiple bullet holes.

He convulsed a few times, feeling his life trying to leave him. But he couldn't let it go. Not yet. If there was one ounce of life left in him, one fiber of resolve, he was going to find it, and drag it and his body to the bitter end.

There was still Damien Smith. And he was still breathing.

Charlton Fields, little Charlie, opened his eyes.

# CHAPTER 51

D amien Smith could see the lights of the emergency vehicles dancing through the trees. He squatted down in the tall grass, panic flushing his face red and widening his eyes.

The sound of the sirens was getting louder now. They would be here in mere moments.

His heart beat so loud in his ears that it damn near started to drown out the sound of the blaring horns. His eyes darted around, frantically searching for something, *anything* he could hide himself in.

Nothing.

He stood to make a run for it, despite his elderly physique and lack of physical fitness. Sweat beaded across his brow, streaking for his eyes. The salt burned and blurred his vision. He wiped his eyes with the sleeve of his shirt. His chest heaved.

*"You..."* he heard a voice say.

It sounded like someone gurgling water and talking at the same time. A horrible voice.

He turned to see Fields standing there, ten feet behind him, a large survival knife in his hand. The blade was down in a stabbing position, white knuckles clenched over the hilt.

Damien's pale skin relieved itself of all color.

Blood poured out of Fields, from multiple wounds in his body, and it oozed from his mouth as well. There was a rather horrifying wound on his face and his eye looked like something out of the darkest of nightmares.

"Oh, God!" Damien screamed.

Fields managed a blood-soaked chuckle at this.

*"He's not coming for you,"* he scoffed, shaking his head. *"But I am!"*

Fields stumbled forward. Every step he took was unbalanced, crooked, bizarre. The man could barely stand, and Damien had no idea how the psychopath before him was able to move at all. But there he was, doing exactly that.

Damien's body froze. He couldn't move. Couldn't even breathe, much less react. Fear gripped every muscle and tendon in his body, and his nervous system refused to send the necessary signals to affect his escape.

His body had gone into total lockdown.

Fields continued to laugh as he hobbled, crimson tar splashing out of him, dripping, gushing. Damien had never felt fear like he did in that moment. Paralyzing terror, unlike anything he could ever have imagined, engulfed him from the inside out.

*This* was horror.

Fields got within a few feet and Damien finally managed to get his brain activated just enough to create movement, but it was all for naught. His first step was backwards, and his foot landed unevenly.

He toppled over to his back. Gazing up, he could see the monster Fields, the monster *he* had created, limping and dragging and hobbling ever closer, the knife in his hand rising into the air more and more the closer he came. The sight was an abortion of reality before him.

*"Oh, dear God! What have I done?"* Damien whined.

Suddenly there was a thunderclap and Fields's body tensed. His eyes became confused and infuriated all at once as even more blood flew from his mouth.

Damien sat up on his backside, propping himself with his hands, confused. He had no idea what had just happened.

Then Fields collapsed.

He fell merely two feet away from Damien's feet, the knife still clutched in a white-knuckled death-grip.

Damien gulped audibly and felt adrenaline and spent fear shudder through his body. His gaze took the scene in for a moment and then he looked up, past Fields's body, and saw one of the cops who'd been chasing them, the younger one, on his side holding a smoking shotgun. Blood was smeared all over his chest and face, and he coughed up more as Damien stared in wild-eyed disbelief.

The cop racked another shell into the chamber of the gun, and with a sigh, laid his head over on the ground roughly.

Damien Smith sat in awe.

Fletcher heard the shotgun blast and it jarred him from his intimate moment with his family.

His head jerked around towards the door, eyes wide and alert. Helen's mouth quivered.

"Harry?" she said, unable to contain her concern.

He jumped to his feet and drew his weapon.

"Stay here!"

He darted for the door, leaping over the dead beast on the floor, forcing wondrous thoughts of what the thing could be from his mind as he went. There was no time for that now.

He sprang through the door and past the burning body of the gunman. The fire was starting to spread from the charred corpse to the beams that supported the weight of the roof.

*No time!*

His eyes trained on the vehicles in the meadow surrounding the cabin. Fields's car was there in the front, behind which burned the exploded car of the gunman. Beyond those was the car he'd taken from the officer in town, bullet holes and blood spatter all over the windshield.

Then he noticed the passenger door was open.

Sirens wailed and he could see lights of red and blue dancing through the woods around the drive that entered to their meadow of horrors.

He sprinted towards the farthest car, angling around to the left so that he could get to the open passenger door.

*"Benson?"* he screamed as he ran.

Then he saw it.

Benson on the ground, struggling for breath, shotgun clenched in his hands, the barrel still smoking. Past him was Fields's body, face down just a couple of feet away from Damien Smith, the cock-sucking pervert who'd created the whole nightmare. He felt a rush of red fury rise in him at the sight of the man. The man he'd trusted. The man he'd arrested.

The man who'd gotten away with it all.

Fletcher rushed to Benson, pushing his rage aside and keeping his weapon aimed in the general direction of the other two.

"Benson?" he bellowed, not realizing how loud he'd just been.

Benson looked up at him, coughing blood.

"Harry," he gurgled. "He just won't stop, Harry!"

Fletcher looked up at Fields, face down, unmoving.

"I think you got him, partner."

Benson managed a smile, streaked with crimson, his teeth coated in blood.

"Now I'm your partner?"

They smiled at each other momentarily until a loud *whoosh* of flame diverted Fletcher's attention back to the cabin. He stood suddenly and looked back. The whole deck was catching fire, save for the end by the doorway. The roof was now ablaze and it was only a matter of time before it would be entirely engulfed.

*"Girls!"* he hollered.

Just as he started to rush back, he heard a moan. At first, his mind associated it with Benson, on the ground, bleeding and hurt badly. But as he turned his head back, he realized it wasn't Benson at all.

He snapped his eyes up and saw Fields's head rising, and his hand, holding what appeared to be a hunting knife, began to slide towards him.

He looked back at the cabin, then again at Fields and Damien Smith. Damien was immobilized with fear, seeing the monster Fields refusing to die.

Fletcher was suddenly faced with the thought of leaving Damien to his fate with Fields and just rush back to his family. He had decided to do just this when he saw Helen carrying Heather out of the cabin, Heather's arm wrapped around Helen's neck. They were coming out of the cabin and would be clear in plenty of time. He exhaled a huff which was drenched with both relief and frustration.

He turned back to Fields.

---

Fields could barely see now. Black spots blocked his vision. But he could *feel* Damien Smith, the man who'd destroyed his family and his life—and murdered his baby sister, let's not forget about that—still in front of him. Locked in place by pure horror.

He knew he was in his final seconds of life. He knew in a few moments, he'd be taken off to whatever horrible eternity that awaited him at the hands of Trocephus and his ilk. But none of that mattered now. All that mattered was completing his mission, finishing his crusade, ending his rage, avenging his family.

Avenging sweet Sophie.

He lifted his head from the ground with a monumental effort. His hand clutching the knife began to curl towards him.

He smiled at Damien. From what little he could see, he saw unadulterated terror on Damien Smith's face.

Blood was flowing at phenomenal rates from his body. He had no idea how he still had any left in him. But apparently, he still did, and he would use every goddamned drop of it to kill the monster in front of him.

But he knew he could only savor the moment for so long.

He dragged himself, excruciatingly, towards Damien. Every inch felt like a mile and every movement like pure torture.

Yet he savored it. Every bit.

He reached Damien's knee and grabbed the man's collar with his free hand. Using the leverage, he made his way to his knees, and managed to raise the knife over his head.

Fires blazed behind him. The sound was almost soothing, and he welcomed the warmth that drifted to him from the flames. He was very cold now.

He pulled Damien's face, petrified with fear, within an inch of his own.

"Now you pay for what you did to Sophie!" he hissed, spitting blood all over the man.

He raised his head up again, along with the knife, and he heard Damien scream.

Fields's eyes blazed with madness.

Harry saw Fields moving towards Damien.

He was at war within himself over intervening. Damien Smith was as much a monster as Fields. He didn't deserve pity. He didn't deserve salvation.

He deserved nothing but what Fields was bringing.

Even still, he began to rush towards them, gun raised. Fields was clutching Damien's shirt now, hauling himself up above the pervert. He saw Fields hiss something in Damien's face, spewing blood all over him in the process.

Fletcher's pulse quickened. He moved faster. Time seemed to slow down.

Fields was rising over Damien. The knife went into the air.

The first set of headlights from the emergency vehicles broke through the tree line.

Damien began screaming.

Fletcher drew down on Fields.

---

Damien Smith urinated on himself.

Fields was over him, hissing into his face, spraying him with blood and saliva.

Then the knife went into the air.

Then he saw Fletcher, the same cop who'd been drawn to him before everything had come out about the children all those years ago. He was also the same cop who'd arrested him after the fact. The fucking asshole hadn't bought his story, never had. But fucking asshole or not, here he was, now, gun raised and aimed at Fields, about to save his life. Only...

Only he was hesitating.

Fields had the knife in the air, nearly at the apex of reach, about to drive it down into him. And Fletcher was hesitating? What the fuck could he be hesitating over? He was a cop, god-damnnit! It was his job to protect him!

Even in the moment, mere seconds from getting stabbed to death by a bleeding maniac, Damien Smith managed to get filled with his own brand of indignation.

"Shoot him, Fletcher!" Damien screamed. "You have to save me!"

But as Fletcher's eyes met his, fresh terror filled Damien Smith's bowels.

---

Fletcher locked eyes with Damien as the old pervert bellowed at him.

And Harry Fletcher realized his decision had been made for him.

His ex-wife and daughter were somewhere behind him, as was his dying partner. Beyond Fields and Damien, lights were spilling into the meadow from emergency vehicles and backup. Eyes were on him, he knew that. But still, in that moment, he didn't care. He didn't give one solitary fuck just then. Twenty years of bitterness and fury were finally coming to a head within him, and his eyes blazed out at Damien Smith with pure disgust fueling their fire.

Fletcher dropped his gun to his side.

"Reap your whirlwind, Damien!" he said, and smiled. "See you in hell!"

"*Sophie!*" Fields said in a gurgling hiss, which came out as *Show-fee* through his ruined face, and blood speckled the face of his flaccid nemesis.

Damien had just enough time for his mouth and eyes to form perfect *OHs*, and then Fields's knife was sinking into the fleshy part of the old man's throat. All the way to the hilt. Blood spurted and splashed out of him in violent sprays, and Fletcher knew that the man's jugular had been severed.

The pervert tried to scream, but all that came out was a wet grunt. Fields ripped the knife free and brought it down again, this time into Smith's chest, and there was a fleshy splitting sound. Terror filled the old man's confused eyes, which were now void of indignation.

Then a gunshot cracked through the night and Fields's head vanished from the nose up in a red mist. Chunks of yellow-gray meat speckled Damien's face as he went over with Fields.

Fletcher turned, shocked, and saw Benson holding a smoking pistol in his trembling hand. He dropped it to the ground as his eyes met Harry's. His eyes were cold. Distant. Disapproving.

Fletcher looked beyond Benson to his ex-wife and daughter, and was met with the same look from them, but theirs were coupled with a certain kind of pain.

*They watched me kill him,* he thought. *I didn't kill him myself, but I let him die. And they watched.*

Any fleeting hope he'd had for mending things with his family was gone now, and he decided he could live with that. Hell, he'd managed to live with it this long, hadn't he? What was the rest of his life after twenty years?

Nothing.

He turned back to the bleeding monsters in the field and walked towards them, holstering his gun as he went. Fields was dead. No doubt about that. But Damien was still gurgling weakly. He knelt next to the old man.

Damien's terrified eyes met his, swimming with tears and pain. Blood spurted from his mouth and throat and chest around the blade that still protruded from him. He was trying to speak, but couldn't.

"Don't you say a fucking word," Fletcher said to him, scared by ice he heard in his own voice. "Don't you dare spoil this moment."

And then, Fletcher watched him die.

It didn't take long. He was old, and he'd been slashed badly through his artery. Still, it was a satisfying moment for Fletcher. It felt like triumph. Evil had been taken out. He finally felt as though there might be some justice in this world.

He stood to his feet, and was washed in the lights of an ambulance. Several other emergency vehicles were spilling in all around them, police, fire, paramedic. The cavalry was here, just a few moments too late for the show.

Fletcher turned once more and looked at Benson and his family. Benson was in bad shape, but still managed to shake his head at Fletcher. Helen and Heather did the same, apprehension and fear now on their faces as they looked at him.

And Harry was surprised to find that it seemed to hurt less this time. Even if they couldn't understand it, he knew he had done the right thing. At least he *thought* he had.

Perhaps he would have to mull it over for the rest of his life. Who knew? But he could live with it.

The ice on his heart told him he could.

# EPILOGUE

Fletcher stood over the grave of Marvin Gaston.

The grave—a modest, flat marker—was in a cemetery about two miles outside of Longview, surrounded by a wrought-iron fence with a majestic entryway marked with tall stone pillars and beautiful rose bushes. Beyond the entry about thirty yards, the trail split in two directions, circling around a large plot of graves in the center. There was another large plot off the back end, and a mausoleum in the far-left corner, holding caskets and urns of those whose families decided not to put their loved ones under the earth.

Fletcher was in the center plot, not too far from the edge. He'd laid a fresh bouquet of flowers down on his old partner's grave. A tear collected in his eye as he reminisced his friend and partner, the man who'd never shown concern for his own life, but heroically charged into danger on multiple occasions to save the weak and to stop evildoers.

He smiled remembering his fallen comrade.

After the events at the cabin with the gunman, the monster, and Charlton Fields, Fletcher had been a changed man. Whether or not this change was a good thing was up for debate, even with Fletcher himself, but he was nonetheless changed. Forever.

Something had broken inside of him at the end. Something which had been fragile to begin with, dating back twenty years, when Smith had been revealed as the monster. When Fletcher got his first taste of true injustice. The event had bruised the inner part of him, damaged it to a great extent. But it hadn't broken. Not then, anyway.

Perhaps, he often thought now, he had still held on to some belief in redemption, no matter how buried he had kept it. After all, even as Fields had been on his rampage, Fletcher had found himself just shy of cheering the man on in his crusade. There had been justice in it, no matter what society thought about it, or what morality had to say. There had been justice. There were innocents slain, and he didn't justify that. *Couldn't* justify it, not that he'd wanted to. But in the five men who had destroyed Charlton Fields's life—not to mention that of the poor boy's family—justice had been served. Not in a court room, not in a jail cell, but with bullets, knives, and blood.

*Blood,* Fletcher thought, as he wiped the stubborn tear away from his eye and raised a flask to his mouth to take a drink.

Heat flushed his throat, his chest, his stomach. The whiskey warmed him on this cool day, and it deadened the pain in his mind. The part within him that screamed for balance and justice in a world which wasn't black or white anymore. Wasn't even gray, for that matter. No, this world was full of every color in rainbow, and no matter how society or church philosophy tried to make things plain, it simply wasn't.

*But blood*, he thought again as he winced against the whiskey's heat. *Blood paid it all in full.*

That was the irony of it all, at least in Fletcher's view. The blood. Through the whole ordeal, Benson—Mr. Jesus-freak himself—had been going on, and on, and on about God's sovereignty, His plans, His ways. Blah, blah, fucking blah. Pitiful attempts to make some sense of Damien Smith and his perverse actions, his creation of monsters. Fields had been nothing more than the outcome, not the cause. Damien Smith had been the real monster.

*And monsters breed monsters.*

That was the hell of it all. Despite all that had happened, Fletcher didn't blame Fields. He thought that under similar circumstances, he may have done the same thing himself. In fact, he thought quite a lot of people would have. And for all Benson's religious ramblings, he had been right about at least one thing. Blood really had covered a multitude of sins.

None of the men Fields had killed had been outed. None of their cover-ups, their perversions, their lies. None of it had come out. They died as beatified saints in the eyes of the world.

The thought forced the flask back to Fletcher's lips for another long gulp.

*One went down a monster, the rest as saints,* Fletcher thought and shivered at the thought, despite the warmth of his drink.

He took a final look at Gaston's grave, nodded and gave a mock salute to his old partner, then ambled on from there.

*Fucking monsters,* he thought aimlessly as he moved.

And what a lot of monsters had come to be through it all. As he strode about, looking this way and that at different tombstones, not really reading the inscriptions upon them but simply glancing at them, he thought about the thing he'd seen in the cabin when he'd come through the door after his ex-wife and daughter. Just moments before that damaged part inside of him had broken completely.

A demon. That had been all Helen would say about it. In fact, that was the very last thing she had said to him at all. After what had happened at the end, she hadn't been able look at him the same. In the fire which had followed, any evidence of her demon had gone up with the cabin, but he never doubted it had been there. God was real, he knew that now. And it followed there would be something working against such a force. Something which had been released from Damien Smith's perversion.

But now, Helen couldn't look at him at all, not after all that had happened. It was okay, he supposed. She couldn't understand. She was too full of the mercy and kindness theology, all too common in the Bible-belt, to really grasp why he'd done what he'd done. His daughter was the same way, though she could stand to talk to him on the phone, if not see him in person. She still called him, had wished him a happy birthday when his time came around to get one year closer to his inevitable death. But see him? No, she couldn't do that.

This forced another drink, and he stumbled as he tilted his head back to let the amber liquid slide down his throat, heating him with its warmth. He didn't think he was drunk, but there was an unmistakable swirl in the back of his head, and just the hint of blurring at the outer edges of his peripheral vision. But no matter. This was common for him now. After all, what else was there?

He'd lost his job. He hadn't been fired, though he was sure if he had stayed on it would have been as inevitable as death and taxes. But he had lost it all the same. When Captain Felt had begun grilling him with questions in the days following, fueled with the contemptuous testimony of Benson, Fletcher had relinquished his badge then and there without a second thought. There was no second thought to be had anyway. The department was an off-shoot of society, and simply would not—*could not*—understand. Never would, he reckoned. Yet he'd kept his gun. It was his, not the department's, and he'd be damned if they'd take it from him. Even now, it was tucked neatly in its holster under his left arm.

Fletcher's thoughts drifted to Benson then. Benson had gone in to surgery immediately after arriving at the hospital in the ambulance which had raced away with him out of the clearing that night, one year ago now. He'd been in surgery for nine hours, and he had flat-lined three different times. Fletcher didn't know how, perhaps divine oversight, but he'd come back every time. He made it and came through to make a full recovery. It had taken several months, but he'd come back on the job, and was now partnered with Ernie. Ernie had nearly died himself after getting shot in the throat by Fields, but had managed a full recovery himself. Bert, on the other hand, had been reduced to full-time desk-duty. His hand was ruined, and the whole event had killed the part inside him which made him a good cop. He couldn't function on the streets anymore. He and Fletcher still saw each other, got together for drinks frequently, and it seemed to Fletcher that Bert was the only one who really understood why Fletcher had done what he had done.

"That fucker Fields," Bert had said one evening over their second pitcher of beer, "he fucked up my hand, fucked up my whole career, for that matter. But if what you tell me is all true, about Damien and his partners in crime at that god-forsaken church of theirs, well..." He had raised his glass in a toast. "Well then, God bless him...if there *is* a God."

Fletcher nodded at the memory, a covert smile spreading across his face, and thought again of Fields.

Fletcher went back to Gaston's grave, stooped down, and grabbed a single rose from the bouquet he'd left for his partner, and began walking amongst the tombstones again. His eyes darted to and fro again, this time looking for a specific grave.

It took him several minutes, but he finally found what he was looking for.

It was little more than a marker really, not an actual tombstone, about the size of a sheet of paper. It was propped up at an angle on a metallic arm driven into the earth.

# CHARLTON FIELDS

That was all it said. Nothing more.

Fletcher shook his head ever so slightly as he looked at it. In the past year, as he'd reflected on all that had occurred, he'd come to understand Fields. Not condoning everything he had done, but enough. Enough to have respect and pity for the man whose life had been destroyed by the actions of monsters and hypocrites, and a society unable or unwilling to acknowledge the truth. Fletcher thought about what he might have done had he been in Fields's shoes, and could never say with absolute certainty what he may have become.

*Monsters are created. And they're created by monsters.*

Damien Smith had been a monster, alright. So had the pastor and the other elders who'd covered everything up.

Fletcher never speculated on the condition of Damien Smith's soul when he'd died. He didn't have to. There was no regret. No sorrow for what he'd done, for what he'd created and set in motion. Only self-preservation and self-righteous indignation. It was in that moment Fletcher had known that if he stopped Fields, Damien would have gotten away with it all again. He would have been venerated and revered as some sort of hero, the man who had survived the psychopath's rampage to tell the tale. He knew it would have been spun into a hypocritical morality tale, one which Fletcher simply could not stomach.

And that had been all it took.

He looked again at the small marker signifying the burial place of the killer Charlton Fields. He felt the tear he'd contained at Gaston's grave collect again in his eye. He squatted down on his haunches, the rose in his hand.

"I'm sorry, little Charlie," he whispered, staring at the marker. "I'm sorry I couldn't have done more when they took your family. I'm so sorry."

He laid the rose on the grave as the tear escaped his eye and streaked down his face.

He took a moment more, then stood, sniffed, and wiped the tear clear of his face. He took another drink, then considered the flask in his hand. After a moment, he smiled, and held the flask out at arm's length. He tipped it over, and poured a few drops on the grave.

"I don't blame you, Charlie," Fletcher said as he righted the flask and took another sip from its mouth. "I really don't blame you."

He stared down at the marker for a moment longer, nodded, then moved on again. He was heading for his truck, ready to head back home, put his feet up, and enjoy the company of Jack Daniel's. They had much to talk about, he figured, and he had come to enjoy their frequent visits.

As he moved along, he saw a large tombstone, a rather extravagant piece, depicting some holy-looking individual on a gallant steed rearing back on its haunches, the rider grasping the reigns in one hand, the other extended forward as if leading a charge. Fletcher paused and frowned deeply, for he knew whose grave it was before ever looking at the inscription. He had seen it on the news, in the papers, and social media. It had been paid for by the church he had been a part of twenty years ago, by a congregation full of willing sheep.

It was the grave-stone of Damien Smith.

On it, there was an inscription that made Fletcher's stomach roll over.

*'Here lies Damien Smith, mentor, giver, Saint'*

Fletcher physically gagged as he saw it for the first time in person, and had to take a long pull on his flask, emptying half its contents at once. His whole body shivered as he did, and he winced again as he gulped it down.

It helped. His stomach, that was, not his psyche.

As he stared at the graven abomination before him, he was overcome with a rage that swelled within him like a tidal-wave, flushing his already red cheeks to a dark crimson.

He spat on the marker.

"You're no fucking saint!" he screamed in the deserted graveyard. "I hope you're burning in hell!"

But the marker made no reply, and except for a murder of crows which fled in the back plot of the graveyard, flapping their wings and fluttering off into the darkening sky, there was no sound except his echoing curse.

*A murder of crows,* he thought, relishing the irony as he compared it with Fields's crusade against these so-called *saints*.

"Fly high, assholes!" he said to the crows as they fluttered away, his hand rising to reveal his middle finger jutting out like an iron spike.

*Crows. Black, ominous creatures that flutter around, devouring the flesh of the fallen.*

This thought made Fletcher laugh in a bitter tone that might have chilled him if not for the whiskey in his blood.

*Devouring the flesh of the fallen. Just like these saints.*

He laughed bitterly again as he replaced the flask to the inside pocket of his jacket, his hand brushing against the butte of his pistol, tucked neatly in its shoulder holster. When the flask was safely stowed away, he glared up at Damien Smith's grave-stone for several long moments, feeling the rage swell within him.

That was when he realized he needed to take a piss.

His first thought was to get into his truck, get back to his house—he only lived ten minutes away—and relieve himself. Get home and just put this out of his mind with a few swigs of Jack and something on the TV.

But then, he thought better of it.

*Why be uncomfortable when you don't have to be?*

He unzipped his fly, hefted his penis in his hands, and pissed for a long time on Smith's grave.

*"You're no fucking saint, Damien,"* he said as he glared up at the dead man's grave. *"But then again, neither am I."*

He could have been, though. Hell, he almost had been, or so he often liked to think, usually when he was knee-deep in cheap bourbon and stewing over all he'd lost, which was happening more and more often now. But then Damien, that sick, old fool, had tipped him back. He had lost his faith once, thanks to the same bastard, all those years ago. He had just started getting it back when the end had come. That one, solitary moment. Fletcher could have stopped Fields. He knew that. But...

But Damien. The one he'd let drag him down before, had done it again. With one look, not of repentance, but indignation, and his self-righteous demands for salvation. That had been what pushed Fletcher over the edge. That one moment had defined everything for the rest of his life. A life that could have come with a good job, a new partner he genuinely cared about, a woman he still loved back in his life, and a daughter that could look him in the eye and proudly call him her father.

Or a life without any of that.

As the yellow stream flowed from him, steaming the air and graying the white stone of the grave-marker, he reached back inside his jacket, this time grasping the butte of his pistol and removing it from the holster. He'd done this many times in the past year, but never with this much surety and purpose, not to mention resolve. His fingers wrapped tightly around the handle, his knuckles draining of color as they clasped the metal as though they were holding on to a ledge a hundred stories in the air for dear life. He placed the barrel against his temple. Tears welled fresh in his eyes and spilled over on his cheeks. In that moment, home, Jack, and TV seemed the farthest things from his mind.

He pinched his eyes shut and sighed harshly.

*That's a huff Har—*

"Shut the fuck up!"

No. He was no saint. And sainthood, he believed, was forever out of his reach.

*"God-damn you, Damien!"* he growled, his teeth gritting tightly together. *"And God-damn me!"*

No saints had died in the rampage of Charlton Fields. None which Fletcher recognized anyway, least of all himself.

Or maybe, that was precisely what happened.

# THE END

# ACKNOWLEDGEMENTS

Dr. Rathburn, Gena, and Destani. Your input and feedback were invaluable to this endeavor. Without your help, this work would be a total mess. Thank you for your patience and keen eyes. I am eternally grateful.

# ABOUT THE AUTHOR

C hris Miller attended North East Texas Community College and LeTourneau University, where he focused on creative writing courses. He is the superintendent of his family-owned water well company and has enjoyed a life-long passion for reading and writing. Chris and his wife, Aliana, have three children and live in Winnsboro, Texas.

Follow Chris Miller Online:

**Twitter:** @CMWordslinger
**Instagram:** @cmwordslinger
**Facebook:** Chris Miller—Author @
facebook.com/chrismiller1383
**Website:** www.chrismillerauthor.com